THE
SHAMAN
LAUGHS

ALSO BY JAMES D. DOSS

The Shaman Sings

THE
SHAMAN
LAUGHS

JAMES D. DOSS

ST. MARTIN'S PRESS
NEW YORK

Grateful acknowledgment is made to The Putnam Publishing Group and the Estate of Robert W. Service for permission to quote from "My Highland Home" by Robert Service on page 117.

Library of Congress Cataloging-in-Publication Data
Doss, James D.
      The shaman laughs / James D. Doss.
            p.   cm.
      "A Thomas Dunne book."
      ISBN 0-312-13601-3
      1. Police—West (U.S.)—Fiction.   2. Ute Indians—Fiction.
   I. Title.
   PS3554.O75S47   1995
   813'.54—dc20   95-31795

First edition: December 1995

10 9 8 7 6 5 4 3 2 1

For Martha, Bret, and Kirk
and for
Rolling Thunder
May he lie down in green pastures

/pitʉku-pi/ were usually good-natured, though on occasion they could be grouchy.

—ANNE M. SMITH,
ETHNOGRAPHY OF THE NORTHERN UTES

THE
SHAMAN
LAUGHS

COLORADO, SOUTHERN UTE RESERVATION
CAÑON DEL SERPIENTE

From a distance, the lone monolith has the sinister appearance of a peglike tooth, set firmly in the mouth of the Canyon of the Snake. A close examination reveals that the top of the sandstone projection is remarkably flat. Suitable, perhaps, for a table. Or an altar.

Near the center of this surface, there is a cavity. In the age of the woolly mammoth and giant ground sloth, it was only a shallow depression that caught a few drops of rainwater; barely enough for a sparrow's bath. But that was then. Now it is larger. Deeper. But the sparrow no longer comes to bathe in this place.

In a time known only to lingering ghosts, the basin was put to practical use by resourceful women of the Anasazi. They would fill the natural metate with hard grains of blue and yellow corn, then grind the maize into a coarse meal with heavy granite *manos*. Over a score of generations, their labors gradually enlarged the cavity and gave it a measure of symmetry. These were the fat years, before the great thirst visited the land. Drought did not travel alone; Hunger and Sickness strode along hand-in-hand, only a few faltering steps behind. At the appointed time, Death would come in the form of a small gray owl and sit on the heads of those who were called away to the world of shadows. Many were called.

During the centuries after the Anasazi had passed into the whispers of romantic myth, the bowl-shaped cavity reverted to its original function as temporary home to the occasional goat-faced spider or silverwing cricket. But that was during the dry season. When booming thunderstorms rumbled over the sinuous canyon, the cavity would catch a precious store of water. Flittering yucca moths, even sleek ravens would come to drink. It might have remained so for a thousand millennia until the sand-laden winds finally eroded the monolith to dust.

It did not remain so.

On this day, the cavity in the stone is filled with a warm liquid. It is thicker than water.

The long finger dips into the viscous fluid, then touches the tip of the tongue. Yes . . . delicious. The finger dips once more, then moves in slow, deliberate strokes over the grainy canvas. The drawings on the sandstone table in Snake Canyon are simple, but the subjects are unmistakable. The original figure was a bull elk. There are also mule deer, a few horses, a scattering of domestic cattle.

But the slaying of animals has never been more than a preparation for the ultimate goal . . . and the incomparable delicacy.

These new sketches in scarlet represent human beings, the second much larger than the first. The left hand of the smaller figure grasps a rectangular object. To the casual observer, it might be a purse. Or a book. To identify the larger of the intended victims, the stained finger executes a short arc over the stick-man's shoulder. Among those who possess knowledge of such matters, there will be no misunderstanding of this archaic sign.

It is a crescent moon.

THE SHAMAN'S HOME: CAÑON DEL ESPIRITU

Daisy Perika leaned on the aluminum sill of her kitchen window. She stared at the stark outlines of the great stone women perched on Three Sisters Mesa, that five-mile finger of sandstone that separates the Canyon of the Snake from the Canyon of the Spirit. The old woman did this whenever she was troubled; it helped to calm her spirit.

But something moved. She blinked at the ghostly figure of mist descending the mesa's crumbling talus slope. The vaporous Whatever It Was took each step with exaggerated care, as if a fall might cause serious injury. How curious; this comic behavior brought a slight smile to her wrinkled face. The specter seemed to raise a wispy arm in a hesitant greeting, then ventured forth in starts and stops as if unsure of itself. Would the phantom approach the Ute woman's home uninvited? Perhaps this shadow wished to talk. To whisper sly myths into the shaman's ear; tales of times when the earth was young. Before the People were. Many spirits, like human beings, had a tendency to exaggerate. Not a few were incapable of telling the truth. But the apparition paused, then turned away, apparently drawn to the shelter of the sandstone walls of *Cañon del Espíritu*. Wandering spirits, even ghosts of human beings, were common enough in this place. Such appearances did not trouble or even surprise the old woman. This was a lonely spot, where even the ghosts thirsted for conversation with the living.

Matters of far greater consequence than this shy apparition occupied her mind. But, since Nahum Yaciiti had disappeared so mysteriously in that awful storm, who was there to talk with about such deep things? Daisy had almost forgotten about her cousin; Gorman Sweetwater sat at her small kitchen table, sullenly nursing a cup of brackish coffee.

Gorman longed for a smoke and, as was his habit, was feeling sorry for himself. He figured he ought to be able to smoke if he wanted to. Hadn't he driven all the way out here to bring his cousin a load of stuff she needed from town? The Ute rancher thought about rolling himself a cigarette, then he thought again. The old woman was in a foul mood tonight. And he didn't want to get Daisy started with all that endless talk about how bad smoking was for his lungs and it would be the death of him for sure and didn't he care that poor little Benita would be left all alone without a Daddy and besides who would take care of his precious cattle then? Gorman slammed his coffee cup down hard enough to get her attention.

Daisy Perika was startled by the noise; then she remembered the groceries her cousin had brought to her remote trailer home at the mouth of *Cañon del Espíritu*. She lifted a carton of eggs thoughtfully, as if weighing them. "Something ain't the way it ought to be." She snapped at Gorman like it was his fault.

"That woman at the store said"—a dry cough rattled Gorman's lungs— ". . . said them eggs is jumbo grade A and still warm from the hen." He stuck an unlighted pipe into his mouth; the taste of stale ashes lifted his spirits. "Take a sniff, I bet you can still smell the chicken's—"

"I don't mean the eggs." Gorman could act so stupid! Or maybe it wasn't an act at all. She opened the refrigerator and carefully placed a dozen eggs into their oval receptacles in the door shelf. "It's the air that don't feel quite right tonight," she said almost to herself, "I won't be able to sleep good."

Her cousin raised an eyebrow. "What's wrong?" Sometimes, Daisy could see tomorrow. And the day after.

"It's like *Kwasigeti* comes for somebody. Somebody I know."

At the mention of the demon, the pipe slipped from Gorman's lips and clattered onto the linoleum floor. "Somebody you know?" He hadn't been feeling all that well lately. . . . Maybe the old woman could see a deadly sickness coming to snatch his soul from his body. He pressed the question as he retrieved the beloved pipe. "You mean . . . like one of your relatives?"

She refilled his cup with black coffee. Charlie Moon, her favorite nephew, was out there somewhere in his squad car, patrolling the rutted back roads of the Southern Ute Reservation. "Not you, Gorman."

With great relief, the old rancher released the breath he had been holding. "You always did worry too much. Me," he pointed at his chest with the pipe stem, "I figure when a feller's number's up, it's up." He leaned back and stuck the pipe between his teeth. "When old St. Peter toots that big horn, why I'll just saddle up my pony and go and meet Gabriel at them purple gates."

Daisy sighed. Like most old men, Gorman got sillier with every passing year. The shaman squinted through the open window at the approaching midnight. She hugged her shoulders and sniffed at the night air. The breath of the canyon was still warm, but it was not sweet with the usual aromas of sage and juniper and piñon. "I don't know what it is, Gorman . . . something just don't smell right."

Gorman Sweetwater, whose reprieve from the cold fingers of Death had improved his mood considerably, glanced over the rim of his coffee cup at his cousin. He smiled only with the wrinkles at the corners of his eyes, "Maybe it's that old *pitukupf* who lives up the canyon in his badger hole; I doubt if that little fellow has took himself a bath for . . . prob'ly twelve or eight hundred years. More or less."

The old woman pretended not to hear this foolish talk. Her cousin, who had once lost a good horse because he didn't show proper respect to the *pitukupf*, should know better than to make jokes about the dwarf-spirit. But Gorman, like most old men, was apt to forget the hard lessons he'd learned in life.

And then there was Charlie Moon. There would be no point in telling the policeman that she sensed something terrible out there. Her nephew would treat her with respect, but he would pay little attention to a warning based on her intuition. Daisy Perika closed her eyes and tried to see into the darkness. Tonight, she knew, sleep would not come at all.

THE POLICEMAN'S HOME ON THE BANKS OF THE LOS PIÑOS

It was almost midnight when Charlie Moon finally unbuckled his cowhide cartridge belt and draped it over the back of a heavy oak chair. He pulled off his boots. The Ute policeman's thoughts drifted to Benita Sweetwater. Any day now, Gorman's daughter would be home from Fort Lewis College in Durango. He could almost see Benita's dark eyes, the flash of her sweet smile. But such thoughts were distracting and would rob him of sleep. Moon forced his mind to other matters. Such as Police Chief Severo's upcoming vacation and his replacement by Scott Parris for those few weeks. Moon smiled at this thought; it would be good to spend some time with his friend again. The Ute also considered his unfinished adobe home; there was so much work be done, and never enough time. And finally, Charlie Moon let his thoughts drift to his aunt Daisy. It wasn't good for the old woman's mind, living by herself at the mouth of that haunted canyon. It was a place that more prudent Utes preferred to avoid. The isolation turned her thoughts inward, made fantasies come alive and dance around her little bed after the sun slipped behind the mesa. But there was no use talking to her about moving. The old woman was stubbornly fixed on the notion that because she had entered into this world at the mouth of *Cañon del Espiritu*, from that sacred place she would also depart.

But Charlie Moon did not entertain those troublesome thoughts that keep less fortunate souls sleepless far into the depths of night. For this reason, the Ute policeman was usually asleep within a minute after his heavy frame hit the mattress. On this night, Moon rolled over in his bed and was soon lost in the infinite, ever-changing landscape of his mind. As a finger of cold moonlight reached gently through the window and touched his face, the dream began innocently enough, without any hint of that which was to come.

The dreamer walked along a much-used trail. Without knowing how it could be so, Charlie Moon was certain that his feet had made this path.

This place was unremarkable except for its striking familiarity.

Before him was a field of black basalt boulders, scattered patches of juniper and piñon, and irregular clumps of fringed sage. White four-petal fendlerbush blossoms waved at him, mountain bluebirds and yucca moths were on the wing, tireless honeybees droned from pink rose to purple aster. The Ute paused to watch a buffalo cow grazing on the lush grasses; her mate drank from the waters of the rolling stream. And what was his grandmother's name for this creek that churned its reddish-brown waters through the shallow valley? Sweet Waters of Forgetting? Blood of Manitou? Tears of the Sky Virgin? He could not remember. But one landmark was unmistakable. The stark profile of the Cochetopa Hills rose into a morning sky that was a whitish blue. But the dreamer could see over the horizon—far to the east, this endless sea, this sky-blanket over the earth patched with billows of clouds that rolled and swelled—great vaporous waves driven before an unseen storm that had not yet reached its full fury. A small wooden ship pitched upon the rolling surface of this sky-sea, square sails bent before the winds. A craft that would bring the fierce Blue Eyes to this land of the grandmother of all his grandfathers. Some of these first would be killed, a few would be enslaved, fewer still would be absorbed into the confederation of tribes who lived in that place where the sun came up. But there would be many others who would come over the cold waters. Many beyond counting. The ship vanished into a deep fog.

The Ute knew that he had walked this trail many times, a thousand winters before the People had been given the horse, even before the bow and arrow had replaced the flint-tipped dart and atl-atl throwing stick. Charlie Moon also knew that he would be here again. Soon. Before the Apache Plume gave her last petals to North Wind. He heard a low rumbling sound, like summer thunder over the San Juans. It was the buffalo bull; the great animal pawed the sod nervously as he bellowed his words to the clouds. The cow continued her grazing.

Moon was suddenly distracted from the buffalo; he turned to see an old man, dressed in leather breeches and a spotless white shirt with silver buttons. His legs were bowed, his short form bent forward. The man's long hair was straight and coarse—coal black tinged with streaks of snowy white. The face was ancient and wrinkled, the nose flattened, the skin dark like polished walnut. The beaded band around the old man's head was a marvel to the dreamer; this ornament shimmered with more colors than a rainbow—amber and turquoise and cornflower and jasper and rose quartz and a dozen other hues that Charlie Moon had never seen nor imagined and would not remember after this dream.

The old man's lips sighed, then formed soundless words. "Son of Buckskin Moon, son of Alice Winterheart . . . will you look upon what I must show you?"

Moon nodded. There was something hauntingly familiar about this elder, but his identity was hidden from the dreamer.

The venerable figure raised his arm; he pointed to a small forest of piñon and juniper. He stared at the young Ute with an expression of unutterable sadness, then turned away. The stooped figure left the path and walked into the small forest of evergreens. Moon was not eager to follow, but he found that his legs were in charge. They made long, heavy strides.

In Middle World, thunder rolled down the broad valley, along the muddy banks of the Los Piños, off the rocky face of Shellhammer Ridge, over the painted steel roof of the house where the dreamer slept. The west wind sighed heavily, rippling the waters of the Piños, bending the limbs of great cottonwoods and limber willows along the river's banks. Just above the foaming rapids in the elbow of the river, in the home built of adobe bricks, the dreamer heard the thunder speak. Charlie Moon also heard the nervous chatter of the cottonwood leaves, the dark whisper of the willows. He stirred uneasily, but did not escape the prison of his dream.

Moon was now aware that he was running. He wanted to turn away, but the dreamer's legs were like great pumping pistons, driving him toward some uncertain dark shore. But now, in a clearing among the juniper and piñon and scrub oak, his legs slowed to a walk. But it was very strange—the light of the sun did not touch this place of dark mists! Worse still, the old man was not here.

There was a small half-alive tree isolated in the center of the clearing; even the dry grasses did not grow near its roots. . . . The big Ute moved toward this tortured growth and was suddenly stopped as if by a wall of smoky glass. Barely visible through the folds of darkness, Charlie Moon could see a form suspended from a branch in the tree. It must be an animal. A fresh deer carcass waiting to be butchered.

The mists parted for a moment. . . . No . . . oh no . . . it was a human being . . . naked . . . hanging by the ankles. The face, twisted in pain, was unrecognizable through the swirling mists. The Ute could not tell whether this was a man or a woman . . . but he had a sense that he knew this person well. In the same way that he knew himself.

As the thunder rumbled over his sleeping body and the cottonwoods shuddered and rattled, Charlie Moon realized that he was struggling in the depths of a strange nightmare. But there was little relief in this knowledge.

The wretched prisoner called out to him, but Moon could not understand the words. From the darkness, a second figure appeared. But this was neither human nor animal. This apparition had matted hair, short muscular legs that terminated in shining black hoofs. And a great shaggy head. Blood dripped from the grinning lips of the beast, and fire flashed like lightning off the curved horns above its ears. The shaggy figure approached the naked upside-down human being. The right arm was raised—a slender blade of blue flame appeared in the hairy fist. As the dreamer watched in horror, the horned beast began, very deliberately, in the manner of a skilled butcher, to dismember the struggling victim.

Charlie Moon tried to break through the invisible barrier and come to the aid of this human being, but his efforts came to nothing. The hanging figure screamed and begged and screeched and pleaded. But the beast was without mercy. Now, the human being made one final cry and the pitiful sound was like that of a helpless animal being ripped apart by the claws and teeth of a merciless predator.

Moon roared in defiance at this abomination; he directed his protests to the heavens that seemed so far away from this dark place. There was no answer from the heavens. But the horned creature paused in its bloody work, then turned to observe the dreamer. There was a slight cocking of the beast's head. A recognition.

With a spasmodic jerk of his spine, Charlie Moon awoke on his perspiration-soaked sheet. His body was stretched, like the poor wretch hanging from the tree. His mouth gaped . . . his chest heaved as he gasped for breath like an asthmatic. The big Ute was ashamed; even as a child no nightmare had brought such raw fear. He gritted his teeth and willed the terror to depart. Oh, so gradually, he relaxed. The rainless storm of wind and thunder rolled away to the South. But a vicious gust of wind had slammed the branch of an aspen against the window and there was now a short, curving crack in the pane. The cold moonbeam slipped in through the window once more. Refracted by the fracture in the glass, the finger of light painted a cunning geometry onto the pillow, just above his shoulder. It was a short arc . . . a crescent. A sign.

Now the circle was closed.

THE SHAMAN'S HOME: CAÑON DEL ESPIRITU

Daisy Perika sat up in bed, her arthritic fingers clutching desperately at the frayed cotton blanket. Her prayer was a solemn chant. "Oh God . . . Great Mysterious One . . . protect Charlie Moon . . . cover him in the shadow of your wings."

EAST OF IGNACIO, THE BUFFALO PEN

The old bull paused, forgetting a mouthful of half-chewed gamma grass. The cow, unaware of his sudden unease, continued to graze in peaceful bliss. The bison raised his immense head and sniffed as the breeze whipped at his beard. At first, he detected nothing more than the pungent aroma of piñon. He braced his legs, stood perfectly still and listened; there was only the warm whisper of the west wind and the ripple of sweet water over the shining rocks in the river. A deep bellow rumbled in his throat; he blinked and scanned the familiar horizon. He watched the sea of dry grass, thirsty waves rolling and swelling as the breeze troubled the surface of the pasture. The animal raised his head to blink at the thin blue layer that separated his world from the infinite vacuum of space. A pair of red-tailed hawks circled over a giant cottonwood on the bank of the Los Piños. They floated without effort, as if lost in a dream. The smallest detail of his domain appeared to be exactly as nature had ordained. But it was not. Something watched.

And waited.

Homer Tonompicket was maneuvering Charlie Moon into just the spot where he wanted him, and this put him in an exceptional mood.

The Game Warden threw his head back and bellowed the latest melancholy ditty from Nashville:

"Now sweet Sally's gone . . . my heart I would of give her . . .
She'd swallered enough gin to pickle all the catfish in Mud River . . .
Sally's eyeballs they turned yeller, she'd shake and she'd shiver . . .
But the bartender told me: 'What killed her was her liver!' "

Homer stopped to catch his breath and glanced at the driver of the Blazer. "Old Gene Autry—now there was a singin' cowboy that could ride and shoot and rope."

Charlie Moon grinned. For one of the People, Homer had a peculiar fascination with cowboys.

"And," Homer reminded his companion, "Gene always got the pretty girl." A dark scowl fell like a curtain over the game warden's face. "Dammit, Charlie! Why ain't there no more singin' cowboys?"

Moon eased his boot off the accelerator. "I guess nothing stays the same." The policeman turned off the blacktop of County Road 321; he shifted into second gear and steered the Blazer down the rutted incline toward the fenced forty-acre pasture.

"Old Gene, he give up his singin'," the game warden whispered in a tone of disbelief. "Went and bought hisself a baseball team." Homer, who was a purist, had terminated his annual pilgrimages to Nashville after "they" moved the Grand Ol' Opry out of the small downtown theater and into the gaudy suburban acreage dubbed Opryland. This had happened decades ago but to the recalcitrant old man it was only yesterday. Disneyland in Tennessee, that's what it was. All that was missing, he had told everyone in Ignacio who would listen, was that big black mouse that talked like a girl. "It's the end of real country music, that's what it is," he complained bitterly to other Utes who wondered why Homer cared what those *matukach* yodelers did in Tennessee.

Moon shifted into low. "You ready to tell me what this little trip is all about?"

The tribal game warden pointed a stubby finger across the dashboard and shouted over the roar of the V-8 engine. "Over there, Charlie."

Charlie Moon braked the Blazer to a lurching stop near a stack of baled hay and cut the ignition. He followed Homer Tonompicket toward the gate in the barbed wire fence. "There," the game warden said, pointing at a heavy chain that secured the dual steel gate at the center. "You see that?"

Moon leaned over and squinted at a new Master padlock. "This lock looks okay to me." He straightened up and looked down at Homer's face, which was partially hidden under the black Stetson's dusty brim.

"That's the whole point, Charlie. That lock ain't broke. You're my witness."

"You brought me out here at sunrise to show me a padlock that's not broke?"

"Now," Homer said, "take a look out there in that pasture. Whadda you see?"

Moon scanned the fenced forty-acre pen. There wasn't much to see. Some gamma grass, a few clumps of sage, the crumbling ruin of a house at the northwest corner. And, of course, Never Stops Talking. The aged buffalo cow stood near the rectangular stock pond, oblivious to the presence of these official representatives of the Southern Ute Tribe. Except for a slight wagging of her head, she might have been a statue. The old buffalo cow had earned her name by her habit of snorting and bawling almost continually. This morning, she was unnaturally quiet. And very still, more like a taxidermist's product than a living creature. Moon frowned at the game warden. "I see an old buffalo cow. Why didn't you move her to the new pasture, with the rest of the herd?"

"Decided to leave her here. Figured Rolling Thunder needed himself a female companion."

Charlie Moon understood. A younger bull would service the herd in the big pasture, so to keep the peace the old bull had to stay behind. Homer Tonompicket, a romantic to the core, had figured that Rolling Thunder needed some female company. Homer's house was empty now, so he would know something about being lonely. Moon stretched his neck, giving the pasture another inspection. "Where's Rolling Thunder?" A dozen years earlier, there had been a contest to name the first buffalo calf born on the reservation.

"Now," Homer said grimly, "you see what I mean. He's gone without a trace. And the gate ain't been touched. It's like . . ." Homer raised his arms to the sky, ". . . like he just up and flew away. Like old Nahum Yaciiti."

"Buffaloes don't fly, Homer." Moon's stern tone hinted that he did not welcome the reference to the old shepherd who had vanished in a freak windstorm. There was still no sign of Nahum's remains, and unfinished business made the policeman uneasy. And prone to bad dreams. And there was the nightmare vision . . . of a helpless soul suspended upside down from a tree limb, all trussed up to be butchered by . . . Moon dismissed the picture from his mind. "Who's got keys to that padlock?"

Homer's voice went flat and stubborn. "I got the only set." Maybe the big policeman was wrong this time. Maybe buffalo could fly. If they had some help.

Charlie Moon was looking across the river; the sun was illuminating Sky Ute Downs in a soft yellow glow. The policeman turned to squint at the sunrise, blooming like a fiery flower over the eastern range. The bottom of a heavy cloud was a vast field of glowing embers, threatening to rain molten drops of gold onto the mountains. Fire from heaven. Or some place. He didn't look at Homer when he spoke. "You walk the fence?"

"Sure I did," the game warden snapped. "Fence is in good shape." He waited for the policeman to speak, but Moon was ominously silent. "Dammit, Charlie, I know what you're thinkin'! No, I didn't go off and leave the gate open, come back and find the buffalo wandered off, and then lock the gate and call my old friend at the po-leece and tell him a bald-faced lie."

Charlie Moon was embarrassed that the game warden had so easily read his thoughts. "Okay, Homer." He patted the old man on the shoulder.

"Then," Homer demanded, "tell me what happened to a full grown bull buffalo!"

"Well," Moon said, "I expect somebody wanted some meat. Maybe a skin to sell. They probably waited until R.T. was rubbing his hide against the fence so they wouldn't have to move him very far, then shot him."

"How'd they get half a ton of buffalo over the fence? Tell me that."

"Maybe they had a truck with a winch." He would ask Officer Sally Rainwater to check on some of the local wrecker trucks. Maybe somebody had rented one. "Or, maybe they cut him up in chunks and pitched 'em over the fence."

The game warden leaned on the fence, grasping a rusty strand of barbed wire with both hands. He nodded toward the buffalo cow. "Maybe that's the way it was, Charlie. But what about Never Stops Talking?"

Moon knew exactly what Homer meant. If someone was going to go to all this trouble and risk for some fresh meat, why not take both buffalo? Even if they couldn't haul away that much meat, the old cow would have been a hazard to anyone who spent enough time in the pen to butcher Rolling Thunder. It would make sense to shoot the cow, but there she was. "When did you move the rest of the herd?"

"Let's see," Homer scratched nervously at the gray stubble on his chin. "What's today? Thursday? Yeah. We moved 'em out on Monday. Took most of the day, I guess we got the last of 'em out about sundown. I'm sure it was Monday 'cause it was just before the big rain on Tuesday morning." He squinted at a long bank of clouds. "That sure was some gully-washer."

Moon left Homer leaning on the fence; the policeman walked around the south side of the pen, then the west side that paralleled the river. He poked around inside the ruined house; Homer had filled most of it with alfalfa hay. It took him almost half an hour to circle the pen. He paused several times to study the ground; it was still soft from Tuesday's rain. There were occasional tracks of coyote and raccoon. Even wild turkey. But no human prints aside from Homer's pointy-toed size-seven Tony Lamas. And no tire tracks. There were more questions than the locked gate and unbroken fence. The sensible way to kill a buffalo was with a rifle; but a gunshot would almost certainly have been heard. This was a quiet spot, and the veterinarian who lived up the hill near the county road didn't miss much. Only last month, Harry Schaid had called the police after midnight to report a "big ruckus down at the buffalo pen." Officers Sally Rainwater and Daniel Bignight had answered the call. Sally's report said they had driven off a pack of stray dogs that were worrying the buffalo. No, if there had been a shot near the pen, the veterinarian would have called it in. Or maybe Doc Schaid wasn't at home that night. Nothing was simple.

Homer was waiting at the corner post, stuffing his jaw with chewing tobacco. "Find anything?"

Moon nodded. "Not much." But it was clear that Rolling Thunder had vanished sometime before the rain washed the sign away. And, of course, after the other members of the herd were moved to the new pasture. Sometime between sundown last Monday and two or three the next morning when the rains came.

Homer blinked and rubbed the back of his hand across his eyes. "I'm gonna miss that cranky old bastard." The aging bull was irritable and, when annoyed, dangerous. But Homer, who was getting old and cranky himself, had loved the animal. Tonompicket felt a pang of disappointment at the policeman's casual treatment of the disappearance; he had hoped for more. With Moon on top of this, there should have been a good story to tell and retell and embellish during the long winter nights when the freezing winds spilled down from the mountains and whistled through the pines.

But Homer realized that he would have to be patient. Police Chief Roy Severo always said that Charlie Moon might take his own good time to figure things out, but that in the long run, he generally got the job done. The Utes were proud of their big policeman's remarkable ability to make sense of actions that, on the surface, seemed to have no meaning. Only last year Moon had figured out why someone broke into the grocery store over on Goddard Avenue and took fifteen bottles of mouthwash without touching nearly two hundred dollars in the cash register. And just this spring, Moon had immediately understood why someone had felled the flag post in front of the Ignacio post office. And understanding why had revealed "who." But for the moment, Homer mused, it looked like the big policeman had his mind on something else.

Charlie Moon pushed his hands deep into his jacket pockets. Normally at this moment, the Ute policeman would have been enjoying a plate of *huevos rancheros* at Angel's Diner. And his third cup of black coffee. He gazed across the waters of the Los Piños toward the racetrack. Moon had a feeling. . . . He would see Benita today.

Never Stops Talking interrupted his reverie.

The policeman turned his attention back to the old cow. Never Stops Talking had begun to talk. She puffed and snorted; her lungs rattled as she exhaled a warm mist. It was as if she had suddenly become aware of the Utes. The old cow wagged her shaggy head, then pawed the ground. *Dare to come near,* she announced in a language that could not be misunderstood, *and I will make short work of you!* Moon watched the animal with the innocent fascination of a child. *If only you could talk, then you could tell me what happened here.* In the old days, there were Utes who spoke to the buffalo. And the buffalo, the old men insisted, spoke to the People. The policeman's eyes locked with those of the great shaggy animal. Moon was mesmerized; unable to look away. Never Stops Talking suddenly shifted her head and looked toward the Los Piños. What were those enormous, unblinking brown eyes staring at? He scanned the river bank. A morning breeze was beginning to stir the cottonwoods; the leaves rattled like dry bones. Then, the buffalo turned to glare past Moon toward the highway. She snorted, flipped her head, and pawed at the grass.

Homer chuckled. "I think she likes you, Charlie. Maybe she's tryin' to tell you something."

Maybe she was. Something peculiar had happened here, and he could still sense the remnant of its presence. Like a bad odor. The Ute policeman had an unsettling sensation—he had felt unseen eyes staring at the back of his head since he arrived at the buffalo pen. Aunt Daisy would say: "Pay attention to your spirit when it talks to you, Charlie. Sometimes it sees what your eyes can't." Maybe. But the wrong kind of imagination could get in the way of good police work. He grunted and turned toward the Blazer. "Let's go find some breakfast."

Homer Tonompicket followed, pleased at what he had accomplished by involving Moon in this mystery. The dead buffalo was now a police matter; it would be Charlie Moon who would write the official report. Moon would have to face the tribal chairman who sat in the chamber under the mounted head of the great buffalo, presiding over the affairs of the People. Tonompicket shuddered at the scene his mind painted. The chairman would be flanked by irate members of the tribal council, who would demand to know how Rolling Thunder had been lost and who was to blame. But Charlie Moon would cover for the game warden; Homer's face had recovered its customary smile. He drifted off into nostalgic recollections of Ernest Tubb and Roy Acuff and Little Jimmy Dickens. And, most of all, old Hank Williams. Under his breath so Charlie wouldn't hear, Homer sang a few lines about a man who was so awful lonesome he might as well just lay down and die. He felt the tears well up in his eyes; the tight knot in his throat choked off the sad song. Homer was remembering someone . . . his quiet little wife. Elisabeth had finished washing the breakfast dishes on that gray day in March. Then, she simply walked out the front door. He thought she was going to get the newspaper, but she didn't come back. He'd heard gossip that his wife was living with a school teacher in Albuquerque. Or with a truck driver in Fort Collins. Or that she had died from the tuberculosis in Kansas City. It was more than three years now, but Homer still expected her to show up any day. He sighed and shook his head in bittersweet sorrow. "You know, Charlie," he rasped hoarsely, "there damn sure won't never be another Hank Williams!" Or another Elisabeth.

Moon turned onto the blacktop and thought about it. Homer was right. Old Hank had crossed that deep river a long time ago. And now Rolling Thunder was gone. Vanished. Like night mist in the morning sunshine. But the Ute policeman had sensed something; this piece of work had the character of . . . a *message*. He had no idea who had written this letter, but there was no getting around it—the name on the envelope was Charlie Moon.

2

CAÑON DEL ESPIRITU

It was early morning. The pale moon was still hanging in the western sky and the rising sun was blocked by a heavy bank of clouds. Daisy Perika bent over to pour cold well water from the galvanized pail onto the thirsty roots of a Better Girl. "There, there, sweet little *tumátis*," the old woman sang soothingly to the scrawny tomato vine, "have yourself a long drink." She would have felt foolish if anyone could have heard her speaking to a plant, but there was not a living soul within a mile of her little trailer home at the mouth of *Cañon del Espiritu*. The shaman was not concerned that one of the multitude of ancient ghosts might venture forth from their peaceful rest in Spirit Canyon to eavesdrop on an old woman's conversation. You learned to live with the *uru-ci* like you learned to live with the nervous little prairie rattlesnakes. You let them alone, respected their right to be where they were, they wouldn't harm you. Well, most of the time they wouldn't.

With some difficulty, she stood upright and straightened her aching back. What the half-dozen blighted tomato plants needed was a taste of fertilizer, but she had already used up the last of the blue powder from the box of Miracle-Gro and would not be able to buy more until the social security check arrived in her mail box. It would be cheaper to buy tomatoes at the grocery store in Ignacio, but their tart taste didn't compare to her sweet vine-ripened Better Girls.

As Daisy was wondering whether her little vegetable garden could endure for another week without fertilizer, a small cloud slipped over the white disk of the moon. Into the shadowy stillness, a gust of wind was exhaled from the yawning mouth of *Cañon del Espiritu*, whipping the old woman's wool skirts around her arthritic knees. The wind was deathly cold. She turned to gaze intently toward the mouth of the canyon. The shaman was certain that in her mind's eye, she could see the male spirit of this icy wind—a billowing gray form that beckoned to her. This was, as her grandmother would have told her when she was barely twelve, a sign to be read. Daisy turned her gaze upward to a small dark cloud that moved stubbornly against the winds. While great cumulus clouds were drifting to the east, this dismal blemish of frozen vapor was attached to the face of the moon as the great orb fell toward the western horizon. Yes, the cold wind from the Canyon of the Spirits was certainly a sign. And the wrong-way cloud was also an omen. But what did it mean? Daisy Perika thought she knew.

"Charlie," she whispered, "Charlie Moon . . ."

INTERSTATE 25, SOUTH OF DENVER

Scott Parris hadn't spoken ten words during the long drive to the airport. Anne Foster unbuckled her safety belt and moved close to him, resting her head on his shoulder. He tried to ignore the soft waves of strawberry hair, the scent of honeysuckle. The policeman glanced at Anne's safety belt, now useless on the passenger seat. "I oughta give you a ticket for that."

She whispered in his ear. "For snuggling? Not even the chief of police would be so unromantic."

In spite of his glum mood, he smiled briefly and put his arm around her. "You'll be a long time gone." And so far away.

"Oh, I don't know. It'll pass quickly enough for you, with all your official duties to keep you occupied." She pretended to pout. "You'll probably forget all about me."

"Yeah," he muttered, "when pigs learn how to fly."

"When they do," she countered, "you could wing out to see me. I'd love," she added in a husky whisper, "to entertain you."

He pulled her close, and grinned. "From time to time, a man does need a bit of entertainment."

Anne had little to say on the rest of the trip to Denver International, and he had less. He checked her bags and picked up her boarding pass. As they hurried toward the gate, Parris held her bulky carry-on in one hand, squeezed her little hand in the other. His thoughts were on an earlier journey. The airport that time had been O'Hare. It had been Helen who hung on his arm and promised that the brief visit to her mother in Canada would just "whiz by." His wife had died in Montreal in a freak traffic accident. This catastrophe had sent him into a deep abyss of depression and triggered his early retirement from the Chicago police force. That trip to the airport had started a tragic chain of events that eventually led him to Granite Creek in Colorado where he had now served almost two years as chief of police.

He kissed her, then watched her slender form disappear into the mouth of the long tunnel that disgorged its contents into the belly of the sleek airplane. Scott Parris stood by the plate glass window; he frowned at the greasy stains on the engine cover and wondered whether the near-bankrupt airline could afford proper maintenance. He also wondered when he would see her again—*if* he would see her again. The policeman turned away, angry with himself for these absurd, neurotic imaginings. Of course the engine wouldn't fall off the wing. Of course she would be back. And if the deep lonesomes moved in to stay, he would say good-bye to Colorado and show up at her door. This fantasy was immensely calming.

He was in the parking garage when he heard Sam Parker's booming voice.

"Parris! Scott Parris, you trout-fishing sunnuvagun, is that you?" Parker burst from a crowd of travelers, the image of a successful attorney in his expensive three-piece suit.

Parris grabbed Parker's outstretched hand and pumped it with enthusiasm.

The special agent in charge of the Denver Field Office was, he explained from the corner of his mouth, just returning from a trip to Boston. On some unmentioned Bureau business. "Why don't you come over to the house this evening, spend the night with us," Sam said. "I'll broil some steaks so rare, there'll still be ticks on the hide."

Parris grinned and glanced at his watch; the morning was slipping away. "Sounds hard to pass up, but I've got to get back to Granite Creek and get things shipshape at the station before I head for Ignacio."

Parker dropped his suitcase at his feet and leaned a long cardboard cylinder against the wall. "Oh, yeah. I heard you were going to be acting chief cop for the Southern Utes while Roy Severo's away on vacation." He searched Parris's face in an effort to detect some clue to his feelings. Parris had seen the same expression when Sam Parker sat in a bass boat, reading meaning into the ripples on Navajo Lake. "I'm surprised Granite Creek can do without you for that long."

Parris leaned against a steel column. "No problem, actually. Got a leave of absence. Leggett will be taking care of the shop while I'm away. He'll probably have my job before I get back."

Parker tilted his head quizzically, a sure sign he had something on his mind. "Frankly, I'm surprised the Utes didn't appoint Charlie Moon as acting chief. Or Sally Rainwater. She's been around since Moses parted the waters."

"I don't know about Sally, but Moon turned 'em down flat," Parris said. "Charlie said he didn't want a desk job. He suggested they ask me to cover for Severo. So, they made me an offer."

Parker nodded. "Sergeant Moon's a good cop. Only one thing I have against him," he said with earnest dismay, "he's a *bait* fisherman." He faked a shudder. "Night crawlers, crickets, grasshoppers."

"I figured a change of scenery would be good for me. Nothing's happening in Granite Creek. Anne just left for Washington, won't be back for weeks." Maybe months.

"What's Anne Foster up to in the District?"

"She's in demand since her piece on the 'Sunday Morning' show last year. She's landed some kind of contract with CBS." His eyes had a faraway look. "Anne speaks several foreign languages, so I expect the network will find lots of ways to keep her busy. She'll probably be wined and dined at the best embassy parties." Parris was suddenly ashamed of the bitterness he heard in his voice; he wondered if he sounded like a small boy whose mommy had left him at school for the first time. "I figure I'll spend a few weeks with Charlie Moon, find out where all the good fishing holes are down there. With any luck, the whole thing will be a vacation. When the stint's over, I'll take a week or two of real vacation, show up on Anne's doorstep. Maybe if I'm good," he said earnestly, "she'll adopt me."

Parker was entirely lost in thoughts of his seven-pound line cutting the water like a hot wire through butter, a bristly Joe's Hopper trailing in intermittent jumps at the end of an invisible meter of nylon tippet. He could almost see a fourteen-inch native brown, its glistening body breaking the surface to take the hand-tied fly, then diving to bend the rod double. "Maybe I'll get a chance to drop by Ignacio myself." He patted the cardboard cylinder as if it was a friendly puppy. "Bought me an antique bamboo rod last week in Connecticut—an Edward's Quadrate." He paused to let this sink in.

old woman followed behind, working hard to keep up with the big man's long strides. "I know where Nahum kept his key hid, but I wouldn't never use it myself." It was much too high for her to reach. "But you're a policeman and a Ute Indian like Nahum, so I guess it would be all right if you wanted to go inside and poke around some."

He was certain that Armilda remembered that he had examined the house on the day after Nahum disappeared. "Why don't you come in too?" The Ute looked thoughtfully at the skinny old woman in the plastic raincoat. "Maybe you'll spot something I missed."

"Well, maybe I will come inside," she said between short gasps for breath, "if you think it'd help."

Moon stepped onto the low porch steps; the unpainted pine boards creaked under his weight. He counted the two-by-four porch rafters until he was seven from the south end. The Ute ran his fingers along an unpainted rafter, wiping away a thin veil of spider webs. He found the tarnished brass key where he had left it last year, hanging on a galvanized roofing nail. Nahum had not been a careful man, but he had been lucky. The windows were unbroken, the door lock showed no signs of tampering. There was no indication that vandals had entered the house. Maybe it was because of the persistent rumors that Nahum came back to sleep in the loft of his log cabin every night. And that he drank gallons of whiskey and would surely shoot anyone who was foolish enough to enter his home. But local folks craved such stories, and many believed Armilda's fantastic tale of a band of angels that carried the old shepherd up to heaven. Swing low, sweet chariot! It was all nonsense, of course. Self-delusion. But the Ute's stomach tightened as he opened the door.

Armilda did not expect to find Nahum Yaciiti in the house; she followed the policeman in quickly and flitted about the dusty space like a ragged old moth, touching this, rubbing dust off that, muttering her amazement that ". . . a man could live in such squalor."

Moon thought the place was reasonably tidy. The downstairs was a single large room. A heavy redwood table had been placed at the west window, which had a view of the rolling waters of the Animas. This sturdy piece of furniture served for eating and, judging from the scattering of papers and lead pencils on its surface, as a desk. And everywhere, there were books. A tattered family bible. An English-Spanish dictionary. A cookbook entitled *The Complete Book of* *_____g*.

"Too many books, too much reading," Armilda tapped her temple

"You're kidding." Parris's envy was written all over his face. "One of the numbered series?"

"Serial number five-zero." Parker grinned, displaying a set of over-sized teeth that would have looked just right in the mouth of a Neanderthal. The rod had set him back a week's pay. "Can't wait to flick some dry flies in the Piedra. It's about time for the browns to get hungry." Parker paused, choosing his words carefully. "While you're in Ignacio, you'll likely end up working with my people. From time to time."

"Yeah, guess I might at that." Parris waited. The FBI had jurisdiction for major crimes on Indian reservations. But he sensed that Parker had something specific on his mind.

"You know our guys in Durango?"

"Sure," Parris said. "Stan Newman. George Whitmer. First class guys." The Durango office had the responsibility for the pair of Ute reservations along the southern Colorado border.

"Newman had to go in for knee surgery a couple of days ago. He'll be laid up for at least two months. Whitmer's tied up in at a federal trial in Salt Lake, then he's off on a job in Arizona. Don't know when he'll get back." Parker avoided eye contact. "I've sent a new man down there. Expect you'll meet him pretty soon after you set up shop in Ignacio."

"Fine," Parris said. "Look forward to it." He could have cared less, but it seemed an appropriate response.

"I'd appreciate it if you'd introduce him to Charlie Moon and the rest of the Ute movers and shakers. Kind of grease the skids for him."

There was something odd about this request. It seemed so reasonable, but there was a worried look in Sam's eyes. Parris nodded. "No problem. Me and Charlie Moon, we'll take care of your new man." And, in a way that neither Parris nor Parker could have foreseen, they would.

Scott Parris was halfway to Granite Creek when he realized that Sam Parker had not mentioned the new agent's name.

NEAR BONDAD, ON THE BANKS OF THE *RIO DE LOS ANIMAS PERDITAS*

Charlie Moon folded his arms across his chest and leaned against the fender of the big Bronco. And remembered. It was now most of a year, since Nahum Yaciiti had vanished. The old man had disappeared on the same night his sheep had been slaughtered in the violent storm. There had been nothing but rumors about Nahum's whereabouts, but the Ute policeman stopped every time his duties brought him south of Durango along this stretch of Route 550. He stood in silence and surveyed the small section of earth that had been home to Nahum and provided marginal pasture to his few sheep. It was less than a dozen acres, this sharp wedge of land that pointed to the south. The low bank of the Animas, dotted with tall cottonwoods and bushy willows, was the western boundary. The two-lane blacktop between Durango and Aztec formed the eastern limit. Armilda Esquibel's land abutted the Yaciiti property on the north, and the old woman could see everything from her adobe home that hung precariously on a clay bank above Nahum's bottom land. Moon wondered if the troublesome woman was peering at him from her bedroom window. Sure. If Armilda was alive, she was watching.

The Ute policeman put his hands in his jacket pockets and walked slowly down the lightly graveled driveway toward Nahum's small log house. No smoke came from the stone chimney, and a sheet of steel roofing was loose and rattling in the occasional gust of wind. The shepherd's dilapidated Dodge pickup was parked out back of the house near the small corral, exactly where it had been on that morning after the twister came through. Things were much the same, except now the rusty truck was covered with a thin coat of yellow dust. And it had been much colder on the morning after the storm. It had been October, that time of year the old people called Moon of Dead Leaves Falling. Nahum's sheep had fallen like dead leaves. The pasture was dotted with bleached bones scattered by coyote and buzzard. Occasional snatches of dirty wool still hung on a few tumbleweeds.

Moon leaned with both hands on a creosote-soaked timber that served as a heavy cross member in the sagging corral fence. A relative from Towaoc had taken Nahum's skinny Appaloosa mare to shelter in his own barn until the old shepherd returned. But the smell of the animal still hung on the corral. The presence of Nahum Yaciiti was also strong.

The policeman did not hear the presence behind him, but he felt something like a feather sweeping over the back of his neck. Moon turned slowly, unconscious that his right hand was moving upward toward the bone handle of the heavy revolver holstered on his belt.

Armilda Esquibel was both amused and annoyed at this policeman who had never believed her eye-witness accou shepherd's remarkable disappearance. "Don't need to be afra man. I'm only a harmless old widda woman." But she had kled right hand in the pocket of her plastic rain coat. H were wrapped around the black grip of an antique Remin ringer that had not fired any .41 caliber rim fire cartridges when Armilda shot a fat Apache woman in the thigh.

Moon grinned and tipped his hat. "You're pretty lig feet." Sneaky was more like it. He warily watched the twit in the coat pocket. He thought about dying. A policema little glamour; his death none at all. According to the F he was far more likely to be shot by a deranged old wom vicious bank robber.

She chewed on a tiny plug of Red Man tobacco in relaxed her grip on the hidden derringer. "Since that was taken away to heaven by them angels, there ar galoots and pumpkin-heads comin' around here to car thing that ain't nailed down." She removed her little raincoat pocket and pointed toward Nahum's grape dozen excavations pockmarked the clay. "Them chuc think old Nahum buried his greenbacks out there. Th sometimes and they dig for it . . . like gophers they tobacco juice very near Moon's left boot and grinned joke. "I come down here," her little brown eyes spa chase them thievin' bastards off."

"You should call the station," Moon advised ge care of any trespassers." Most likely, protect them dictable old woman.

She grunted to show her derision. An honest wi not wait half a day for the Utes, who operated on make an appearance and then treat her like she Besides, Armilda enjoyed chasing the thugs away tion made her feel young again. Like she might li she hoped that one of these vandals would give him right between his beady little eyes. "You g house?" On her television screen, policemen al around inside the house of a missing person to derful clue. Armilda Esquibel also wanted to se

Moon didn't answer, but he headed toward

with an arthritic finger and assumed a sage expression, "that was Nahum's problem. Made him think too hard and the poor old man just wore out his mind."

Moon opened the cookbook to a page that had been marked with a slip of yellowed paper. Macaroon Hats. Hazelnut Fingers. Ginger Snaps. Vanilla Paisleys. One and three quarter cups of flour. One half cup ground almonds. Margarine for greasing the pan. The Ute shook his head and smiled. It was hard to picture old Nahum spending his evenings baking cookies. But you never really knew people.

He carefully placed the cookbook back into the rectangle of dustless space on the table and turned to study the room. It was just as the policeman remembered it. A large RC Cola calendar tacked to the wall over the sink displayed an impossibly pretty brunette. A long, shapely leg was draped over a red bicycle; she held a bottled soft drink near barely parted lips. The Winchester carbine Moon had found in the Dodge pickup and hung on a rack over the back door was still in its place. There was a kerosene lamp on the thick pine mantle over the stone fireplace; the scarlet fuel in the glass chamber looked like cheap wine. A painted iron bed stood in a corner, the fine patchwork quilt still turned back on a blue sheet, inviting the old shepherd to rest his bones. An antique vacuum-tube radio in a varnished wooden cabinet sat mute in a dark corner.

The policeman found his notebook and turned the dated pages back toward that cold autumn morning last year. Moon had made a record of the contents of the log house, including a detailed inventory of the food stored in a rough pine cupboard in the corner. Now he compared his notes to what he saw. Six cans of Bush's Best pinto beans, eight small tins of Hatch green chili. Ten cans of a generic store brand of sweet corn. There was an unopened five pound bag of whole-wheat flour. A two gallon tin of corn meal. A glass jar filled with brown sugar. A plastic bottle, half-filled with maple syrup. And an unopened glass jar of Aunt Nellie's Corn Relish. It was all there, just as it had been last year. Waiting for the owner of the household to return.

A small refrigerator still hummed by the back door. Probably needed defrosting. A dual wire basket hung from the ceiling; one section was filled with yellow onions that had sprouted months ago. Another with shriveled potatoes that needed throwing out. Almost enough supplies to feed an old man through the long Colorado winter.

The Ute climbed a ladder and peered into the dusty attic. Pale sunlight filtered in through the single four-pane window; a black mouse scurried for cover under a pile of yellowed newspapers. There was an old cedar chest missing a hinge, odd bits of lumber, stacks of books and magazines. There was also another iron bed, but this one had no mattress on the sagging springs. The policeman made his way down the creaking ladder.

Armilda Esquibel was watching him and wondering what this silent Ute might be thinking about. Most likely, nothing at all. He was a man, so he probably had about as much brains as a peckerwood.

Moon turned for one last look. There was nothing he had not seen before. Most of the old man's belongings were here. But not all. Nahum's gray felt hat with the band of half-dollar sized silver conchos was not hanging on the wooden peg by the front door. Neither was his blue wool coat. There was no sign of his rawhide boots. Wherever he had gone, Nahum had been fully dressed.

Nahum Yaciiti's saddle hung from a stout oak peg by the rear door. This Christmas gift from his wife was a special treasure. The old shepherd had oiled and saddle-soaped the leather every Saturday night. Moon rubbed a fingertip along the dusty leather. Tiny cracks were opening in the shiny surface of the polished cowhide; it hadn't been oiled in a month of Saturdays. It didn't look like Nahum had been back. Or would be.

Charlie Moon stared at the old saddle and whispered to himself. "Well, old man . . . where do you ride tonight?"

3

CAÑON DEL ESPIRITU

Oblivious to the stark beauty of the crisp, deep shadows cast by creamy moonlight, the tiny deer mouse paused to sniff tentatively, interrupting its nibbling on a pungent juniper seed. The rodent tilted her furry head and oriented oversized ears toward the source of the barely audible sounds. Scuff-scuff, the sounds said. After a brief silence, the peculiar sound would repeat. Scuff-scuff. The wee creature, long acquainted with the threat of the heat-sensing rattler and sharp-taloned pygmy owl, sensed that something even more sinister approached along the floor of the canyon. The mouse scampered up the trunk of a venerable piñon. It slipped into its nest of shredded bark, which was expertly wedged into the crotch of a forked branch. Emboldened by the relative security of this hideaway barely a yard above the earth, the rodent watched with mesmerized apprehension as the source of the scuffing sounds approached. The little creature blinked its luminous black eyes in puzzlement at first sight of the *thing;* this unnatural apparition that moved in undulating motion like a shadowy wave over the moonlit sand of the canyon floor. At first, the shape of the intruder was indistinct, an amorphous patch of dark fog floating over the ground. Then, as if it could change its shape at will, the presence seemed to take on substance and form. The thing paused, raised itself to a standing position . . . like a great bear. But it was not a bear. . . . This shaggy-haired creature had broad shoulders, no neck, and a peculiar, flattened head. The head had horns. And a single red eye. Now it would glow brightly, like an ember in a fire. Then it would dim, as if the creature had blinked. The mouse could not deal with abstract concepts, like Good and

Evil. But there were primitive instincts deep within its breast that drummed an urgent warning: Be still, be still!

A mosquito whined lazily around the dark form, confused by a peculiar mixture of scents that was alien, yet strangely inviting. The insect lit and immediately drove her long proboscis deep into the surface of the creature. There was no hint of blood . . . no evidence that the phantom was alive; the mosquito departed to search for a prey whose heart pumped the warm, nourishing substance of life.

Something rippled underneath its fur, then the apparition moved away ghostlike through the fringed sage and Apache plume toward the dusty wallow under the old juniper where the great spotted animal slept. To the deer mouse, this choice seemed reckless. The great bellowing animal who ruled over this canyon would be annoyed if awakened; its great, sweeping horns would make short work of this mysterious intruder.

A pygmy owl in a crevice on the canyon wall stopped its whoop-whoop call; even the leg-scraping chirp of the fat black crickets fell silent. The night creatures were unnaturally quiet, as if all the canyon's life had felt the approaching shadow of death. For a moment there was total silence, as if the mouse had gone deaf.

When the terrible shriek filled the sinuous canyon and echoed off its towering sandstone walls, the deer mouse jerked its little head inside the bark nest and trembled spasmodically in elemental terror. The rich, sweet aroma of fresh blood slipped over the moonlit landscape like a heavy fog.

The soft glow of the morning sun was barely touching the horizon when Gorman Sweetwater shifted the pickup down to second gear, then glanced sideways at his daughter. Benita was almost as pretty as her mother, and she was the only close family left since his wife had died. He dreaded the thought that she would meet some young man at the college in Durango, get married, and move far away. Then he'd be alone.

Gorman grunted to get his daughter's attention; he jerked a thumb toward Daisy Perika's trailer home.

"Kitchen light's on, Daddy. That means coffee's perking." Benita patted him on the arm. "You intend to stop and gossip with Aunt Daisy?"

"Business before gossip. We'll check on the stock first."

He continued for another hundred yards, then braked his pickup to a stop at the mouth of *Cañon del Espiritu;* Benita got out and opened the flimsy barbed-wire gate that blocked the dirt road. After his daughter was beside him again, the Ute rancher shifted into low and released the clutch. He chugged along the rutted lane, blinking into the morning haze as he searched the brush for a glimpse of his small herd of purebred Herefords. It was not that they needed checking on, but the animals were a source of joy to the rancher. Several times every week he would leave his home before dawn and drive to the canyon to admire their handsome forms. And talk to them. Gorman knew every animal; each had its own personality. He had loaded three bales of alfalfa hay into the pickup, but this was just an excuse to make the trip.

The rancher was familiar with their habits. On cold nights, the Herefords usually slept in the piñon grove along the sandstone shelf on the north side of the canyon. It was a good place; the sandstone was covered with petroglyphs, the sacred markings of the Old Ones whose spirits rested peacefully within these towering walls. There was, of course, the *pitukupf* as well, but the dwarf had not done any real harm for many years. Not since Gorman's horse had grazed too close to his underground home. The rancher pushed this unpleasant memory from his mind. The Ute wondered if the *pitukupf* was, like himself, getting too old to cause any serious trouble. He smiled at the thought; Daisy Perika claimed that the *pitukupf* was full of years beyond counting, and Daisy knew something about this subject. Daisy had the Power. The Old Power. She was probably the only Ute left who could hear the voice of the *pitukupf*. Most of the younger generation didn't believe in the dwarf's existence. Many of the youngsters, unlike Benita, couldn't even speak the language of the People. But with the new Ute language program in the Ignacio public schools, that would change. A few went away to Fort Lewis College and learned the *matukach* view of Native American history. What else did they learn from the whites? The thought troubled him; what would come to pass in another twenty years? There were barely more than a thousand Utes on the southern reservation, fewer still on the Ute Mountain enclave. Would anyone be left who understood the ways of the People? Daisy Perika was very old; after she departed for the next world, who would talk to the dwarf-spirit? The rancher wondered if the *pitukupf* was ever lonely. Gorman was lonely every day Benita spent at Fort Lewis College; this was another reason he visited his cattle and stopped by to visit with Daisy.

He set the brake on the pickup, filled his brier pipe with a wad of Prince Albert, and touched a flame to the fragrant tobacco. The rancher took a deep draw, then pursed his lips to blow a puff of gray smoke toward the windshield.

Benita put on her stern face; little wrinkles rippled across her forehead. "You ought to give up smoking." Unconsciously, she imitated her mother's tone.

"I'm trying to get used to the pipe again, it's not so bad as the cigarettes. Anyhow," he added with an air of self-righteousness, "I don't impale."

Lately, he was having trouble finding just the right word. "You don't *inhale*," she corrected gently.

"That," her father said, "is why it don't hurt me none." Gorman exhaled smoke from deep within his lungs. Benita studied her father's profile; when she wasn't around to keep an eye on him, did he roll a new cigarette every ten minutes?

Gorman was considering how much he had to be thankful for when he heard the sound. It was something between a howl and a hoot, from somewhere on the cliff above the canyon. Was it a cougar . . . or another type of beast altogether? The rancher put his pipe on the dashboard and lifted an old 30-30 caliber carbine off the rack over the rear window.

"Stay put," he said. It would not have occurred to Benita to question this solemn instruction. Gorman slid from the pickup seat and planted his big feet on the sand of the canyon floor. He tried to remember a prayer. When he was younger, he had memorized a half dozen of the prayers in the tiny black book he found in his uncle's medicine bag. Gorman's memory was fading; he reverently repeated the one prayer that he could remember. He was whispering ". . . deliver us from evil" as he moved toward the piñon grove. He squinted at the mesa ridge, more than a hundred feet above the canyon floor. "For thine is the power. And the glory. . . ." The old man could see nothing unusual on the rim, but he felt it. Watching him. ". . . for ever and ever." He gritted his teeth and cocked the lever-action carbine. "Amen," he grunted.

From the edge of his visual field, he thought he saw something move above him, on the edge of the cliff. It could have been imagination. Probably something ordinary, like a coyote or a wandering *uru-ci;* there were many ghosts in this place. He moved along the path in the sage. There was fresh manure on the sand by a Gambel oak, and other signs that the Herefords had slept in the piñon grove. He moved closer to the canyon wall, brushing aside the freshly bloomed Apache Plumes. Then, there was an odor that penetrated the chill morning air. Blood. Freshly spilled blood! Gorman rested his finger on the trigger and moved against the light breeze that drifted down *Cañon del Espiritu*. He saw the carcass as he rounded the face of a squat sandstone pillar. The big animal was on its side, legs protruding stiffly, belly beginning to bloat with gas.

"No, no," he pleaded, "Please, God, don't let it be my bull." He stopped and closed his eyes, hoping the dreadful apparition would vanish. "God, listen to me. I can do without a cow or a steer, but I need my bull!" He opened his eyes. The animal was still there. Gorman's feet were like lead as he forced himself close enough to inspect the carcass. "Oh . . . no. Oh, please, no." It was the bull. Or had been. The mouth was open, tongue lolling out, as if the animal had bellowed. The ears had been removed. There was something terribly familiar about this. Yes. That bull elk up in the Never Summer range. Gorman's legs wobbled; he forced himself to move close to the carcass. He used the carbine as a staff to steady himself as he squatted to discover the final horror. Before he looked, he was virtually certain of what he would see. He looked, then closed his eyes and swore. The butcher had also removed the bull's testicles!

There was a wailing howl from atop the mesa. Gorman wheeled, set the carbine stock firmly against his shoulder and fired in the direction of the sound. "Damn you!" He cocked the carbine and fired again. And again. The cracks of the shots echoed back and forth between the canyon walls until the sounds dissipated into the morning mists. Then, total silence. Gorman squatted by the dead animal and leaned his old carbine on a piñon snag. And wept.

Daisy Perika was frying a thick slice of ham in the iron skillet when she heard the faint echo of distant rifle shots. Was her cousin taking a deer out of season? If so, she knew she would get a share. She imagined sliced deer-liver with diced onion in her skillet and the vision made her mouth water. No, more likely Gorman was shooting at a cougar. Not likely he'd hit anything; the cataracts in his eyes were gradually dropping a milky curtain over his world.

Only minutes earlier, she had heard her cousin entering the canyon. There was no mistaking the old GMC pickup; it had a loose tail pipe that rattled against the frame when Gorman jolted over ruts in the dirt road. Even without that clue, it had to be Gorman. Who else visited *Cañon del Espíritu* at the crack of dawn? Then, in the stillness of the morning, she heard the truck engine start. This morning, he'd cut his visit short. Gorman was usually in Spirit Canyon for at least an hour, gloating over those fat cattle. But wait—the truck wasn't lurching over the bumps; someone with a more delicate touch than Gorman was driving. Daisy smiled with satisfaction; Benita was home from Fort Lewis College in Durango. The shaman had already placed an extra plate on her kitchen table for her cousin; she added another plate for Benita. Gorman always stopped to visit on his way out of the canyon. It was invariably the same routine: Daisy offered breakfast, he would refuse. Then after she urged him, he would grudgingly accept. "If you're going to keep after me," he would say, "I might as well have some." Gorman was one of life's constants.

Daisy opened the door of her trailer home as she heard Gorman's heavy step on the wooden porch. He had those dirty rubber boots on; she frowned at his big feet. Gorman leaned on the porch railing while he pulled them off. Daisy moved forward to embrace Benita. "How are you, little girl?"

Benita's eyes were moist. "Fine, Aunt Daisy." Gorman was obviously in a foul mood and Benita was shaken. Daisy waited impatiently to learn what they would tell her. If it was a family dispute, the Sweetwaters would keep it to themselves. It would be bad manners to pry, but if it came to that, Daisy would pry.

Benita noticed the third setting at the table. "But how did you know I'd be here?"

Daisy assumed a solemn expression and touched a forefinger to her temple. "I have my own ways of knowing these things." The shaman was rewarded by a wide-eyed expression of awe from the young woman. It was best to stay a step ahead of these college kids. Kept them in their place.

Gorman sat down heavily at the table. Daisy poured a cup of pitch-black coffee into his favorite mug, the one with the Nestlé bunny that appeared after the cup heated. Benita didn't drink coffee; said it made her nervous. Children nowadays behaved so strangely! Gorman had a tentative sip.

"You two want some breakfast? I'm making a cheese omelet and some ham. Got a jar of maple cream from my friends in New York State. Goes good on the hot biscuits."

Benita glanced at the lard can on the biscuit-board and realized these were old-fashioned biscuits; she nodded her polite rejection of this offer. "Thanks, Aunt Daisy. I don't have much of an appetite this early."

Gorman rested his face in his hands. His voice croaked when he spoke. "Ouray is dead!"

Daisy tilted her round face and raised her eyebrows. Had he been drinking this early in the morning? Who did Gorman think he had shot? "Well, it's a bad thing, I guess, but you ought to be over it by now. Chief Ouray's been dead way over a hundred years."

Gorman looked up, wide-eyed and outraged. "Dammit, Daisy, not *that* Ouray. My registered Hereford bull, Big Ouray, he's dead!"

Men, the old woman sighed, they were all alike. They loved their pickup trucks and their animals. And ignored their wives. She wondered what she should say to comfort her cousin. "They say you should never give an animal a name unless it's a pet." This brought no response. Daisy poured an extra dash of coffee into his mug. "That the bull you bought back in January?"

Gorman grunted. Benita started to say something, then clamped her mouth shut.

Daisy adopted a more sympathetic tone. "How did it happen?" That bull, with his enormous horns and nasty temper, was a dangerous brute. No cougar or bear would dare mess with him. "He eat some poison weed?"

Gorman shook his head; he felt a need to cleanse his thoughts. "This is a bad thing. Somebody cut him up. Took his ears and balls. Like that elk in the Never Summer range."

She remembered the story about the mutilated elk in the alpine pasture. Some Utes figured it was witches. The crazy *matukach* woman in Durango insisted the culprits were little silver-clothed people (with long ape-like arms!) who came from the stars in flying ships that like looked like huge cigars. But nobody really knew what had happened to the unfortunate animal.

Daisy sat down beside Gorman and patted his shoulder in a motherly fashion. She had always tried to look out for her lanky cousin, ever since they were children. He was like a brother. "A Ute wouldn't do anything like that," she offered. "Sounds like some crazy *matukach* at work. Some of them are filled with superstition; who knows why they do the things they do?" Daisy noticed Benita's smile and was puzzled. Who could understand young people? Maybe Benita had spent too much time with the *matukach* professors, learning a lot of foolishness.

Gorman rubbed at his eyes with a dirty red bandanna. "I don't know. White people in the canyon? It happened late last night; he was still warm." He looked out the trailer window. "The only way into Spirit Canyon goes right past your place. . . . Wouldn't you have noticed if somebody went up the lane?"

"I didn't hear a car or truck." Daisy was searching for an answer. "Maybe the animal got sick and died; coyotes eat what is easy to get, like the tongue and privates and . . ."

"Big Ouray still had his tongue, and coyotes don't eat ears." He eyed her curiously. "I heard something. Howling." Gorman swirled the coffee in his cup. "You don't think . . . that little man who lives in the canyon might have had something to do with this?" This question embarrassed Benita, but Gorman didn't care.

Daisy shook her head to dismiss this troubling question. The *pitukupf*? No. The dwarf would never mutilate an animal. The shaman's brow furrowed. Would he?

"Daddy," Benita began firmly, "there isn't any such thing as a *pitukupf*, it's just an old tribal myth, like the Water-Baby." The young woman was pointedly ignored by her elders.

Gorman stuck his brier between his teeth. He looked through the kitchen window and into the yawning mouth of the great canyon. "The dwarf—he killed my best horse a few years back."

"That was different," Daisy retorted sharply. "Your own fault. You shouldn't have hobbled him so close to the little man's home. You know he doesn't like that." She got up and opened a small sack of flour. "Anyway, I put tobacco by his home every new moon. He wouldn't do anything bad to me. Or my relatives." She adjusted the propane flame under the coffee pot and gave Gorman a sideways glance. "What'd you shoot at?"

"Nothing," he said. "Shadows."

"Gorman the great hunter," she mocked, "bring some shadow-meat with you next time, I'll make you a shadow-breakfast."

Gorman ignored the insufferable woman's jibe. "I'm in bad trouble. Big Ouray was a twelve-thousand dollar registered Hereford. And he's only half paid for. I needed him to build up my herd, start selling registered animals instead of hamburger meat." He thumped his fist on his chest. "Can't take much more of this." His voice took on a pitiful tone. "I'm an old man, not goin' to be in this world many more winters." He glanced at his daughter to see if she understood the gravity of his pronouncement, then turned to watch Daisy putter about the small kitchen. "I expect my heart will just stop thumpin' some dark night. It runs in my family. You know my third cousin . . . Sally Bitter Horse who lives with her mother over at Hondo Fork?"

Daisy was devoting most of her attention to a mixing bowl. She added a cup of buttermilk, two large gobs of lard, and a pinch of salt to the dough. "Sure. Sally works in the high school over there."

"Mrs. Bitter Horse," Benita said, "teaches mathematics and music."

"Well Sally," Gorman continued, "the way I heard it, she was learnin' them kids some 'rithmatic, when she had an attack from one of them cor-uh . . . corollaries and she damn near died from it."

Benita sighed. "She had a *coronary*, Daddy."

He glanced at his daughter, wondering why she was repeating what he had just said. Maybe she was getting a little bit deaf, like her mother had been. He turned toward Benita and spoke a little bit louder: "And I could have me one of them corollaries myself. An' then," he pointed at her with the pipe stem, "you'd be a orrifun." This image brought a tear to his eye.

Benita leaned over to kiss him on the cheek. "Daddy's complained about his heart for twenty years. But the physician at the clinic says he's in good condition for his age."

Gorman grunted. "Hmmmpf. Blue-eyed *matukach* from Robe Island." He sucked hard on the pipe. "What's he know?"

"You better go by the tribal police station," Daisy said. "See my nephew, tell him about the dead animal." She added another gob of lard to the dough. "He's in charge of the whole outfit while Chief Severo's away, and," Daisy added with quiet pride, "Charlie Moon always takes good care of family."

Benita nodded vigorously; her bright expression made it clear that she considered this a very sensible suggestion.

"After I call on the vet, I'll talk to your nephew the big-shot policeman," Gorman said.

The old woman turned away from her work to squint at her cousin. "Ain't it a little late to call the animal doctor?"

"Doctor Schaid is required to examine the carcass," Benita said, "before he fills out the insurance forms." She had already explained this to her father.

Daisy found her rolling pin; she pressed the dough onto a polished maple board until it was no thicker than her thumb. "So. You got insurance on that bull?" She was surprised that Gorman had demonstrated such foresight.

He drank the last of the coffee and belched. "Sure. Bein' a rancher is a perfession just like any other perfession." Benita had badgered him into buying the insurance.

"Since you give 'em all names, I thought maybe they was your pets." Daisy grinned and Gorman kept a poker face. "Who you got insurance with?" He ducked his head and she knew. "Not Arlo Nightbird . . ."

Gorman avoided her sharp eyes. "He's the cheapest."

Daisy winked at the girl. "You know what the *matukach* say: 'you get what you pay for.' Anyway, you're the stingiest man I ever knew, except for my second husband." She hurriedly crossed herself. "God rest his pitiful soul."

Benita chimed in. "Father never throws anything away. My history professor, she says that people who grew up during the Great Depression—"

"What's done is finished," Gorman interrupted. "I don't need no lecher from either one of you." It would be best to change the subject. "You heard about Arlo Nightbird's plans for the canyon?"

"I don't pay no attention to rumors," Daisy retorted. She searched a cabinet drawer until she found the soup can with the sharp rim. "You listen to all that tribal gossip, you'll hear something that'll keep you awake at night." The old woman, waiting anxiously to hear the gossip, used the soup can to cut the biscuit dough into neat discs.

"This ain't just talk," Gorman said. "The Economic Development Board's workin' on a deal with the government. Want to put some kind of garbage in *Cañon del Espiritu.*"

"Garbage? In the sacred canyon?" She refilled his cup. "They'd never do that."

"It's not exactly garbage," Benita said, obviously proud of her knowledge, "it's well . . . waste. Radioactive waste from nuclear power plants."

Daisy paused and looked blankly at the greasy propane stove. "Why would the tribe want to do something like that . . . in my canyon?" She slid the tray of biscuits into the preheated oven, then lit a burner with a butane cigarette lighter.

"It's not all that bad," Benita said. "They put worn-out nuclear fuel elements into big tanks of water, then they put concrete slabs on top of the tanks. The water and concrete stops the radiation. You could sleep right beside it every night for your whole life, no problem." She watched doubtful expressions spread over the faces of her elders. "It shouldn't be any danger to our cattle."

Her father squinted at her. "What did you say that stuff was?"

Benita repeated her words slowly: "Nuclear . . . fuel . . . elements."

The old man added a pinch of tobacco to the brier bowl and relit his pipe. "If them knuckle filaments is so damned safe," he asked, "then why don't they just keep 'em where they're already at?"

Benita opened her mouth to reply, read the combative expression on her father's face, and thought better of it.

"You two need some breakfast," Daisy said quickly.

Gorman put on a sad demeanor as easily as some men slipped into a coat; it was carefully designed to generate sympathy. "Don't know if I can eat. What I seen in the canyon kinda took my appetizer away." He glanced at the black iron skillet and sniffed hopefully at the fetching aroma of the ham slab swimming in the popping grease.

Daisy played his game. "I made enough cheese omelet for all three of us. And there's a big slice of sugar-cured ham. And hot biscuits with maple cream." She paused to give him time to think about it. "But I expect you'd be better off to go home and have some oatmeal. They say oatmeal's good for old men's bowels. Cheese and eggs, they might stop up your plumbing."

Gorman sighed. "Well, if you're gonna keep after me, I guess I might as well have a bite."

"Maybe," Benita asked, "you have some cereal?"

"I got ham and I got eggs," Daisy replied sharply. Her tone said *take it or leave it.*

4

Charlie Moon, a half cup of coffee in his fist, was standing outside the police station. Away from the crackle of the short wave radio, the incessant ringing of telephones, the whining complaints of a drunken prisoner who insisted that he was a very important man in Denver and a "damn good friend of the governor." Moon sniffed at the pungent scent of pine in the air; he squinted at a half dozen ravens gliding in a wide arc through the pale morning sky. How could a Ute ever leave this place? But many of the People had.

Before he saw it, Moon heard Gorman Sweetwater's pickup pass the Sky Ute Motel and turn the corner at KSUT radio. The old GMC lurched into the tribal police headquarters parking lot. The policeman was not particularly pleased to see Gorman's pickup truck until he noticed Benita sitting next to her father. So she was back from college for the summer. For the past two years, he had wanted to say something. He had planned a dozen artful ways of letting her know that she was always on his mind, but he never knew quite what to say to this pretty girl. In her presence, Moon always ended up playing the role of uncle.

The big policeman leaned on the door and grinned at the rancher. "Gorman, you still didn't get that tail pipe fixed. And worse than that, you're parked in Homer Tonompicket's spot."

The rancher snorted. "I'll worry about the tail pipe if it falls off, and you can go piss on the game warden."

Moon touched the brim of his hat. "Mornin' Benita. It's a good thing you inherited your momma's sweet disposition." He wanted to add "and her good looks," but the words hung in his throat.

Benita smiled and glanced uncertainly at her grumpy father. Charlie Moon was the best catch on the reservation. Maybe in Colorado. "How's your new house coming along, Charlie?" Maybe he'd ask her to come out and see it.

Moon avoided the old man's suspicious glare; he pushed a gravel pebble with his toe. "Still a lot of work to do." Maybe he should invite her over to have a look at the place. But what if she didn't come? He took a deep breath. "Maybe, sometime when you have some time to kill . . ."

She was about to accept this unfinished invitation when her father interrupted.

"I got me some trouble."

The policeman backed away as Gorman opened the door and slid to the gravel surface. "What kinda trouble?"

"The bad kind. Something . . . somebody's killed Big Ouray."

The policeman thought hard and came up with nothing. "Who's Big Ouray?"

"My registered Hereford bull, dammit. And don't tell me I shouldn't give my stock names. They're my cattle and I can damn well do whatever—"

"Now don't lose your water." Moon gestured toward the station door with his cup. "Let's go inside and have some coffee. You can tell me all about it." Gorman lost a beef every year or so, and he always waved his arms and yelled until he was hoarse.

"Don't need more coffee. We just had breakfast at your Aunt Daisy's. That woman pushes greasy food at me every time I stop by; I won't be able to eat nothing again before suppertime. All them eggs and pork is gonna cause me to have," he thumped his chest, ". . . one of them cor-uh . . . cor-oll . . . ahhh . . . coronations."

"Well now that'd be the day," Moon said earnestly. "I expect the whole tribe and half the town would show up to watch it happen."

Benita clamped a hand over her mouth to suppress a giggle. Gorman cocked his head and blinked curiously at the big policeman. Charlie Moon was supposed to be so damn smart but sometimes he said things that didn't make no sense at all. "What're you gonna do about my dead bull?"

Moon adopted his official tone. "Tell me what happened."

Benita watched them through a sand-blasted windshield. She barely winked at Moon; the big Ute ducked his head shyly.

The old man pushed his hands deep into his overall pockets. "Not much to tell. Big Ouray was dead when I got there just about sunup this morning. Ears and balls gone." Moon felt the hair stand up on his neck. "And," Gorman added quickly, "don't say it was coyotes; it wasn't no coyotes—somebody done it with a knife." He looked glumly toward the place where the sun comes up. "A razor-sharp knife."

"You see any tracks?" Moon knew what the answer would be.

"No tracks." Gorman lowered his voice almost to a whisper. "I heard a noise, though, from up on the mesa. Kind of a . . . a wail." No point in mentioning he'd shot at the sound, that would only bring a stern lecture about gun safety from the big policeman.

Moon nodded. Gorman had probably heard a cougar. Maybe. "How about the rest of your cattle, they all right?"

"Didn't find 'em. Expect they're holed up in them little draws way up the canyon." He scowled at the policeman. "I sure as hell can't afford to lose no more beeves so you better see it don't happen again! In the meantime, I'm gonna go over to Arlo's place and file a claim on the bull. That animal," Gorman sighed with bitter regret, "cost me a fair pile of money."

"Arlo Nightbird carrying the paper on your animals?" Moon's tone was just critical enough to irritate the rancher.

"That's right," Gorman snapped, "and I don't want no lip from you about who I buy my insurance from. I already had a belly full from your Aunt Daisy. She thinks I should go up to Durango and buy insurance at one of them *matukach* agencies. Arlo ain't no saint, but," Gorman added in a virtuous tone, "he's one of the People and I try to give the People as much business as I can." Arlo was cheap.

Moon held his hands up in mock defense. "Hey, you want to deal with Arlo, it makes me no never mind."

"I'll take care of my ranchin' business," Gorman pointed at Moon's chest, "you take care of police business."

"I'll go up to Spirit Canyon and check things out." Moon stole a quick look at Benita over Gorman's battered hat. "Then," the policeman said, "I'll write up a report." He waited for the predictable response.

"Well, that's just dandy! A report. That'll do me a helluva lot of good." Benita offered Moon an apologetic look; Gorman slammed the pickup door and roared off in low gear, the tail pipe dangling on a single rusty hanger.

Moon watched the pickup disappear. "You're welcome." He waved. "We're here to serve!" Sooner or later, Benita would show up in town without her cranky father. Then, Moon promised himself, he'd manage to be where she was. Then—he kicked at a pebble— then he'd probably choke again.

At Benita's insistence, Gorman Sweetwater kicked some of the dried mud off his boots before he pushed the plate glass door under the sign that announced: NIGHTBIRD INSURANCE AGENCY. Herb Ecker was sitting behind a battered desk, carefully inking words into a bound notebook. Gorman waited impatiently as the young man closed his eyes and repeated the words aloud: "I dance the dance of the old ones."

Gorman shuffled his feet to announce his presence, but Herb, blissfully alone with his imagination, continued: "I dance the dance of remembering."

Gorman cleared his throat. "You'd best forget the dance, kid, and tend to your business."

The insurance salesman jumped to his feet as if launched by coiled springs. "Good day, Mr. Sweetwater, how may I be of service to you?" Herb looked hopefully at Benita, who flashed a lovely smile in return. The young man looked at the floor, his blond hair flopping over his forehead like a mop.

Benita stifled a giggle. She adored his blue eyes. "How are you, Herbie?"

Ecker blushed. "I am quite well." He glanced uncertainly at the old rancher, then at the daughter. "Thank you."

"Your hair," she said, "looks a lot nicer since you let it grow out. You writing poetry?"

The exchange student had been nearly bald when he arrived in Ignacio. Ecker started to reply, then hesitated when he saw the dark expression spreading over Gorman Sweetwater's face.

Gorman glared at the young man, then turned his harsh stare on his daughter. "You two know each other?" It had the unmistakable tone of accusation.

"Sure, Daddy. Herbie was in two of my classes last year. He's one of the smartest students at Fort Lewis College." She beamed at the young man. "Next semester, Herbie's enrolled in graduate school at the University of New Mexico."

Ecker's blush deepened. He looked as if he was about to apologize for sharing a class with Benita.

Gorman snorted. "New Mexico, huh?" Were Colorado schools not good enough?

"Yes, sir," Ecker replied with a spark of confidence. "Anthropology major."

The rancher scowled suspiciously at the distraught young man. Gorman decided that Herb was entirely too pretty to be a boy, and this made the rancher nervous. He wondered if this kid really liked girls. Rumor was, Herb took an unhealthy interest in his boss. Some Utes jokingly referred to Herb Ecker as "Nightbird's shadow." But it was time to get down to business. "My bull," he cleared his throat, ". . . he died."

Herb raised his eyebrows in a puzzled expression. "Your bull—you say it died?" His peculiar Germanic accent annoyed Gorman, who was suspicious of almost everyone. Especially foreigners.

"Yeah, died." Gorman leaned forward menacingly. "That's what happens when you drop off to sleep and you don't wake up no more." He was disappointed when the young man showed no sign of being offended. "You oughta remember him: Big Ouray. Registered Hereford. You sold me the policy, even came out to take them pictures of my animals."

Herb nodded and smiled politely. "Of course, I do remember now. I am very sorry about your loss, Mr. Sweetwater." Herb clasped his hands in the manner of a mortician comforting the bereaved. The blond kid had bounced from job to job to earn his tuition and a meager living. Part-time tutor in German and mathematics, veterinary assistant to Dr. Schaid, now peddler of insurance. Maybe, Gorman mused, Herb had put in a stint with a funeral parlor.

Gorman suddenly lost interest in baiting this sickly-pale foreigner; he was eager to finish his business and leave. "I'm here to file a claim."

"Certainly. I do not handle that part of the business, you understand. I sell the policies. Mr. Nightbird, he processes the claims."

This sounded like a run-around. "Arlo does that? I thought he spent all of his time working up big moneymaking deals for the tribe. Where in hell is that little crook?"

Herb glanced uneasily at a closed door. "Mr. Nightbird is busy. I'll tell him that you—"

Gorman marched toward the closed door. "He'll see me right now. Benita, you wait here." Herb was frantically pressing the intercom button when Gorman stomped into Arlo Nightbird's office.

Arlo had his immaculate ostrich-hide boots propped on his desk. He was watching a pornographic video while, between puffs on an oversized cigar, he sucked on a silver flask of expensive bourbon. Arlo pressed the PAUSE button on his remote control and glared at his visitor. "Can't you read English, Gorman? It says PRIVATE on that door, and that's damn well what it means."

Gorman nodded toward the naked figures frozen on the television screen. "From the looks of *that*, it should say PRIVATES."

Arlo scowled and pointed his cigar at Gorman's feet. "And your boots, your big damn rubber boots! What'd you do, wade the river? You're tracking mud all over my brand-new antique Persian rug!"

Gorman dropped his lanky form into a chair and removed his hat to reveal long, unkempt wisps of iron-gray hair. He scratched at his scalp. "My bull. Big Ouray. He died last night."

"Well, hell, Gorman, I'm just heart*broken*." Arlo switched off the television. "We'll have to round up some Irishmen and throw us a wake. Maybe we can invite a few cows, some that was mounted by your bull." Arlo rubbed the turquoise stud in his left earlobe and waited for a reply that didn't come. Gorman's silence unnerved him. "What do I care if your damn bull croaked? Go tell your blackbird priest; it's none of my business."

"Don't bad-mouth Father Raes. And it is your business. I'm here to file a claim."

Arlo was wide-eyed. "You're kiddin' me. We wrote a policy on your damn cattle? I don't believe it."

"Believe it, piss-ant." Gorman pitched a scuffed blue envelope on the oak desk.

Arlo opened the envelope, eyed the policy suspiciously, then bellowed. "Ecker, you write this big ass-hole a policy on his swayback cows?" Under his breath: "Dumb Kraut son-of-a-bitch."

Herb appeared at the office doors. "Yes I did, Mr. Nightbird."

Nightbird muttered to Gorman. "Damn Europeans been nothin' but trouble since Christopher rowed his boat ashore." Arlo buried his face in his hands and groaned. "Why'd I go hire a foreigner?"

Gorman imitated that superior air he had often seen on his daughter's face since she had become a college student. "Probably 'cause he came cheap." You get what you pay for.

Arlo was practically pulling the turquoise stud from his earlobe. "Damn, I feel heartburn coming on!" A ray of hope flashed across his face. "Is the policy paid up?"

Ecker approached somewhat uncertainly; he offered his boss a folded computer printout from a legal-size file folder. "Yes sir. In effect through next December for twenty-four animals."

Arlo squinted uncomprehendingly at the printout; Gorman watched his face and was reminded of a weasel. "How do we know the policy was written on your dead bull? Maybe," he glanced sideways at Gorman, "you got two hundred cows, you only insured two dozen?"

Herb Ecker produced a piece of blue paper. "The photographs and ear-tag numbers are all here, Mr. Nightbird." The young man pointed at a color photo stapled to the list. "That is Big Ouray. Ear tag number 101."

Arlo glared at the color photograph of the sullen bull, then unfolded the policy and read it through the bottom of his bifocals.

Gorman grinned. Arlo was boxed in; maybe he'd get a major case of heartburn. Maybe even one of them coro-whatzits.

Arlo folded the papers and dropped them on his desk. "So how'd your damn old bull die?" He tried hard to sound casual. "Some city-boy hunter mistake him for an elk?" That would void the policy.

"Elk season," Gorman said, "ain't till October." The rancher smelled a trap; he looked down at his muddy boots. "Big Ouray's stone dead; that's all that matters. I want my money."

Arlo sensed a weak spot. "Policy only pays on death by natural cause. Terminal belly ache, lightning strikes, baseball-sized hail stones, predators, that kind of thing."

Gorman looked up quickly. "It was a pred—predabiter."

"What kind of predator? Mountain lion, bear?" Arlo grinned. "Sasquatch?"

"Don't know." Gorman shifted uncomfortably in his chair. "Whatever it was didn't wait around for me." Or did it? The blood-chilling howl from the mesa top still rang in his ears.

Arlo chewed on his cigar, allowing Gorman time to sweat a bit. "You'll need some evidence. The insurance adjuster, maybe he'll think *you* killed the bull." He saw Gorman's massive fists clench. "Now don't get edgy. I didn't say *I* believed you'd try to cheat the insurance company, but you know how nit-picking these adjusters can be."

"You tell the adjuster it was a predabiter. Then he'll pay."

"Okay. Tell me what kind of animal killed your bull."

"Don't know for sure."

"There must have been signs, tracks. What the hell kind of Indian are you, Gorman, you can't tell from the signs. . . ."

Gorman raised his big frame from the chair and leaned over the desk, waving his hand as if he might grab Arlo by the throat. "What the hell kind of Indian are *you*, Arlo, trying to cheat one of the People? You little thief, I ought to—"

Arlo backed his chair up against the wall. "Now calm down, I didn't mean to upset you, but I got to go by the rules. Have Doc Schaid examine the animal."

"I called the vet already; he's on his way to the canyon by now."

"If he says its natural causes, we'll pay. I guarantee it. You have Arlo Nightbird's word."

Gorman grimaced. "I'd sooner have a bad case of the piles."

Arlo let the insult pass. There was a rumor that, in his youth, Gorman Sweetwater had killed a knife-wielding Apache with those huge hands. The cigar bobbled in Arlo's mouth as he talked. "Dammit, Gorman, you ought to retire from this cattle business anyway. Can't make any real money at it, not with the import quotas from Argentina going up every year. Before long, you'll likely have to move them bone-bags out of Spirit Canyon anyhow."

Gorman was stunned. "What do you mean? I've had an allotment in *Cañon del Espiritu* for my whole life; my father had it, and my grandfather . . ."

Arlo hung his thumbs over his alligator-skin belt. "You read the *Drum*, you'd know I'm the new chairman of the Economic Development Board. We're going to shake the federal government's money tree. They need a temporary site to store radioactive wastes from nuclear power plants. We're going to propose using Spirit Canyon. Indian reservations are a natural; the state legislatures don't have much to say about what we do on our own land."

The rancher's doubtful expression annoyed the entrepreneur.

"Listen, Gorman, the Skull Valley Goshutes in Utah and the Mescalero Apache down in New Mexico got a big head start on us, but I think we got a good chance to beat them out with our canyon site. I've been working on the Phase One proposal for weeks now; its only for fifty thousand, but there's big money for whoever finally gets the installation."

"I heard about it, but I don't see why my cattle couldn't stay in the canyon if that knuckler crap is as safe as they say it is."

Arlo took another sip from his small flask of bourbon, scratched his crotch, and belched. "Government rules say we have to keep domestic animals and people away from the site."

Gorman stared out the window at passing traffic. "The tribe wouldn't never allow the *matukach* to put garbage in the sacred canyon."

"Sacred bullshit. I'll tell you what's sacred. Greenbacks, deutsche marks, yen." Arlo rubbed a beautifully manicured finger against his thumb. "That's what pays the rent. Anyway, it's not like it'll hurt that useless old canyon. I hear they'll cover the waste with enough concrete to build a freeway from here to hell and gone. And it's only temporary. When Yucca Mountain is ready, they'll move it all over to Nevada."

"When would that happen?"

Arlo ducked his head. "Oh, not too long." Fifteen, maybe twenty years. Maybe never.

The rancher turned to leave. "You see I get paid for Big Ouray."

Arlo followed him to the outer office. "Hey, is that Benita? She sure has filled out."

Gorman saw the leer on Arlo's piglike face. It had been a very bad day, and this was finally just too much. He wheeled on the smaller man. "You better get control of it, Arlo, before somebody snips it off." The rancher's hand made a cutting motion across his crotch.

Louise Marie LaForte, an elderly French Canadian who had stopped by to renew her fire insurance, watched through slit lids. "*Oui*," she whispered to Herb Ecker, "a warning to take seriously."

Arlo raised his hands in apology. "Hey, I didn't mean nothin' . . ."

Ecker fumbled awkwardly with a sheaf of papers; he avoided looking at Benita.

The rancher, with his daughter leading the way, stomped toward the door.

Arlo's mouth dropped open. "Get a hold of yourself, old man, all I said was—"

Gorman slammed the door hard. The plastic sign listing the daily hours of the Nightbird Insurance Agency popped loose and clattered onto the floor.

Arlo watched Ecker replace the small sign on the door. "Hard-nosed old bastard," he muttered.

Herb Ecker cleared his throat; he moved close to his boss. "I'm about to take the mail to the post office. Is there anything you want before I leave?"

Arlo waved his cigar impatiently. "Yeah, you Kraut Boy Scout, I want you to take some friendly advice. Sell insurance on automobiles and houses. Move some term life whenever you get half a chance." He glanced toward Louise Marie but didn't bother to lower his voice because any fool knew that all old people were half deaf. "Scare the old grannys into spending every penny they have on supplemental health insurance. But you sell one more policy on somebody's good-for-nothing livestock, and you can find yourself another job. I could replace you like that"—he attempted to snap his stubby fingers—"salesmen are a dime a half-dozen and overpriced at that." Arlo clamped his teeth, almost biting through the fat cigar. "Maybe you'd like to go back to Doc Schaid and clean up after the animals for minimum wage. I imagine he likes Krauts."

Herb's back stiffened; there was a momentary hint of defiance in his eye. "I am not German, Mr. Nightbird. I am Belgian."

Arlo leaned forward, his unblinking eyes like fried eggs, and shook his finger in the young man's face. "Wops, dagos, Krauts, Frogs," he rasped, "they're all the same European immigrant white trash to me."

Louise Marie LaForte momentarily forgot that she was pretending not to hear; the mouth-filling oath spilled out between her pursed lips. *"Cochon . . . stinking little swine!"*

Arlo slowly turned his head and focused his bloodshot little eyes on the old woman, who clamped a tiny hand over her mouth. Louise Marie was certain that she would live to regret this error.

And she would. But in a way that she could not have imagined.

Daisy Perika stretched out onto her bed. She imagined what Father Delfino Raes would say about what she was about to do, then pushed the St. Ignatius Catholic priest from her thoughts. The old woman relaxed for several minutes, then closed her eyes and remembered the rhythmic chant that was centuries old when the Pharaoh's astronomers still believed the earth to be flat. Over and over the words pulsated in her consciousness . . . a song sung by women in trances who had heard the whisper of the Spirit. After hearing, they had used sharp awls of fish bone to stitch the tough walrus hides together. Their men had stretched the walrus skin over skeletons of green birch to fashion the sturdy little boats. The First People had chanted the words to the rhythm of their whale bone oars as they rowed their tiny craft across the dark waves among the floating mountains of blue ice. To a land that was harsh and sweet, old and new. To a world that, for two hundred centuries, would belong to their sons and daughters. But the song, which was to pass through a thousand generations and a score of languages yet unborn, remained fresh and vital.

Now the shaman chanted the sacred psalm of the people who had heard the urgent voice of the Spirit:

> *That Great Mysterious One . . . listen*
> *it is he who whispers*
> *whispers to our women*
>
> *We would stay here . . . ooh*
> *near the graves of our fathers*
> *in the arms of our mothers*
>
> *But he whispers to us . . . listen*
> *he whispers to us*
> *and we hear his voice*
>
> *Now across the dark waters . . . away*
> *we go away forever*
> *from the graves of our fathers*
>
> *Under the face of the moon . . . see*
> *we go away forever*
> *from the arms of our mothers*
>
> *These cold winds carry us . . . far*
> *away like leaves*
> *away like dead leaves*

The old woman's throat was dry; Daisy licked her lips and swallowed. She waited for a moment and the words began to flow again, like sweet water from a spring of ages.

> *That Great Mysterious One . . . listen*
> *he calls us to this quest*
> *a hard journey to a far land*
>
> *To another world . . . away*
> *into a darkness*
> *into a great darkness we go*

We are now become . . . new
children without fathers
infants without mothers

We are now become . . . old
grandfathers of tribes
grandmothers of nations

We who were last . . . see
we are now become
the First People

Now the song was sung. Her whispered words were replaced by a thumping sound, in rhythm with the beating of her heart. It was like the hollow fump-fump call of the Lakota medicine drum, the rawhide relic that now hung on the wall in her kitchen. Since her second husband had died, there was no one to tap his palm on the drum, to aid Daisy's entry into the misty edges of Lowerworld. By necessity, the shaman had trained herself to hear what must be heard.

As the imaginary drum beat filled her consciousness, Daisy gradually lost awareness of her surroundings. The gray shadows in her bedroom were replaced by the familiar streaks of colored light and the heady odor of moist black earth, that rich soil found under the shadow of rotting pine logs. Daisy felt herself floating; then, without warning, she was falling. The shaman instinctively grasped for a handhold, but there was nothing solid in the dazzling array of flashing lights. She was under the branches of towering ponderosas . . . then passing through the earth, along the roots of an ancient juniper in *Cañon del Espiritu.* Her journey ended abruptly, the flashing lights were replaced with a flickering yellow glow. Firelight. She was in that place that other Utes whispered about in campfire stories—the subterranean abode of the *pitukupf.*

The dwarf seemed surprised at the sudden entry of this creature of Middle World into his subterranean domain. He was busy sewing up a tear in his green shirt. He paused from his chore, dropped the deerbone awl into a sandstone pot with a humpbacked red rabbit painted on the bottom. The little man pulled his pipe from under his badgerskin belt. Daisy watched silently as the *pitukupf* stuffed a wad of dried *kinnikinnik* into the clay bowl; the dwarf used the inner bark of the red willow when he had no real tobacco. She would remember to bring a gift of Flying Dutchman. He lit a splinter of dry piñon from a glowing ember on his hearth, and touched this to the pungent *kinnikinnik*.

When he was ready, the *pitukupf* nodded to indicate that his guest should sit on the floor by the fire. Daisy held her hands near the embers and relished in the warmth; her fingertips and toes always became terribly cold when she made these trips. The shaman wanted to ask the dwarf whether he had killed Gorman's prize bull, but hesitated. If the *pitukupf* had killed and castrated the bull, he would probably deny any knowledge of the deed. If the dwarf was innocent of the killing, he might be insulted by the implied accusation and become sullen. It was important to take just the right approach with this unpredictable creature. "My grandmother told me long ago: 'The powerful *pitukupf* in *Cañon del Espiritu*, he knows everything.' " Her grandmother had actually said: "That grumpy *pitukupf*, the one who lives in the badger hole in the canyon, he *thinks* he knows everything." But the flattery was not wasted.

The little creature solemnly nodded his agreement with this accurate assessment of his knowledge of deep matters.

"Tell me, if you know," she continued cautiously, "who was it that killed my cousin's bull?"

The dwarf stuck his hand into a tiny stone pot of red ocher; he touched his bony thumb to Daisy's forehead and left a scarlet print. An eye to see with. He whispered into her ear, telling her that the bull had been visited by an evil presence, but that he, the *pitukupf*, could not help his human friend in this matter. The answer was not in Lowerworld, but waited for her in another place, much farther away. She could go there if she was invited, but, he told her with some bitterness, it was forever forbidden for the *pitukupf* to enter into that domain.

Daisy covered her eyes with her hand. If only Nahum Yaciiti were here; the old shepherd might tell her how to get to this strange land where answers waited. "Ahhh . . . Nahum," she whispered, "this is very hard . . . what shall I do?"

First, there was a dizziness, followed by a sense of floating. Daisy felt a warmth enter her old body, then a tingling, as if many needles had pricked her skin. She opened her eyes and realized that she was no longer in the home of the dwarf. At first, there was only a vortex of pale green light; she fell into this whirlpool and tumbled like a leaf caught in a swift stream . . . until she was on a wide plain, knee-deep in moist grasses of every description. There was no path here; the eternal dew on the grasses wetted her skirt as she walked. She marveled at lovely flowers that were lavender and orange and white, with attending bees that buzzed and darted among the fragrant blossoms. The rich brown soil of the plain was visible between tufts of grass, and the ground was littered with beautiful stones of every shape and color; she picked up chips of mottled gray flint, pink quartz and mica-speckled granite. This great sea of grass seemed to go on forever under a cloudless sky whose amber light did not come from a sun. There seemed to be nothing here but grass and wild flowers. The shaman was wondering about this experience, as she often did. Were these strange journeys taking her to actual places? Or perhaps they were merely visits to dark lands in her mind. She was turning these thoughts over when she heard the rumble of thunder. But no . . . this was not thunder.

The massive form of the buffalo appeared on a low rise, his hoofs striking sparks on the flinty soil. The great animal paused and gazed down at the aged shaman, whose form was now that of a slender young woman.

In a way that Daisy did not understand, the buffalo spoke to her. She did not hesitate at his summons; the young woman ran to the animal and leaped onto his broad back. The shaman held on with both hands to tufts of coarse hair in his shaggy mane. She could feel his great muscles ripple under her thighs as Rolling Thunder bolted across the grassy plain toward a dark wood. Here, the beast paused, puffing great billows of moist breath that became a fog over the forest floor. The sky was hidden from her view; great trees spread their branches over a barren floor that, except for a sickly gray moss, was devoid of any living plant. The largest trees were petrified, with leaves of glass, curly bark that had the texture of black granite. She was astonished to see many animals standing in this eerie forest. Deer. Elk. And cattle. They appeared to have been placed with great care. Some had postures that suggested movement: a poised hoof there, a lifted head here, nostrils that seemed to sniff the still air. But these creatures did not move. Nor did they breathe. Were they, like the trees, also made of stone? Big Ouray, Gorman's brawny Hereford bull, stood among them. His stout legs were spread in a wide stance, his head raised high. The bull's mouth yawned open in a silent bellow.

The shaman slid from the broad back of the animal. Then, the buffalo began to walk among the lifeless creatures. The old woman in the young woman's body followed the great beast.

She reached out to touch the glossy coat of a bull elk. No. This hide was quite real, but she could feel no ribs beneath the soft skin. And for the eyes—the eyes were cold. Dead. Gingerly, Daisy touched the tip of her finger onto the shining surface of a large brown eye. The orb was hard, exactly like a polished stone. A glassy eye that stared. At nothing.

She heard a clicking, a dry rattle. The sound was behind her, near the great buffalo. Daisy turned, "Ayyyaaa . . . ," the shaman muttered, "*núu-oo-vu* . . .!" Terrified that she would attract attention to her presence in this place, Daisy clamped a hand over her mouth. What she saw was a human skeleton, with pale bones like dirty chalk. The thing squatted on the moss, taking no notice of either the shaman or the enormous buffalo. The apparition clasped its bony hands together and held them close to a cage of ribs—as if it held something quite precious. Now the hands moved forward; the contents of the skeleton's fingers dropped upon the moss, and the dreadful skull was tilted quizzically as if to observe the objects through those empty eye sockets. Daisy, in spite of her loathing, was drawn toward this creature with neither flesh nor sinew. She leaned with her hands on her knees, to examine the treasure the skeleton had dropped. There were three potsherds, rectangles whose edges had been ground smooth. The chips of clay were white, like the creature's bones. Each potsherd was inscribed with red dots and black lines. She gazed up hopefully at the buffalo. What did this mean? The buffalo's eyes were now like embers of fire. She turned to see whether the skeleton had retrieved the potsherds, but now the bones were disarticulated and strewn across the moss.

She heard the buffalo snort, then bellow—the force of the blast from his roar snapped branches off the petrified trees and knocked Daisy to the ground. He pawed at the moss with a hoof that glistened like polished brass; the blue fire that he struck from the flinty ground was like lightning, and thunder boomed over the forest. The shaman screamed and clamped her hands over her ears in a vain attempt to shield herself from the terrible sounds. Then, deep silence. The enormous buffalo was now also a statue; with glassy eyes that stared blankly.

A heavy, smothering darkness fell over the dead forest. The shaman felt her young woman's body dissolve like mist. Daisy Perika was happy to leave this place.

5

Nancy Beyal looked up from her paperback romance to see a tall man with a silly grin on his face. She grinned back. "Hello, Scotty . . . I mean Chief Parris." She turned to a uniformed officer who appeared to be in her late forties. "Meet Sally Rainwater. She's been around a long time. Knows just about everybody in Ignacio."

Sally offered Parris her hand and nodded toward a husky young man with a neatly trimmed crew cut who was pretending to read the log book. "This is Daniel Bignight. He's a recruit from Taos Pueblo. Been with us about a year." Bignight looked up and smiled shyly.

Nancy pushed her chair away from the radio console. "We were expecting you. Glad you're going to sit in for Chief Severo." She hid the lurid cover of the book with both hands.

"Well, Nancy, I hope to do a little more than 'sit' while I'm here." He raised an eyebrow at her book. "What're you reading today?"

Nancy hesitated, then removed her hands from the cover. "It's a sort of a historical novel." Romantic thriller.

Parris glanced at the sensational illustration on the cover. A pale but handsome vampire was licking blood from a lovely woman's throat. He read the title aloud. "*Aldea del* . . . uh . . . *Sombras.* What's that mean?"

"Roughly translated," she said, "it means Village of Shadows. There's this really terrible dentist from Mexico City who hypnotizes these poor country girls, see, and then he . . . well, it's a part of my correspondence course in conversational Spanish." Nancy opened a drawer to reveal a stack of cassette tapes, "but I don't guess you're much interested in—"

"Sure I am. Maybe I could borrow the tapes when you're done.

Picking up a little Spanish might help me on the job." Might impress Anne, who was fluent in several languages.

Nancy closed the drawer. "You want to see Chief Severo's . . . I mean *your* office?"

"Later. Right now I'd like to see Charlie Moon."

"He's at Angel's Diner," Nancy Beyal said, "feeding his big face."

"Then I'll drop by and have lunch with him. Anything much going on?"

Nancy smiled again. "You mean crime-wise?" She paused to search her memory. "Nothing much, I guess. Slow, like usual. We picked up a drunk cowboy from Cortez last night; he was takin' a pee right in the middle of route one fifty-one. Bozo threw up all over the floor. I'm the jailer too, so I had to mop it up. That's about all I guess."

Parris noticed that she was looking over his shoulder and smiling her official smile. "May I help you sir?"

Parris turned to see a thin man, decked out in highly polished cowboy boots, new jeans, and a beautiful fringed leather jacket. Topped off with an expensive felt hat that a prosperous cowboy might wear to a funeral. But there was something about the way the fellow carried himself; a cold aura of confidence surrounded him.

The stranger flipped the leather cover to display his credentials. His words were clipped and precise. "James Hoover. Special agent, FBI."

Parris coughed to cover a grin; Hoover's lips went thin.

Nancy brushed around Parris to have a close look at the I.D. "Hmmm." She mouthed the words as she read the credentials. "James E. Hoover." She glanced quickly at the face under the Stetson. The special agent's expression was a mixture of apprehension and defiance. *One smart remark,* the hard eyes said, *and you'll regret it!* This J. E. Hoover's face was thin and pale. Eyes with cold, fishlike retinas. No resemblance to the round, cherubic face of the Old Man.

Parris offered a hand, which was accepted after a momentary hesitation. The man's palm was cold, his fingers long and delicate, almost feminine.

"I'm Scott Parris, I'm going to be—"

"You," the pale man interrupted easily, "are acting chief of police until the real chief returns from his vacation. Until then, you are responsible for the operation of this . . ."—Hoover glanced glumly at his surroundings—"this . . . ahhh . . . this establishment of law and order." Rainwater and Bignight had vanished.

Parris grinned apologetically at the young woman. "This is Nancy Beyal. She's the dispatcher and, most of the time, the person who actually keeps the place shipshape."

Hoover's gaze slowly took in the room. Shelves filled with worn manuals and leather-bound law books. A scarred oak table with an electric hot plate and a half-dozen coffee cups. A scattering of gray metal desks, all littered with papers. He glanced into the chief's unoccupied office; there was a hat rack without a hat. But there was a loaded revolver hanging on a gun belt. And muddy boots in a dusty corner. He returned his attention to the young woman in front of him. The dispatcher was slipping a paperback novel into a desk drawer. The special agent almost smiled; the only sound was the clicking of a large wooden clock on the wall. "Keeping this place shipshape must keep you pretty busy."

"Where's Newman?" Nancy asked meekly, "he's been our contact at the Durango FBI office for years."

"Agent Newman is on sick call," Hoover said, "I'll be his replacement until he mends."

Nancy's fingers found a rosary in her purse; she would pray for Newman's speedy recovery.

"Where is Sergeant Charles Moon?" Hoover asked in an uninterested tone. "I understand he's the senior cop around here."

"He's having lunch up the road at Angel's Diner; come on up for a bite and I'll introduce you." Parris turned and winked slyly at Nancy. "I'm sure Charlie will be happy to meet you." The FBI hired and trained its agents with uncommon care and, as a consequence, had remarkably few sons-of-bitches. This surly one, with the unfortunate moniker, had probably been sent to the boondocks to get him out of Parker's hair.

When they were outside in the cold glare of sunlight, Parris turned to block Hoover's path. The special agent stared at him quizzically. "Nancy, Charlie Moon, all the Ute cops are top notch," Parris said evenly. "They'll be a great help to you." Would this cold man get the point?

Hoover's voice was flat, like his eyes. "The Bureau is grateful for this piece of information." He turned and slipped into a gray Ford sedan. "I've got to check in with the Denver field office. I'll be at that greasy spoon in twenty minutes to meet Sergeant Moon." He glanced meaningfully at Parris before slamming the door. "You be there."

Parris watched the Ford disappear; he didn't realize that his right hand was clenched into a fist. "Well," he muttered, "there goes a man Will Rogers never met."

Special Agent James E. Hoover slammed the door to his room on the ground floor of the Sky Ute Lodge; he immediately threw the deadbolt lock and attached the brass security chain with a hand that trembled. He sat down in a padded chair, and began to rock. Back and forth, a hundred times, then a dozen more. He began to shiver, as if it was cold. The temperature in the room was eighty degrees. The coldness was inside the man. The coldness had been there since he was a child, raised by a father in whose mouth butter would not melt. But now, in the man who had been noted for his raw courage, there was a formless, throbbing fear. And a growing darkness.

Hoover fumbled in his briefcase until he found a small plastic bottle that had been purchased in Juarez, Mexico. It had no label, but there were yellow tablets inside, somewhat smaller than aspirin. He stumbled toward the bathroom. Hoover placed two of the pills on his tongue; the taste was bitter. After a moments hesitation, he added a third tablet and washed the trio down his throat with a glass of water. He waited for the effect. It came, but it was not enough. Not enough to drive the Darkness away. With fingers that trembled, the thin man removed a panel from the inside lid of his suitcase. Under the panel was a zippered leather pouch. Inside the pouch was a brown glass bottle containing a clear liquid. There were also three tuberculin syringes in the pouch. He withdrew two cubic centimeters of the transparent liquid, rolled up his trouser leg, rolled down his white sock, and injected the liquid into a vein.

He sat down on the bed, closed his eyes, and hugged a pillow to his chest. "Ahhh . . . oh yes . . . yes."

Charlie Moon heard the familiar sound of Scott Parris's measured stride. He looked up from his plate of roast beef and mashed potatoes. The policeman smiled. "What's cookin' pardner?"

Parris scooted into the booth and grinned across the table at the big Ute. A couple of minutes with Hoover had seemed like a week; it was good to see a friend's face. He grasped Moon's giant hand. "I appreciate you setting this job up for me, Charlie. I can use a few weeks away from Granite Creek. It's been hectic."

"You need to slow down some." Moon passed a menu to his friend.

"Give your shadow a chance to catch up with you."

At this moment, a thin man wearing a four-day beard and a tattered black trench coat appeared. Most of the fingers were missing from his brown cotton gloves. He saluted Moon in a stiff military fashion, but took no notice of Parris. "Top o' the morning to you, Sergeant-Major." He had the barest trace of a British accent.

Moon nodded. "And a good morning to you, Taxi. How's the writing career getting along?"

Taxi pulled a sheaf of papers from his coat pocket. "It has taken three decades of intensive research, but I have," he announced dramatically, first looking over his shoulder to see if anyone overheard, "finally unraveled the mystery of the so-called Kennedy assassination."

"That's good," Moon said. "Lots of folks would like to know who did it."

He leaned over to whisper in Moon's ear. "It was not John Fitzgerald Kennedy who was shot in Dallas, but merely a look-alike. A stand-in. The president," he continued with a mad glint in his eye, "is alive today, living in Newfoundland. He operates a modest fleet of lobster boats, turns quite a tidy profit."

Moon didn't smile. "Well, now. That news will sure turn some heads."

"I have an excellent literary agent now, who resides in Dewy Rose, Arkansas. She will sell this manuscript to the highest bidder, and then it's Hollywood for me." He turned suddenly and waved a grimy hand at Parris. "You need not take notice of me. I am . . . the invisible man." Taxi swept away without further comment; he planted himself at a nearby table. He licked the tip of a stubby pencil and began to scribble marginal notes on his manuscript.

"I may safely assume," Parris said, "that was not the superintendent of schools."

"That was Taxi," Moon said. "Drifted in a couple of years ago. Nobody knows what his real name is. But he's harmless enough—just a writer."

"He doesn't look overly prosperous," Parris said.

"I doubt if he makes any money writing. We call him Taxi," The Ute said, "because he's also a taxidermist. Stuffs everything from squirrels to trophy elk. I guess he does pretty good during the hunting season."

Parris, a policeman to his core, unconsciously surveyed the other occupants of the restaurant. Angel was spewing Mexican curses at the jammed cash register drawer. A matched pair of pot-bellied truck drivers sat in a corner booth, gloomily sipping canned beer. A trio of high school boys leaned on the antique juke box and leered at a slim girl who passed by outside. "Nancy says nothing much is happening, crime-wise."

Moon thought about that for a few seconds. "It's been fairly quiet."

"That's too bad. The new FBI agent, the one assigned to the Durango office, just showed up. It would be nice if you had something serious he could sink his teeth into." Like a ripe cow pie.

"Well," Moon said, "a rancher stopped by this morning. Says he found his Hereford bull dead up in *Cañon del Espiritu.*"

Parris raised an eyebrow. "Is that police business?"

"This time it is. Gorman Sweetwater says somebody killed the animal, then mutilated it. A few days ago, one of the tribe's buffalo came up missing."

"Sounds like a story the newspapers will love, but I doubt it'll interest our Bureau boy."

Moon frowned and shoved a forkful of beef between his lips. "This new S.A.—what's he like?"

Parris didn't meet his friend's curious gaze. "I expect he's well qualified for his job." Angel appeared at his side and filled a cup with coffee.

"Are you," Moon asked suspiciously, "holding out on your pardner?"

Parris put on his best poker face. "He should be here any time now; you can judge for yourself."

Moon pushed his fork under a mound of mashed potatoes. "Never met anyone from the Bureau I couldn't get along with. Now you take Stan Newman, George Whitmer. First-class lawmen. Sam Parker is all right, except he's kind of a snob about fishing with nothing but dry flies."

The man had approached quietly. He flashed his credentials at Moon. "I'm Hoover, FBI." The Ute nodded as he read the I.D. "James E. Hoover?"

There was a brief silence as the special agent anticipated the inevitable smart remark about his name. Taxi materialized at his side. "Excuse me, Mr. Hoover." He grabbed the pale man's hand and shook it. "I knew your father, knew him well. And I don't believe any of those absurd things they're saying about him."

Hoover withdrew his hand and glared at the grubby intruder. "Who the hell are you?" He wiped his fingers on his shirt.

"I," Taxi announced with injured dignity, "am a well-known writer. Estonian cookbooks. Thrilling exposés about the Martian bipeds who live in a great glass bubble under Lake Erie. Humorous greeting cards. And," he stretched to his full height, "the occasional erudite article for the *New England Journal of Medicine*. Less than eight years ago, I was a very successful cardiologist with a busy practice in Miami. Alas, I got crosswise of certain unsavory elements in the Cuban community and was forced to leave that profession behind. But enough about me! Where was I? Oh, yes—I was not always a writer, you know. In your father's day, I worked with Elliot Ness. I was—can you believe this—an undercover informer on the Capone organization." He held two fingers close together. "Frank Nitty and I, we were like that. But poor Elliot was somewhat overrated as a lawman." He paused and squinted at Hoover. "Do you know that John Dillinger is still alive?"

Hoover blinked. "Dillinger?"

"Indeed. He is now a prominent member of the president's inner circle." Taxi touched the tip of his nose with a grimy finger that protruded from the ragged glove. "Department of Justice. Check it out, laddie." With this, Taxi headed for the door, his tattered coat-tails flapping behind him.

Hoover watched him go. "Evidently, the local asylums are overfull."

"Taxi," the Ute said, "is harmless. Kind of a local character."

"You are Sergeant Charles Moon, I presume?"

"That's me. You must be the new G-man in Durango." The Ute eyed the man from the spotless gray Stetson hat down to the purplish hue of the expensive bull hide boots. "Well, now. I see from your outfit that you are a cowboy."

Parris fought to choke back a grin.

Hoover didn't recognize the line from the old song. "Whenever I move into a new area, I prefer to dress like the locals." Moon offered his hand to the special agent; there was a slight pause before Hoover accepted it. The Ute pumped the cold hand once, then let go. Hoover slid into the booth beside Parris; he sniffed at the mixture of greasy odors that hung over Angel's Diner like a permanent fog. "I'm running the Durango office while Newman's on the sick list." He waited for a response from Moon, but the Ute's face betrayed nothing. "I'll be having a close look at the police force operations on the Southern Ute and Ute Mountain reservations."

Moon stared quizzically at the newcomer.

Parris found his voice. "I'm sure you'll find that Roy Severo runs a good shop. All his people are first rate."

Hoover, who pretended not to notice Parris, directed his remarks to Moon. "Maybe you could give me a rundown on recent criminal activity."

"Don't usually have much serious crime on the reservation." The Ute's tone was mildly apologetic. "We had a bank robbery a few years back."

"I heard about that," Hoover said. "Understand the suspects got away."

Moon was about to point out that the bank was the jurisdiction of the Ignacio town police. But that would sound like an excuse. "I was at a trial in Denver that week," he said meekly.

"You must have break-ins, burglaries."

The Ute nodded. "Every now and again. Last March, a couple of hard cases from Flagstaff broke into the Texaco station. Cleaned out the register."

Hoover leaned forward expectantly. "You apprehended them?"

Moon avoided Hoover's searching gaze. "It was my day off." He brightened. "But they were picked up by Kansas cops over in Coffeyville when they broke into a hardware store."

Hoover's face mirrored his disappointment and his suspicions that the Southern Ute Police Department was in sad shape. "What about tribal politics," he said, "fill me in on any controversies."

"Well . . . tribal council's split over a recommendation by the Economic Development Board," Moon said. "The EDB bunch, led by Arlo Nightbird, wants to go after some federal money."

Angel appeared again, pouring coffee into the newcomer's cup.

Hoover pretended to be interested in his coffee, but his gray eyes glistened under oddly reptilian lids. A snake about to strike. "Federal money? What for?" The special agent licked his lips; he could taste the sweet possibility of fraud and corruption. And promotion.

"Arlo Nightbird's cronies, they want to do a study up in *Cañon del Espiritu*," Moon said. "If it works out, maybe they'll be able to store some nuclear waste up there. Big money in it for the tribe, but most of the council members are worried about messing up the canyon."

"And you," Hoover said, "how do you feel about storing nuclear wastes on the reservation?"

"Don't know," Moon said. "I generally like to hear both sides of an argument before I make up my mind."

Parris could sense the big Ute closing up. If Hoover pushed too hard, Moon would tell him nothing of value.

"Interesting," Hoover said, "federal money. That project will bear watching."

"Whatever you guys want for lunch," Moon said as he waved at Angel, "it's on me."

"Thanks," Parris said, "I'll have the Navajo Taco."

Hoover reached for a menu, jammed between a napkin dispenser and a sticky ketchup bottle. "They serve any authentic Ute cuisine in this place?"

"Well," Moon offered congenially, "it's mostly Mexican and American but there are a couple of Ute dishes. I'd recommend the three-meat stew."

Hoover frowned as he scanned the menu. "As long as it's not that old-fashioned Ute stew." He grinned without humor. "I don't normally eat horse meat."

Parris closed his eyes. Maybe, when he opened them, Hoover would be gone. Like a bad dream.

Moon's fork stopped halfway to his mouth; he cocked his head sideways and blinked at Hoover. "Horse meat?"

"I understand that when times used to get tough during the winter, Utes would eat their dogs first, then their horses." Hoover glanced up from the menu; the grin on his face was as genuine as the "turquoise" stone in his string tie. "Guess I won't have to worry about what I eat until the cold weather comes."

The Ute thought about this for a moment. "Well, not necessarily," Moon said amiably. "When beef gets a little pricey, Angel might buy a couple of nags that came in last over at the Downs."

Hoover pretended not to hear. He studied the menu and wondered about some of the unfamiliar words. What the hell did *fajitas* mean? And *sopaipillas*?

Parris pointed a spoon over Moon's shoulder. "Someone wants to see you." An old, gaunt Ute was fidgeting at Moon's side. The Ute policeman turned to look at the grumpy man. "It's sure nice to see you again." He glanced behind the rancher, but Benita was not with her father. "You want something to eat, Gorman?"

The rancher was turning his battered felt hat in his hands. He leaned over Moon's shoulder, and spoke slowly into the big man's ear. "I'd think twice about having my eats in *this* place."

Hoover's ears pricked up.

Moon had heard the story three times, but he knew the old man wanted to tell it again. "And why's that?"

Gorman glanced toward the counter where Angel was wiping at the greasy Formica surface with a paper towel. "You never know what you'll find in Angel's grub. Maybe," he said, "you'll get the salamander!"

Parris hid a grin. Special Agent Hoover leaned forward, straining to hear. "Did I understand you to say . . ."

"Damn right," Gorman said, jerking his thumb toward the smelly kitchen where Angel concocted the grub. "Salamander," he muttered darkly. He glared back at Moon. "You know my third cousin Sally Bitter Horse, from over at Hondo Fork?"

Moon nodded. Everybody knew Sally. The Navajo woman was always suffering with some new and wonderful ailment.

"Well," Gorman whispered hoarsely, "Sally, she told me she got that salamander right here, in some of Angel's chicken salad three Sundays ago. That night, Sally took the chills. And then," he lowered his voice, "she had the squirts for most of a week." He hitched his thumbs under his overall bib. "That's what she says."

Hoover stared uncertainly at the rancher. "Even in this dump . . . surely no one would put a . . ."

Gorman shook his head sadly at the ignorant tin horn. "Nobody *puts* salamander in the food, sonny. When you're not watchin', they just crawls in there all by theirselves." City folk. They never did understand hardly anything about nothing.

Hoover glanced quickly toward Charlie Moon, then at Scott Parris. Both men were hanging on every word from the old man's mouth. These dumb cops would believe anything. But the special agent looked into the dim chamber that was Angel's kitchen. On the far wall, there was a shelf lined with large jars. Jars filled with dill pickles. And pickled cauliflower. And shriveled pigs feet. And what else? Hoover pushed the menu aside.

Gorman leaned over and whispered in Moon's ear. "I need to talk with you."

Moon wiped his mouth with a paper napkin and looked up at the rancher. "About Big Ouray? I already told you I'd go and check it out."

"Well, that's just the thing," Gorman said with forced casualness, "it's like I told you this morning—I called Doc Schaid. He'll go have a look. He'll work out what happened and write it up on one of them forms. You don't need to bother yourself about it no more."

"That's fine," Moon said, "but I'll go over to the canyon and nose around anyway. If somebody killed Big Ouray, it's police business."

At the mention of a killing, Hoover's back straightened. "What did you say?"

Gorman had practically wadded his old hat into a ball. "Just leave it alone, dammit. If death wasn't by natural causes, there won't be no insurance money. If there ain't no insurance payment, I'm wiped out." Moon sure was awful slow to catch on. Big men were like that. Slow.

Hoover fairly shouted. "Killed? Damn it all, who was killed?"

Moon ignored the visitor from the Bureau. "Okay, Gorman. I've got to poke around a bit, but I'll try not to queer your insurance settlement."

The rancher nodded his thanks and bolted away while Hoover sputtered. The special agent was trying vainly to get Moon's attention. "What happened to this . . . Big Ouray?"

"Yeah," Parris said, "you didn't mention anything about—"

"Sure I did, just before Mr. Hoover got here. Gorman Sweetwater, the fellow that just left, he found Big Ouray dead this morning. Over in *Cañon del Espíritu*."

Hoover's voice was almost shrill. "How was the victim killed?"

Moon didn't look at the special agent. "Victim?"

Hoover slammed his palm against the table. "The homicide, dammit! Was it by gunshot, a knife, blunt instrument, what?"

A tiny light sparkled in Moon's eyes. "Well, we don't know exactly how Big Ouray met his end." He wrinkled his brow in pretended concentration. "Could be something he ate. Maybe some Jimson weed."

A muscle twitched in Hoover's jaw. "You suspect he was poisoned?"

The Ute sipped at his coffee. "Could be," he said, "we won't know until the car . . . the remains are examined by Doc Schaid."

Parris was trying hard to understand, then he put it together. Big

Ouray was the dead bull Moon had mentioned earlier. This had to be stopped. "Hoover, I think you've mis—"

"I'll handle this," the FBI agent snapped. He glared at Moon. "Any marks on the body?"

"Yeah," the Ute replied, "from what Gorman told me this morning, you could say there were marks."

The special agent found a small leather-bound notebook in his coat pocket. "Well? What kind of marks?" Hoover didn't attempt to hide his impression that he was dealing with an oaf.

"Well, let me see," Moon said. "Oh yeah. His ears."

"Ears? What about his ears?"

"Gone, both of 'em. Like politicians right after election day."

Hoover paled. "You mean . . . purposely removed?"

"Snipped off." Moon took a long drink of coffee. He leaned forward dramatically and lowered his voice to a hoarse stage whisper that could be heard across the restaurant. The truck drivers had forgotten their beer, the teenagers had lost interest in the jukebox. Taxi was scribbling furiously on the margins of a coffee-stained manuscript page. "That's not the worst part."

Unconsciously, Hoover flattened his back against the plywood booth. "What . . ."

"Big Ouray's balls. Sliced off slick as a whistle." Moon made two quick knifelike motions with his hand. "Both of 'em. At least that's what Gorman says."

The notebook slipped from Hoover's fingers. "You haven't viewed the body yet?"

"Only heard about it this morning. I'd planned to get out there this afternoon, but Gorman says Doc Schaid will take care of everything. I guess there's no hurry now."

Hoover closed his eyes and bowed his head. "This is simply astounding. A Ute has been murdered and mutilated, and you're sitting here, calmly having lunch. . . ."

"Well . . ." Moon paused thoughtfully, then replied, "I never exactly said he was a Ute. You can't always tell by looks. Fact is, Big Ouray's got a whiter face than yours." He took a quick drink from his coffee cup. "I'd say he was from Anglo stock."

Hoover was slightly embarrassed at his presumption. "With a name like Ouray, I naturally assumed . . ."

Moon appeared sympathetic with Hoover's confusion. "These days, you can't tell by a name. Now there's a little Filipino woman who lives just north of town. Calls herself Blue Bird Feathers, but she's no Indian, Ute or otherwise. Reads the stars, predicts the future, sells magic potions and garlic candy. Stuff like that."

Angel stopped by to ask if Hoover was ready to order. The special agent waved the man away. "We can't sit here until the corpse rots. Get a camera, all the analytical equipment you have available. And understand," he pointed at Moon, "I am officially taking charge of this investigation."

"Look," Parris said, "I don't think you understand. Before you go off half-cocked—"

"Perhaps *you* don't understand," Hoover snapped, "murder on an Indian reservation is a matter of federal jurisdiction."

"Well, we don't know for sure it was murder." Moon wiped at his mouth with a paper napkin and raised his massive form slowly. "But as far as I'm concerned, whatever you say goes."

Hoover started to reply, then his hands trembled. He clenched his hands into fists, then turned quickly and headed for the door.

Moon cupped his hand to his ear. He frowned at Scott Parris. "Is it just me, or did you hear that thumpity-thump sound?"

Parris listened intently. "Hear what?"

"Opportunity," the big Ute said with a merry twinkle in his eye, "opportunity knocking."

6

Charlie Moon watched Hoover's Ford sedan in his rearview mirror. "Road's going to get kinda rough for that little street car. Not near enough clearance."

Parris reminded himself that he was acting chief of Southern Ute Police. Among other duties, he was responsible for maintaining good relations with the Bureau. "You'd better tell Hoover the truth about that bull."

The Ute assumed a pious expression. "Nothing I told him wasn't the truth."

Hoover followed the tribal police Blazer into the mouth of *Cañon del Espiritu;* he felt the muffler dragging as the little Ford struggled through deep ruts. When Moon stopped for Scott Parris to open the gate, the special agent abandoned his sedan and slid into the front seat beside the Ute. Parris closed the barbed-wire contraption after Moon drove the Blazer through the gate, then climbed into the rear seat of the four-wheeler. The Ute nosed the squad car slowly up the canyon in low gear, examining the landscape to the right of the dirt lane.

Hoover was leaning forward with both hands on the dash board. "How far is it to this Ouray fellow's house?"

"Big Ouray had no use for houses," Moon replied. "Always lived out of doors, night or day, rain or shine."

"Remarkable," Hoover said, "a real eccentric. Was he a loner?" He loved this job.

"Wasn't acquainted with him myself," Moon said, "but those who knew him said he was kind of hostile. Liked bein' with cows more than with people."

Parris dropped his face into his hands. Moon was determined to do this thing.

"The sexual mutilation," Hoover said with a professorial air, "is a classic giveaway. Ten to one it's his wife."

"He didn't have himself a wife," Moon said with an air of sadness. The Ute adjusted the rearview mirror so he could watch Parris's face.

"If the victim wasn't married, look for a jealous girlfriend. Or her husband. Of course," Hoover added thoughtfully, "maybe he wasn't interested in girls. You know anything about his sexual preferences?"

"From what I hear," Moon said, "Big Ouray's . . . what I guess you'd call . . . uh . . . straight."

Parris groaned as the Ute winked in the mirror. In more than one way, the acting chief of police was just along for the ride.

As they rounded a heavy stand of scrub oak, Moon stomped the brake pedal. A green Dodge van was blocking the road.

The Ute cut the ignition and muttered under his breath. "Doc Schaid's truck. Didn't expect him to get here so soon; Gorman must have really leaned on him."

Hoover leaned forward expectantly. "The medical examiner?"

"What passes for one," Moon said.

A heavily built man appeared through the sage, followed by a small woman dressed in a man's shirt, faded jeans, and high leather boots. The veterinarian, who carried a small tripod-mounted camera in one hand, was returning to his truck. Moon noticed that he walked somewhat unsteadily. His companion, an attractive brunette with a rich olive complexion, was lugging his black bag of instruments and medications. Schaid was a hulking man whose stooped posture belied his six-foot-four height; the picture of him carrying only the camera while the tiny woman strained at the heavy medical bag was ludicrous.

Moon opened his door. "You fellows sit tight for a minute. Doc Schaid's more likely to talk if it's just me and him."

"I guess that's okay for now," Hoover agreed doubtfully, "but I'll need to interrogate him as soon as—"

"Hey, Harry," Moon yelled, "what's cookin'?"

The veterinarian's response was a sullen grunt.

Moon was irrepressible. "How did you talk Mrs. Nightbird into doin' duty as your packhorse?"

Emily Nightbird smiled sweetly. "I needed something to keep me busy, Charlie. And," she added tenderly, "I love to be around the animals."

Schaid scowled, leaned the tripod against a dwarf oak, and displayed a bandaged right hand. "Got injured. Short-handed, gotta make do." Moon sniffed the faint odor of whiskey. So the rumors were true; the vet was hitting the bottle. According to the stories that floated around Angel's Diner, Schaid's marriage had gone sour. The local gossips also whispered that the vet's wife had found herself a rich boyfriend. Barbara Schaid hadn't been heard from since her husband reported that she left to visit her ailing sister in Virginia. The veterinarian had evidently realized that his wife, who served as his surgical assistant, wouldn't be returning soon. He had hired Herb Ecker to assist him in the surgery. The Belgian exchange student had stayed with the veterinarian for barely a month, then left to sell insurance for Arlo Nightbird. Now Arlo's wife was working with Schaid. The Ute studied the bandages. Schaid also limped slightly. "What happened to your paw, Harry?" Veterinarians who worked with large animals were injured almost as often as rodeo cowboys.

The veterinarian hesitated before answering. "Damn mare stepped on it." He moved the bandaged hand behind his back. "Who'd you bring with you?"

Moon nodded toward the Blazer. "That's my pardner Scott Parris in the back seat. He's chief of police up at Granite Creek; he's pinch-hitting for Severo." He pointedly ignored Hoover, knowing this would raise the veterinarian's interest.

Schaid, who was always suspicious of strangers, squinted at the squad car. "Who's that city cowboy?"

Moon dropped his voice and nodded toward the car. "Oh, him? He's down from Denver."

"Denver?" Schaid's face was a question mark.

Moon gingerly nudged a pebble with the scuffed toe of his boot. "He's determined to examine the carcass." The hint of a smile flitted across the Ute's face. "I just didn't know how to say 'no.' "

Neurons began to misfire under the veterinarian's thick skull. Big Ouray had been a valuable animal. The insurance company might send an expert consultant to perform an examination. Schaid cleared his throat and spat. "City boy. Probably couldn't find his ass with both hands." The last thing Schaid wanted was a qualified veterinary pathologist nosing around this carcass. This was his turf. *His* carcass. "He here representing the insurance company?"

"No." The Ute looked away, toward the towering figures of the Three Sisters sitting in eternal comfort atop the mesa. "He's representing the government."

"Government?" Schaid had a habit of repeating key words.

Hoover had waited long enough; he ejected himself from the car and flipped his I.D. wallet open to display his credentials. "Hoover. Special agent, FBI." He snapped the wallet shut. "I'll inspect the body. Right now."

Schaid stared blankly at the special agent. "Body?"

Hoover pocketed his credentials. "I'll want a signed copy of the autopsy."

The veterinarian's voice dropped to a whisper. "Autopsy?"

"And," Hoover nodded at the woman, "I'll want to interrogate your assistant."

"Interrogate?" Emily decided that enough was enough. "What is this all about, Mr. . . . ."

Hoover tipped his hat at her. "The Bureau investigates all major crimes on Indian reservations, ma'am." He had seen all the John Wayne films and knew that western gentlemen addressed ladies as "ma'am." "I'll need to find out everything you know about the Big Ouray murder."

"Murder . . . Big Ouray?" Emily's brows made inverted Vs over her lovely brown eyes. She glanced at Moon. The Ute avoided her eyes.

Hoover blinked at the woman. There was no shortage of empty heads around here. Must be inbreeding. He turned his attention back to the "medical examiner." "Where," he demanded, "is the body?"

"Body?" Schaid looked helplessly at Moon.

The Ute policeman pushed his hat back and allowed himself a quick grin. "Mr. Hoover wants to have a look at what's left of Big Ouray."

The veterinarian pointed toward the general direction of the carcass.

Emily watched Hoover's back disappear through the brush. "You have some very strange friends, Charlie." Scott Parris got out of the car and slammed the door. He tipped his hat at the pretty woman, and was rewarded with a shy smile. She reached for Schaid's instruments, but Scott Parris grabbed the heavy bag. "Allow me," he said gallantly. He followed her to the van.

"Why," Schaid growled as he watched Emily chatting with Scott Parris, "does a fed want to look at a dead animal?"

"Those FBI types," Moon said with an air of mystery, "don't tell us ordinary cops more'n we need to know. Could be," the Ute added in a conspiratorial tone, "this dead animal is tied into some bigger case he's working on."

Schaid hitched his thumb under his belt to steady a rhythmic twitching in the injured hand. "Old Gorman may have a hard time collecting his insurance money on that dead bull, unless I can make a good case for natural causes. Don't you let that fed screw things up."

"Harry," Moon asked, "do you know who wrote the policy on Gorman's cattle?"

The veterinarian used his uninjured hand to wipe perspiration from his forehead. "Gorman didn't say when he called, but it don't matter much. They all want the same information, only the forms are different. You want a guess, I'd say the policy was written on National Farmer's Union. Gorman probably used one of the agencies in Durango or Pagosa."

"Afraid not," Moon said. "You know Gorman Sweetwater, always lookin' for a way to save a buck. Arlo Nightbird's agency wrote the policy, probably on some little fly-by-night company in South Clawhammer, Nebraska, that don't have the money to pay its phone bills."

Schaid's mouth slowly dropped open. "I didn't know Arlo wrote any paper on cattle. Oh damnation, why didn't Gorman tell me?"

"He probably didn't know Arlo's wife was working for you. Didn't know myself until a few minutes ago."

"Well," Schaid said thoughtfully, "Emily's seen the carcass . . . but I'll ask her to keep mum about it."

Moon sensed a tenderness in Schaid's voice when the vet mentioned Emily—something about the way he spoke her name. The delicate little woman, unlike her husband, was popular in Ignacio. She organized the annual blood drive, gathered clothing to distribute to the poor, collected money for an endless list of good works. "How come," Moon asked, "one of the richest women in the county is doing your dirty work? Can't be the pay."

"Maybe she's bored from sitting at home." The veterinarian's tone hinted that Moon should keep such questions to himself. "I ain't about to ask. She's good with the animals."

"What about Big Ouray . . . how'd he die?"

The vet avoided eye contact with Moon. "Won't know for sure

until I do some tests on samples from the stomach, but the big brute probably ate a bushel of poisonous weed," Schaid said, "then fell over and died. Happens every day with cattle. One minute they're right as rain, next thing you know they flop over dead as a stump. I'll check out the flora on the canyon floor. Likely as not, we'll find some loco weed or death camas."

Moon nodded toward the camera. "You take pictures of the carcass?"

"Yeah," Schaid said. "I'll get you some copies if you want 'em."

The Ute policeman watched Schaid's face carefully. The fix was in; Gorman would collect his insurance. "If it was bad weed that killed him, what happened to Big Ouray's ears and balls?"

A muscle twitched under the veterinarian's left eye. "Hard to say. Coyotes. Buzzards. Raccoons." Schaid turned his head to watch Emily Nightbird, who was combing tiny burrs from her dark hair, carry on an animated conversation with Scott Parris. They were smiling. Like friends. Good friends. He clenched his fingers into fists, ignoring the pain from the injured hand. "Beeves die for no reason at all, then the predators come for lunch. I'm surprised you've got time to waste on stuff like this."

"Maybe you could keep me posted on what you find." Moon watched Schaid's face closely. "It'd help to know . . ."

"I got more'n enough on my plate, treatin' the sick animals. Don't have much time left over to spend with dead ones." With that, the veterinarian stumbled off toward his van. He nodded at Emily, who said something to Scott Parris before she got into the van. Moon frowned thoughtfully as Schaid pulled around the Blazer and left a trail of dust floating over the rutted dirt lane.

Emily was waving. "That," Parris said to Moon as he waved back, "is a nice looking little woman. Awfully pretty eyes."

The Ute grinned at his pardner. "When did Anne leave? Must be hard to be without a woman for a whole day."

Parris felt a pang of guilt. "I just said she was awfully pretty."

"She's also awfully married," Moon said dryly. "Emily's husband is Arlo Nightbird. Arlo owns an insurance agency; he carried the paper on Gorman's cattle. Also finagles government grants for the tribe." Moon didn't mention that Arlo had a half-dozen local girlfriends and was a regular customer at a chicken ranch in Nevada. Emily Nightbird deserved a lot better than Arlo.

Parris was watching the veterinarian's van disappear around a curve. "Is she a Ute?"

"Nope. Half 'Pache, other half Mexican," Moon said. "Her momma was one of the Roanhorse 'Pache bunch down at Dulce. Good family, made some money with gas leases. Emily's dad is Fidel Sombra; runs a hog farm up by Oxford."

Parris glanced toward the sandstone cliff and sighed. "Wonder what'll happen when Hoover finds the dead bull?"

Moon grinned. "Let's go see." Parris followed the Ute's giant strides through the clumps of fringed sage. Judging from Moon's direction, the FBI agent had wandered off course. The Ute led Parris to a grove of ancient piñon. Parris saw the remains of Big Ouray as soon as Moon broke a path through a thicket of Apache plume.

The Ute stood over the carcass and looked at the ground. The veterinarian and his assistant had made enough tracks to obliterate any evidence that might have remained of the mutilator. Crossed strips of white tape covered the incision where the veterinarian had inserted a tube into the animal's stomach. "Nuts, ears, sliced off clean as a whistle," Moon said, "this wasn't done by coyotes."

"Yeah," Parris said. He fought off a threat of nausea. "Who'd do something like this?"

Moon squatted by the carcass and thought about what had happened. Maybe he should have come out this morning to look for some sign. But who would have expected Schaid, who had a busy small-animal practice, to respond so quickly to Gorman's summons? The Ute kneeled by Big Ouray's head; he ran his hand over the bull's neck. "Didn't bleed much." He looked up at Parris. "Bull must have been dead when somebody cut him or the arterial pressure would have sprayed blood all over the place." He ran his fingers over a slight abrasion between the horns and the eyes. "Wait a minute." Moon pressed his thumb against the red hide; there was a depression where the bone had been crushed. "Somebody smacked this big fellow on the head."

Doc Schaid should have noticed this; unless the alcohol was fogging his brain. But even if he did, it wouldn't be in his report. The veterinarian, who depended on local ranchers for much of his income, would leave out any detail that might endanger Gorman's insurance claim. So there it was.

Moon took a dozen steps away and walked a wide circle around the dead animal. There were only a few footprints. Unfortunately, they all matched the ones Harry Schaid had left at the carcass. The vet was probably attempting to find some bad weed to blame the animal's death on. In this canyon, that shouldn't be hard to do. The Ute returned to the carcass and stood in silence, gazing intently at the remains of an impressive animal.

Hoover appeared unexpectedly. "Help me find the man's body; we've got more serious business than some stinking dead cow!"

"Not a cow," Moon replied evenly. "That's a bull." Or what had been a bull.

"Fine. Cow, bull, whatever. The important question, is where in hell is Mr. Ouray's body?"

Moon nodded toward the carcass. "That's him. Mr. Big Ouray. Gorman Sweetwater's prize Hereford bull."

An blank expression spread over the special agent's face. "This is some kind of joke?" It had never occurred to Hoover that a mere tribal policeman would dare to trifle with him.

Parris put his hand on Hoover's shoulder. "I tried to warn you. Charlie Moon can't pass up a chance to have a little fun."

"Fun?" Hoover was nibbling at his lower lip; his hands trembled. "Hey, it's what I should have expected out here among the mentally deprived. Country yokel plays a prank on the city boy." The special agent was breathing in short, rapid puffs.

Moon grinned at Hoover. "I never said he was a man; everything I told you about Big Ouray was the gospel. . . ."

Hoover sucked in a deep breath and exhaled slowly. He fixed his icy stare on the Ute and enunciated his words with great care. "You overgrown . . . inbred . . . shit-for-brains asshole!" Hoover whirled and marched away.

The Ute policeman shook his head in mock dismay. "Overgrown, am I?" Moon glanced sideways at Parris who wore an "I told you so" expression all over his face.

"He's a bit irked," Parris said as they watched Hoover stumble over a sage bush.

"Uh-huh." Moon shook his head sadly. "Nervous little feller. Walks like he's stompin' post-holes."

"I expect he has a long memory, Charlie. Sooner or later, he'll find a way get even with you. Can't say I'd blame him."

"He doesn't," the Ute observed, "have much of a sense of humor."

An hour later Charlie Moon and Scott Parris were comfortable and warm, basking in the inviting aromas of Daisy Perika's tiny kitchen.

"So what killed Gorman's bull? An animal or a man?" Her suspicious eyes were focused on her nephew's face.

"Hard to say," Moon said, "didn't find much out there. You have any notions?" There wasn't much that happened in *Cañon del Espiritu* that Daisy didn't know about. Or have an opinion about.

She stirred a cedar spatula in the iron pot, then turned the propane flame down until the yellow ring turned to a blue flicker. "I figure it's some crazy person." The shaman thought about the rusty twelve gauge in the closet. Might be a good idea to load the gun. Just in case.

Parris sniffed at the aroma. "Smells fantastic." Marvelous what fresh air would do for your appetite.

"The vet's report," Moon said, "will most likely say Big Ouray ate some bad weed. That coyotes chewed off the missing body parts. I guess maybe that's what happened."

Daisy dipped a full ladle of lamb stew into each of three plastic bowls. "Don't play that game with me, Charlie Moon. Whenever you try to fool me, you blink your eyes a lot. If you don't want to tell me what happened, it don't matter the least bit to me."

Charlie gave her an enthusiastic bear hug, lifting her little feet off the linoleum. "Auntie, I never tried to fool you in my whole life." He sat her down, and unconsciously, blinked several times.

Daisy Perika elbowed her nephew sharply and fought back a smile. "You'll never grow up, you big buffalo." She watched Scott Parris taste his stew, but directed her question to her nephew. "You figure whoever killed Gorman's bull and cut it up like that . . . could be somebody we know?"

A frown passed over Moon's face. "Hard to say." It had to be someone who was willing to attack a full-grown bull with some kind of club. Someone who was a little crazy. Or . . . someone who could get close without alerting the animal. A troubling possibility occurred to the policeman, but he dismissed it.

Moon went to the bathroom to take a shower; Scott Parris occupied himself with a copy of the *Southern Ute Drum*. As she washed the dishes, Daisy's thoughts were on her nephew. Charlie Moon was a fine, honest man, and everyone said he was a good policeman. He attended mass at the Catholic church every Sunday morning but his aunt suspected that he had retained some interest in the way of their ancestors. Most of the Utes were at least nominal Catholics, but a few kept the old ways too. Daisy remembered how Charlie got his Ute name when he was a little boy.

Lois Winterheart was Charlie's grandmother. Daisy's mother had told incredible stories about Lois—said the old woman could "change herself, become like the spirits who moved about without need of a body." Daisy could picture her mother, as she described Lois, moving her hand in a floating motion, "and she could drift through the trees . . . you couldn't see her, except maybe you might see her shadow." Daisy remembered the delightful thrill as she would lean closer to hear her mother whisper: "But if you paid attention, you could feel something like a gentle breeze drifting through the pines, whenever Lois would pass by. Some of the old people," mother would continue, "said Lois had a power to make the wind fall still, then start up again. But you couldn't hear nothing at all when she was on the move. All the birds and everything, they would get real quiet when Lois used her power."

Her father had dismissed this as a foolish woman's idle tale, but Daisy would never forget what happened those many years ago, during the Moon of Great Hunger. It was when the heavy snows came. The February snowflakes were like wet goose-feathers; they fell without pause for three days. Then, the moaning winds rolled in from the northwest. When the storm finally moved away toward Chama and Tres Piedras, the drifts were big enough to lose a team of horses in.

It was that awful winter when Lois Winterheart had moved into the adobe house down on the banks of the Piedra, ten minutes (in good weather) from Daisy's trailer home. Lois needed to borrow fuel for her cooking stove, but a person needed snowshoes to navigate wave after wave of drifts. Despite these obstacles, old Lois appeared on Daisy's front porch in her tattered woolen shawl and beaded moccasins, asking to borrow any coal oil her neighbor could spare. Lois had waited patiently in the kitchen, sipping a cup of strong coffee while the shaman poured kerosene from a five-gallon can into a glass jug. Lois had departed with the jug under her arm. A moment later, when Daisy had hurried outside with the shawl that her neighbor had forgotten, the old woman was gone. And there were no tracks in the deep snow. None coming, none going. And everything was deathly silent . . . it was as if the whole earth and all its creatures had, for a few moments, held their breath.

And that wasn't the end of it. Daisy remembered it like last week.

Back in nineteen and sixty-eight, Lois had taken sick with pneumonia and was making ready to go to the other world. On the far side of that deep river. Daisy paused as she remembered, gazing blankly at the wall. She could almost see the misty edge of that other world. Before Lois passed over, she had summoned little Charlie Moon to her bedside. Charlie was her favorite grandchild. Daisy had watched Lois put her right hand on her grandson's head and gave him some of this power she had. And a secret name.

Daisy sighed. She had a suspicion that Charlie could hear the songs the old ones sing. But maybe he tried not to listen. The shaman paused and listened; she could often hear the songs that wafted down the Canyon of the Spirit. But Charlie was drifting away, losing touch with the old ways that had sustained the People since time began. Her dark eyes snapped fire as she turned from her dish-washing to glare, almost accusingly, at the white policeman who was reading an article about Miss Southern Ute in the *Drum*. "Charlie acts more like a *matukach* every year. You know he got himself a subscription to the *Wall Street Journal*, then bought some stock in a fruit juice company down in Georgia?"

"Charlie never mentioned it to me," Parris said with a straight face, "don't suppose he'd want that kind of information spread around."

She nodded; her scowl said that of course Moon would keep such shameful activities concealed. Daisy dried the last cup; she pulled her shawl around her shoulders and closed her eyes. "I had a bad dream about Charlie last Friday, woke me up in the middle of the night. Couldn't get back to sleep for worry."

This at least, Parris understood. Those who were close to policemen often dreamed of gruesome deaths at the hands of ruthless criminals. "Something bad happen to Charlie?"

"It was awful." Daisy shuddered at the distasteful memory. "Dreamed he'd taken up golf."

7

The morning sun illuminated the crumbling wall of Three Sisters Mesa; the air was heavy with a damp, gray mist. Gorman Sweetwater rolled the truck window down and sniffed at the sweetness of the crisp morning air. He lifted his boot off the accelerator pedal and glanced toward Daisy's trailer to see if her kitchen light was on. It was. He watched the trailer door open, framing the old woman's stooped form. She moved carefully down the porch steps and waved. Gorman shifted down to low gear and turned into her lane. By the time he switched off the ignition, she was leaning on the truck door.

"Good morning, cousin. Come to check on my cattle." The ones, he reminded himself bitterly, that remained.

"Stop for a few minutes. I got a skillet full of scrambled eggs and pork sausage and Hatch chili."

"I'm not all that hungry," Gorman lied. Benita kept nagging at him about how eating rich food would cause something to clog up his arteries . . . but what was it? Since she'd been to college, Benita had so much to say it was hard to keep track of it all. But suddenly it came back to him; Gorman was certain that he remembered his daughter's exact words. "Anyhow," he said, "them eggs and sausage would be bad for my castor oil level."

Drained of patience, Daisy turned away and waved a hand to dismiss this nonsense. This old man got sillier with every year.

He sniffed at the rich aroma drifting from her kitchen window. "But," he said with a pious tone, "I'll come in and have some eats if it'll make you feel better."

"Check the railing on my porch. It moves when I lean on it." Those who eat should also work.

"Got a hammer and crowbar in the truck, maybe some nails. I'll see what I can do." He knew that her last husband had been a pitiful excuse for a carpenter and Daisy never missed a chance to maneuver her cousin into the odd job.

"Charlie was here yesterday. He went up the canyon to look at your dead animal."

"Figured he would," the rancher muttered. With the report he expected from Doc Schaid, the insurance payment was practically a done deal. Why couldn't Moon leave it alone?

"Scott Parris, that policeman from up at Granite Creek, he was here too."

Gorman grunted. He had no interest in this *matukach* cop. He gave the porch railing an expert once-over. "You hear about the tribal council meeting last night?"

"How would I hear? I got no phone and don't get a newspaper but once every two weeks."

Gorman shook the railing. A couple dozen number ten nails should do it. Maybe an extra cross brace. Or maybe two. This called for a smoke. He fumbled in his shirt pocket for the fixings. Daisy waited patiently while he poured tobacco from a worn leather pouch into a cigarette paper that was thin enough to read through. "The council decided to let Arlo Nightbird send them dockamints in to the government in Washington." Gorman licked the paper and sealed the assembly into a misshapen cigarette.

"What'd you say?" Daisy knew what he meant, but she wished to delay the full realization of this news.

"Dockamints . . . papers to get a study done on putting that nukuler power plant garbage here in *Cañon del Espiritu*," Gorman said sourly. He thumbed the wheel on his butane lighter and touched the dancing yellow flame to the twisted tip of the homemade smoke. "I expect Arlo Nightbird is happy as a maggot in road kill."

"I expect he is," Daisy agreed. "What about your cattle?"

Gorman turned and gazed at the first light of dawn filtering into the canyon; the sacred refuge where his cattle were just waking. "Most likely, I'll have to move 'em out. Over to the winter range at Bondad." He cleared his throat and wiped a moist eye. "Jimson weed, blood-sucking ticks big as a dime, and mostly alkaline water, but," he added bitterly, "they say I can't stand in the way of progress."

"That's bad," Daisy said simply. The shaman was shivering from the cold, and also from a sense that when the sun was high, darkness would remain. As the old woman turned to retreat to the warmth of her kitchen, she spoke over her shoulder. "I made biscuits too."

Gorman sniffed at the kitchen aromas. Daisy's lard biscuits sure beat those that came in a can. "Don't feel hungry, but I guess I could eat a little bit if you want some company." Hog lard, he knew, could stop up a man's veins just like a wad of coffee grounds could block the drain pipe under a sink. And that would bring on the dreaded heart attack. But the old man pushed the image of the dreaded *corollaries* from his mind.

Nancy Beyal greeted her favorite policemen with characteristic cheerfulness. "Good morning, fellas."

Moon glanced toward a spare office, informally reserved for the FBI. "Where is he?"

"Mr. Hoover? Haven't seen him since late yesterday." Nancy thought she saw something odd in Moon's expression. "He came in, picked up his stuff, and cut out. I suppose he's off to Durango, or," she added hopefully, "maybe Denver." Timbuktu wouldn't be far enough.

"Can't imagine why he left so soon." Parris winked slyly at Nancy, "we were having us a fine old time."

"Did you hear," Nancy whispered, "about Gorman Sweetwater's threat to . . . to castrate Arlo Nightbird? Louise Marie LaForte heard the whole thing; it's all over town." Such stories were a sweet tonic that eased the tedium of her job at the tribal police station.

"Gorman gets hot under the collar," Moon said, "but he cools off pretty fast."

The telephone rang; Nancy answered it, then gestured to Parris. He pressed the receiver to his ear, and heard Sam Parker's voice. "Hello, Scott. How are you doing?"

"Fine, Sam. How are you this morning?" Had Hoover already complained about Moon's prank?

"Still hittin' on eight cylinders. You taking good care of . . . Hoover?"

"Sure." Parris dismissed a twinge of guilt. "He's getting special treatment."

"Anything happening down there . . . law and order related?"

"Nothing much," Parris said cautiously, "we had a cattle mutilation."

Parker, who specialized in kidnapping and armed robbery of banks, snickered. "Wow. Wish I'd been there."

"It was a valuable animal," Parris said defensively. "Worth over ten grand. Somebody cut off the ears. And testicles."

"Did it happen on reservation land?" Sam Parker was familiar with the crazy-quilt layout of the Southern Ute Reservation.

"Yeah. Moon's investigating."

"Well, you have a good time. Anything I can do to help, you let me know."

Parris watched Moon; the Ute was at the coffeepot, well out of earshot. "There is something, Sam. It's about this fellow you sent to help us. James E. Hoover."

"What about him?" Parker's tone was wary.

"Everybody here loves him and he's one helluva cop. Matter of fact, local opinion is that J.E. could do your job. After he had a frontal lobotomy."

"Watch out what you say, you smart-mouthed bottom-fisher," Sam Parker said over a chuckle. "Mess with me and I'll assign Hoover to cover Granite Creek until he retires."

Parris was hanging up when Charlie Moon, at a cue from Nancy Beyal, picked up a telephone and was patched through to the emergency line. "What is it?" he grunted. The Ute listened quietly for some moments before he interrupted. "Louise Marie, how many times have I told you? Don't call me . . ." He waited again. "Yeah. I'll come out. But this is absolutely the last time." He hung up nodded at Parris. "Let's go, Acting Chief. It's time you met some of the local citizens."

They found the old woman sitting on her front porch swing, busily shelling dried peas. The yellowed husks matched the hue of the skin stretched over the purple veins crisscrossing her plump hands.

Moon touched his hat brim. "What's cookin', Louise Marie?"

The elderly woman looked up, smiling benignly at the big Ute.

"Louise Marie, this fellow is Scott Parris. He's standing in for Chief Severo for a few weeks." Moon nodded toward the placid figure in the swing as he spoke to Parris. "This little dumpling is Louise Marie LaForte. She's not a Ute, not even an Indian. In fact," Moon pretended disdain, "we're not sure she's even a United States citizen. Louise Marie came from up in Quebec. One of them Frenchies." Louise Marie allowed herself a coy smile as Moon continued. "Doesn't matter to Louise Marie that I'm only supposed to answer calls on reservation property. She gets me out here every week or so, just to waste my time."

Her peas all shelled, she looked up through the thick lenses of her spectacles at the Ute's towering form. "It was so nice of you to drop by, Charles."

"When," he demanded with feigned gruffness, "are you going to stop calling me? You should be bothering the Ignacio police anyway, you're not even in my jurisdiction. If you want to harass me, Louise Marie, you're going to have to join the tribe and move onto the reservation."

"I only call you because I like you, Charles Moon." The town police ignored her many calls. "You're lucky I'm fond of you, I don't generally care all that much for the *gendarme.*" She patted the cushion beside her, indicating that he should sit. Parris watched while Moon seated himself, wondering whether the rusty chains that suspended the swing from a pair of crooked eye-bolts in the porch roof would support the big Ute's weight.

Moon folded his arms and closed his eyes, preparing for the inevitable assault on his rationality. "What is it this time—is Taxi bothering you again?"

Louise Marie glanced across the yard at the ruin of a two-story frame house where Taxi had squatted since he arrived in Ignacio from goodness knows where. "No, it's not Taxi. I wish he'd get out of that taxidermist work—I can smell the stink from his place when the wind blows just wrong." She shook her head in despair. "He still peeks at me sometimes, out of that upstairs window. But he mostly keeps to himself since you had your little talk with him." No point in mentioning the stuffed squirrels the lunatic had left on her front porch. Moon would tease her about having a boy friend if he knew about the gift. She carefully placed the aluminum pan of shelled peas on a stool at her knees. "I saw it, just before daylight this morning. Down by the river bank." She nodded toward the general direction of the Los Piños, waiting for Charlie to ask what *it* was.

The Ute remained silent.

Parris waited as long as he could. He stepped onto the porch and leaned on a supporting column; the powdery paint soiled his jacket sleeve. "What did you see, ma'am?"

Louise Marie looked up as if she was aware of his presence for the first time. "Who are you?"

The acting chief of police nodded toward the Ute and grinned. "I work for Charlie. Sort of help out from time to time. Did a prowler bother you, is that why you called? . . ."

"I got my dead husband's old pistol to take care of prowlers," she snapped. "Wasn't no prowler. It was the hairy one." Her voice dropped to a whisper. "It was the *loup-garou.*"

Parris leaned over to hear more clearly. "The what?"

She blinked her eyes, looked up and down the weed-choked gravel lane to make sure no passerby overheard. "That *loup-garou.* All hairy. *Oui*, with a long tail, him. And," she added ominously as she held a gnarled finger beside each temple, "with horns!" She started to tell them about the other strange feature on the monster's face and thought better of it. A *loup-garou* was one matter; they were common enough. But who would believe that she had seen a terrible red eye, an eye like a coal of fire?

Parris looked hopefully at Moon for an explanation. "Loo Guru?"

Moon cleared his throat. "A *loup-garou,*" he said with an almost imperceptible touch of sarcasm, "is actually a fellow with a serious problem. He's an ordinary citizen by day, a dangerous animal by night. Usually half wolf and half man. The man half is generally French, so he shows himself to Louise Marie. She's the only Frenchie in the neighborhood."

The elderly woman nodded vigorously. *"Oui, oui,* he was hairy as any ape you ever saw but this one wasn't no wolf! He had horns on his head!" Louise Marie shivered. "A bad one, him!"

Parris realized that Charlie Moon was happy to leave the interrogation to his "pardner." He hesitated to ask, but there was no turning back. "What did this . . . loo . . . um . . . hairy fellow do?"

"Well," she said, "he crawled along the river bank on all fours, sniffing at the ground like a great dog, wagging his big head, dragging his tail on the ground behind him." Her voice rose to a shrill pitch. "Isn't that the sort of thing you police are interested in?"

Parris opened his mouth, but couldn't think of an appropriate response. Moon got up from the swing and patted the old woman on the shoulder. "Sure we are, Louise Marie. Keep your doors and windows locked." He patted his sidearm. "We'll be on the lookout for your *loup.*"

"You can't kill *loup-garou* with ordinary bullets," she said, shaking her finger at the Ute. "In Quebec, my father would load a shotgun

shell with exactly twelve rosary beads. One for each of the Holy
Apostles!"

As they drove away, Parris watched the little figure in the porch
swing. "What's the story here?"

"Louise Marie," Moon said, "married an Iroquois up in Quebec by
name of Henry Gray Dog. He brought her here thirty-odd years ago.
Worked in the oil fields down by Farmington. Did some guide work
for the elk hunters; I heard he was a first-rate tracker. Back in ninety-
one, Henry left for a hike one morning. Hasn't been seen since.
Louise figures he'll come back someday; that's why she never went
back to her family in Canada." Moon paused to wonder what had
really happened to Henry Gray Dog. Dead, most likely. "She's lone-
some. Probably drinks a little too much homemade wine. I stop by
to check on her from time to time."

"Sounds like she's a lot of trouble for you," Parris said.

Moon didn't reply. He was wondering about Louise Marie's *loup-
garou*. What had the old woman seen?

8

Scott Parris, flat on his back, squinted at an electric light that was suspended on a long brass chain from the ceiling of the gymnasium. He gave up a vain attempt to find a comfortable position. He did find some comfort in the knowledge that the big Ute was on the next table. Herb Ecker appeared at his elbow, rolling his sleeve down. "This is the first time I have donated blood," the insurance salesman said in a Germanic accent. "It was not so difficult."

"Nah," Parris agreed. "Kinda like a bee sting." The nurses who inserted the needles always said that. Like a bee sting was nothing.

"You should have seen Dr. Schaid," Ecker said. "The veterinarian told them to take an extra pint."

"Doc Schaid's a sissy compared to my pardner," Moon chimed in. "Now Scott Parris, he's not afraid of hollow-point bullets or needles big as your thumb."

Ecker smiled and left with some comment about how it was a good feeling to give a part of yourself to help others. Parris turned his head to see Moon, whose boots extended well over the edge of the six-foot table. "I thought we were on our way to see this guy up in Durango. You didn't say anything about getting bled."

Moon folded his hands over his chest. "Our civic duty, pardner. Besides, we got a kind of competition with the Ignacio town cops. Last year, they gave two more pints than the reservation police."

Parris closed his eyes when Cecelia Chavez, the public health nurse, pushed his sleeve up and wrapped a section of surgical rubber tubing around his arm. "You look kind of pasty. You feel all right?"

"Pasty is my normal complexion."

Cecelia grinned as she tapped on his arm to find a suitable vein.

"All you big men are such babies when it comes to such a teeny little pinprick." She nodded toward her right. "You see Emily Nightbird over there?" Parris opened one eye but could not see the pretty woman. "Emily organizes the Ignacio drive every year, and she's always the first one to donate blood. And Nancy Beyal, bless her little heart, she was here an hour ago. If Nancy can give a pint, we ought to get a quart from you." Cecelia scowled toward Charlie Moon. "And someone the size of this big horse ought to give us a good half gallon." The public health nurse nudged Parris's ribs with her elbow. "You know what Charlie did a few years back? When he didn't want to give blood?"

Parris was eager to distract himself from this nervous woman who wielded a needle with hands that fluttered like aspen leaves in the wind. "I'm only interested if it's something that'll sully his reputation."

"That big galoot," she whispered, "filled out the donor's form with a pack of lies. Said he had every disease from hepatitis to TB. We took his blood anyway."

"Oh, I don't know that he was joking," Parris replied without smiling. "I've heard nasty rumors about Charlie and some kind of awful social disease. . . ."

"After you get his pale *matukach* blood," Moon muttered to Cecelia, "see if you can snap the needle off in his arm."

Emily Nightbird appeared, and placed the tips of her fingers lightly on Parris's hand. "Hello, again. It's so kind of you to help us."

Parris tried to nod, but it was a difficult maneuver with his head resting on the stainless steel table. "My pleasure," he lied.

Emily leaned over. Her dark hair fell close to his face; he caught the scent of a deliciously fragrant perfume. "I hope you don't mind the procedure . . . some donors are bothered by the needle."

Parris forced a hearty chuckle. "Needles? Nah. No problem." He winced only slightly as the nurse shoved a stainless cylinder into his forearm, completely missing the vein.

"Now squeeze that rubber ball I put in your hand," Cecelia commanded. "Pump, pump!" She sighed with disappointment. "Well, well, you got little bitty veins like a girl. No flow at all. I'll give it a couple more tries. If that don't work, we'll have to jab the other arm."

Daisy Perika was trudging up the incline from her mailbox when she heard Gorman's pickup behind her. The rancher pulled over and got out. He reached into his coat pocket and produced a crumpled envelope from the Nightbird Insurance Agency. "Look," Gorman growled, "at this."

Daisy removed the contents and frowned at the perforated blue paper; her lips moved as she read the figure on the check. "Four hundred and twelve dollars. And twenty-two cents." She looked up at her cousin's grim face. "Big Ouray was worth thousands, is this all the insurance will pay?"

"There won't be no payment on Big Ouray. That's a refund on my policy; it's been canceled." He coughed, threw a half-spent cigarette butt onto the path and ground it viciously under his boot heel. "Arlo claims there was a mistake when them papers was filed. Says that Ecker kid wrote one number wrong when he copied Big Ouray's registration. I figures he's doctored the papers, but that makes my insurance not worth a shiny dime."

"Arlo's found a way to keep from paying, then," Daisy said with stoic resignation.

Gorman's hands shook as he produced a tobacco sack and attempted to pour its contents into a flimsy cigarette paper. "That little bastard—he always finds a way." The old man spilled half the tobacco and muttered a curse. "I should of got my insurance with one of them outfits up in Durango, instead of trying to save money on the premium."

Daisy opened her mouth to remind her cousin that she had told him this, but decided to remain silent. Gorman was suffering enough right now. Later, he would be feeling much better. Then she would remind him.

"So," Parris asked, "this Oswald Oakes is a friend of yours?"

"Oz," the Ute said thoughtfully, "is a guy I play cards with." Friends were few and far between, and Oz didn't quite make the grade. Moon pulled the Blazer to the curb behind a blue Miata convertible. The towering house perched uncertainly on the crest of a forested hill that sloped gently toward the rocky banks of the Animas. "His main interest is collecting stuff. Old books. Antiques. Prehistoric artifacts." Moon reached to the rear seat for his wide-brimmed Stetson and jammed it down to his ears. "Oz is a pretty good source of information." And, because he'd never quite gotten the hang of five-card stud, a pretty good source of income.

"Information?"

"On odd things." Moon switched off the ignition. "UFO reports. Monster sightings."

"And let me guess—animal mutilations?"

The Ute nodded as he set the emergency brake and opened the door. "He keeps a set of files. I guess it's kind of a game for him." For Oz, everything was a game.

Parris pulled his hat brim over his forehead to shield his eyes from the stinging rain. "You figure he'll help us sort out this bull mutilation?"

"Could be," Moon said as he made giant strides up the red brick sidewalk toward the front door.

Parris shoved his hands deep into his coat pockets; his cold fingers found a roll of antacid mints in one pocket, aluminum foil packets of Alka-Seltzer in the other. He stood behind Charlie Moon while the Ute policeman banged on the door. They waited. Moon pounded again, rattling the ivory-tinted lilies on the stained-glass panes. "Hey, Oz . . . open up, it's raining on my new hat!" Presently they heard muffled sounds of footsteps from somewhere deep inside the three-story Victorian house. An angular, bony man dressed in old-fashioned woolen trousers and a blue silk shirt opened the door. He removed his gold-framed reading glasses, dropped them into a shirt pocket, and blinked uncertainly at his visitors. Parris peeked past Moon at the man who leaned lightly on a cane. Oswald, who was almost as tall as Charlie Moon, sported a well-groomed goatee and a faultless mustache that appeared to be lightly waxed at the tips. He removed the stub of a cigar from his mouth and pointed the smoking end at his visitors. "Well, now, what do we have here," he said amiably. "From your unkempt appearance, you certainly are not a pair of itinerant Mormons."

"We're the law," Moon said grimly. "And we're here on official business."

Oswald laughed soundlessly and made a sweeping gesture of welcome with the cane. "Come in. But wipe your boots on the mat." He eyed Parris with an almost childlike curiosity. "You are not a Ute. Do I know you?"

"Oz," Moon replied, "say hello to my pardner, Scott Parris."

He had already heard about the Ute's new friend from Granite Creek; perhaps Charlie would not be coming around so often now. It was rumored that this pair of policemen spent all their spare time angling for trout in the mountain streams. Oswald could not fathom the attraction of such a pointless activity. He looked hopefully at Parris. "Are you a player? Cards, I mean."

Parris shook Oswald's outstretched hand. "I enjoy the occasional hand of poker."

Their host raised an eyebrow. "What is your game? Five Card Stud? Seven?"

"In Granite Creek, some of the cops have a Tuesday night game. Mostly, it's Five Card Stud or Spit in the Ocean." But there had been other games, in other places. "Mexican Stud, or Shotgun," he said in a barely audible voice, "that's what we played in Chicago." Chicago. The very name of the city had power to resurrect sharp memories, both sweet and bittersweet. Crisp lake breezes scented oh so lightly with the aroma of dead fish. Polish sausage sandwiches at the Ninety-third Street drive-in. Faithful comrades on the force whose coarse jokes and loud laughter would be heard nevermore. And, of course, Helen. Who was nevermore. So much was gone.

Oswald, sensing that Parris had drifted away, turned to Moon. "Charles, I must confess—I am tiring of poker." He had lost too many hands to the Ute. "We must try a new game."

Moon, who had been expecting this complaint about poker, hung his new hat on the stilettolike antler of a pronghorn antelope trophy. Once you got to know Oz, the patterns of the old man's moods and thoughts could be anticipated, and this predictability was his fatal weakness as a gambler. Their gaming had begun with checkers. Then chess. Then straight pool. Finally, poker. But Oz tired of any contest when he hit a losing streak, and began talking about a "new game." "What'd you have in mind?"

Oswald took Moon's jacket and hung it on another antler. "I would prefer a new contest . . . one that challenges the intellect."

The Ute policeman had financed most of his new house with winnings from these games. And it wasn't like Oz couldn't afford it. "When you decide, let me know what your fancy is."

Oswald brightened. "You have not been around for awhile. . . ." He glanced uncertainly, almost jealously, at Scott Parris, then back at Moon. "Are you sure you will be available?"

"I'll have to check my work schedule. Between the SUPD and my unfinished house, I don't have much time for anything but work." Maybe that was why he hadn't made an effort to visit Benita. Or maybe work was just an excuse. He promised himself to visit the Sweetwater ranch tomorrow. Or maybe sometime next week.

Parris, who picked up the occasional arrowhead, gaped at a display case filled with a half-dozen pieces of "killed" Mimbres pottery from New Mexico, exquisitely chipped obsidian blades crafted by the Hopewell mound builders in Ohio, carved shell jewelry from the Baja, and other odd bits and pieces that he could not identify. After their host offered a brief summary of this portion of his artifact collection, the policeman followed Oswald down a paneled hall that opened into a large parlor. The centerpiece of the room was a pool table. The balls, racked in a triangular array on the felt-covered slate, awaited players. Around the table, a dozen pieces of mismatched antique furniture were scattered over a heavy carpet. One wall was decorated with old Navajo rugs and a pair of broad windows that overlooked the shady lawn; two walls were filled floor to ceiling with books. Not one of the books looked new. Moon, who was at ease in any environment, dropped his heavy frame onto a flimsy looking Queen Anne chair. The chair creaked ominously as its delicate cabriole legs spread slightly.

Oswald winced. "Please be careful, Charles. That chair was constructed by highly skilled craftsmen in 1708. I would like it to see the New Year."

Parris stood uncertainly, scanning the parlor for a chair with a sturdy appearance. Oswald pointed; "try the Chippendale; it is middle Georgian." Their host stroked the varnished arm of the chair like another man might caress the neck of a favorite dog. "Wonderful mahogany, don't you think?"

"Nice piece," Parris said. "My wife loved antiques."

Oswald noticed the past tense. "You are . . . separated from your wife?"

Parris tried to swallow the lump forming in his throat. "Helen died. Almost three years ago." He saw the question on the old man's face. "Automobile accident."

Oswald nodded sympathetically. "My mother, bless her sweet soul, passed away eleven years ago this past June." It had been cancer, but he could not utter the cursed word. He felt a moistness gathering in his eyes. "Not a day goes by that I do not miss her. But," he added brightly, "my many activities fill my days." The loneliness hung over his hours like a dark curtain. "Excuse me, fellows. I'll go get some refreshment."

Oswald disappeared for a minute, then they heard a teakettle's shrill whistle. Their host returned with a large silver tray that needed polishing. He placed the refreshments on a marble-top table. "This is first-rate Darjeeling. I get it from an importer in San Francisco." He made the initial offering to Parris, first the tea, then a plate of cookies. "I normally serve the biscotti with a very special white wine, but, in deference to Charles, I will refrain from offering any alcohol."

Parris pretended not to have noticed the comment; if Moon was a recovering alcoholic, that was his business.

"You must dip the biscotti into the tea, but quickly. It is," Oswald added gravely, "a very *civilized* thing to do." A gentleman was obliged to attempt, against all odds, to civilize these rough fellows.

Parris dipped the thin cookie into the Darjeeling. Quickly. He took a bite of the moist pastry and found the experience to be rewarding. Moreover, he reminded himself, it was very civilized. "Not bad," he said, and licked his fingers.

Their host sighed; he accepted this response as the best that could be expected. "Now tell me; what undeserved twist of fortune brings a pair of policemen to my door on this gloomy day?"

"It's your lucky day," Moon said, "we brought you a present."

Oswald leveled a mock scowl at Parris. "Ask the Navajo or the Apache; they will tell you it is written on the stars"—he lifted his arms dramatically and gazed upward toward a ceiling of varnished oak panels—". . . shun Utes bearing gifts."

Parris raised his cup in salute and grinned. "Saw it last night, right beside the drinking gourd."

Moon sat in placid silence, waiting for the tension to build in the old man.

Oswald shifted his weight in the cushioned chair. He crossed his legs. Drummed his fingers on the polished New Hampshire marble table at his elbow. Uncrossed his legs. Finally, it was too much. He looked out a window and pretended to watch a low cloud drift by the hilltop. "Ahhh . . . so what is this gift that you bring?"

Moon reached for the cookies. "Something for your little computer to chew on."

Oswald twisted a pointy mustache tip in nervous anticipation. "Ah—wonderful! But don't tell me . . . let me guess. A UFO report?" Moon's face said *no*. "A Sasquatch sighting? No? Wait, I know, you have finally decided to request my assistance in solving the mystery of the old shepherd who vanished in such an unusual fashion last year. Something Yaciiti . . . was that his name?"

Moon groaned inwardly; why did everyone have to beat their gums about the Nahum Yaciiti disappearance? "We had an animal mutila-tion."

Oswald's tea cup didn't quite get to his lips; his brows lifted ever so slightly. "You don't say. Some little old lady's kitty was . . . ?"

"Hereford bull," Moon said. "Big fellow."

"Aha—much better! You were quite right to come to me about this mutilation. Now I'll do my imitation of Sherlock." Dramatically, Oswald Oakes closed his eyes and placed a palm on his forehead. "This crime occurred on reservation property, or you would not be investigating the incident. It was probably in a remote area. . . ."

"That was a pretty safe guess, Oz. It was way up a canyon. Lone-some place." Moon popped two cookies into his mouth. These things were pretty flat. "You got some Oreos stashed away somewhere?"

Oswald leaned forward, the cigar clenched between his teeth. "Let us sweeten this inquiry with a wager. I'll give you two-to-one I can describe precisely how the bull was mutilated . . . precisely."

Moon shook his head and frowned. "You're getting way too big for your britches, Oz."

Ceremoniously, the old man removed a crisp twenty dollar bill from his wallet and waved it in Moon's face. "Put your money where your impertinent mouth is." He blew a smoke ring that drifted toward the ceiling.

The Ute laid a ten dollar bill onto the coffee table. "Okay, Sher-lock. My Hamilton sees your Jackson." A man could not refuse free money.

"Ahhh . . . an interesting wager at last." Oswald closed his eyes and pressed his long fingers lightly against his temples. "Let me visu-alize what you have found. Ahhh . . . I can see it all now. The bull was missing its testicles."

The Ute grinned. "Good guess, Oz, but it's more complicated than that." He reached for the bills.

"But wait," Oswald said quickly, almost as an afterthought, ". . . did I forget to mention the ears?" He blinked at Moon and slapped a palm against his forehead. "Oh my, of course—the ears will certainly have been removed. And, needless to say," he added with an air of smug triumph, "the unfortunate animal will have been dispatched with a forceful blow to the skull." He lowered his voice to a soft monotone. "Is that sufficient, Charles, or shall I provide you with the name of the mutilator?"

Moon couldn't take his eyes off the pair of greenbacks. "A name. That would help."

"Then, because you are such a good loser, a name you shall have." Oswald smiled brightly and inserted the bills into his wallet. He leaned back and clasped his hands behind his neck. "I have been keeping records of mutilations for years. West of the Mississippi, there are only three mutilators of large animals who practice this arcane trade with any regularity. I know their habits and personalities well enough to assign names to each. Picasso rarely operates east of Utah, and almost never in the summer season. Butcher has not mutilated an animal in more than four years. Therefore," he snapped his fingers, "the mutilator must be Cain. And," he continued with an air of genial triumph, "Cain has a very characteristic method of mutilation, which I have already described. Of course, 'Cain' is not his actual name . . . merely a convenient identifier that I have assigned for . . . ahhh . . . reference purposes." He watched disappointment spread over the policemen's faces. Moon was, as always, patient. But this Scott Parris fellow seemed mildly annoyed. "Did you, by chance, bring along a photograph of the carcass?"

Moon reached into his shirt pocket. "Doc Schaid took these."

The old eccentric accepted the photos gratefully. "Harry Schaid is a fine veterinarian and a passable photographer. He has been quite helpful in my mutilation research." Oswald's eyes brightened as he inspected the photo of the hind quarters. "Of course. The very mark of Cain. Clean, straight incisions . . . like a skilled surgeon's work."

"Doc Schaid," Moon said, "is trying to help Gorman with an insurance problem; I expect he'll say the mutilation was the work of hungry coyotes."

Oswald dropped the spent cigar stub into an onyx bowl and removed a fresh Havana from a varnished walnut box. "He will say it was coyotes. But you will know better, Charles." He snipped the end off the cigar with a small scissors, and lit it.

"Well," Moon admitted, "coyotes don't normally have ears for breakfast when there's fresh beef tongue on the menu. And besides," he added, "the bull didn't die from what you'd call 'natural causes.' "

Oswald inhaled the fragrant tobacco smoke deep into his lungs, and coughed. "Of course not."

"Aside from his mutilation techniques," Parris asked, "what do you know about this 'Cain'?"

The old man was looking out a bay window at the sheets of driving rain. "I shall help you as much as I can," Oswald said dreamily, "but I doubt you will ever lay a hand on him." He took a long drag on the cigar, then went to his rolltop desk and rummaged around until he found a leather-bound journal. He pushed the reading glasses along the bridge of his nose, and grinned at the Ute policeman. "How about these odds, Charles—five to one. One hundred dollars to your twenty, that you will not apprehend Cain before he strikes again."

"Thanks," Moon said, "for the vote of confidence." But he would pass on this bet.

Oswald raised his hands in a defensive gesture. "I meant no insult, Charles. As a technical gambler, I always go with the statistics. If the mutilated creature had been a chicken or a puppy, you might get lucky and discover a foolish teenager playing at Satanism. But in the United States and Canada, virtually no one has ever been arrested, much less convicted, for the mutilation of a large animal."

Moon knew that Oswald had a point. The chances of arresting this space cadet was somewhere between zero and very small. He sighed, interlaced his fingers, and rested his chin on his hands. He wondered what Benita was doing. Right now. Probably helping her daddy round up the rest of their Hereford cattle. Or maybe . . . washing her hair. Maybe brushing her hair. Benita had beautiful hair.

Oswald noticed this prayerful posture. He also took note of the small wooden crucifix suspended on a silver chain around the Ute's neck. "Charles, if you are to have any chance of arresting Cain," he said in a mildly mocking tone, "perhaps you should resort to prayer . . . for a miracle." Oswald's eyes twinkled with barely suppressed merriment. "Those clever television detectives are invariably rewarded with a full disclosure of misdeeds when they confront the guilty party with some little shred of evidence. Yes, yes . . . have faith . . . surely the mutilator will confess his crimes to you." The old man chuckled, then blushed lightly. "I am sorry, Charles, I suppose that was impolite . . . but you must forgive me. Life has become rather tedious; I must find my amusement where I can."

Moon briefly lifted his teacup with both hands, as if it were a sacred chalice. "I forgive you, Oz." The Ute closed his eyes; his lips barely moved, as if in silent prayer.

Oswald was never quite sure when Moon was teasing him. Perhaps that was why the big Ute was so difficult to defeat at poker. "I will want to get some information recorded," he said, "for my data base."

He opened his notebook and held a gold-plated mechanical pencil over the page. "The owner of this deceased bovine is . . . ?"

After a long pause, Moon raised his head. "The bull belonged to Gorman Sweetwater."

Oswald printed the name at the top of the page. "When did the mutilation of this bull occur?"

"Last Wednesday night; maybe early Thursday morning."

The old man was writing carefully, in a neat script. "Please describe the animal."

"Like I told you, Hereford bull. Registered stock. Gorman called him Big Ouray."

"Big Ouray." He pursed his lips as he wrote. "How very appropriate." Oswald abruptly left his chair and headed across the room toward the rolltop desk. He sorted through a box of computer disks until he found the one labeled MUT/AN. Oswald removed a laptop computer from his desk and brought the machine to a Queen Anne settee. He switched the computer on, slipped the floppy disk into the drive slot, and pressed a key with the eraser on his mechanical pencil.

Parris leaned on the small couch and watched over the old man's shoulder.

"I have," Oswald said with an air of weary virtue, "been gathering information for this mutilation data base for almost three decades. More than six hundred animals, mutilated in forty-two of the United States, and sixteen foreign countries."

"Impressive," Parris said without conviction. It was sad that an old man did not have better things to do with the few years he had left. But Parris wondered . . . what would *he* be doing in another twenty years? Or ten? It was a depressing speculation that he attempted to dismiss.

Oswald pressed the space bar to stop the rolling display. "Consider this. In the category of animals with ears and testicles removed, no more, no less, there are precisely sixteen cases. Excluding your Hereford bull, of course. Twelve of these mutilations occurred within five hundred miles of Durango, most were to the north and west. I am certain that Cain is responsible for all of them."

"This includes," Moon asked, "that elk, up in the Never Summers?"

Oswald highlighted the spreadsheet entry on the screen. "Right there, you see? Bull elk, discovered two years ago last September in the Never Summer range. Approximately thirty miles from Estes

Park, on Forest Service land. Killed by unknown means. Ears and testicles removed. I was able to find the carcass shortly after Dr. Schaid called me to report the discovery of the mutilation."

"Could be the same guy that cut up Big Ouray," Moon said.

"Recently," Oswald offered in a cool, clinical fashion, "there has been evidence that this mutilator drains blood from the wound. Perhaps with some type of catheter. I am certain," he added grimly, "that Cain drinks the blood of his victims. This can only be the act of a mystic." You see, he pointed the mechanical pencil at Parris, "Cain absorbs the strength of the bull by consuming its blood."

Moon was about to put a cookie into his mouth; he returned it to the silver tray.

Scott Parris was mildly amused at the old man's naive belief that he could imagine the mind of the twisted person who did this thing. Oswald was a typical ivory-tower theorist; he had sufficient confidence in his intellect to confuse his educated guesses for certifiable facts. "What I can't understand," Parris muttered, "is how a man gets close enough to club a full grown Hereford bull."

"The way I figure it," Moon said, "some guy, let's call him Cain, hiked into the canyon, probably around midnight. The moon was up; there would be enough light. He's been there before, scouted the canyon, so he knows where the animals sleep. He comes in quietly, from downwind. The break in the skull was kind of irregular, so I figure he picked up a good-sized rock, maybe a chunk of sandstone." Oswald raised an eyebrow at this. Moon knew the look, but continued as if he hadn't noticed. "He takes his time, moves right up to the sleeping bull, conks him on the head. Then, he cuts—"

Oswald nodded impatiently. "No, no, Charles." He held his palms outward in a gesture that pleaded for reason. "Which of your ancestors would strike a large animal with a rock held in his hand? An experienced hunter would want some leverage, to effectively lengthen his arm." The old man waited for some sign that these policemen might understand his point. There was no sign. "Cain," he said as he made a chopping motion with his right hand, "would use an instrument with a *handle*."

"A bull that size," Parris said, "I'd imagine it'd take at least a ten-pound sledge hammer to—"

"Butcher . . . now he might use a sledge," Oswald frowned thoughtfully, "but Cain . . . no. I am certain that he would not. This particular mutilator has a certain . . . refinement that would be reflected in his choice of instruments." The old man sighed and rubbed his eyes. "Cain would select a weapon that was appropriate for the ceremony. And I assure you, that this is a *ceremonial* killing." He paused, as if recalling something, and his face brightened. "Wait, let me show you something to demonstrate my point." Oswald pushed himself up and took quick strides out of the room.

Parris muttered, almost to himself. "I don't see what's wrong with a sledge hammer."

Moon ate the last half-dozen cookies.

Oswald returned triumphantly, carrying a heavy staff of hard wood. A grooved stone was attached to one end with thin strips of bark and a dark, sticky substance. "I picked this wonderful artifact up in Mexico several years ago. A Mayan girl discovered it in a limestone cavern in Yucatan. Within five kilometers of the classic ruins at Uxmal." He offered the artifact to Moon. "I estimate it to be late tenth or early eleventh century." He glanced at the Ute's crucifix. "Of the Common Era."

Charlie Moon accepted the club with a sense of reverence. In the days before the Spaniards came, the People had made similar weapons to kill Navajo and Apache, even Sioux. The head of the club was formed by laboriously pecking a small granite boulder until it was egg-shaped and about twice the size of a softball. Then, a deep groove was fashioned around the stone, and a stout oak handle was attached with wet rawhide and pine pitch. This Mayan club was fashioned in much the same way, except that the stone head was a smoky yellow quartz. Moon gripped the club in both hands and slowly swung it in a chopping motion.

Parris watched the Ute, who seemed fascinated by the artifact. "Cain'd have to be a pretty strong guy to crack a bull's skull, even with a club like that."

"Not necessarily." Oswald puffed impatiently on his cigar. "A healthy twelve-year-old could do the job. It is," he said with an air of authority, "a matter of steady nerves and accuracy, not brute physical strength." He went to a shelf, withdrew a thick volume, and blew a puff of dust off the covers. "Here. In Sisson and Grossman's *Anatomy of Domestic Animals*. You see?" The old man placed the open book on the marble table. "Examine this figure." The lawmen leaned forward to see an ink drawing on a yellowed page that was labeled SKULL OF OX: LATERAL VIEW. Oswald was enjoying his role as teacher. "The brain of a bovine is, compared to the size of the skull, relatively small. Your mutilator would have to land a blow within a circle. . . . I would estimate . . . hmmm . . . certainly no more than five, maybe six centimeters in diameter . . . situated on a bisecting line midway between the eyes and the horns on the frontal bone. Right here." He tapped the pencil eraser on the sketch to identify the lethal point.

Moon nodded. "That's just where he smacked Big Ouray."

"Except for an internal central ridge, the bovine skull is less than a centimeter thick in this region. A moderate blow would do the trick. But, of course," Oswald said as he saw lingering doubt on the lawmen's faces, "the blow must be carefully aimed."

"Yeah," Moon said, "if he misses, he's got himself a mean-tempered bull with a bad headache. Maybe he gets disemboweled." The big Ute shook his head in awe. "This guy must not be afraid of anything."

"Cain, you see, draws strength from the danger associated with his task." Oswald rolled his cigar between two fingers. "He is calm. Calculating. Limited by neither mercy nor fear. That," he gazed thoughtfully at Moon, "is why Cain does not miss his target. It is the power of intellect over emotion."

"A sane man," Parris muttered, "is afraid of being gored to death. And only a lunatic," he glanced at Schaid's color photographs, "would cut up a dead animal like that."

"Lunatic," his host said patiently, "is a word we use to describe an unusual mind. The mutilator, within his own frame of reference, is quite sane."

"If he's sane," Parris pressed, "then what's his motive?"

"Motive?" The old man paused and considered the question. "Motive. Such a serious word . . . a policeman's word." He patted Parris's hand. "But it is only a game, don't you see?" It was clear from the policemen's puzzled expressions that they did not see. "The testicles and the ears are trophies—a tangible celebration of the victory of the hunter's intellect and courage over the animal's instinct and brute strength. The only *motive*, gentlemen, is to win the game." He reached for the onyx bowl, and tapped the fresh ash off his cigar. "Life is a game that we all must play. A contest of both wit and chance, even bluff. Not unlike poker." Oswald gazed out the rain-streaked window at a willow dancing with the wind. "To use a card player's term, Cain has sweetened the pot." The old man felt a cold draft; he shivered.

"When word about Big Ouray gets out around Ignacio," Moon said with a faint smile, "some folks won't believe it was a human that did it."

"I have heard all of those fantastic rumors that float around after an animal mutilation," Oswald said softly. He turned to look over his cigar at the Ute. It was no surprise that Charlie Moon was tainted with a touch of superstition. All men were. "Let me assure you—this mutilator certainly was not the *pitukupf*. Or one of those old Anasazi spirits defending his resting place. This was a man. A man with an excellent mind, capable of meticulous planning."

Scott Parris's thoughts drifted away from this nonsense; he wondered what Anne was doing in Washington. Right now. At this moment. Maybe she was thinking about him. Wondering what he was doing. He got up, hoping Moon would take the hint and make his good-byes. "Looks like we've got our work cut out for us."

Oswald snapped the book covers shut. "I doubt it will happen, but if either of you should happen to come face-to-face with this mutilator, I advise you to be very prudent. Cain . . . I am sure that he is getting bored with killing animals. Some day soon, he will begin stalking"—almost imperceptibly, the old man shuddered—"the ultimate prey. What you are involved in," he blinked at Moon through watery eyes and his voice quavered, "is a most deadly game."

The Ute patted the old man on the back and smiled. "Thanks for the warning, Oz."

"This is starting to sound like pretty serious business. Maybe," Parris glanced slyly at his friend, "we should call in the FBI to give Charlie a hand."

Oswald Oakes watched Moon disappear down the tree-lined brick walk; the white man trailed behind the big Ute. He shook his head with the sad resignation of one who has tried to communicate and failed. Surely, the game had already begun. But who could prevent it! Not this mismatched set of policemen. If anything was to be done to influence the outcome of this affair, it was up to him. Filled with conflicting emotions, Oakes shuddered and tried to dismiss a multitude of fanciful worries from his mind.

On that very evening, as other old men drifted gratefully into the misty world of dreams, he would resist the gentle call of night. Finally, in the small hours, his resistance would fail. At first he would nap peacefully enough. But soon Oswald's eyes would begin to shift and flutter under his lids. He would dream dreams. Of being watched. Stalked. Of running . . . a formless, relentless hunter in close pursuit. The dream would end as it always did. There would be sharp pains, like hot fire ripping through his flesh. Rivers of warm blood. His violent death at the hands of the huge, shadowy form that pursued him through a forest of stunted, twisted trees.

And without knowing how he knew, Oswald Oakes knew this: The one who stalked him was not a stranger.

Outside the museum atmosphere of Oswald Oakes's Victorian home, the sun was breaking through the overcast, throwing a pale filtered light on the wet, emerald lawns. Parris rolled his window down; the moist, clean air was delicious. As they drove slowly through the old residential section of Durango, Moon glanced at his pardner. "Old Oz can't imagine an ordinary lunatic killing an animal and cutting it up just for the fun of it." He sounded almost apologetic. "He doesn't meet the sort of folks we have to deal with." Moon suddenly pulled onto the shoulder. He switched off the ignition.

The Ute seemed to be watching someone, or something, past a thin grove of lodge pole pine. Parris looked, but saw nothing unusual. "What is it, Charlie?"

"Funny," Moon replied dreamily, "never thought about it before, but that kinda looks like fun."

Parris followed Moon's gaze to the pair of men strolling across the manicured grass. "Surely you jest."

"Oh, I don't know," the Ute said, "I get some spare time, I may take up golf."

9

Daisy Perika awoke long before daylight; she had thought she heard a deep rumble of thunder in the west, but maybe it was a dream. No . . . there it was again. The storm was somewhere south of Durango but still west of Ignacio. Just about over Bondad. The old woman settled her head onto the rumpled pillow and sighed. Sleep would not return. She stretched her legs in a futile attempt to drive away the stiffness and the painful cramps that drew her toes under her feet. The shaman imagined that the faraway thunder was, as her grand-mother had told her when she was barely five summers old, the great buffalo-hide drum of Man-in-the-Sky. She heard his palm slap the hide of the drum once more, with a solid crack that reverberated off the earth. Gradually, the drumbeats became synchronized with the pounding of her old heart, echoing across the dim memories of her many years. She whispered the shaman's song that her uncle, Blue Humming Bird, had taught her:

> "Carry me over the clouds
> Carrry me over the great snow mountains
> I will hear the sound of your wings
> Carry me there on your shoulders
> Carry me down to Lowerworld
> I will hear the sound of your wings . . ."

Daisy felt herself covered with a heavy fog, then she drifted away with the sound of the drumbeat. She seemed to float through the aluminum roof of her trailer home, then saw the San Juan range far below—rounded peaks covered by thin wisps of silver cloud that flitted ahead of the west winds. The shaman was carried higher, until the horizon curved gently, and she could see a soft boundary in the Kansas prairie where the morning sunlight was sweeping in from the east. Abruptly she felt her body plummet toward Lowerworld, but the shaman was not afraid. This had happened many times, more times than she could remember.

Without any sensation of landing, she was in a deep forest of vines and ferns and trees that were old beyond reckoning. She found herself in the eternal twilight of Lowerworld; a trio of pockmarked orange moons cast strange, flickering patterns over the fluttering leaves and twisted vines. At first, the shaman felt rather than saw the presence above her. A shadowy form moved slowly above the mossy forest floor, floating like a kite under the branches of the trees. Fascinated, she watched the shadow transform its amorphous darkness into another shape, the form of an animal with wings. It was now a great bird, like an owl, with pitiless yellow eyes and curved yellow talons that ached for prey. The feathered creature dropped behind a mass of ferns, as if to make a kill. Daisy heard a scream. The awful shriek, which gradually fell to a low, pleading moan, left her trembling with horror. Was she the next victim? When the enormous bird arose with a ponderous flapping of wings, its talons were crimson—dripping with blood! Daisy shuddered as the great feathered creature circled under the limbs of the ancient trees. While she watched, the bird was gradually transformed . . . it was once again a flickering shadow, without discernible form, darting to and fro like a great moth among the mossy trunks of the trees.

The dwarf appeared on the forest floor, puffing smugly on his clay pipe. She heard the voice of her power-spirit; the *pitukupf* spoke in the archaic Ute tongue. Daisy rearranged the words in her mind and translated most of the prophesy into English, the tongue she used from long habit. The words hinted of a dark personality—someone, some*thing*, who would commit a barbarous, taboo act.

> "One *who was* Aváa,
> Is not Aváa,
> Will become Aváa *again after spilling* nuu-ci *blood*."

His final warning made the blood run cold in Daisy's veins. One of the People would surely die, and the manner of death would be horrible. So unspeakable was the crime, that the *pitukupf* refused to describe it. "Who is the Ute who will die, little man, and who . . . what is it this flying shadow that kills one of the People?"

His answer was silence, punctuated by occasional puffs of Flying Dutchman smoke. As she was wondering how the dwarf might be encouraged to tell her what he knew, Daisy felt herself slipping away. Back. Upward toward Middle World. In a moment, she was once again inside her old, arthritic body, her head resting on a sweat-soaked pillow. With some effort, she swung her aching legs over the edge of the mattress and pushed her feet into a pair of worn leather slippers that had belonged to her second husband. "Sleep has left this house," she said aloud, "I might as well get myself up." She felt an urgent need to hold fast to Middle World. It would be good to do something ordinary. Make a pot of coffee, fry an egg in the iron skillet. Then, the vision would not seem so real. So compelling.

Arlo Nightbird felt good. Very good. He steered the Mercedes along the gravel road with one hand and searched for his bottle with the other. There was one last problem to deal with before the government money began flowing into the reservation like the waters of the Piños. Then, he would be the most influential man in Ignacio. After that . . . who could say what his future might hold? Maybe an appointed office in state government. Maybe more. Ben Nighthorse-Campbell, the Northern Cheyenne, had made it all the way to the United States Senate. Arlo grinned. If an honest man like the Cheyenne rancher could go that far, what was the potential for a clever businessman who was willing to break a rule here and there? His potential, Arlo decided, was limited only by his imagination. And his will. And the immediate impediment in his path to glory was a pathetic old woman. Hardly, he thought, a worthy challenge.

Daisy had felt the presence of the storm since before daylight, long before there was a fragrant hint of rain in the breeze from the west or the least hint of cloud in the pale cobalt sky. Now, the rumbling gray clouds were rolling over the crest of Three Sisters Mesa. She sniffed at the damp air whipping her kitchen curtain. A heavy storm was coming, with rain that would produce rushing torrents in the arroyos—thunder that would rattle the aluminum walls of her flimsy trailer home, lightning that would snap like a great whip of fire across the mesas. She pulled her shawl around her shoulders and waited for the first drops of rain. The old woman was surprised when she heard the sound of the engine; it was well muffled. This was not Gorman's old pickup truck, neither was it Charlie Moon's big four-wheel-drive police car. This was something else. The old woman pushed the frayed cotton curtain aside and rubbed a little circle of moisture off the window. Yes, the car was turning into her lane, but this was an automobile she didn't recognize. It was long, and sleek, and the color of wild strawberries. Or, she thought with a ripple of apprehension, of freshly spilled blood. This was an expensive automobile, and she wasn't acquainted with folk who drove expensive cars. Daisy waited at the window to see who would get out. She sucked in a short breath when she recognized Arlo Nightbird. He stepped out of the car, pulled his expensive breeches up over his belly to raise his cuffs above the dirt in her yard, then almost tiptoed toward the trailer.

Daisy listened to the old wooden steps creak as Arlo mounted the porch. He impatiently kicked aside the tools left behind from Gorman's half-finished repairs. Daisy entertained a fanciful picture of Arlo stepping through a weak plank and breaking his leg. He didn't. Instead, he pounded hard on the aluminum door. "Daisy," he bellowed, "you in there?"

For a moment, Daisy Perika considered not opening the door. If she had taken this course of action, the future of the Southern Ute Tribe would have been altered in unimaginable ways. But she opened the door, and the die was forever cast.

"What do you want . . . Arlo Nightbird." She spat the words out, mouthing his name as if it was a distasteful obscenity.

Arlo grinned stupidly; she smelled whisky on his breath. "Caught you in a raw mood, did I? Just came by to bring some news. All right if I come in?" He glanced over his shoulder. "Looks like rain."

"Rain's a minute away. Don't expect you'll be here that long." Daisy stepped onto the porch; better not to let him into the house. If Arlo was drunk, he might pass out, or throw up on the linoleum.

He had lost the dumb grin. "I came by to offer some help."

"Help . . . from you?" In spite of her nasty mood, Daisy found this statement unaccountably amusing. She smiled. "Guess there's got to be a first time. Help away."

Arlo relaxed. He used his boot-tip to shove the crowbar to the edge of the porch, and leaned on the pine railing. It swayed. Daisy wondered if it might break. She imagined this little peacock falling off backward and her grin spread wider.

He drew a deep breath. Best to get it done. "You heard that the tribal council approved the Economic Development Board's proposal?" Daisy's face was blank. "The plan," he continued, "to get government money to study the feasibility of storing nuclear waste in Spirit Canyon."

This little apple even sounded like a *matukach*. Red on the outside. White on the inside. "Gorman told me," she muttered, "you gonna make him move his cows out of the sacred canyon?"

"Ain't my idea, it's one of them government requirements," Arlo said, "they'll all have to be out in the next couple of weeks."

"If that garbage is so safe, why can't Gorman keep his stock in the canyon? He gonna get two-headed calves?"

"It's perfectly safe," Arlo said, "it's just that the feds won't perform a study on any site with animals or people living nearby."

Daisy felt a sickness deep in her abdomen. "People? There's no people in *Cañon del Espiritu.*"

Arlo removed a three-page memorandum from his coat pocket and held it near Daisy's face. "These are the rules. No domestic animals, no endangered species, no human domiciles within two miles of a proposed storage site."

She squinted at the tiny print. "What's dom-eye-ciles?"

"Houses where people live on a regular basis. Like your place."

"My place?" The sickening sensation became nausea; the old woman backed up against the door for support.

"Yeah, Daisy, your place. You live too damn close to the canyon site. But don't worry. . . ."

"Don't worry?" She stared at Arlo's pudgy face in disbelief. "I've lived here for most of my life. . . . Before we had this trailer, my first husband built an adobe, over there . . ." she pointed a trembling finger at the pitiful ruin, but Arlo ignored her pleas.

"What I mean, Daisy, this is a real piece of luck. Since you have to move for this deal to stick, the tribe's going to pay for all your moving expenses, and provide you with a new house in that development south of Ignacio. Running water, electricity, cable television. . . ."

"I got electricity here," she said defiantly, "and I got a fine well with a good Sears-and-Roebuck pump. I could have had one of those cardboard-box houses anytime I wanted it."

Arlo was determined. "But cable TV, Daisy, real good pictures, even the Movie Channel."

"Cable TV is for folks who want to watch naked people," Daisy snapped. "I don't need none of that trash." She folded her arms resolutely. "It's a free country. I'm staying put, right here."

"You got no choice," Arlo said with a dark scowl, "you got to get out and you got three weeks flat. You don't move, I'll send the police out to arrest you."

Daisy drew herself up to her full height, which was an inch greater than Arlo's. "Listen to this, you poor imitation of a Ute, you're not one of the People, you never have been. I've got a *matukach* friend that's three times the Ute you'll ever be and he's chief of police until Severo gets back. And you think Charlie Moon is goin' to throw his aunt out of her own house?"

Arlo opened his mouth to reply, but stammered impotently.

"Listen, you little wart on a pig's belly," Daisy continued, gathering steam, "don't let me see your homely face on this land again or I'll reach down your throat, grab your little ass, and jerk you inside out!" She leaned over stiffly and picked up the crowbar.

Arlo backed against the railing, the rotten pine gave way with a heavy groan, and Daisy saw the soles of his boots fly upward as he tumbled backward. The man hit the ground with a dull thump; he tried to speak but the breath was knocked from his lungs. When he got up on one knee, he found some of his wind. "You pushed me . . . tried to kill me, you damned old witch. That's . . . that's *assault.*" He drew a deep breath and coughed. "I'll have you thrown in jail, you'll never see this dump again. . . ." Daisy was standing on her porch, gripping the crowbar like a baseball bat, muttering weighty curses in archaic Ute.

Arlo instinctively reached for his sheath knife. This offense was too much for the old woman to bear; she raised Gorman's rusty crowbar over her shoulder. Arlo's eyes widened. "Don't . . . no . . ." He managed to get to his feet, backed toward his expensive red automobile, attempting to shield his face with both arms.

The shaman muttered an old incantation for victory over her enemies, then flung the crowbar at Arlo Nightbird with every ounce of strength in her frail body. There was a scream followed by a sickening crunch as the heavy steel implement impacted. Daisy stood, openmouthed with surprise as she viewed the startling consequence of her fury. No . . . no . . . this was not at all what she had intended. Arlo was finally, for the first time since he learned to speak, at a loss for words. He made no sound, none at all, and this frightened her far more than his threats. Now, she knew, there would be the devil to pay.

As Daisy considered what she should do next, the rains came.

Emily Nightbird dialed the number at her husband's Economic Development Board office and waited. Ten rings. Fifteen. No answer. She dialed another number. On the second ring, she heard Herb Ecker's greeting. "Nightbird Insurance," he announced with European formality, "how may we be of service?"

"It's Emily Nightbird. I'm surprised to find you at work so late."

"I have considerable paperwork to catch up on."

Herb had no apparent social life. Arlo thought Herb, who donated hours of free overtime, was a bargain. Emily found him to be somewhat . . . *peculiar.* She tried hard to make her inquiry sound casual. "Is my husband there?"

There was a hesitation before he answered. "No, Mrs. Nightbird. He was here immediately after lunch, then . . ." No. It was not his place to reveal to this woman where her husband went. Arlo had made that crystal clear the last time he "blabbed." Herb cleared his throat. "I am uncertain precisely where he is . . . at this moment."

Emily nibbled at a stubby fingernail. "Did he say when he was coming back? We have a reservation at the Strater in thirty minutes." She immediately regretted this admission.

"I am sorry," Herb said. "He did not tell me when he would return."

She said good-bye and slammed the receiver down. Tears welled up in her eyes. Emily clenched her fists. "I will not cry. I will not!" Thirteen years ago, when she had told her parents about her engagement to the richest man in Ignacio, her father had spat into the fireplace and made his warning. Emily remembered his exact words. "I've knowed about Arlo Nightbird since he was a little boy. He's mean as sin and a skirt-chaser and won't make you a good husband." Daddy had been right. Emily dropped her face into her hands and wept.

The telephone rang. She grabbed it. Before she could speak, Emily heard her father's voice. "Hello, little girl."

She cleared her throat. "Hello, Daddy."

"What's wrong? You don't sound—"

Emily drew a deep breath. "I'm fine."

"Called to wish you a happy anniversary."

"That's kind of you." Her voice broke.

"Let me guess . . . it's your weddin' anniversary, and the little horse's-ass ain't there, is he?"

She gripped the telephone with white knuckles. "Daddy, I wish you wouldn't refer to Arlo as a . . . in that vulgar manner."

Fidel Sombra chuckled. His daughter had entirely too much of that fancy education. "I s'pose it *is* an insult to horses everywhere. Put the mule's ass on the line, maybe I'll apologize." Maybe, he thought, I'll ask him if he's picked up the clap from one of his whores.

"Arlo's not here. I expect him any minute now. We have a reservation at a restaurant in Durango." Emily paused as she heard the doorbell. "Just a minute." She carried the cordless extension to the door. She was disappointed, even irritated to see Cecelia Chavez. Why couldn't people call first if they wanted to visit; drop-ins were such an awful nuisance. The public health nurse appeared to be exhausted. "I'm very busy right now," Emily said curtly.

"It's about the blood drive. . . ." Cecelia was on her way in.

"Could it wait until tomorrow? I'm speaking to my father on the telephone."

Cecelia seemed not to have heard; she passed by and dropped her angular figure onto a sturdy couch.

Emily turned her back on this guest and lowered her voice as she spoke into the telephone receiver. "Cecelia Chavez is here; I expect she wants to give me the blood drive figures. From the expression on her face, we must be short of our goal again this year."

The old man snorted. "So where is your husband?" Out whoring around, he thought.

"I don't know where he is." Emily hoped Cecelia couldn't hear the conversation. A few months back, there had been talk. The nurse, the gossip was, had spent a few of her evenings with Arlo Nightbird. "I called Herb Ecker, but he doesn't know where Arlo is. Or won't say."

"I'll give him a call, and he'll damn well tell me where that worthless bastard is!"

"You leave Herb alone. I'll be fine." She tried to distract him. "And how are you, Daddy?"

"Hard as flint, tough as old rawhide."

"I appreciate your call. Really."

"I got hogs to feed. I'll come by tomorrow morning." He hung up.

Emily stared blankly at the telephone and wondered what to do. If Arlo didn't show up soon, she'd call the Strater and cancel the dinner reservations. She turned to the nurse. "Now," Emily asked with pretended cheerfulness, "what can I do for you, Cecelia?"

As the rain fell in sweeping torrents and the earth trembled under her feet with each deep rumble of thunder, Daisy struggled up the steep path across the talus slope toward her destination on Three Sisters Mesa. There was a sharp crack only yards ahead as a zigzag of lightning snapped the top of a piñon snag. The flash illuminated the concave shelter in the sandstone cliff. She slipped on a wet stone, stumbled to her knees, then pushed herself upright with the stout oak staff. Daisy clung tenaciously to her precious plastic bag. "Another two hundred steps," she wheezed, "and I'll be there, where it's always dry. One step at a time." She raised her staff. "Go away, *tona-pagay*," the shaman shouted to the lightning, "fly away to your home in the great mountains of the North, do not waste your powers to harm an old woman who," she added with a pitiful tone, "will die soon anyway." Heavy drops pelted the old woman, turning her path into slippery mud, but the lightning paused in its high-step across the mesa.

Daisy Perika stumbled and slipped and grunted and tripped, but she did not pause. When she finally reached the cliff overhang, it seemed that her pounding heart might stop. The shaman fell on her side by the old brush shelter that she had used for long meditations and special visions. Now that she was safe, the lightning struck once, then twice, along the talus slope, exploding a juniper into splinters. "Thank you, *tona-pagay*," the shaman gasped, "thank you for giving me time."

When she could breathe easily, Daisy crawled inside the willow structure and carefully emptied the contents of the plastic shopping bag on the sandy floor. Kitchen matches in a waxed box, a wool blanket, canned peaches, stale lard biscuits—it was all there, and remarkably dry. There was an armload of firewood remaining from her last sojourn in the cliff hideaway; she scraped dry bark from a juniper branch with her thumbnail and lit this tinder with a wooden match. The flames sprinkled her face with dancing flashes of amber light, the warmth on her hands and knees was wonderful. Gradually, Daisy began to feel better and to consider her predicament. If she had stopped after Arlo Nightbird fell off the porch, she would have been safe from the law. But once the crowbar left her hand, everything had changed. When the police came, there would be indisputable evidence of her crime. There would be no way out. She would be sent to jail, never again to see her sweet home at the mouth of *Cañon del Espiritu.*

The shaman bowed her head and pressed her palms against closed eyes. Nothing good would come of this day's work. Daisy pulled the blanket over her tired body; she immediately fell into a deep, dreamless sleep. A sleep that not even the booming thunder would disturb.

JoJo Tonompicket paused on the deer path and nodded toward his brother. "Archie . . . you hear that?"

The other young Ute leaned on his antique Springfield 30.06 and listened. "Yeah. I bet it's Uncle Homer. He finds us out here with these rifles, there'll be hell to pay and then some." Archie was a born worrier. "He'll take our guns and throw us in jail."

JoJo nodded. "Yeah, he'd do that sure enough." Homer Tonompicket took his job very seriously. Just a couple of years ago, the tribal game warden had caused comment when he arrested his brother-in-law for keeping two cutthroats over the limit. But then Homer wasn't too fond of his brother-in-law. "Don't sound like Homer's truck," JoJo whispered. He moved behind a juniper and waited until he could see the battered GMC pickup lurching along the rutted lane.

Archie dropped to one knee and watched. "Comin' out of *Cañon del Espiritu.* Movin' right along, too."

JoJo grinned. "Faster'n first-class mail." It was five hundred yards, but he recognized the old pickup with the loose tail pipe. "Wonder why old Gorman's haulin' ass in such a big hurry?"

10

Scott Parris was drifting through a strange dream. Daisy Perika, who was much younger in this fantasy orchestrated by stressed neurons, had prepared a picnic lunch and packed it in a basket. They walked together, hand in hand, deep into *Cañon del Espíritu*. He spread a red and white checkered oilcloth onto a flat spot under a large cotton-wood by the stream bed. Fat speckled trout darted through the rolling green waters. Daisy opened the basket and displayed its contents with pride; it was filled with acorns. "Eat one," she said urgently, "and you'll be given the Answer, eat two and you'll understand the Question." Parris desperately wanted to understand these mysteries. He bit into the soft pulp of a plum-sized acorn. It was terribly bitter. "That didn't help," he told Daisy, "I don't understand anything. I don't understand why my wife had to die, why Anne must be so far away." The young version of Daisy laughed and blew him a kiss.

Parris awoke to the sound of thunder and blinked into the half-light. It took him a moment to realize that this was not his familiar bedroom in Granite Creek. He was in Ignacio, the tricultural city in the center of the patchwork Southern Ute Reservation. On the ground floor of the Sky Ute Motel. On a firm mattress, under a heavy orange quilt. He rolled off the bed and pushed the curtains away from the window. He blinked and gazed upward. The crystal blue was gone this morning; the sky was low, sodden, and uncharacteristically gray. Ominously gray. As he watched, a few drops of rains splattered on the cement walkway in the courtyard. The intermittent drops gradually multiplied into a light shower; within seconds a heavy gray rain was falling in vertical sheets. The drops stuck to the window like porridge and seemed to coagulate, as if the rain had turned to blood.

This was a bizarre observation; he mustn't be fully awake. He ran his hand through his thinning hair and wondered whether it was raining in Bethesda, where Anne had her apartment. He glanced at his watch; it was two hours later in the District of Columbia; she would have been at work for some time by now. Probably interviewing Very Important People, people who made things happen. Senators. Handsome senators. Rich handsome senators. He wondered if Anne ever wondered about him. And cared about what he was doing. And with whom. As if in mocking answer, thunder rumbled a low, hearty laugh directly over the Sky Ute Motel. He didn't like the sound.

Parris was brushing his teeth when Moon pounded on the door and boomed out in a voice that reverberated between the walls. "Up and at 'em, pardner. Time to do some police work!"

They were pulling into Angel's gravel parking lot when the dispatcher's voice crackled over the short-wave radio. "Car three-thirty-nine. Charlie?" She waited. "You there Charlie?"

Moon picked the microphone off the dashboard hook and pressed the key. "What's on your mind, Nancy?"

"Just had a call from Emily Nightbird. Wants you to come by and see her."

"Urgent?"

"Don't think so," Nancy replied. "She said to come over at eleven."

"I'll check it out." Moon hung the mike onto its hook.

"You must be happy," Parris said sarcastically, "this call won't interfere with your breakfast."

Moon's face wore a puzzled look. "Breakfast can wait. Let's go see what she wants."

Moon parked the Blazer under the branches of a huge elm and switched off the ignition. He nodded toward a black Honda parked in the broad asphalt driveway. "That belongs to Doc Anderson."

Parris raised an eyebrow. "He makes house calls?"

"For the Nightbirds," Moon muttered bitterly, "we all make house calls."

A uniformed maid opened the door and frowned at the policemen. Moon removed his hat; Parris followed suit. "Emily called," Moon said, "said she wanted to—"

"Mrs. Nightbird"—the maid emphasized the proper address for her employer—"doesn't expect you until eleven." She waited to see if they would leave. They would not. "Come have a seat in the parlor," she said through thin lips.

They followed the maid to a room filled with massive Spanish furniture. The couch looked like it would support a Buick. Moon sat; he seemed lost in thought. Parris wandered into the hall and glanced into the library just in time to see the physician withdraw a syringe from Emily's arm. He ducked back into the parlor. "Doctor just gave her a shot." The physician passed in the hall, noticed the policemen, then hurried through the front door without speaking. The maid appeared; with a subtle nod, she indicated that they should follow.

Emily blinked uncertainly at the policemen. The delicate woman was pressing a piece of cotton against her forearm. "My doctor . . . just gave me an injection to help me relax. I've not been sleeping well." She glanced at the mother-of-pearl face on the grandfather clock. "I didn't expect you until eleven." Visitors should arrive precisely on time. Early was worse than late.

Moon looked at the hat in his hands. "Well, we have some other things on our plate, have to stop by when we can." The Ute had no intention of being summoned like a servant.

Emily understood that this early arrival was his way of informing Mrs. Nightbird that her husband didn't own the tribal police. She smiled weakly at Parris. "I'm sorry Cecelia had so much trouble getting blood from your arm. It must have been rather painful, all that poking around with the needle."

Parris grinned foolishly. "Stuff like that don't bother me." This woman smelled wonderful, and her lovely brown eyes were so . . . so enormous!

Moon shuffled his big feet and nervously shifted his weight from one leg to another. "What can we do for you, Emily?"

"It is a rather personal matter," she said carefully.

"Look," Parris said, feeling more than ever like an outsider, "if you two would rather discuss this alone . . ."

"No," Emily said wearily, "that won't be necessary. It's nothing that will surprise this community." A moist hint of tears glistened in her soft brown eyes. She sat down. As her green silk skirt slipped well above her knees, Parris couldn't help but notice that she had attractive legs. Very attractive legs indeed. He averted his gaze to a bad painting of yellow aspens in a cherry frame. How long had Anne been away in Washington? A few days, or a few weeks?

"This," she continued hesitantly, "is somewhat embarrassing for me."

Moon nodded. And waited.

"It's Arlo," she said. "He didn't come home last night. Or," she added with a sigh, "the night before."

Moon looked at his boots and cleared his throat. It was his turn to be embarrassed. "I don't know quite how to say this, but . . ."

"I know," she said quickly, "my husband often vanishes for days. I know where he goes, the awful things he does, and I know everybody in Ignacio gossips about it behind my back." She jutted her chin defiantly. "I've learned to live with that. But this is different. He's been working very hard lately, on that proposal to use *Cañon del Espiritu* for storage of nuclear waste. It's all he talks about, all that's on his mind."

"I wouldn't worry too much," Moon said confidently, "he'll show up in a couple of days. Always does." With his tubes all cleared out.

"My husband, despite the appearance of spontaneity, plans his 'disappearances' well in advance," Emily said stiffly. "His little flings never interfere with business. Not ever."

"And," Parris said, "he had some special business planned?"

"Indeed," Emily said, "early this morning, he was to meet with an official from the federal government's Commercial Nuclear Waste Agency. I'm certain that Arlo, no matter what he was up to, would show up at the Economic Development Board offices to greet this visitor. He didn't. She called here at nine-fifteen, wanted to know where he was. So you see, this is different. Nothing could have kept Arlo away from that meeting, unless . . . that's when I called your office. Your dispatcher . . . Nancy Beyal said she'd get in touch with you. I'm so happy you came—I don't know what to do."

"When," Parris asked, "was the last time you saw Mr. Nightbird?"

Emily patted her eyes with a lace handkerchief. Parris resisted an absurd fantasy of taking this delicate woman in his arms and comforting her. "Arlo left right after breakfast. Day before yesterday. We had dinner reservations at the Strater."

"That's a fancy watering hole," Parris said. "Special occasion?"

"Our wedding anniversary," Emily attempted, without success, to smile. "When he didn't show up, I called his EDB office but there wasn't any answer. Then, I called the insurance agency; Herb Ecker said Arlo had left."

Moon scribbled a few notes. "Wouldn't expect Arlo to miss his anniversary celebration." It was a polite lie. "Did Herb know where Arlo was?"

"Herb wouldn't . . . didn't tell me." Emily pressed little fingertips against her temples in a vain attempt to fight off the first waves of a migraine. Parris noticed that her nails were bitten off to the quick.

Moon pocketed his notebook. "We'll stop by and see Ecker. I'll be in touch soon as we learn something."

Moon was in the squad car, notifying the dispatcher about his plans to search for Arlo Nightbird, but Parris lagged behind. "I wouldn't worry. Nine out of every ten missing persons turn up perfectly safe, with a reasonable explanation for their disappearance." Well, maybe five out of ten.

Emily took his hand and squeezed it. Parris felt a sensation like an electric shock ripple along his arm. "You're so very kind," she said softly. She was still holding his hand when Moon poked his head in the doorway. "You done here yet, Chief?"

Parris blushed and made a hurried departure. He was certain that Emily Nightbird had hesitated, ever so slightly, to release his hand. Just a little. Maybe. He pretended not to notice the wide grin split-ting Moon's face.

"Must be rough on you with Anne so far away," Moon observed with pretended compassion as they slogged through the rain toward the squad car. "I got this third cousin I could introduce you to. Never has had a boyfriend, and she's about your age. Only drawback," the Ute said, "is she's kind of muscular and has this little mustache. Best thing, though, she's not a *married* woman."

"No wonder," Parris said, "sounds like she's twice the man that you are."

Moon chuckled as he slid under the wheel. "Let me fix you up with a date, then you can tell me."

The big Ute was getting to be a sharp pain in the ass, but he was right. It was time to call Anne. First thing this evening. To hell with this temporary job with the Ute cops. He'd grab the first plane to Washington.

The young man was busy writing in a bound notebook when Moon's voice boomed over his head. "What's cookin', Herb?"

"Oh, nothing . . . just writing a few lines." He hurriedly closed the cover of the notebook.

Moon nodded toward his pardner. "This is Scott Parris. He's standing in for the chief for a few weeks."

Herb got to his feet and offered a polite, continental handshake. "I have already met you . . . when we were donating blood."

Parris pumped the hand. "Yeah. I remember." The policeman had a tattoo of tiny bruises on both his forearms.

Moon sat on the desk. "I have to know where Arlo went a couple of days ago. He hasn't showed up and his wife is worried." He leaned close to Ecker. "Don't give me any stuff about not knowing where your boss is, just spit it out."

Herb avoided Moon's frank gaze. "I'm sorry I couldn't tell Em— Mrs. Nightbird. Mr. Nightbird gave strict instructions that I was always to be discreet about his . . . whereabouts."

"I understand," Moon said patiently. "Just tell me what you know."

"He went out to that place . . . Spirit Canyon, to see Mrs. Perika."

Moon's brow twisted into a puzzled frown. "Aunt Daisy? What about?"

Ecker reddened. "I am sorry. I believe it was about an eviction notice. In connection with the tribe's plans for Spirit Canyon."

Moon grunted as he pushed himself erect. Deliver an eviction notice to Daisy Perika? Arlo was either very stupid or very brave. No. He was very stupid. "Okay. We'll go have a look; ten to one there'll be some simple reason why he didn't get back. Maybe he had a flat tire up by the canyon. Daisy doesn't have a phone, so he's probably still there." Moon suppressed a smile at the thought of Daisy making a bunk for Arlo Nightbird. She'd sooner keep a scorpion in her pocket.

Parris read the upside-down title on Ecker's notebook. The letters spelled out POETRY by H. Ecker. "You a poet?"

Herb blushed. "Not a very competent one." The young man waved his hand to indicate the row of books on his desk. "But I read a lot. I am memorizing some of my favorite poets. . . . I repeat the lines during my spare time."

Most of the two dozen books were paperbacks that showed much wear from constant use. Parris squinted at the titles. Whitman. Dickinson. Frost. Burns. Poe. "You really remember a lot of that stuff?"

"Actually," Ecker said earnestly, "I have memorized almost every line."

Parris raised his brows. "In *all* those books? I don't see how anyone could."

Ecker appeared to be injured by the skeptical tone. "If you doubt it, you may select any volume. Open to any page, pick a line at random, and read it aloud. If I cannot recite the next line, I will pay you twenty dollars. If I succeed, of course, you would pay me twenty dollars."

Parris smiled uneasily. "That's a tempting proposition, kid, but I don't think it'd look right. You know, the chief of police gambling on the side."

"Then," Ecker said, "forget the money. If I win, you must memorize a poem of my choosing and recite it, without error, within say . . . six weeks of this date."

"And if you lose?"

"You select a work by any poet. I will memorize it in a single reading and recite it without error."

Parris looked doubtful.

"To make it easy on you, Mr. Parris, I will turn my back when you select a volume. Does that provide you a sufficient advantage? Maybe," he said with the mildest hint of a taunt, "you are a man who prefers to avoid risk." Ecker sat down. His glum face mirrored his disappointment at the policeman's reticence.

Parris rubbed his chin and looked at Moon's impassive face. "What do you think?"

"I think," Moon said, "you should take the young smart-aleck on."

He whispered: "You think I can take him?"

"Pardner, it's a sure thing if I ever saw one."

Parris had noticed something interesting on Ecker's desk. There was a brown paper bag with a book in it. A brand new book. An unread book. "You're on," Parris said, "turn around." After Ecker ceremoniously turned his chair to face away from the desk, Parris quietly removed the volume from the paper bag. It was *The Best of Robert Service*. He opened the book; the new pages practically stuck together. Parris grinned at Moon, who winked back. He read aloud. "Now a promise made is a debt unpaid and—"

". . . and the trail has its own stern code," Ecker interrupted. He leaned back in his swivel chair and laughed. "That's too easy. 'The Cremation of Sam McGee.' You want to hear it all, from the beginning?"

"Hold on," Parris muttered, "that didn't count. I was just practicing." He looked imploringly at Moon. "Wasn't I just practicing, Charlie?"

"Sure you were, pardner. Now throw Herbie a really tough line."

Parris searched through several pages, then paused. "You ready?" Ecker nodded. Parris cleared his throat. "Although I supped on milk and brose . . ."

". . . and went to bed by candle-light, I pored on noble books of prose, and longed like Bobbie Burns to write. Now in this age of the machine . . ."

"Oh, stow it." Parris groaned as he slammed the book onto Ecker's desk. "I know when I've been hustled."

"That was the second stanza of 'My Highland Home.' Three stanzas of eight lines each, found on page two hundred and eight." The young man turned around to face Parris, a wide grin displaying perfect teeth. "Most people choose the Robert Service book when they accept this wager. I think it is because I keep an unused copy in the bag on my desk. They assume I have not read it. I earn about a hundred dollars every month with this bet. Pity you would not play for cash."

Parris scowled at the big Ute. "Dammit, you said this was a sure thing."

"It was," Moon said, chuckling, "you never had a chance."

"Well, name my poison."

"Since you represent the local authority," Ecker said, "I will make it extremely easy for you. How about 'The Shooting of Dan McGrew.' You can recite it for me a few months from now . . . let us say no later than Christmas Day." The acting chief of police would be gone from Ignacio long before the holidays; this would allow him a graceful way to forget his obligation.

They were a few miles north of Arboles on Route 151 when Moon shifted down to second gear and turned left off the paved road onto the gravel lane. The Ute glanced at his companion. "You gonna have any trouble memorizing that whole poem?"

"Cripes," Parris groaned, "I can't even remember my Social Security number."

The Blazer had barely topped the first rise on the gravel road when they saw the red convertible parked on the shoulder. In spite of the intermittent rain, the top was down. The car had been heading away from *Cañon del Espritu* toward the blacktop. Toward Ignacio. Toward home, and, presumably, Emily. Emily, with the rich olive complexion, the luminous brown eyes, the fetching legs. Emily with the electric touch! Parris felt absurdly jealous of Arlo Nightbird. As they pulled closer to the sleek automobile, Parris whistled. "That's some fancy car." This Nightbird guy had everything.

"Five-hundred SL," Moon said, "that's Arlo's wheels all right. Showy little sunnuvagun, ain't he?" He flipped the switch for the emergency lights; the alternating blue and red flashes reflected off the Mercedes chrome. "Let's go have a look."

Parris squatted at the Mercedes bumper and ran his finger around the sharp edges of a broken headlight.

Moon grunted. "Didn't happen here. No broken glass under the headlight." The Ute sniffed, then dropped to a prone position. "Hey. Have a look at this."

Parris poked his face under the bumper and saw the sticky green puddle. "Antifreeze?"

The Ute rubbed a sample between his fingers and sniffed at it. "That's what it is."

Parris peered through the grille. "There's a puncture in the radiator . . . couple of inches from the bottom. Coolant must be about gone. Looks like Mr. Nightbird stopped here when his engine overheated."

Moon inspected the sodden interior of the Mercedes. He picked up a half-full bottle of bourbon whisky off the floorboard. "Booker Noe's single barrel stuff. A fifth of this juice costs about fifty bucks." Moon dropped the bottle onto the seat. He turned and surveyed the rugged landscape. "Wonder which way he went? Paved road is a mile away; maybe he hiked to the blacktop and caught a ride."

"He didn't get home, though," Parris said. "Maybe after he broke down here, he walked back to your aunt's place."

"I don't know," Moon said, "they weren't on particularly good terms. And if he came out here to tell Aunt Daisy about an eviction notice, I don't expect he'd be entirely welcome. No," Moon said almost to himself, "I imagine she would have kicked his butt halfway to Ignacio."

"Maybe the radiator was punctured at the same location where the headlight was broken," Parris offered. "That would explain why there's no broken glass around here, and why he—the car got this far before the engine overheated. Could be that someone wanted us to think there was an accident here, but they forgot to bring the broken glass along."

"Daisy, Daisy," Moon whispered, "what mischief are you up to now?"

"I guess we better go see your aunt. Maybe," he added hopefully, "she saw somebody with Mr. Nightbird."

Moon's expression was grim. "I sure hope she's got a good story."

Moon parked the Blazer at the dirt lane leading to Daisy's trailer. Parris followed him down the lane as the Ute policeman studied the old ruts. The rain had been heavy; there was no sign of tire tracks. If Arlo's 500SL had been here, the heavy rains had washed all traces away.

"There," Moon said. A reflection of the filtered sunlight had caught his eye. He knelt and used his pocket knife to pry the shard from the clay and held it up for Parris to inspect. "Five'll get you ten," the Ute policeman said, "this chunk of glass is from Arlo's broken headlamp."

"There's a lot more glass than that missing," Parris said. "Where's the rest?"

"It looks like someone cleaned it up, only they missed this little chunk. But why would someone want to hide the fact that Arlo had been here?" It was a rhetorical question. And they both knew who "someone" was.

"I imagine your Aunt Daisy has a perfectly good explanation," Parris said lamely.

"Sure," Moon shook his head and sighed, "my Aunt Daisy has a good explanation for everything. Maybe the *pitukupf* did—did whatever was done." He climbed the porch while Parris waited several paces away in the light rain.

The *matukach* policeman didn't want to hear the conversation between aunt and nephew. If Daisy had something incriminating to say, it might be best if her nephew was the only witness.

Moon pounded on the door. "Aunt Daisy, it's Charlie." No answer. He counted to ten, then pounded again. "Aunt Daisy, open up. Need to talk to you." He turned to climb down the creaking steps, then stopped. The porch railing was leaning against the steps. Moon squatted; he picked up a claw hammer, a heavy screwdriver, and a crowbar. "Gorman's tools. He was going to fix the porch for Aunt Daisy. Guess he hasn't got around to it yet."

Their eyes met, then both men turned toward Three Sisters Mesa.

The cleft, high on the side of the cliff, was barely visible in the swirling mists. Parris remembered the crude brush shelter from a previous visit; Daisy had hidden there at least once before. Would she hide there from the law?

"I wonder," Parris said with a thin smile, "where she could be."

Moon grinned at him and clasped a hand on his shoulder. "You better not stay on the Rez too long, *matukach*. You're starting to behave like one of the family."

"Well," Parris said, "we're here to find Mr. Nightbird. Where should we look?"

Moon shrugged. "If Arlo didn't go out to the main highway, and he's not holed up in Aunt Daisy's trailer, maybe he went up the canyon."

Parris suddenly felt cold. And tired. And lonesome. "There's nothing up there. Why would he go into the canyon?"

Moon shook his head. "Maybe he was drunk, and wet, and wanted a place to sleep. There are some dry shelters in the canyon, close to the petroglyphs. Maybe he's up there sleeping it off."

Parris climbed back into the Blazer. "Let's get it over with. When we get back to town, I've got things to do."

"What things?" Moon asked innocently.

"Isn't there a jukebox at Angel's Diner?"

"Sure."

"Well," Parris announced loudly, "I'm gonna buy myself a twelve-ounce RC Cola and a Moon Pie."

The Ute grinned. "Somebody name a pie after me?" It seemed appropriate.

"Then you know what I'm gonna do?"

"Can't hardly wait to find out."

"Drop a nickel in the jukebox, play 'Maple on the Hill.' " The old song wasn't on the juke, a nickel wouldn't buy the time of day, and there were no Moon Pies at Angel's. But these were merely facts.

"What's 'Maple on the Hill'?" Moon asked.

"A classic country song." Decades ago.

"Not in Ute country, it ain't." Homer Tonompicket, that Grand Ol' Opry buff, probably had the song on a 78 rpm disk.

"And after the juke slides the record back in the stack, then I'm gonna hop a plane, plop my tired behind into one of those cushy first class seats and zip over to Washington where I will spend as much time as I can with Anne. I'm tired of living alone, Charlie." Parris slapped the dashboard so hard it made his palm sting. "Dammit, I feel fantastic! I may even ask Sweet Thing to marry me. She's making enough money for both of us; I could retire and become a bum!"

"You don't never do any useful work, so you're already a bum." Moon replied cheerfully. "But marrying Anne is the only smart idea I've heard from you in a long spell." Moon slowed to a crawl and shifted into four wheel drive. When the mud turned to deep muck, he shifted into low four wheel drive and the squad car groaned as it pulled along at an old man's pace. When they were near the site where Big Ouray's carcass had been discovered, the Ute cut the ignition. He glanced at his companion. "There's not a chance in a thousand we're going to find anything up here, but we'd best go through the motions and put it in a report. Why don't you stay in the car while I have an official look around?"

Parris, who had been entertaining visions of Anne, was experiencing a manic mood swing. No more J. E. Hoover. Lots more Anne. "No way, bub. You gonna slog along in the mud, your pardner slogs along in the mud beside you."

Moon pulled his hat brim down over his forehead. "Suit yourself," the Ute said, and slammed the door.

Parris slogged along behind as Moon led the way through the fringed sage toward the petroglyphs. When they reached the nearly vertical cliff wall, the Ute searched a half-dozen of the lower crevices that would provide decent shelter for a sleepy drunk. There was no sign of Arlo. Parris entertained himself by imagining Anne's reaction when he called. "Oh, darling," she would say, "I'm so thrilled that you're coming. I'll cancel my appointment to interview the First Lady. . . . We'll spend all our days . . . and nights . . . together."

Parris was jarred from this optimistic fantasy by a gruff announcement. "He's not where I thought he'd be," Moon said. "Let's go home. If he doesn't turn up in a couple of days, I'll put an all points out."

"As Acting Chief of the Southern Ute Police, I hereby give advance approval to all your sage decisions," Parris said. He slogged along again, following the Ute to the squad car. Parris was opening the door when he spotted something a few yards up the lane. "Wait. Up there." He pointed. "What's that . . . that white thing under the bush. . . ."

Moon couldn't see the object through the steamy windshield. "You want to check it out?"

Parris felt a sudden feeling of dread sweep over him. "It's probably nothing. A piece of paper."

Moon put the key into the ignition switch. "You won't be satisfied until you find out what it is."

Parris trudged up the road, forcing his feet to make each step. The white object became clearer as he drew near the dwarf oak. It was only a sock. A white cotton sock with two red rings around the ankle. But there was something odd about the shape of the sock. Parris stopped in the middle of the muddy lane.

"I don't like this," he said quietly. Moon didn't hear. "I don't like this!" he yelled.

Moon got out of the Blazer. "What is it?"

"A sock."

"Sock?" Moon's voice was flat. The Ute did not move.

"Doesn't look like an empty sock," Parris yelled. "Looks like it's got a foot in it."

Moon looked down at the mud caked on his boots but didn't answer.

"Did you hear me? I said it's got a *foot* in it." Parris took one step closer and leaned over to get a better view. "I can see part of a leg!"

The Ute policeman felt the cold to his marrow. Why was Daisy hiding? Why had she broken a headlamp on Arlo Nightbird's 500SL, then cleaned up the glass?

Parris waited for an eternity. Finally, Moon was at his side. "You're right. It is a sock."

"With a man's foot in it," Parris reminded him. He pointed at the leg to emphasize this significant point.

"Yeah. Hairy leg."

"Way I figure it," Parris said, "there's a whole body attached to that leg."

"I sure hope so," Moon responded earnestly. "Why don't you have a look?"

Parris tried without success to tear his gaze from the hairy leg. "I hereby resign as acting chief of tribal police. You have a look."

"I don't much like to get close to dead bodies," Moon said. "It's kind of a thing with Indians. Bad luck to touch a dead body. Causes soul sickness."

"I was under the impression," Parris reminded him curtly, "that you didn't believe in that sort of thing."

"I don't," the Ute replied solemnly, "but you get sick whether you believe it or not."

Parris moved closer to the bush and pulled back a branch. The first thing he saw was another leg, twisted under the first. This foot was bare. It was several seconds before his brain would fully comprehend the scene burned on his retinas. "Oh no!" He turned away and felt his legs go wobbly.

Moon shoved his hands deep into his coat pockets. The cold didn't go away. "Tell me."

Parris cleared his throat, forced himself to answer. "Male. Light olive complexion, dark hair. Maybe fifty to fifty-five. About five-five or six. Flabby."

"Sounds like Arlo Nightbird. Look, I'm sorry I pushed you into checking out the body. I had no idea you had such a thing about viewing a corpse. . . ."

"Wasn't just that," Parris said, "the body's been . . ." He felt a fresh wave of nausea sweep over his viscera.

"Been what?" Moon knew what the answer would be.

"Castrated," Parris said weakly.

Moon put a massive hand over his eyes. "Dear God."

Parris squinted at the cloud-fingers touching the mesa tops. It did seem to be an appropriate moment for prayer.

The Ute found his voice. "Look at his ankles, Scott."

Parris leaned forward, forcing himself to this task. "I'm looking, Charlie."

"Are there any marks"—the Ute clenched his fists—"like a cord was tied around his ankles?"

Parris's voice was thin. "No. Not that I can see." He turned away from the corpse and studied his friend's face. "You know something you aren't telling me?"

The Ute barely heard Parris's voice; his whole attention was absorbed with that awful vision from the nightmare. A human figure strung upside down from a tree limb. Waiting . . . waiting to be butchered by the horned beast and his blade of blue fire. Moon had not the least doubt that it was a premonition. Still waiting to be fulfilled. And it would not wait much longer.

But that awaited him in the dark world; in this world of sunshine and cleansing rain there was police work to be done. First, the identification must be made. He clamped his hand on Parris's shoulder.

"Does he . . . does the body . . . have a turquoise stud in the left ear-lobe?"

"No way to tell," Parris said.

"You couldn't see his left ear?"

It was a long time before the *matukach* policeman answered. "Whoever snipped off his balls," Parris whispered, "also took his ears. Both of 'em."

Cain had earned his name.

11

The old shepherd was oblivious to the vast space beneath his dangling feet. Nahum Yaciiti sat lightly on the dead pine branch that hung over the canyon wall; his back rested on the scarred trunk that had been stripped of bark by repeated strikes of lightning. He watched the policemen on the canyon floor as they covered Arlo Nightbird's body.

Charlie Moon, having looked at the body, sat down heavily in the squad car. The Ute policeman felt oddly hollow as he watched his *matukach* friend drive wooden stakes in the dirt lane. Parris strung yellow POLICE—DO NOT CROSS tape along the stakes, then draped it around the bush that sheltered the mutilated corpse. The Ute silently surveyed the canyon floor, wondering if there had been tracks near the body. Before the rains came and erased such evidence away forever. Why hadn't the killer done this work after the rain, when the soft ground would have preserved a few footprints? Probably because the murderer wasn't stupid. Moon thumbed the plastic button on his radio microphone. "Base, this is three-thirty-nine. You read me, Nancy?"

There was a burp of static as the dispatcher answered. "Read you, Charlie. Signal is weak."

"I'm in a canyon. Don't have line of sight between our antennas." He hesitated. "Call in all patrols, notify the state troopers. We've got us . . . a situation."

"Will do. What kind of situation?" Nancy's internal antennae didn't need line of sight.

"Found a body in *Cañon del Espiritu*. No positive I.D. on the victim."

"Is it Arlo?"

"I said we don't have a positive I.D.!" He was immediately sorry he had snapped at Nancy. The dispatcher, who knew almost everything worth knowing about Ignacio, had learned that Arlo was missing. "It's a homicide. We'll guard the site until the rest of the troops show up. Contact the BIA police in Cortez. Then call Sam Parker in Denver and ask him to send in some Bureau people. You copy that?"

Nancy hesitated slightly. "We normally call Durango for FBI assistance."

"Call Denver. I say again, Denver! You copy that?"

"Ten-four, Officer Moon. Stand by."

Officer Moon. That was Nancy's way of letting him know that her feelings were hurt. The Ute policeman watched the second hand tick on his Timex Quartz. Three minutes and forty-four seconds, and Nancy's voice returned. "Base to patrol three-thirty-nine. Our fellows are headed for the canyon. Rainwater was at Twin Crossing, checking on some stolen sheep, her ETA is forty minutes. Bignight was at the restaurant at Arboles; he should be there in fifteen minutes. State police should show up in an hour. Haven't been able to raise anybody at BIA."

Moon breathed deeply and answered in a casual tone, as if they were discussing a routine call about a barking dog. "That's good, Nancy. You talk to Parker?"

"Yes, sir." Moon didn't like the sound of this. "Officer Moon" had been a mild reproach. But Nancy never called him "sir." This didn't feel right.

He pressed the mike key. "And?"

"Mr. Parker is sending . . . somebody. Should arrive pretty quick."

Somebody? Moon braced himself. "Who's Parker sending?"

Nancy told him the bad news.

Parris leaned on the door and peered through the open window. "Well, the body's fenced in. You got help coming?"

"Yeah," Moon shot back, "couple of hours, we'll have a regular circus in the canyon."

Parris glanced over his shoulder at the shrouded remains of Arlo Nightbird. "I assume you notified the Bureau."

"They're sending Hoover." Moon's face was impassive, but he flexed his big hands slowly as if trying to grasp for something. Something solid to hold onto.

"It's his turf," Parris said reasonably, "he runs the Durango office till Stan Newman's back to work."

"I kind of hoped Parker might have time to come down himself," Moon said.

Parris was about to respond when he saw something on the mesa top. "Look . . . up there. What in blazes . . ."

Moon shielded his eyes with his hand. "Where? What do you see?"

Parris blinked. "Looks like a man . . . up there sitting on that limb." He pointed to a dead ponderosa on the mesa.

Moon squinted, then produced a pair of binoculars and scanned the crest of the mesa. "What limb?"

"That big dead tree, over the petroglyphs. He's on the second branch from the bottom. Dammit, I don't know why you can't see him."

Moon offered the binoculars to his friend. "Take a look."

Parris peered through the prisms at the blurred image of the pine. "Charlie, you're not looking at the right tree." He adjusted the focus. The form of the man was no longer there. The lawman felt his face blush warm. "Well shoot, Charlie—he's gone." Or maybe he was never there. Maybe.

This *matukach* was full of surprises. The barest hint of a smile slipped across Moon's face, but the Ute saw nothing funny in this white man's illusion. "You sure you saw somebody up there . . . ?"

"Cross my heart and hope to . . ." Parris left the childish oath hanging in mid-air. Here in *Cañon del Espiritu*, yards from a horribly mutilated body, it seemed unwise to tempt the Principalities and Powers with casual promises.

Two hours later, a gray Jeep Wagoneer with U.S. government plates roared up the muddy canyon road. Special Agent James E. Hoover dismounted. He was outfitted in a camouflage jump suit, freshly polished combat boots, a blue cotton jacket, and a matching blue baseball cap. Both jacket and cap had large white letters that spelled FBI. He marched up to Parris, who was leaning on the Blazer. "Give me the short version."

Parris's feet were cold, his head was aching, and a troublesome wisdom tooth was beginning to throb. And now, here was this obnoxious little twit, demanding a report. Mentally, he shrugged away his pain and annoyance. He would treat the special agent with the respect his position deserved. "I was with Charlie, we were looking for this missing person. Arlo Nightbird. Last report we had, he'd been on a routine errand to see Mrs. Perika, who lives at the mouth of the canyon. Anyway, we found his Mercedes on the gravel road. . . ."

"I passed it on the way in," Hoover snapped.

A sharp pain shot through the roots of the cracked wisdom tooth; Parris rubbed his jaw tenderly. "Charlie . . . he thought we should check out the canyon. Then we found this body. . . ."

"I hope," Hoover glanced at Moon, "something's left for the Bureau team to examine." He turned his face away and muttered just loud enough to be heard. "Unless this pair of Keystone Kops already screwed up the crime scene."

Parris's head was now throbbing with every beat of the pump in his chest. "Now just a damn minute . . . !" He took a quick step toward Hoover, who held his ground. Neither man blinked.

Hoover jutted his chin out defiantly. "You shopping around for trouble, I can provide you with a wide variety." If the big cop swung at him first, in front of witnesses, he would break both the yokel's arms. It would be self-defense, clear and simple; the Bureau wouldn't discipline him for defending himself.

Moon's face was dead pan; he watched thoughtfully, wondering whether Parris would flatten the special agent. Now that would be some story to tell.

A state trooper leaned to one side and whispered to Sally Rainwater: "Twenty bucks on the little guy in the jump suit." This tough little G-man clearly wasn't afraid of hell or high water. And he was at least ten years younger than the cop from Granite Creek.

Sally assented with a slight nod. The acting chief had shoulders like a buffalo; he would break this little snot in half!

Daniel Bignight bought ten dollars of the action because he felt an obligation to show solidarity with his fellow Native American officers. The boss was tough enough, but he was slow. The fed would chop him up.

Parris nodded toward a deer path that meandered off into the pines. "Mr. Hoover, I suggest we discuss our differences in private. Let's you and me take a little walk." Because he did not know what else to do, the special agent followed Parris, who stopped when they were barely out of sight and removed his jacket. He dropped his shoulder holster onto the jacket, and turned to face Hoover. "It's high time we got this sorted out."

"I'd like nothing better," Hoover said evenly, "soon as I'm off duty." There were now no witnesses to testify that the cop had started a fight. This was not good.

"We are," Parris said evenly, "going to settle this now."

Hoover's face was like flint. "I taught hand-to-hand combat at Quantico."

"Thanks for the warning." It *was* a useful piece of information.

There was no delaying the inevitable. Hoover sighed and shook his head; he had no choice but to teach this thick-headed cop a hard lesson. The special agent unbuttoned his jacket; his arms were still entangled in the sleeves when he saw Parris launch a right hook. He tried to duck. Too late. The heavy blow landed on his jaw, the sunlight went out, and the cold ground slapped him hard on the back. The special agent drifted helplessly, somewhere in that dim world just this side of utter nothingness.

Parris leaned against a piñon, and waited. He rubbed his sore knuckles. They ached terribly. They felt good. He felt better.

Hoover's leg twitched; he grunted. He sat up, gingerly rubbing his jaw, then struggled to get to his feet. "This isn't over."

Parris gripped Hoover's arm to steady him. "Yeah," he said gently, "I know." He followed the groggy man back to the throng of expectant policemen.

When the state trooper saw the lumpy bruise on Hoover's jaw and his staggering gait, he glumly passed a crisp twenty dollar bill to Sally Rainwater, who wasn't surprised. Daniel Bignight was greatly relieved; he gloated openly as he pocketed a pair of fives.

Parris's head had stopped throbbing, the dull pain in the wisdom tooth was barely noticeable. He interrupted the embarrassed silence as if nothing unusual had happened. "What we have here, Mr. Hoover, is the body of Mr. Arlo Nightbird. He's been struck on the head." On the forehead, to be exact. The mark of Cain?

"Anything else?" Hoover unconsciously pushed his tongue against a loose molar.

Moon smiled merrily at the special agent. "You remember Big Ouray?"

Hoover's eyes widened with suspicion. "If this is another snipe-hunt, I'll—"

"The body," Parris interrupted, "has been mutilated. Exactly like the Hereford bull!"

Hoover was open-mouthed, momentarily forgetting the throbbing jaw. "You mean somebody sliced off his ears and his . . . his gonads?"

"That," Parris said sadly, "is about the size of it." His feet were still cold and he desired nothing more than a long sleep. Sleep without dreams.

The special agent frowned, deep in thought. "Was he married?"

"He was," Parris said. Hoover certainly had a single-track mind.

"Did the victim . . . fool around?"

Moon sighed. "Only when he was awake."

"It'll be his wife," Hoover said. "Statistics show, sixty-one percent of the time in cases where philandering husbands are offed, it's the old lady that did it."

"I've met her," Parris said with open sarcasm, "she's a born killer."

Hoover eyed these thorns in his side with undisguised hatred. "You two must be all worn out. Maybe you'd like to go home and get some rest."

"Thanks," Moon said cheerfully, "we've sure appreciated spending this quality time with you."

Charlie Moon held the speedometer at sixty; he glanced sideways at his friend. "You okay?"

"Why shouldn't I be?"

Moon's tone was gentle, understanding. "Guess you don't want to talk about it."

"About what?" Parris snapped.

"Pickin' a fight with a guy half your size." He chuckled. "Guess I'd be embarrassed too."

Parris glared at the Ute. "Nobody likes a smart-ass, Charlie." He rolled the Blazer window down. The sky over the reservation was an infinite vault of perfect blackness, sprayed by a random array of blinking diamonds. The moon was still an hour below the horizon, but a coyote, eager for the appearance of the silver orb, yipped hopefully from the crest of a low ridge.

The Ute smiled at his reflection in the windshield. This *matukach* hard case had a fair dose of grit. Moon lifted his foot off the accelerator when he saw the large brick house on a knoll well off the highway. "Nightbird place is up there on the right. You think we should stop and tell Emily, or wait until the Bureau checks his fingerprints?"

Parris considered the house with a mixture of sadness and apprehension. The porch lights were on; the faithful wife was waiting for her husband's return. Not realizing that she was no longer a wife, but a widow. "You have any doubt the corpse is Mr. Nightbird?"

Moon tried to blot out the picture in his mind. "It's him." What was left of him.

"It's your territory, so it's your call, but I'd let her know right away."

"Suits me, pardner. You want to come in?" Emily had taken a shine to this *matukach*; it might make the job easier.

"Sure," Parris said. No cop wanted to break the grim news to a brand new widow without backup.

Moon tapped his knuckles gently on the door, then stepped backward as if to distance himself from the despair to come.

Parris shivered and jammed his hands deeper into his coat pockets. "Don't think she heard you."

Moon tapped again, even more lightly.

There was a muffled sound of footsteps. Emily cracked the door and looked up at Charlie Moon; his form towered above her. She pulled the lace collar of her pink satin nightgown close to her throat and glanced at Scott Parris, who removed his hat. Neither man spoke; neither would meet her direct gaze. She knew.

Emily's hand trembled as she unhooked the brass security chain and swung the door wide. The woman started to speak, then covered her mouth with a jerky motion of her delicate fingers. She disappeared down a dark hall, her steps quick and decisive. Moon wiped his boots on the fiber mat, then followed the woman into her kitchen. Parris trailed behind, wishing he was far away. With Anne. What was Anne doing now?

Emily waved her hand nervously at the cushioned Early American chairs under her dining table. The policemen ignored the invitation; they stood awkwardly, trying to decide what to say. How to say it. Emily wheeled on them, frustrated to the edge of fury. "Sit!" she barked, "sit down, both of you."

Obediently, they sat.

She filled an enameled kettle with water and slammed it onto a burner. "It's about Arlo?" It was more a statement than a question.

Moon cleared his throat. "Yes, ma'am. . . ."

"Don't 'ma'am' me, Charlie Moon. Makes me feel like an old

woman. Is Arlo . . . is he . . ." She paused and put her hand over her mouth.

"Arlo's dead," Moon said flatly, "I'm sorry."

She was silent for some moments, then began to scurry around the kitchen. "I was about to have some tea. I'll make some for you fellows," she said. "Did he have an accident in his fancy car?"

"No," Moon said.

Emily placed three china cups on the ecru linen tablecloth and poured boiling water into the cup by Moon's clenched fist. "Well," she said as if they were exchanging ordinary gossip, "are you going to tell me?"

Parris watched Emily drop a tea bag into his cup. He was surprised to hear himself answering her question. "It was . . . homicide." Homicide. A fine word. It sounded much less brutal than "murder."

Emily finished her task, then sat down across the table from the policemen. Parris thought the tiny woman looked smaller than ever, as if she was in the process of shrinking. Ninety pounds, eighty pounds . . . soon there would be nothing but a sigh in the pink satin nightgown. She blinked at Parris. "You were there . . . you have seen . . . Arlo?"

He ducked his head, afraid to meet her eyes. "Yes."

"Scott," Moon said gently, "found the body."

She ignored Charlie Moon. "How was my husband killed?"

Parris put his hand over hers. "I'm sorry. I can't say anything about it."

Her eyes widened, her olive skin stretched tight over her skull. "But I'm his wife. . . ." She gripped Parris's hand.

"Emily," Moon said softly, "it's standard procedure in a homicide. We can't reveal anything about how the victim was killed. It could complicate the investigation."

"Do you have anyone to stay with you?" Parris asked gently. Her hand felt cool on his . . . it was a comfort to him.

"If you need some company," Moon added, "I could ask Nancy Beyal to come over. . . ."

"No. I'll be all right." She put a trembling hand to her throat. "I'll call Daddy . . . he'll be here in twenty minutes."

12

The morning sky over the San Juans was a wild spray of pale pink, the anemic tint of almost ripe watermelon, but the policemen were unaware of this stunning sunrise. Parris braced himself against the dashboard as Moon bounced the squad car over the rutted gravel road. The Ute hadn't spoken since he picked Parris up at the Sky Ute Lodge; the *matukach* policeman tried to gulp a swallow of black coffee from a Styrofoam cup, but spilled it on his boots when Moon hit a deep pothole dead-center.

"Better stop and back up so you can try again," Parris said cheerfully. "You missed a bigger hole on the left side of the road. On a scale of ten, would have been worth . . . maybe eight points."

Moon muttered something that was unintelligible under the roar of the V-8 engine. He jammed his foot on the brake pedal and careened into the dirt lane that led past Daisy Perika's trailer into the mouth of *Cañon del Espíritu.* "I'll feel better when the sun gets high over the mountain," Moon said with a scowl. "Didn't sleep so good last night." He saw a light in the trailer. "Looks like Aunt Daisy's back. I'm gonna have a word with her." Parris understood that he wasn't invited. Moon climbed the porch, slapped his palm on the aluminum wall. Daisy opened the door immediately and Moon disappeared inside. He sat down at the kitchen table while his aunt poured warmed-over coffee into Gorman's bunny cup. "Tell me about Arlo Nightbird."

Daisy folded her arms and spoke through thin lips. "I don't have nothing to tell you about that jackass."

Moon tipped the sugar bowl over his coffee; the crystalline stream of sweetness disappeared into the surface of the dark liquid. "Arlo is dead." He watched her eyes—Daisy showed no sign of surprise. "I already know Arlo came up here to see you. But he never came home that evening. We found his car about a half mile down the gravel road, but his body was up in Spirit Canyon." Charlie Moon was torn; the police officer had a job to do, but the Ute nephew was afraid to hear what his elderly relative might have to say. "What do you figure happened?"

"I got nothing to tell you." *Maybe later*, her eyes said. "Drink your coffee."

"If you don't want to talk to me, that's fine," Moon said slowly, "but there's an FBI man up in the canyon who'll be by here any time to see you."

"He's already come by," the old woman said.

Moon felt his stomach churn. "What'd you tell that . . . I hope you didn't—"

"I didn't say nothing." Daisy's eyes twinkled. "I opened the door, but I made like I don't understand English. He even tried a few words in Spanish, sounded like *'comprender Español?'* but I just shook my head and blinked at him. I guess he thinks I only speak Ute."

"You," said Moon proudly, "ought to be ashamed of yourself."

When Moon returned to the Blazer, Parris wanted to ask whether the shaman had said anything about Arlo Nightbird, but he didn't.

The Ute cranked the engine to life. "She's not talking," Moon said, "and there's no use pushing her."

Hoover was supervising the transfer of the body into a BIA van when Moon pulled off the dirt lane. The bruise on the special agent's jaw was now a dirty mixture of yellow and purple. Hoover pointedly ignored the presence of the policemen until they were within spitting distance. "So," he muttered to himself, "Tom and Huckleberry have returned." He raised his voice so they could hear. "You two might as well make yourselves useful." He squinted up at Moon, who stood with his back to the sun. "I expect you could tell me something about who Arlo Nightbird was—what he did."

Moon rocked back and forth, his arms folded. He was certain that Hoover had already picked the brains of the Ute cops who stood by watching, but it would be necessary to go through the motions. "Arlo was the richest man on the Rez. Ran an insurance agency, big mover and shaker on the Economic Development Board. Was working with the Feds to turn this nice place," Moon swept his hand to indicate the canyon, "into some kind of nuclear waste dump. Meant big money for the Tribe."

Hoover turned his back on Moon. "What about his wife?"

"Emily," Moon said. "Well educated—couple of degrees from the university up in Boulder. Her Dad is Fidel Sombra; he runs a little farm north of Ignacio."

"The victim have any children?"

"No children." At least not by his wife.

"Enemies?"

"Well," Moon said slowly, "when they have his funeral, there'll be no trouble finding a place to park."

"Let's narrow it down a bit," Hoover said. "Was there anyone who'd kill him?"

Moon glanced wryly toward the plastic body bag in the BIA van. "Evidently."

The special agent glowered at the Ute policeman. "We haven't found his trousers, but we found his belt. There was a sheath for a knife. Must have had a five and a half or six-inch blade. We didn't find the knife."

"Maybe," Parris offered, "the guy who did him in took it with him."

"That would make the killer pretty stupid," Hoover said hopefully.

"Could be," Moon said thoughtfully. "Or maybe this one isn't much worried about getting caught." Maybe he should tell Hoover about Oswald Oakes's theory about Cain. Oswald would love to have a visit from the FBI, and an opportunity to demonstrate his knowledge about animal mutilations. But that could wait.

Hoover flipped the pages of his notebook. "I understand that one Mr. Gorman Sweetwater recently had a heated dispute with the victim." The special agent had made the comment casually. Too casually. Somebody was doing a lot of talking to this fed. Moon glanced at Sally Rainwater, who was leaning against the side of the BIA van, then at Daniel Bignight. "Local gossip, that's all." Moon said.

"From what I hear, this Sweetwater guy was all pissed off about an insurance scam that Nightbird wouldn't buy. Sweetwater reported that an insured bull had died of natural causes, wanted a quick insurance settlement." A cold smile twisted Hoover's mouth. "You remember the bull? Name was Big Ouray."

Moon's fingers were toying with the .357 magnum cartridges on his belt.

"Problem is," Hoover was getting up to speed, "the bull had been mutilated by unnatural means, so a natural death wasn't a legitimate claim. There were also some technicalities about how the insured animals were identified; the policy may not have covered the bull in question. When Mr. Nightbird refused to recommend payment on the bogus claim, this Sweetwater fellow, who probably killed his own bull to collect the insurance, threatens to castrate him! Now, Mr. Nightbird turns up extremely deceased in the same canyon where the bull was found, and Mr. Nightbird is also minus his family jewels and his ears, precisely like Sweetwater's bull. Ear for an ear, ball for a ball." Hoover paused to gloat. "Now, Officer Moon, would you say that Gorman Sweetwater was a prime suspect?"

Moon stared down at Hoover. He stared until Hoover blinked. "Well," the Ute policeman replied thoughtfully, "since you put it like that—no. Even if Gorman killed his bull for the insurance, it doesn't make any sense for him to mutilate the animal—that would only queer his insurance claim. Not only that, half the people in Ignacio hated Arlo more than Gorman did. And the whole town knew about that castration threat Gorman made against Arlo."

Hoover turned away and dismissed Moon with a wave. "Never mind. I shouldn't expect you to see what is so damned obvious. But"—looking doubtfully over his shoulder—"maybe you'll still be of some use. There's a weird old broad who lives near the canyon entrance. . . ."

"That weird old *lady*," Moon said softly, "is my aunt Daisy."

"Figures," Hoover said, "I guess everyone around here is related to everyone else, like in the Ozarks." Hoover wanted to say that this could explain a lot, but his throbbing jaw was a painful reminder that a man must measure his words. "Since she doesn't speak English, I'll need a translator." He looked innocently at Moon. "I assume you speak a word or two of Ute."

"Sure as you're a *waa-pi*, G-man," an unseen Ute policeman muttered. Moon gave no sign that he had heard this insult. Daniel Bignight, who had picked up a few Ute words, turned his back. His frame shook with suppressed laughter.

Hoover flushed; he opened his mouth, then snapped it shut. He had barely heard the remark and didn't dare ask for an explanation. He was certain that someone would provide one. He retreated toward the van and instructed the BIA driver to take the body away.

Parris was watching Hoover when he spoke softly to Moon. "What's this nonsense about your aunt only speaking Ute? She speaks better English than half of my relatives."

Charlie Moon grinned, but didn't reply.

"I'm beginning to wonder," Parris said, "whether this job's worth the pay."

Moon thought carefully about this. "The benefits," he observed thoughtfully, "are mostly spiritual."

Daisy opened the door while Hoover was knocking. She smiled and gestured that he should enter. He was followed by Moon and then by Parris, who nodded politely. The old woman was silent as she poured three cups of strong coffee and ladled out steaming posole into plastic bowls. She gestured again to indicate that the lawmen should sit at her kitchen table, then placed the coffee and posole in front of them. She muttered something in the Ute dialect to Charlie Moon, then sat down and folded her arms in Buddha-like serenity.

Hoover tasted his coffee, grimaced at the brackish flavor, then leaned forward and smiled at Daisy. He spoke loudly, as if volume would help the communication. "I," he pointed at his chest, "represent the government in Washington. I am here to help the Ute."

Parris turned his head and coughed to stifle a snicker.

Charlie Moon spoke in Ute to his aunt: *"This guy is manure in your path, so don't step on him."*

Daisy nodded placidly, but didn't reply.

Hoover clasped his hands prayerfully. "When Mr. Nightbird came to the canyon—can you tell us anything about what happened?"

Moon began his translation, which was another pointed warning to his aunt.

Daisy interrupted and nodded vigorously. "Ah . . . Nightbird." She continued her comments in Ute.

Moon interpreted. "She says Arlo stopped by late in the afternoon, in his fancy car. Talked to her about the waste project for the canyon, then he left."

Hoover scowled at Moon. "That's all?"

Moon nodded. "That's all. He came, he left."

"Ask her if his car was damaged when he showed up."

Daisy listened to the query from Moon, then shook her head.

"Ask her—did she see anyone else, before or after he left?"

Moon muttered a few Ute syllables. Daisy answered; her monologue lasted almost three full minutes.

Hoover was leaning forward expectantly. "What did she say?"

"She said she don't remember too well."

"Shit, man, she gabbed that Indian pig latin for five minutes, she must have told you more than that!"

"She's kind of old and her memory's going," Moon explained apologetically. "It takes a lot of time for her to try to remember what happened on a particular day."

"Good grief," Hoover groaned, "why don't these old biddies learn to speak enough English for simple communications with the civilized world?" Unaware of the slight scowl on Daisy's face, the special agent stirred a spoonful of the posole and inspected the greasy brew with a worried expression. "This looks like hominy. I don't care much for hominy. Gives me gas. And what's this stuff floating around in this muck?" He scowled and muttered, "Hmfff. Probably dog meat."

"Dammit," Parris snapped, "watch your mouth!"

Hoover regarded Parris coldly. "What the hell for? The old woman doesn't understand English." He turned to the Ute policeman with a pained expression. "But if I've offended Officer Moon's delicate ethnic sensibilities, please accept my abject apologies." He affected a slight bow toward Moon.

The Ute policeman grinned. "Oh, no need to apologize. My aunt's getting kind of old and simple-minded." Daisy remained poker-faced. "No telling what kind of meat she put in the pot." The Ute sniffed at his bowl. "Might be *prairie* dog. No," he sniffed, then tasted a morsel, "don't think so, tastes kind of whangy, more like . . . ummm . . . porcupine." He winced as Daisy kicked his shin under the table.

Moon and Parris were finishing their posole when Hoover pointed at the door and shouted at Daisy. "Good-bye." He saluted her in military fashion. "The president in Washington thanks you!" Hoover paused by the door when he noticed a copy of the *Southern Ute Drum* on a small chest of drawers. Daisy Perika's name was on the newspaper mailing label. "What's this doing here . . . if she doesn't understand English?"

"It's the pictures," Moon said, "she likes to see pictures of her friends."

Hoover grunted; he frowned suspiciously at the silent woman before he left the trailer home.

Daisy watched Hoover hurry back to his Jeep; she punched Moon in the ribs. "Old and simple-minded, am I?"

"Sorry, Auntie. Just old, I guess."

Parris cleared his throat. "Mrs. Perika . . . I guess we'll be going. Unless there's anything you want to tell us." He was certain that this old woman knew something about Nightbird's murder. Maybe she even knew who had drawn the blade across . . . but the image was an obscenity.

The shaman's eyes went flat; the seconds ticked away while Moon waited patiently. It seemed as if Daisy might remain mute, but she turned to Scott Parris. "Most of the *matukach* think our old ways are foolishness. Some of my own people," she glanced accusingly at Charlie Moon, "say the *pitukupf* is just an old campfire story to frighten naughty children. But you"—she pointed at Parris's chest—". . . you know different."

She was, he knew, referring to his last trip to the reservation. Parris looked at the cracked linoleum on the floor and fidgeted. He had not actually *seen* the dwarf. Except in his dreams, where the *pitukupf*, who smoked a clay pipe, had the appearance of a wrinkled Irish leprechaun. Absurdity stacked upon absurdity.

"There's something you two need to know," she said. "I've seen it with my own eyes." She paused, closing her eyes to better recall the vision. "There was this big dark thing, like a black shadow. The shadow . . . it became a big bird with sharp claws, kind of like an owl." She imitated claws with her wrinkled hands, and slashed at a startled Parris, who leaned backward. "It killed somebody behind a bush. There was blood on its feet."

Parris couldn't take his eyes off her imitation claws. "Blood? On its feet?"

"Sure," she said, holding her hands forward with thin fingers curved under her palms. "On its claws. Blood, dripping off onto the moss. I think it killed one of the *Nuuci.*"

Parris felt the hint of a headache surge under his temples. "The owl killed a . . . um . . . nooch?" Maybe a *nooch* was some kind of animal.

"*Nuuci,* one of the People," Moon said. "A Ute."

Daisy nodded. "I'm sure now, it killed Arlo Nightbird. And that's not all."

"There's more?" Why were these predictions always reported *after* the event? Parris glanced at Moon, whose face did not betray his thoughts.

"Sure," the shaman said, "that big owl, it changed back into a dark mist. Like a shadow." She waited for Parris to respond, but the policeman was at a loss for words. Daisy patted Parris's arm affectionately. "You and Charlie, maybe you'll figure out what it means."

Parris nodded politely. He wasn't good at puzzles.

Moon leaned on the aluminum door frame and looked at the sliver of moon, suspended like a silver earring from the largest of the Three Sisters. The policeman part of his mind suggested that maybe this was Aunt Daisy's way of telling them what she had seen in the canyon when Arlo was murdered. The Ute part said maybe not.

13

Scott Parris sat across the table from Charlie Moon; he watched the Ute policeman fork a massive chunk of Angel's homemade banana cream pie into his mouth, then wash this down with a gulp of scalding black coffee. Moon had already consumed half a fried chicken. Parris was both fascinated and somewhat envious; half of Moon's diet would have made his trousers shrink at the belt line. The big Ute showed no sign of a bulge around the waist. Angel brought fresh coffee and grinned at Moon; the Ute with the prodigious appetite was far and away his favorite customer. "How 'bout another piece of pie, Charlie? Banana's all gone, but we got some blueberry and pecan."

"No, thanks," Moon said between swallows, "I'm not so hungry today."

Parris was trying to think of an appropriate barb when he saw a Jeep Wagoneer skid to a halt outside the plate-glass window; James Hoover swung the Jeep door open and banged Moon's tribal police Blazer. Moon didn't look up when the special agent came through the swinging doors. Hoover's pale face was flushed; the bruise on his jaw was now covered with an inexpert smear of beige makeup. He sat down and leaned his elbows on the table, unconsciously imitating the relaxed posture of Charlie Moon. "I interviewed the Nightbird widow. She wasn't a lot of help." He checked his watch. "You guys get through feeding your faces, we got some police work to do."

The Ute wiped his mouth with a paper napkin. "Can't speak for my pardner, but I love police work."

Hoover flipped through the pages of his notebook. "First, I need to interview Mr. Herbert Ecker. Arlo Nightbird's employee." He put the notebook into his pocket and drummed his fingers on the table while the men finished their meals with what seemed to be deliberate slowness. He checked the face of his wristwatch a dozen times, cleared his throat a half dozen. Finally, it was too much. He sprang to his feet. "You can catch up with me at the Nightbird Insurance Agency." Then he was gone.

Moon waved at Angel. "Put mine on my tab." He nodded toward Parris. "Charge my pardner's to the station tab."

Angel's jaw dropped. "But Charlie . . . the station don't have no tab!"

"Then open one," Moon said thoughtfully, "maybe I'll use it too." Parris gave Angel a handful of dollar bills.

Moon hummed an obscure tune as they followed Hoover to the Nightbird Insurance Agency. As they arrived, Herb Ecker, with a paperback book under his arm, was mounting an aged black Harley-Davidson. Hoover was already flashing his credentials; Ecker paled at the knowledge that the FBI wanted to talk to him, but he seemed happy to see Charlie Moon's cheerful face. The Ute policeman nodded toward Hoover. "Herb, this fellow is Mr. J. E. Hoover, special agent from the FBI office in Durango. He's investigating Arlo's death. You help him any way you can, I'd appreciate it."

Herb swallowed hard; his Adam's apple bounced. "Yes, sir, I always cooperate with the authorities."

Hoover glanced at Moon with just a hint of appreciation, then turned his attention back to Ecker. "When was the last time you saw Mr. Nightbird?"

Ecker hung his head and mumbled his answer. "Wednesday, sir. About half past two. He was on his way up to that place the Utes call Spirit Canyon."

"For what purpose?"

"I think . . . to visit Mrs. Perika."

Hoover scribbled in his notebook. "Uh-huh. And what was his business with Mrs. Perika?"

Herb saw Moon's expression harden; he hesitated before he answered. "Something about the use of the canyon for storing nuclear wastes, I believe. He wanted to help arrange for Mrs. Perika to . . . to move to Ignacio."

"So," Hoover pressed, "she was moving out?"

"Yes . . . I would assume so. To a much nicer house."

A brief grin flashed over Moon's face; Herb relaxed.

"Now," Hoover said gently, "tell me about the interaction between Mr. Gorman Sweetwater and your employer."

Herb raised his eyebrows. "Sir?"

"The insurance scam—about the bull!"

"Oh, that. Yes, Mr. Sweetwater filed a claim on his bull, Big Ouray. I—we had written a policy on the Herefords he keeps up in Spirit Canyon."

"There was, I understand," Hoover asked with overdone casualness, "a heated exchange between Mr. Nightbird and Mr. Sweetwater?" Hoover glanced sideways at Moon and was disappointed at his inability to read the Ute's face.

Herb looked imploringly at Moon, who nodded almost imperceptibly. "Yes, they spoke . . . loudly."

"Mr. Sweetwater made threats?"

"Well . . . perhaps. In a way."

"Mr. Ecker," Hoover asked softly, "are you going to tell me precisely what these threats were, or do I get three guesses?"

"I don't remember exactly." Ecker reddened under Hoover's stare; a muscle in his neck twitched spasmodically. "I think Mr. Sweetwater became angry when Mr. Nightbird said something about his daughter."

"Daughter?"

"Benita. She was here when it happened."

"When what happened?"

"When Mr. Sweetwater threatened to . . ."—Herb blushed and averted his gaze to the blacktop under his feet—"to castrate Mr. Nightbird. I do not think he actually meant—"

"That's all, Ecker, at least for now." Hoover closed his notebook and turned to look blankly at Moon and Parris. "The exercise in interrogation is complete, your subsequent education begins henceforth. I'll have a warrant to search the Sweetwater ranch tomorrow morning. I want both of you with me—maybe you'll learn how a murder investigation is conducted on a real police force." Hoover turned on his heel and headed for his Jeep.

Moon leaned sideways toward Scott Parris and muttered: "Well, pardner, you ready to learn about the Dark Side of the Force?"

Parris closed his eyes and groaned.

Ecker, now at ease, smiled at Parris. "Have you made any progress in your memorization task?"

Parris scowled in pretended annoyance. "You don't think I'd welsh on a bet?"

"I suppose not," Ecker replied. "After all, 'a promise made is a debt unpaid.'"

Parris groaned. "Don't rub it in, kid." The policeman had recorded "The Shooting of Dan McGrew" on a microcassette tape; he listened to it late every evening but had memorized less than a dozen lines, and these imperfectly.

The memorial service was in a crumbling brick structure that served as a funeral home. There were three halls for services. Emily Nightbird had rented the largest of these, and it was an error in planning. There were barely a dozen mourners, and they were not mourning. Taxi, wrapped in his tattered trench coat, sat alone in the back row. He was muttering incoherently and scribbling notes for an imaginary article. The other mourners sat stiffly, waiting for a few words from the tribal chairman who was eager to get away after putting in a perfunctory appearance. Arlo was not a man with friends, but he was one of the People.

Charlie Moon and Scott Parris took a seat in the second row, behind the widow who sat alone. An elderly man with a grizzled beard appeared with a cup of steaming tea, which he gave to Emily Nightbird. The unkempt man shook hands with Moon, who muttered under his breath to Scott Parris: "This is Emily's father, Fidel Sombra."

Fidel pumped Parris's hand; his grip demonstrated that the wrinkled old man was not as frail as he appeared. "You that lawman from Granite Creek?"

"That's me," Parris said amiably. No one was a stranger in Ignacio for more than a couple of days.

Fidel sat down by his daughter, then turned to continue the conversation with Scott Parris. "I run a first-class swine operation up by Oxford," he said with a breath that smelled of Irish whiskey. "You in the market for any sugar-cured hams or pork sausage, I'm your man." Emily elbowed her father in a vain attempt to restore some dignity to the occasion. "I got some fine bacon," he continued, "and lard by the bucketful."

Parris grinned at the leathery faced man. "I'll keep it in mind."

Fidel put his arm around Emily's shoulders. "That tea hot enough, honeysuckle? I put in two sugar cubes, just the way you like." She nodded the pert little black hat that was fastened onto her hair with a pearl-tipped stick pin. Scott Parris felt a foolish urge to see behind the black veil that covered her face.

The next few minutes were swallowed up by a solemn monologue from the tribal chairman. Parris only heard snatches. Nightbird, according to the chairman, was a "gifted man who cared about his community," a "Ute who had learned how to operate in the white man's world," who had "brought good jobs to Ignacio," and so on.

Fidel Sombra turned to grin at Parris. "That's pure bull shit," he said, "Arlo Nightbird was a good-for-nothing son-of-a-bitch and my dotter is a helluva lot better off with him dead!"

Emily turned to smile weakly. "You'll have to excuse my father," she said with the weary patience of one who has given up her attempts to reform a hopeless case. "Father forgets that I've just lost a husband. And he's had a bit to drink." Her voice carried across the room.

Fidel raised an imaginary glass and cackled loudly. "I'm drunk and Arlo's dead, what more could I ask for!"

The tribal chairman, his dignity offended by this rude interruption, paused to glare at the old man. "Mr. Sombra, is there something you would like to say?"

The mild sarcasm was lost on Fidel Sombra, who got to his feet and surveyed the small group. "Damn right, I have. May Arlo Nightbird's filthy soul rot in—"

"Father," Emily said as her fingernails bit into his arm, "sit down and *shut your mouth.*"

Fidel recognized the menace in her voice and sat down meekly. Moreover, he shut his mouth.

Scott Parris detected an odd smell, much like the formaldehyde in Doc Simpson's laboratory. Taxi had sat down next to him. It would be best to ignore him. The gaunt man scooted closer and barely nudged the lawman with his elbow. Parris turned to see what this strange fellow wanted; mad lights danced like blue fireflies in the man's pale eyes.

He whispered hoarsely in Parris's ear. "Old Nick is back."

Parris raised an eyebrow. "Beg your pardon?"

Taxi drew his finger across his throat. "Aye. Old Nick has come to town and he's in a terrible bad mood."

"Why is Nick in a bad mood?" Parris asked wearily.

"Because to all these people"—Taxi waved his hand to indicate the small congregation of mourners—"Old Nick is invisible." He smiled with a serene assurance that only madmen can know, and retreated to his spot on the rear bench.

Moon leaned over to whisper in Parris's ear. "Now tell me the truth, pardner—aren't you glad you came?"

Parris held on with white knuckles while Moon jammed the accelerator pedal to the floorboard. They roared south on Route 172 toward Rattlesnake Hill, then took a right on 318 toward Bondad. Hoover barely managed to stay within sight of the mud-splattered tribal police car. Just before the rolling grassland melded into the beginning of the canyon country, they turned north into the gravel lane leading to Sweetwater's home. Hoover followed them up the lane through a pasture of gamma grass to a prefabricated aluminum-siding house. The dwelling was nestled in a grove of Russian Olive punctuated with a half-dozen stunted ponderosa pine. The house was flanked on the right with a log-and-slab garage; a rusty blue GMC pickup was parked inside.

Hoover was setting his emergency brake when the Ute policeman banged on the front door. "Gorman! You in there? It's Charlie Moon."

Hoover brushed past Parris, his face flushed pink with excitement. "Knock one more time; tell him we've got a search warrant. He doesn't open up, we kick the door down!"

Moon raised his fist to knock again when Parris interrupted. "Looks like we have some company." They turned to see a red Pontiac station wagon trailing a cloud of white dust on the gravel lane.

"That's Gorman," the Ute said.

"I'll handle this," Hoover snapped.

Moon folded his arms across his chest. "It's your show."

Gorman Sweetwater swerved sideways to a stop behind the Jeep and stumbled out of the car like a man who had hoisted a few too many. Hoover strode briskly to meet the rancher, flashing his credentials. "James Hoover, Special Agent, Federal Bureau of Investigation. I need to have a word with you."

Gorman paused briefly and glanced at the I.D., then at Hoover. "I'm bone-tired, I got no time for this bull shit!" He brushed past the special agent, who turned to follow him, shouting that he had a search warrant. Gorman stopped in front of Moon, who was blocking his way. "Charlie, what in hell is going on here?"

Moon nodded toward Hoover. "Calm down, Gorman. This FBI man wants to talk to you about Arlo Nightbird. You don't have to answer any of his questions, but he does have a search warrant."

The old man turned and glowered at Hoover, who stopped in his tracks. "Arlo Nightbird? I don't have nothin' to say about that little son-of-a-bitch!"

Moon stepped forward and raised both hands in a peaceful gesture. "Arlo's been killed; all Mr. Hoover wants to do is ask you a few questions, have a look around. Then, we'll be out of here."

"I'm damned glad the little bastard's dead," Gorman said, "but I got nothin' to say."

Hoover, determined to regain control of the situation, presented a stapled sheaf of papers. "Mr. Sweetwater, this is our search warrant. Now I suggest that—"

Gorman grabbed the papers, crumpled them in his big hands, and threw them at Hoover's feet. "There's your damned search warrant, now haul your ass off my land."

Hoover stared at the crumpled papers in disbelief. His voice was shrill: "You . . . you can't do that!"

Gorman's jaw was set, his hands clenched into fists. "Lissen close now, cop. You get off my land or I'll kick your ass off. . . ."

"Don't threaten me, you dried up old blanket-ass." Hoover had no respect for the tired old man; that was his first mistake. Furthermore, he wasn't looking when it happened. The special agent was fumbling in his coat pocket for a pair of handcuffs when Gorman's left hook flashed out of nowhere and slammed against his jaw like a sledge-hammer. Hoover fell in a heap, as if his battery had been disconnected. Moon and Parris leaped forward simultaneously; Gorman yelled and swung his right, connecting with Parris's shoulder. Moon grabbed the rancher by the neck and smashed him against the ground. Before Gorman could regain his breath, Parris had snapped cuffs on the old man's wrists. The Ute policeman, resting on one knee, had his hand on Gorman's back. "Now, you old buzz-saw, you let me know when you've had time to cool off, and maybe I'll let you up."

The rancher gasped, then muttered something unintelligible, which Moon accepted as a surrender. He grabbed the old man under one armpit and by the belt, and pulled him to his feet. "You shouldn't have hit that federal man, Gorman. He's got his work to do, just like you and me. Now, he'll be real upset."

Hoover was up on one knee, one hand on his forehead, trying hard to remember where he was.

Gorman drew a deep breath. "I'm sorry." Tears appeared in his eyes and rolled down his wrinkled cheeks. "I've had a bad time, Charlie. Just got back from that hospital up in Durango, ain't slept for two days. Got these pains in my chest."

Moon brushed the dust off his captive. "Sorry to hear it, Gorman. You been sick?"

"It's Benita," Gorman said meekly, "my little girl."

Moon felt a coldness surge in his gut. "What's wrong with Benita?"

"She's got an infection. Doctor says it's bad." Gorman shook his head in disbelief that such evil would visit one so innocent. "I just came home to get some of her things. She asked for her Bible and some night-clothes." He strained at the cuffs on his wrists. "I got to get back to the hospital."

"I'm sorry," Moon said gently. "Hadn't heard about Benita bein' sick. We've been so busy with Arlo's murder, I just haven't had time. . . ."

Hoover was now on his feet, weaving unsteadily. He spat out a bloody bicuspid. "You crazy old son-of-a-bitch," he said in a flat, ominous tone, "you've just made a serious mistake."

"He didn't mean anything by it," Moon said. "His daughter's hospitalized and he hasn't had any sleep."

"I'm sick and tired of this crap," Hoover glanced meaningfully at Parris, "people hitting me in the face like I was some kinda damn punching bag. I want him hauled in and charged with assault on a federal officer!"

"You don't have to arrest him right now," Moon pleaded. "He needs to get back to the hospital and be with his daughter. . . ."

Hoover's eyes were wild with fury. "Save it," he snapped. "Nobody takes a cheap shot at me and just walks away. But first, we'll turn this whole damn place upside down."

Moon looked glum. "Sorry, Gorman, but you've stepped in it. Give me your keys so we don't have to break your door." The rancher, who seemed stunned, stuck his hand into his pocket and produced a ring of keys that were snatched by Hoover, who disappeared into the house. The Ute turned to Parris. "I'll stash Gorman in the car."

Parris nodded. "I'll start on the garage."

"Charlie," Gorman said, "will you get somebody to go see Benita . . . tell her I . . . I'll get there as soon as I can?"

"Don't worry. I'll take care of it personally." Moon was helping Gorman into the rear seat of the squad car when Parris called from the garage. "That Nightbird fellow—any of his clothing ever turn up in the canyon?"

"Not much," Moon said, "you find something?"

Parris was leaning with his elbows on the tailgate of the GMC pickup. "You know what kind of boots Nightbird wore?"

"Sure," Moon said, "expensive ones. Must have had a dozen pairs. But his favorites were custom-made ostrich skin. Bought 'em in Tulsa, claimed they cost over a thousand bucks."

"I think you'd best have a look at this."

Moon leaned over the tailgate. There were four large blocks of salt. But among the tufts of straw and mud was a scattered assortment of clothing: rumpled jockey shorts and expensive gabardine trousers. There was also a pair of ostrich-skin cowboy boots.

Moon whistled. "Looks like Arlo's duds all right." The Ute shook his head in wonderment. "Gorman should have dumped that stuff by now. Old man must have scrambled eggs for brains."

"People who get hot enough to murder other people," Parris said, "sometimes aren't thinking too clearly. They're the ones we catch."

Moon turned to stare at Gorman, who was sitting with head bowed in the rear of the squad car. "I hate to admit it," the Ute said, "but it looks like J. E. Hoover was dead right on this one. Maybe," he said ruefully, "I'll learn something from the little banty rooster after all."

"I guess you'll want to break the news to the special agent," Parris said with a sly grin. "He'll be real pleased."

"I'm gonna go read Gorman his rights," Moon said. "You can tell Hoover what you found."

14

Moon turned right off of Main onto Park Avenue; he lifted his foot and allowed the Blazer to slow to the speed limit.

Parris glanced at his friend; the Ute had not spoken a word since they left Ignacio. "Something wrong, Charlie?"

Moon shifted his weight in the seat and found a more comfortable position. He watched a gigantic bank of heavy cumulus clouds roll eastward from Hesperus. "Don't much like hospitals." The Ute turned into the hospital parking lot.

"Know how you feel," Parris said. "I don't much like anything to do with sickness. One sight of a nurse with a big hypodermic and my belly button sucks in. This young lady," he asked, "she somebody special?"

Moon slammed the Blazer door. "Yeah." He stopped to look over the narrow-gauge railway at the churning waters of the Animas. A pair of buzzards circled lazily above a small island in the river.

A harried nurse with iron-gray hair and sore feet interrupted her work long enough to direct them to Benita's room in the 2E wing. Moon paused outside the door as a candy striper departed with a lunch tray that appeared to be untouched. He looked into the room and saw a small, thin man in a black suit holding Benita's hand as they prayed together. The policemen backed away until the pleas to God were complete. The priest eventually became aware of the policemen waiting in the hall. He left the sick room and shook the Ute's hand. "Charlie," he whispered, "Benita will be so pleased to see you!"

"Well," Moon said carefully, "I hope so." He nodded toward a brown paper parcel under his arm. "Gorman asked me to bring some of her stuff over."

The priest saw something on Moon's face he couldn't quite identify; he had never been able to get close to this big Ute. He held his hand out to Parris. "Who is your friend?"

"Meet my pardner, Scott Parris. He's top cop up at Granite Creek," Moon said, grinning. "But he's agreed to serve as my deputy for a few weeks." The acting chief of police grimaced; this was pretty close to the truth. They shook hands. "Father Raes," Moon added, "is the priest at the Catholic church in Ignacio."

"I've seen it. Nice looking church," Parris said lamely. "I'm not actually a Catholic, but . . ." His words, without support of thoughts, dropped off into oblivion.

"I could tell immediately," Raes said with a straight face. "We Catholics have a secret handshake, you see." The priest turned to Moon. "She's very ill . . . did Gorman tell you?"

"Said she had some kind of infection. But they have all kinds of wonder drugs for that, don't they?"

Raes looked toward the bed. "I understand the bugs are evolving faster than the antibiotics." He cocked his head to one side and considered Moon curiously. "I have more sick folk to see. Why don't you visit with Benita for a few minutes. I'll stop by later." It was the priest's way of respecting what smelled like police business.

Moon touched the brim of his hat in a sign of respect. "Thanks, Father. I'll only be a few minutes. My friend here," he nodded toward Parris, "likes hospitals, but they give me the spooks."

"May God bless and protect both of you." Raes patted Moon's arm and chuckled before he marched off down the hall to bring a touch of grace to another soul.

Parris followed Moon into Benita's room; the Ute pulled a light blue curtain that hid her from curious onlookers who passed in the hall. Except for shallow breaths, the girl was motionless. Like a doll decorating a bed. Her head was resting in a small depression in the center of the pillow. Of her delicate features, it was as if only her large brown eyes were alive. Her eyes smiled when she saw the big Ute. "Charlie . . . ," she whispered dreamily, "Charlie Moon."

Moon knelt by the bed; Parris withdrew to a corner and tried, without success, to appear inconspicuous. Benita looked curiously at the stranger while Moon explained once more who his pardner was.

The Ute's presence gradually infused a little strength into Benita's body. She tried, without success, to raise herself with an elbow. Moon pressed the buttons on the bed until she was elevated halfway to a sitting position. She put her hand on Moon's; Parris was certain that he saw the Ute tremble.

"I'm so weak," she said.

"Your daddy asked me to bring you some things." Moon placed the parcel on the bed. "It's your Bible and some . . . some stuff to wear."

Benita smiled at his reticence to mention her night clothes. "I hope Daddy is getting some sleep. . . . He's been sitting up with me all day and night. He's so tired." A single tear made a wet trace down her cheek.

If he didn't tell her, someone else would. And the trouble her father was in would be greatly exaggerated by Ignacio gossip. If that was possible. Moon looked at the lamp above her head. "I got something to tell you . . . Benita." He wanted to say *sweetheart*, but the word hung in his throat. "Something about Gorman."

Benita's lustrous eyes widened in alarm. "Daddy . . . is he all right? Did he have an accident?"

Moon took both her hands in his and smiled weakly at her pretty face. "Oh, he's healthy enough. It's just that he's . . . uh . . ." Moon looked at the wall behind the bed. "What it is," he sighed, "Gorman's in jail."

Benita made no sound when her lips formed the words: "Oh my God!" She found her voice. "Surely he didn't go back to . . ." Benita bit her lip.

"Now don't you worry. Didn't want to tell you, but you'd have found out anyway when he didn't show up."

Benita licked her dry lips. "Why . . . what did he do?"

"Well, it's up to a jury to decide whether he did anything."

"Charlie," she said with all the firmness she could muster, "what is Daddy charged with?"

"It looks like . . . they think . . . ," Moon struggled to get the words out, "he might have killed Arlo Nightbird."

She gasped and covered her mouth with her hand; Benita's frail body shook with sobs.

Moon turned to look imploringly at Scott Parris. "I've got to go outside . . . get a drink of water." The Ute hurried away. Parris pulled a chair up by the bedside. "We're really sorry to break this news about your father's troubles, Miss Sweetwater. I'm sure Charlie would have rather cut off his right arm than . . ."

Benita was dabbing at her eyes with a tissue. "I know. Tell me . . . why did they arrest my father? Why do they think *he* killed . . . Mr. Nightbird?"

"I really don't think this is the time to talk about that. . . . When you're feeling better, then you can talk to your father. I'm sure this will all be worked out. . . ."

Benita stared at him with her big eyes. Parris didn't want to feel her pain, but he couldn't look away. "You're Charlie's friend, aren't you?"

Parris barely whispered. "Yes. I am."

"I'm his friend too," she said. "So tell me what evidence they have against my father!" The logical element of her argument escaped him, but it was, nevertheless, irrefutable.

"Some of the victim's clothing," Parris said, ". . . was found in your father's truck."

Benita leaned back against the pillow and closed her eyes. "His clothes . . . in Daddy's pickup."

"Could be," Parris said gently, "there's some innocuous reason for the victim's clothes being in your father's truck." That sounded stupid. "I'm sure he'll get a fair hearing. . . ."

"Sure he will," the girl said softly. "And the stars are frozen tears that angels wept." Benita was silent for some time. She finally opened her eyes and focused on the cracks in the plastered ceiling. "Call Charlie. I want him here—right away. And," she said, "there's one other thing."

Parris leaned over the bed expectantly. "Yes . . . and what's that?"

"I want you here too. I have something to say, and I want Charlie to have a witness."

Scott Parris found Charlie Moon sitting in a waiting room; the Ute was rubbing his eyes.

"She wants you, right now." Paris waited and got no response. "Let's go, Charlie."

Moon got to his feet slowly, with all the enthusiasm of a man being escorted to the gallows.

Moon sat in the chair at Benita's right hand; Parris stood on the other side of the bed, wondering what was going to happen. She looked at Moon through her tears. "I want to make a statement."

Parris dug into his coat pocket and found his microcassette recorder. He didn't have a spare tape, but it would be easy enough to make another recording of "The Shooting of Dan McGrew." The tape hadn't been much help anyway. He couldn't get past "Were you ever out in the Great Alone, when the moon was awful clear. . . ." Here, in this stark hospital room, he felt the presence of the Great Alone. Hovering. Parris held the recorder up for Benita to see. "Okay if I use this?"

She nodded. Moon watched the proceedings blankly; he felt like a bystander. Parris pushed the RECORD button and spoke slowly. He stated his name and the date. He glanced at his wristwatch. "It's about twenty past two P.M. I'm at Mercy Medical Center in Durango with Officer Charlie Moon. We're visiting a patient, Miss Benita Sweetwater, who has asked to make a statement. She has agreed to have the statement recorded." He clipped the miniature microphone onto her hospital gown. "That right, young lady?"

"Yes," she said hoarsely, "I want to make a statement."

"You understand," Parris said gently, "that your father . . . Gorman Sweetwater has been arrested for the murder of Arlo Nightbird?"

"Daddy didn't do it," she said firmly.

Scott Parris briefly locked eyes with Moon. The Ute clearly didn't like this development.

"You understand," Parris said, "that anything you say may be used to . . ."

Moon raised a hand and nodded. Parris started to protest, then clamped his mouth shut. The Ute didn't want anything Benita might say to be admissible in any future legal proceedings against her. It was, at the very least, sloppy police work. At most it was a decision that could cost Moon his job. But this was the Ute's territory. And it was clear that this was a very special young woman.

Benita watched them with a curious expression. "You want to know how it happened?"

"Sure we do," Parris said. "Tell us whatever you know." She closed her eyes; Parris wondered if she was remembering. Or fabricating.

"I've lost track of time. I think it was Wednesday afternoon. It looked like rain and the stock in *Cañon del Espiritu* needed some salt blocks. You know . . . Daddy's Herefords?"

"I know about your father's cattle," Parris said.

"Daddy has tendonitis in his shoulders; it started acting up before the rain came. He was hurting real bad. I decided to take the salt up to the canyon myself." She paused to gasp a breath. "The blocks . . . they were already in the pickup, all I had to do was open the tailgate and shove them out."

"Remember what time you left?"

"Not really . . . but it was about the time the rain started. It was a hard rain." She fell silent, picturing the drops pelting the pickup, the wipers smearing an oily film across the windshield.

"Then what happened?" Parris asked.

"I was nearly there. . . ." Benita opened her eyes. "I saw his convertible, off the road . . . on the shoulder. It was raining, but he had the top down and was just standing there with his hands in his pockets. Looked real pitiful. I felt sorry for him."

Who did you see?" Parris leaned over to speak into the microphone.

"Mr. Nightbird. Arlo Nightbird. I stopped and asked if he needed any help. He said his car was running hot and out of water, said he needed a ride back to Ignacio. He was wet and cold."

"And you gave him a ride?"

"I told him I had to drop off the salt blocks for the stock in the canyon, but I'd pick him up on the way out. He said he'd have pneumonia by then, so I said 'get in.' When he got inside the pickup, I smelled the whiskey on him. Told him I couldn't give him a ride when he was drinking, then he said he'd ride in the back of the truck."

"He got in the back?"

"Yes. He laid down on the straw." Benita paused to gather what remained of her strength. Beads of perspiration dotted her forehead. "I thought he'd sleep it off, so I drove into the canyon and found the cattle. When I got in the back of the truck and opened the tailgate, he got up and . . . and . . ." She stopped and grimaced at the memory.

"Benita," Parris urged gently, "tell me exactly what he did. . . . I know this is hard, but don't leave anything out."

"Mr. Nightbird," she said, "had already pulled off his boots. Then . . . he took off his pants."

"Did he say anything?"

"Yes," she shuddered, "he said he'd had his eye on me for a long time. Said he hadn't . . ."—she glanced at Parris who ducked his head in embarrassment for her—"he said he hadn't had himself a 'cherry' for a month of Sundays."

Moon groaned and hid his face in his giant hands.

"What did you do?"

"I got mad . . . told him to get out of the truck. He pulled a knife . . . said he'd cut me up if I didn't . . . cooperate. I guess that's when I tried to run away."

"He chase after you?"

Benita sobbed. "Yes. He caught me and ripped my blouse. I tried to kick him between his legs and he fell down and held onto my ankle. He got mad then, and that's when he did it."

"When he did *what?*"

"When he cut me."

Moon was stunned. "He *cut* you?"

"On my leg . . . right here." She pointed toward her swollen left thigh. "It hurt and it bled, but not too much. I guess it got infected . . . I don't want them to take my leg off."

Moon stared at the tape recorder, as if it were an intrusion into what should have been a very private conversation.

Parris nodded at the girl. "Go on."

"I got away again and ran down to the creek bed. There was already some water in it from the rain. I slipped on a rock and fell in the water. Mr. Nightbird, he jumped on top of me—he was so heavy. Then, that's when I did it."

"You did what?"

"Hit him."

Parris grinned with delight. "You hit the son of a . . . you hit him?"

"With a rock I found on the ground. He fell to one side. I was running back to the road, and he was coming after me, but he was staggering. I sprained my ankle, then I knew I couldn't get away. I stopped and waited for him . . . I still had that rock in my hand. When he got close, I hit him again, real hard. I heard the bone in his head crack and he fell down and dropped his knife. I knew he wouldn't hurt me anymore. Then I got in the truck and drove home."

"There's something I need to ask you about, Benita." Parris searched for the right words. "Something about Mr. Nightbird's body. . . ."

She didn't hear the *matukach* policeman. "When I got home, my leg was hurting something awful." Her voice was weakening; she was a little girl lost in a bad dream. "Daddy saw the blood running down my leg and started yelling. I told him Mr. Nightbird done it . . . that I'd hit him in the head with a rock . . . then . . . then . . ." Benita's head rolled to one side. At this instant, a nurse entered with a tray of instruments and a paper cup with two tiny yellow pills inside.

"Oh," she stage-whispered, "I hope you won't disturb her, she needs to sleep."

Parris pocketed the tape recorder. "Wouldn't dream of it."

Moon gave the nurse his parcel. "I'm a friend of the family; just came by to drop off some of her things."

The nurse unwrapped the package and began to store the nightclothes in a cabinet. She paused as she saw the red Bible. "Oh," she said, "poor little thing's been asking for this. Thank you so much." The nurse turned to look at Moon. "She's been asking for her father too; they're absolutely devoted to one another. Do you know when he'll be back?"

Parris rubbed his chin thoughtfully. "That," he said, "is hard to say."

Moon leaned with his hands on the window frame. There was no earth, no sky. The rain fell straight down, through a still gray fog. He could barely see the bank of the *Rio De Los Animas Perditas*—the River of Lost Souls.

They were halfway to Ignacio when Parris gave voice to what they were both thinking. "There's a big hole in her story."

The Ute nodded. "The missing body parts?"

"I can't believe that little girl mutilated the body," he said.

"No," Moon said. It was unthinkable that Benita would do such a thing.

Parris pressed the point. "But somebody did." It was obvious enough, but he knew Moon didn't want to face it. "Let's say her father takes her to the emergency room at the hospital. He's not too worried about his daughter, not with a superficial wound on her leg. No way he could have known she'd develop a bad infection. He steams awhile, then decides to go to the canyon. He finds Nightbird. Dead or unconscious. Figures his daughter may have some trouble with the law. Maybe he finds Nightbird's knife close by. He gets this great idea: Why not fix Arlo the way someone fixed Big Ouray? That way, it'll look like the nutcase who mutilated his bull also murdered Arlo. What Gorman Sweetwater doesn't know, is that Arlo Nightbird left his boots and britches and underwear in the back of Gorman's pickup truck!"

"Yeah," Moon said sadly. "Could have happened just that way."

"We'll need to have a long talk with Mr. Sweetwater."

Moon, lost in his thoughts, didn't hear him. She *will* get well. Tomorrow, she'll be walking around the room, wanting to go home.

Benita Sweetwater used most of her strength to turn on her left side as the night nurse lifted the covers and jabbed her buttock with a disposable hypodermic syringe. The girl was grateful for the stinging injection; it would soon melt the pain away—at least enough for a precious few hours sleep. She turned onto her back and sighed; the dark-eyed nurse said something about using the call button if she needed anything and was gone. It was then that she felt the presence in the room.

Benita raised herself on one elbow; she stared wide-eyed at the aged figure of a bow-legged man standing by her bed. "Nahum Yaci-iti . . . it's you!"

"It is me," he said simply.

"But everybody thought you were dead since that storm hit your place last year. . . . Some said you'd fallen into the Animas. . . . I must be dreaming. You're not real."

"Touch me and see," he said gently, holding his hand barely above hers.

She raised her tiny hand and touched the warm tips of his fingers. "You're really here." Tears welled up in her eyes.

He sat on the bed and the springs creaked. "Can't stay long," Nahum said. He was a long way from home.

"I'm real sick," Benita said. "The doctor wants to—"

"To take your leg off?" Nahum frowned as he touched her hot forehead.

"I won't let him," she said defiantly. "I won't let him cut my leg off!"

"It's up to you," her visitor said. "You choose the path, then you walk on it."

"I've made up my mind."

He had expected as much. This girl was much like her mother. Nahum slid off the bed. "Then it's a done deal."

"Will you come back and see me again?"

"I'll be back," he said as he patted her hand.

15

Scott Parris arrived at the station as Charlie Moon was hanging up the telephone. The Ute looked up, his face split by a wide grin. "A good mornin' to you, acting chief of the SUPD."

"You are disgustingly cheerful this morning," Parris said, "enough to put me off my breakfast. Any fresh coffee around this place?"

"Read this. Fresh off the fax." Moon offered him the flimsy sheaf of papers.

Parris held the document at arm's length and squinted to get a good focus on the copy.

"You need to get yourself some spectacles," Moon advised.

"Just need longer arms. This a copy of the medical examiner's report on Nightbird?"

"Preliminary report. From the Granite Creek M.E.'s office, but it doesn't have Doc Simpson's signature on it."

"Simpson's on his annual vacation to the South Pacific," Parris observed as he read. "He usually trades off with someone for a couple of weeks when he visits the Sandwich Islands. Let's see . . . says here that Mr. Arlo Nightbird was killed by a blow to the head. We already knew that."

"Try the next page," Moon said.

Parris flipped a page. "Says there were '. . . indications of animal predation on the digits of the right hand and on the lower lip.' That's pretty grim." Parris glanced over the top of a page at Moon, who still wore the look of smug satisfaction. "Don't see why it makes you so happy to hear that one of the People got chewed on by coyotes."

"Read on."

Parris moved his lips as he read, then he brightened. "Well I'll be rode hard and put away wet! The report says 'predators are probably responsible for the mutilation. Coyotes or buzzards . . . could have torn off the ears and testicles.' " Parris felt a sympathetic twinge in his crotch. "But the M.E. only says *probably*—that still leaves the possibility that Gorman Sweetwater went back and castrated Nightbird. . . ."

"Let Hoover try to take that to court," Moon chuckled. "The important point is, the official report says that animals could have done the deed. No way Hoover can make anything stick against Gorman now. Not without some brand new evidence. Everything we have supports Benita's statement. Arlo left his boots and britches in her Daddy's pickup, chased her with a knife. Benita smacked Arlo on the noggin, he gave up his nasty little spirit, then the coyotes showed up and nibbled at him. That's all there is."

"Then what are we waiting for?" Parris said. "Let's drive up to Durango and find Hoover; he'll have to spring Sweetwater and we'll be there to gloat. Of course," he added thoughtfully, "I imagine you'll need a couple of hours for breakfast before you can think about police work."

"I'm not hungry," Moon said. "We'll grab something to eat after we stop by the hospital."

Parris followed him to the parking lot. "Hospital?"

"Gotta tell Benita the good news," Moon yelled over his shoulder. "When she hears her Daddy's in the clear, she'll get better in nothin' flat! Yes boys and girls," he raised his hands to the sky and bellowed off-key: "it's a beee-oooutiful day in the neighborhood!"

The sky had been robin's-egg blue all the way to Durango, and the air was sparkling fresh. But even as they approached the parking lot, Parris sensed something dreadfully wrong at Mercy Medical Center. There was a peculiar, barely visible gray smog hanging over the building; the gloom seemed to permeate into the long, hollow hallways. Parris felt confined by the dismal atmosphere, but Moon didn't notice anything amiss until they were near Benita's room. Then, the snap faded from the Ute's energetic stride. The policemen paused at her door; a short chubby priest was reading aloud from a black leather-bound volume. His voice boomed, as if he were preaching to a large congregation.

"He shall cover thee with his feathers, and under his wings shalt thou trust. . . ."

"That," Moon whispered to Parris, "ain't Father Raes."

Benita spoke through trembling lips in a voice that might have belonged to a child. "I will not be afraid of the terror that comes by night . . . or," she breathed deeply, "the arrow that flies . . . by day."

Moon took off his hat and fumbled with the brim. "Let's stay out here until he's finished."

The priest was reciting something about *the pestilence that walketh in darkness.* "Suits me," Parris said.

Benita's voice rose and fell like swells on the waves of time; they could hear her clearly, then her speech would fade away into a far place: ". . . for He shall give His angels charge over me. . . ."

"They shall bear thee up in their hands," the priest intoned solemnly, "lest thou dash thy foot against a stone."

"I don't like the sound of this," Moon muttered to no one in particular.

They heard Benita's voice. "Surely . . . Goodness and Mercy shall follow me." The young woman used their names in a familiar fashion, as if Goodness and Mercy were her old, dear friends. Finally, the policemen heard the priest clamp the covers of the little book onto its gold-edged pages. Moon watched Benita for a moment; she seemed to be sleeping. The priest crossed himself, then turned to leave.

Moon nodded respectfully at the priest. "You're not Father Raes."

The plump little man raised his eyebrows. "No, that I am not." His speech had the sweet lilt of an Irish brogue.

"Then you must be the Catholic priest from St.—"

"No," the man interrupted, "that I am most certainly not." His blue eyes twinkled.

"I give up," the Ute said, and introduced himself and his pardner.

The priest stuck his hand into Moon's and shook it vigorously. "I'm Father Rory O'Dinnigan, and I hate to disappoint you, but I'm not a Roman Catholic. I'm Episcopalian. Serve as an informal chaplain over at Fort Lewis College. Benita's been attending our Bible study services for more than a year now; Father Raes called yesterday and told me about her illness."

The Ute policeman nodded toward the tiny figure in the bed. "How is she . . . doing?" Moon asked the question haltingly, as if he didn't want to hear the answer.

"Yesterday, the surgeon wanted to amputate her leg," O'Dinnigan said. "Said if he didn't amputate, the infection would spread." Even under the sheet, the infected leg now appeared to be much larger than the other.

"When are they going to do it?" Moon asked.

"Not going to," O'Dinnigan said. "Benita refused to sign anything. I visited her father over at the jail and pleaded with him to sign the papers; he made disparaging remarks about my parentage and made it very clear that if I came close enough he would break both my legs." The priest turned to look at Benita. "Mr. Sweetwater is very bitter; he believes God should not have allowed this awful calamity to fall upon his daughter. Father Raes and I," he said sadly, "represent this God who has failed him."

The Ute was not concerned with Gorman's theological problems. "If they don't take her leg off," Moon asked, "what's going to happen to her?"

"She's going to die." The priest walked daily with Death whispering in his ear.

Benita cried out: "Charlie!"

He was at her bedside in a moment; Benita had pushed herself up on an elbow. Her face was shining with a glow that Moon assumed had something to do with the fever. Parris, standing in the door, could see a pale halo of light developing, swirling like a frosty mist around her head. Father O'Dinnigan was on the opposite side of the bed from Moon, but Benita didn't seem to notice his presence.

She seemed to be blind. "Charlie . . . I heard you talking . . . are you there?"

"I'm here, right beside you . . . sweetheart." He gently lowered her onto a pillow that was soaked with her perspiration.

"Dear Charlie," she said, "Nahum was here last night."

Scott Parris blinked in disbelief at what he saw approaching her bed; he tried to speak but there was a knot in his throat.

Moon, oblivious to the vision unfolding before Benita Sweetwater and, to a lesser extent, before Scott Parris, put his big hand on her forehead. "You're burning up with fever."

She lifted a trembling hand to point toward the foot of her bed. "Can't you see them?"

Moon was troubled by her feverish chatter. "See who? Father O'Dinny . . . the priest is here; my pardner Scott Parris, he's over by the door."

She pointed toward a blank wall, ". . . ooooh," she said with a little squeal of delight, "it is *pían*. Do you see . . ."

Moon attempted to speak but could not.

"She's here," Benita said, "*pían* is here to take me home."

"What did she say?" O'Dinnigan whispered.

"It's Ute," Moon said hoarsely. "It means 'my mother.' "

"Charlie . . . Charlie," she sung as if the sound of his name was sweet music. She laughed. "Kiss me good-bye, Charlie Moon."

The Ute hesitated, then kissed her tenderly on the forehead.

"The Shadow of Death," she said, "it comes near. But I am not afraid."

Charlie Moon was afraid.

The startled priest took her hand. "For the Lamb which is in the midst of the throne shall feed them . . . and shall lead them unto living fountains of waters. . . ." O'Dinnigan's eyes were moist with tears. "And God shall wipe away all tears from their eyes." He wiped away his own tears. "Amen."

Benita slumped; her head rolled to one side on the moist pillow as her lips parted slightly. The priest continued his prayer; the policemen were like statues. Parris could no longer see the apparitions.

Father O'Dinnigan pressed a finger under Benita's jaw in an attempt to feel the carotid pulse. "She has left us," the plump little priest said simply. "May God grant her soul eternal peace."

Moon moved away from the bed and turned his back.

The priest clamped a hand on the Ute's elbow. "Someone will have to tell her father. I don't think he's ready to see a priest. Not just yet."

Moon leaned against the wall, his hand over his eyes. Gorman Sweetwater was the last person he wanted to see.

Parris turned toward the door. "I'll go over and tell him." Any excuse to get out of this room. He was rushing numbly down the hall, barely able to feel his feet hit the floor, when he met Emily Nightbird. She was flanked by veterinarian Harry Schaid and Herb Ecker. Herb was carrying a bouquet of yellow roses; Emily raised a dainty hand to stop Parris. "We've come to see Benita," she said, "poor little thing. How is she—"

"I'm sorry," Parris said, fighting the tightness in his throat, "she just left." He was gone before Emily could respond.

"Mr. Sweetwater . . . I'm Scott Parris. I was with Charlie when you were arrested. . . ." It sounded better than *I helped Charlie slam you on the ground and cuff you.*

The old Ute sat cross-legged on the floor, his lips moving in some silent recitation. He didn't look up at the visitor in his cell.

"I'm afraid I've got some bad news," Parris said gently.

Gorman got to his feet slowly, in the cautious manner of old men whose bones are fragile. He hobbled to the window and nodded to indicate something outside. "You see that big tree?"

Parris looked over his shoulder through the rusty bars. "The cottonwood?"

"This morning, just before first light, he came."

"Who . . . who came?" Parris wasn't sure he wanted to hear this. This day had already been filled with phantasms that might, with the least excuse, come back to haunt him.

"Brother owl," Gorman said. That was what Saint Francis would have called the bird. Brother owl. "He came to see me this morning."

"Oh," Parris said with relief, "an owl." Only an owl.

"He sat right there," Gorman pointed at a dead branch, "and called her name." The old Ute looked up at the *matukach* policeman to see if he understood. "He called out my daughter's name," Gorman said. The Ute would not say Benita's name aloud; it would trouble her ghost.

"That's why I'm here. It's your daughter."

"My daughter's spirit," Gorman said, "is gone. That's why the owl came, to tell me she would leave today, before the sun went down."

Parris fumbled with his hat and looked at an oily stain on the gray concrete floor. The cell stank of urine and disinfectant. "I'm sorry."

Gorman sat down on the wooden bench that was suspended from the green cinder-block wall by a pair of rusty chains.

"Ch—Charlie," Parris stammered, ". . . he's feeling real bad. Couldn't bear to see you right now . . . that's why I came."

"Charlie Moon," Gorman said, "is a good man." He smiled at sweet memories. "Benita, when she was a little girl, wanted to marry Charlie Moon. I told her to wait and find somebody more . . . more . . ." The old rancher removed a red bandanna from his pocket and wiped at bloodshot eyes.

"If there's anything I can do . . . or Charlie . . . ," Parris began.

He put his hands over his face. "I was worried I'd have one of them cor—uh . . . heart attacks and die. And then my little girl'd be a orrifun. Now I'm the orrifun." He looked directly at the policeman for the first time, wondering whether this *matukach* carried a flask in his coat pocket. "You got anything to drink?"

"No."

"Then get me out of this stinking hole so I can find me a bottle."

"I'll do what I can." Parris hesitated. "There's something you should know."

Gorman Sweetwater stared into bitter nothingness. "What's that?"

"Your daughter said that someone"—Parris paused to clear his throat—"Nahum Yaciiti . . . he came to see her last night."

"There was a bad storm last year. . . . They never found his body. She must of seen that old man's ghost," Gorman said with a slight shiver. The notion of a visiting ghost was awful to the Ute psyche of Gorman Sweetwater. But the Christian soul of the old man was not surprised that Nahum's spirit would come to guide his daughter across that deep river. Benita had been close to that peculiar old shepherd. Maybe closer than to her own father.

Parris swallowed hard. "Just before your daughter . . . passed away . . . she saw something." The lawman felt oddly short of breath.

Gorman turned his head; he examined the policeman with a searching expression. This white man *knew* something. "You tell me about it, young man. Then you'll feel better."

"A woman came," Parris said, remembering the shining figures. Impossible phantasms of rainbow light. "Benita said it was her mother." He'd said enough. Maybe too much. It wouldn't do to mention who came with the woman.

16

Hoover rewound the tape and listened to Benita's faltering voice for the third time. His face was without expression except for the customary hardness in his gray eyes.

Parris leaned forward in his chair, straining to hear every whispered word from the young woman who was now spirit.

Charlie Moon sat with his eyes unfocused, his chin resting on clasped hands.

Hoover, twisting a ballpoint pen in his hand, finally broke the silence. "So, let's see what we have. Gorman Sweetwater's daughter makes a confession that she killed Arlo Nightbird. . . ."

"It wasn't exactly a confession," Parris interrupted. "The young woman was defending herself from an attempt at forcible rape."

"She confesses, on her deathbed, to killing Arlo Nightbird," Hoover continued, "thereby giving her father, who has been arrested for the murder of the same Mr. Nightbird, a clean sheet." He tried to read Moon's unreadable face. "Very tidy."

Parris nodded. "The point is—"

"The point is," Hoover interrupted, "that since Miss Sweetwater is now among the deceased, it is not even possible to question her about this"—he waved a hand at the tape recorder—". . . this statement. Far be it from me to suggest that she concocted this whole story to save her father from a long jail term."

Moon sat quietly. Benita was dead. Gone. Nothing much mattered beyond that.

"But it all fits," Parris said. "The wound on Nightbird's head, the clothes he left in her father's pickup. Hell, her father would have thrown that stuff away if he'd known it was there!"

"Let's assume," Hoover said, "that the girl did fight off an attempt at rape and is wounded in the process. She comes home, tells her father what happened and who did it. Nightbird is stranded in the canyon without transportation. Father freaks out, takes off hell-for-leather to the canyon, finds Nightbird, smacks him on the head, and clips off the family jewels. Just like he'd threatened to do."

Moon finally spoke. "It could have happened like that, but it didn't. I've known her since she was knee high . . . she'd never lie to me. Not even to keep her daddy out of jail."

"It's damn lucky," Parris said, "we talked to her when we did. Another day and we may never have known what actually happened to Mr. Nightbird."

"Oh, I don't know," Hoover said. "I suppose we make our own luck." He stared at Moon with an expression of mild derision. "Do you make your own luck, Sergeant Moon?"

"Us Utes," Moon said evenly, "are like the Irish. We have our own leprechauns." He leaned forward, meeting the FBI agent's stare. "And our own luck."

Parris shifted uncomfortably in his chair; the atmosphere was electric with tension. The least imbalance might strike lightning between these men.

"With this confession . . . this very convenient statement, there's no way in hell I can make a case against her father for Nightbird's head injury. But there's still the question of the mutilation." Hoover smiled with thin lips. "The girl said nothing about snipping off Nightbird's ears and balls. Even if her story is true, ten-to-one, Gorman Sweetwater returned to the canyon and fulfilled his threat to castrate Mr. Nightbird."

Parris cocked his head. "According to the M.E., the coyotes tore off the body parts."

Hoover's pale face flushed pink; he didn't realize Parris had seen the report.

"There's no case against Mr. Sweetwater for any part of this sorry episode," Parris added firmly. "Besides, the old guy needs to get out of jail so he can attend his daughter's funeral."

"Piss on her funeral," Hoover snapped.

Parris saw Moon's frame stiffen; the Ute got up from his chair, his big hands clenched into fists. Could he keep the Ute from snapping Hoover's neck? The special agent ignored Moon; he seemed unaware of the danger. Or maybe he wanted the Ute to make his move.

"Look," Parris said as he stepped between them. "There's no justification for holding Sweetwater. Why not cut him loose so he can attend the funeral? If some new evidence turns up, you can get an indictment and throw him back into the cage."

Hoover leaned back in his padded chair, propped an immaculate boot onto his glass-topped oak desk. "Can't cut him loose, even if I wanted too. It seems that Tom Parris and Huckleberry Moon have forgotten about something."

"Oh?" Parris said in a flat tone, "and what's that, G-Man?"

Hoover pulled a long unfiltered cigarette from a silver case. He laughed soundlessly and stuck the white cylinder between his lips. "In the process of resisting arrest"—he rolled his thumb on the striker wheel of a gold-plated lighter—"Mr. Sweetwater struck yours truly—a federal officer." Hoover touched the flame to the cigarette and inhaled. "Even with good behavior, which is unlikely, he'll spend at least eighteen months in a federal establishment for that little indiscretion."

Moon, muttering darkly in the Ute dialect, turned his back on Hoover.

Parris scratched his chin thoughtfully. "Are you sure," he asked, "that Mr. Sweetwater actually intended to hit you?" He paused as if trying to remember. "Or even that he *did* hit you?"

Hoover sprang to his feet. "What the hell do you mean—you guys saw that old blanket-ass take a cheap shot when I wasn't looking. . . ."

"Now that I recall," Parris said, "that's what you called Mr. Sweetwater: 'blanket-ass.' But if you press charges for assault, I expect his lawyer will make a big point of the ethnic slur. Sweetwater may walk, or he may do the eighteen months." Parris pointed at the special agent's chest. "But your career with the Bureau won't last eighteen days."

Hoover turned away; he buried his face in his hands. "I'll turn Sweetwater loose, but if he cuts somebody else up, it's on your heads." His thin frame began to tremble. "You scheming bastards, get out of my office."

"I appreciate you getting Gorman out of jail," Moon said to Parris as they left.

"We were lucky this time," Parris said, "but somewhere, sometime, that little snake is going to bite one of us." He grinned at the Ute. "I sure hope it's you."

Daisy could barely see over the dashboard. "I guess almost everybody will be at her funeral." Neither of them would speak the name of the dead girl.

Moon was silent for some minutes as he steered the Blazer between potholes on the gravel road. When he turned onto the blacktop, he glanced toward his aunt. "Arlo's car had the headlight broken out. There was a hole knocked in the radiator."

Daisy looked away, toward the rippling waters of the Piedra on the west side of Route 151. She began to hum something that sounded vaguely like "Amazing Grace."

Moon continued casually, as if he were discussing the weather. "We found a little chunk of Arlo's headlight in your yard. I figure you picked up all the big pieces. The ones you could see."

The shaman took a quick look at the Ute policeman. "My eyes aren't so good as they was. Think maybe I'm gettin' them cataracts." Charlie was so clever; Daisy was proud of her nephew.

Moon tapped the brake pedal as a wild turkey darted across the road. "How'd it happen?"

Daisy's lips were tight with fury at the memory. "Arlo came to order me out of my home."

Charlie sighed. "So, what'd you do?"

"Heaved a crowbar at him. Missed, though." There was a hint of regret in her tone.

"The crowbar hit his car . . . broke the headlight?"

"And the radiator too, I guess. For awhile, he didn't say nothing at all, acted like he was choking on a bone. Then, he got in his fancy car, swearing like . . . like Arlo always swore when he was drunk." She put her hand on her ears to suppress the memory of this profanity. "Said he'd have me locked up in jail. Or sent to live with the crazy people." She searched Moon's face for some sign of sympathy but found none. "I cleaned up the glass so he couldn't prove the headlight was broke in my place. And then I went up to spend the night with the Three Sisters. Needed time to think. I was awful tired . . . fell sound asleep. Woke up later, thought I heard Gorman's truck go into the canyon, but I didn't know it was his little girl driving. I sure didn't know she had Arlo with her." Daisy shook her head sadly. "Poor, foolish little girl."

"After you heard Gorman's truck," Moon asked, "you hear anything else?"

Daisy tried hard to recall the events of that evening; she knew this might be important. "Don't remember anything after that. Must have went to sleep again; didn't wake up until the middle of the next day."

The cemetery was bordered on the sunset side by the meandering ribbon of the Piños, which was little more than a brook in this season. In the springtime, the silt-laden torrent of snow melt roared by like an endless freight train, but now the sweet waters whispered and laughed over the slippery boulders. On the side of the cemetery where the sun rose, cars and pickups were parked along the shoulder of the blacktop road for a mile. Virtually all of the Utes and not a few of the Anglos and Chicanos in Ignacio had turned out for the graveside service. Daisy Perika shuffled along slowly between Gorman Sweetwater and Charlie Moon; the old shaman held tightly onto her nephew's postlike arm. Scott Parris followed behind, hat in his hand. It had taken all of Daisy's powers of persuasion to convince Gorman to come to his daughter's funeral; the crusty old man wanted "nothing more to do with them priests and their religion that couldn't keep my daughter from dying." When she finally told him that the ceremony would be held with or without him, and that the People would not think highly of a father who didn't show up for his daughter's funeral, Gorman grudgingly relented. The cantankerous rancher had fortified himself with a pint of Canadian whiskey; he muttered darkly as he walked along unsteadily beside Daisy.

The crowd parted to make way for the respected woman and her retinue. Tender words of condolence were offered to Gorman, who showed no sign of hearing. There had been rumors that the old man would "have his say" at the cemetery, and some were attending the services in hope of witnessing a scandalous display that would be the talk of Ignacio for years to come.

Taxi, scribbling furiously on a yellow legal pad, stood behind the major throng of mourners. He nudged Daniel Bignight with a ragged elbow and whispered, "I am taking notes."

The policeman did not respond but Taxi was not discouraged.

"Did you know," he tugged at the policeman's sleeve, "that old Nick is on the prowl?" He tapped himself on the chest. "The Knacker Man will taste blood again. I know this for a fact, and I am writing a synopsis of his activities. A treatment, they call it in the business."

The policeman held his breath and took a sideways step away from this strange man who smelled like road kill laced with some kind of pungent chemical.

Encouraged by this response, Taxi moved closer, his filthy coat brushing against the policeman's immaculate uniform. "I have a new agent, now. She has serious connections in Hollywood. I would," he continued with a sigh, "do *anything* to make it in Hollywood."

Daniel Bignight closed his eyes and prayed silently. *Please God . . . he smells like dead meat. Please make him go away.*

Taxi wandered aimlessly away into a crowd of mourners; they parted in front of him like the waters before the hand of Moses.

Daisy and her party stood before the open grave. Moon stood perfectly still; he would not look upon the coffin. Gorman muttered incoherently to himself; the old man reeled as if he might collapse.

Father Raes stepped in front of the rancher. "Gorman," he said firmly to the slouched man, "look at me!"

Gorman glared coldly at the little priest, but didn't speak.

"Benita has passed over to the other side," Raes said. "She doesn't need this funeral. This gathering is for her family and friends, those who loved her, who still love her. Do you understand?"

Gorman muttered something under his breath and nodded almost imperceptibly.

Raes moved closer and lowered his voice to a whisper. "I know you're bitter and I smell the whiskey on your breath, but I make you this solemn promise: If you disrupt this Holy Service, I will instruct Officer Moon to remove you from this place. And," he added darkly, "you will be disgraced forever in the eyes of the People." Gorman's eyes were slits, his jaw set like granite. The priest turned over his hole card. "Show respect, Gorman, or the Holy Virgin will be offended." He paused, staring the old rancher into submission. "Do you understand me?"

Gorman, who loved the Holy Virgin, was deeply wounded. He nodded meekly and lowered his gaze to the silver crucifix suspended from the priest's neck. He could not erase the picture of his suffering daughter from his mind. Poor Mary, she had watched her child suffer terribly before he died on that tree. With iron nails through his wrists and feet. It was a terribly sobering image.

"Very well," Raes said more gently. "Now let's begin." He returned to the flower-draped coffin and placed his hand on the shoulder of the chubby priest who beamed at the congregation. "This gentleman at my side," he addressed the crowd, "is Father Rory O'Dinnigan from Durango. Father O'Dinnigan is an Episcopalian."

There was a surprised murmur from the Spanish-Catholic element of the crowd.

Raes took a long breath and continued. "Father O'Dinnigan is our brother in Christ and a dear friend of Benita from Fort Lewis College. In light of Benita's experience in drawing nourishment from two branches of the Vine of our Lord, we will have an ecumenical service." Father Raes closed his eyes and prayed silently: *God help me if the Bishop hears of this.*

There were a few whispered comments from older Utes who were not offended by the presence of a Protestant minister, but thought it very bad form to mention the name of the dead.

Father Raes raised a hand for silence. "Later during the service, we will be reciting a Psalm of David. Father O'Dinnigan will read the English translation, I will follow line by line with the Catholic version in Spanish. We're passing out copies of the liturgy and the Psalm for those who wish to read aloud with us."

Harry Schaid, a member of the choir who had been drafted into service by the Catholic priest, was passing out copies of the liturgy. The veterinarian moved through the crowd. He gave copies to Emily Nightbird and her father; Fidel Sombra rolled his paper into a tight cylinder and used the device to scratch at his ear. Schaid gave the leaflets to the tribal chairman, then to Daisy Perika. The veterinarian handed Gorman a copy of the document; the rancher immediately wadded it up and dropped it onto the ground.

Father Raes ignored Gorman and continued. "Many of you know that my knowledge of the Ute language is barely sufficient to carry on a simple conversation"—a few of the tribal members smiled at the little priest's inflated notion of his language skills—"but perhaps one of our Native American members will help me translate the Psalm and the Lord's Prayer into the Ute tongue for future services. Then we will truly live up to our reputation as a tri-cultural community. And now," the priest continued, sweeping his left arm in a broad arc, indicating the multitude of mourners, "remember the words of our brother Paul to those churches at Galatia: 'There is neither Jew nor Greek, neither slave nor free, neither male nor female . . . for you are all one in Christ Jesus.' "

Scott Parris accepted a copy of the liturgy from Schaid; he folded the paper carefully and slipped it into his jacket pocket with a paper clip, two peppermints in cellophane wrappers, and a half dozen credit card receipts for gasoline purchases. And a red plastic toothpick. Items of little value but nevertheless difficult to discard.

Father O'Dinnigan raised his arms in supplication; when the crowd was completely silent, he began: "I am the resurrection and the life, saith the Lord he that believeth in me, though he were dead, yet shall he live; and whosoever liveth and believeth in me shall never die." The priest's voice rolled like thunder over the cemetery, hushing all the idle conversations.

Father Raes smiled and raised his eyes to the heavens. "I know that my Redeemer liveth and that He shall stand at the latter day upon the earth."

"Blessed are the dead who die in the Lord," O'Dinnigan boomed, ". . . even so saith the Spirit, for they rest from their labors."

Scott Parris was surprised by an inrush of joy. . . . He was fantastically light . . . rested from his labors.

Daisy Perika had her eyes closed; her lips moved silently. Charlie Moon was reading the words aloud; but he kept an eye on Gorman who was swaying back and forth like a dry reed in the wind.

"The Lord be with you," Raes shouted to the congregation.

Parris was jarred back to consciousness when the crowd responded in a unison that reinforced their many voices to a swelling roar that swept over the cemetery: "And with thy spirit!" A fragrant breeze rippled among the congregation; women's skirts fluttered, men grabbed the brims of their hats.

"Now . . . let us pray," Raes said. The crowd fell silent, as did the wind.

In some hearts, the phrases danced lightly . . . *mercies that cannot be numbered . . . entrance into the land of light . . . joy and fellowship of thy saints*. Parris was again swept away by a spirit of lightness and joy.

There were a few moments of silence. Only the waters of the Piños could be heard.

"Now," Raes said, "we will read together the Psalm of David."

"The Lord is my shepherd," O'Dinnigan bellowed defiantly to the Dark Powers and Evil Principalities. "I shall not want."

"El Señor me pastorea," Raes called out, *"nada me faltará."*

There was a murmur from the crowd as a few members of Saint Ignatius Catholic Church joined in the reading.

"He maketh me to lie down in green pastures," the Anglos proclaimed joyfully with O'Dinnigan.

"*El me ha colocado en lugar de pastos!*" the Mexican-Americans shouted back. Gorman Sweetwater wept without knowing that he wept; his tears watered the dust at his feet.

Fidel Sombra snorted; he pulled a half-pint of cheap whiskey from his coat. He reluctantly stuffed the bottle back into his pocket when Emily scowled at him, but the old farmer sulked and fantasized about ways to get even with his stern daughter.

"He leadeth me beside the still waters," they chanted.

Parris felt as if he were floating; the sweet words fueled his rhapsody.

Father Raes paused for a moment; he heard something from far away, yet so near. Was it his imagination? Slightly unnerved, the priest continued: "*Me ha conducido junta a unas aguas que restauran y recrean.*"

Abe Workman forgot his shyness, and joined with the chorus: "He restoreth my soul!"

The Spanish-speaking members of the congregation responded: "*Convirtió a mi alma.*"

Parris was barely aware of his body, but he knew that his soul was restored. The next proclamation boomed out: "He leadeth me in the paths of righteousness."

Daisy was trembling; she tugged at Moon's sleeve. "Now," the shaman said urgently, "now . . . very close . . ." The Ute policeman did not hear her.

Harry Schaid offered Gorman Sweetwater another copy of the liturgy.

"Yea, though I walk through the valley of the shadow of death. . . ."

"*De esta suerte, aunqe caminase yo por medio de la sombra de la muerte. . . .*"

Father O'Dinnigan's deep voice boomed over the crowd like a great trumpet: "I will fear no evil; for Thou art with me."

Raes led the Chicanos with equal force: "*no temeré ningún desastre; porque tu estás commigo.*"

"Surely goodness and mercy shall follow me all the days of my life," O'Dinnigan shouted, "and I will dwell in the house of the Lord forever." The Episcopal priest's last word echoed back from somewhere . . . *Forever.*

Charlie Moon made a solemn request to God. Wherever Benita

Sweetwater was, he prayed that Goodness and Mercy were there with her. Forever.

The crowd of mourners had departed in melancholy little clusters of two and three, wiping self-consciously at moist eyes, muttering about the uncertainty of life in this hard world.

Finally, except for the trio of burly men who stood afar with muddy shovels, only the small man dressed in black remained in the cemetery. Father Raes stood by the open grave, his unblinking eyes fixed on the casket. The priest could still hear something very peculiar . . . a whisper . . . a familiar cadence . . . repeated over and over. No, he told himself, it is nothing more than the choppy breeze in the branches of the ash tree over the grave. Or the sound of the waters of the Piños slipping over the rocks. The wind, playing sweet games with my imagination, the shimmering waters of the river, calling to me.

As he entertained this rational explanation, the whispered song trailed off and was silenced. Even though the wind did not cease to rattle the thin branches of the ash, nor did the crystalline waters cease in their long journey toward the great ocean in the West. Father Raes closed the covers of the Book, crossed himself quickly, and turned to walk away from the casket.

The trio of men in overalls now approached the grave with ready shovels.

Father Raes opened the door of his old sedan and turned to look back toward the cemetery. Surely it was only the light breeze in the leaves or the rollicking sounds of the Pinos washing over the rocks . . . enlarged by his imagination. And called upon by the priest's soul, that in his youth had felt the very breath of God. Now, as he passed his middle years, the little priest yearned for even the slightest whisper from the Source of that infinite mystery. But whether it was real or only the peculiar harmony of the winds and waters, the priest missed the sound of the old man's voice.

A voice that chanted the words of King David's sweet song in the guttural chords of the Ute tongue.

17

Charlie Moon was consoling Gorman Sweetwater, who appeared to be on the verge of collapse. The Ute muttered in Parris's ear: "Gorman's got no business driving himself home; he'll likely wrap that old pickup around a telephone pole. I'll haul him over to his place. . . . Would you take Aunt Daisy home for me?"

"My pleasure," Parris said.

Daisy took Parris's arm as they watched Moon lead an unsteady Gorman to the Blazer. This caused a ripple of nervous whispers among the Utes, who wondered whether the cantankerous old rancher might be under arrest again.

"Gorman," Daisy said matter-of-factly, "should give up strong drink." When Parris didn't respond, she elbowed his ribs. "You remember what I told you?"

"About what?"

"What the *pitukupf* showed me."

He opened the Volvo door for her. "The shadow that turns into a bird?"

"Yes." She settled into the seat and buckled the shoulder strap. "And kills somebody, then changes itself into a shadow again. That shadow," Daisy said, "cast its darkness over this cemetery today."

Parris looked down at the little woman in the blue print dress. "Is there something you want to tell me?"

Daisy caressed a rosary, then dropped it into her purse. She searched the face of the policeman for some sign that he sensed the evil presence that was very near to them. The *matukach* could not yet comprehend what had happened today. "No," she said. He wasn't ready to hear it yet. The Book said it and it was true: there was a time to live, a time to die. For everything there was a season.

On the way to her home at the mouth of *Cañon del Espiritu*, Daisy did not speak. After Parris escorted the old woman to her porch, she turned and frowned thoughtfully. "Everybody thinks, after you bury the body, it's all over." Her eyes said that it wasn't over. The policeman didn't answer, but he felt it too. Someone with a relentless will was . . . out there. Waiting. Ever so patiently.

For the first time in days, Scott Parris was able to relax as he drove back to Ignacio. He put Daisy Perika and her elemental fears far away from him. Arlo Nightbird was dead, and that was that. The bastard had gotten what he deserved for the attempted rape. Benita had smacked his skull with a rock. He had died and been chewed on by coyotes. That was grim, but it was a satisfying form of old-fashioned justice. Gorman's spirit, given enough time, would gradually heal. J. E. Hoover would have no further reason to interfere with the operation of the Southern Ute police force. Soon, Severo would be back from vacation. Parris remembered that he was due a couple of weeks vacation himself. He would visit Anne in Washington. Anne. Lovely, sweet Anne. He tried to remember her wonderful smile, the way her red hair flowed in waves over her shoulders. Her luminous brown eyes.

But wait! Anne's eyes were blue. Those radiant brown eyes . . . they belonged to the widow Nightbird. He gripped the steering wheel and tried to remember Anne's eyes, but what he recalled was the electric touch of Emily Nightbird's delicate fingers. When Parris arrived at the Southern Ute Police headquarters, he was still attempting to sweep thoughts of the widow from his mind. Nancy Beyal waved at him from her radio console. He leaned on the door frame and sighed, wondering if the guilt showed on his face. "What's up, dispatcher?"

She rummaged through the papers on her desk until she found the official note pad. "You know a . . . Dr. Simpson?"

"Sure do. Old fishing buddy. He's the medical examiner in Granite Creek."

Nancy squinted at the paper clenched between her painted fingernails. "Dr. Simpson has returned from his vacation; he called about an hour ago. Says you should come up to his place."

"Did he say why?"

"No, but he said to get up there right away." She waved the note like a flag. "It's urgent."

He was in no mood for any of Simpson's abuse. "I'll give him a call."

"He said you'd say that," Nancy replied. "The doctor, he said 'don't call,' just deliver your . . ."—she blushed—"your *self* to his place. Right now."

18

Parris banged on the heavy oak door. After waiting for a sound from inside that did not come, he pressed on the buzzer. Presently, he heard the halting gait of the old man. Walter Simpson pulled the door open and glared under bushy brows. "Took you long enough to get here." The medical examiner turned and waddled down the long hall toward his kitchen.

Parris pushed the front door shut with his boot heel. "It was hard to stay away, considering your reputation for hospitality."

"Old men don't have to be nice," Simpson shot back, "especially when they're bachelors who do their own laundry. I enjoy being a cranky old son-of-a-bitch."

"Then you must be having a great time."

"Tea?" Simpson flicked a kitchen match with his thumb nail, touched it to a burner on his archaic gas stove. The burner hesitated, then burst into flames with an audible *whooomf*.

Parris sniffed the sour odor of a natural gas additive. "You ought to get that fixed. Something's not working right."

"Brilliant diagnosis. You should've been a plumber. Might have amounted to something."

"The wages would've been better," Parris said amiably. "But my services are in demand lately. The Southern Utes asked me to sit in for Chief Roy Severo while he's on vacation."

Simpson chuckled. "I expect you weren't near the top of their list. All the Indian cops must have turned 'em down."

This hit home. "If you merely wanted to insult me, a postcard would have sufficed."

Simpson was searching through an array of colored metal canisters for tea bags. "You know Dr. Sol Addison?"

Parris closed his eyes and searched his memory. "Sounds familiar. He a surgeon over at the hospital?"

"Fine young cutter. Just a couple of years out of University of New Mexico. Bright chap."

"That's nice to know," Parris said with a mild touch of sarcasm. "If I should need a tonsil removed, I'll look him up."

"He's not doing too well financially, just starting out. When I can, I throw some business his way."

Parris suddenly understood. "He the doc who examined the body of Arlo Nightbird while you were sunning in Hawaii?"

"Actually, I went to Tahiti this year. Much less developed. Walked miles of beaches. Met a plump native lass, not a day over fifty. Name of Lea-Lea. Goes topless." He pursed his lips suggestively. "Volunteered to nurse me in my old age."

Parris chuckled. "You are a lecherous, vulgar old man. And I don't believe a word of it."

Simpson pried a sugar bowl from the sticky oil cloth. "Dr. Addison is a sharp young chap. He's assisted me with autopsies on several occasions. With a bit more experience, he could be first rate at M.E. practice."

"But now?" Parris sipped at the tea. It looked weak, but was bitter in his mouth.

"Now," Simpson said, "and I must speak off the record . . . young Dr. Addison still has a wee bit to learn about performing the autopsy."

"Like what?"

"You want some cookies with your tea?"

"What kind of cookies?"

"You like the Girl Scout kind? With peanut butter?"

"My favorite kind."

Simpson rummaged through a cabinet. "Well shoot fire. I'm all out of cookies."

Parris drained the cup. "So Addison did the autopsy on Arlo Nightbird. Did he mess up?"

"We medical doctors"—Simpson peered coldly over his trifocals as Parris—"never 'mess up.' But sometimes . . . being human . . . we make minor errors in judgment."

"And bury the evidence," Parris said. It was a tired old joke, and Simpson pretended not to hear.

"I got back a couple of days ago. Read a copy of Dr. Addison's report to the FBI on the Nightbird autopsy. He concluded that the victim's death was caused by the trauma to the skull."

"A girl he was chasing," Parris offered, "smacked him on the head with a rock."

"I had a look at the remains," Simpson said.

"And?"

"There are head wounds that are consistent with an impact from a rock."

"So?"

"The ears and testicles were not removed by predators. Someone did it with a blade. A very sharp blade. Looks like coyotes or raccoons may have chewed on the wound sites later; I suspect that's what confused my young, less experienced colleague."

"That's bad news," Parris muttered. "We have a suspect who threatened to castrate the victim." Gorman Sweetwater would return to the top of Hoover's suspect list. And it was a very short list.

"There's more," Simpson said ominously.

"Don't know if I want to hear more."

"The trauma to the skull did not result in death."

Parris lowered his cup to the soiled oil cloth. "You've got to be kidding."

"I am a wholly serious fellow when it comes to my professional business. The head wounds seemed to be the only possible cause for the victim's untimely demise. It was a natural mistake, for a beginner. Since Dr. Addison prepared the autopsy, I'll notify him of my findings. Medical courtesy, you see. It'll be up to him to generate an amended autopsy report and submit it to the FBI."

"I assume you'll take care of that right away."

"Little problem there," Simpson said. "Dr. Addison is attending a symposium in Egypt. Then he's off to Pakistan. Won't be back for five or six weeks. Thought you might want to know . . . unofficially . . . before he eventually returns, reexamines the remains, and files the amended report."

"Will you be notifying the FBI?"

"No can do. Not my case. And I expect you to treat this in strictest confidence. Theoretically, my esteemed colleague may decide not to modify his FBI report. It's entirely up to him."

"I'll have to tell Charlie Moon."

"I never agreed to let you pass this on."

"I never agreed not to."

Simpson scowled. "Your daddy must have been a damned Philadelphia lawyer."

"Don't fret," Parris said, "Charlie's the soul of discretion. He'll keep mum until the amended report is submitted. I guarantee it."

"He damn well better, or I'll never do you a favor like this again."

"You still haven't told me how Nightbird died."

"It would appear," Simpson said, "that he died of suffocation."

Parris pushed himself away from the table and got to his feet. "He swallow his tongue?" After trauma to the head, it wasn't all that unusual.

"Quite some time after the man was clubbed on the head," Simpson said, "the 'perp,' as you cops call them, shoved something down his throat, blocking his air passage. Victim may have been unconscious, but he was definitely alive."

"What," Parris asked slowly, "did you find in his throat?"

Simpson opened his refrigerator, searched the shelves that were crammed with a dozen varieties of pickles, moldy cold cuts, and months-old cartons of milk. "Aha," he said, "here it is, behind the cheese." He brought an opaque plastic carton to the table. The medical examiner popped the lid off the plastic box and shoved it across the oil cloth in a casual fashion, as if he were inviting his friend to sample a box of chocolates. "You know what this is?"

Parris leaned over cautiously. He inspected the contents of the box. For a moment, he was baffled. Then, the policeman understood. He felt his stomach churn.

19

Moon was two-finger typing a report on a drunk he had hauled in. The unfortunate man had been reported for exposing himself in the women's rest room at the Sky Ute Lodge. The thoroughly inebriated man insisted that he had thought he was in the men's room. Moon believed him. The Ute looked up to see Scott Parris, who appeared to be lost in thought. "You kind of snuck up on me, pardner." The Ute had heard the worn valves clicking in the Volvo engine before Parris turned into the parking lot.

Parris sat down onto a wooden chair that squeaked. He took off his hat and ran his fingers through a wisp of thinning hair. "I've been up to Granite Creek."

Moon continued his hunt-and-peck style of typing. "You go up there to check on your boys at the station? Bet you thought they couldn't do without you."

"Lieutenant Leggett is doing a bang-up job in my absence. You know my dispatcher, Clara Tavishuts?"

"I better know her, she's my second cousin."

"Clara tells me Leggett's straightened out the files, streamlined the computer booking system. The lieutenant even talked the city government out of enough money to buy two new squad cars."

"Sounds like they get along pretty well without you."

Parris sighed. "By the time I get back, they won't remember my name."

"Sounds fair to me," Moon said. "That why you look so down in the mouth?" The Ute knew it was something else. Nancy Beyal had told him about the urgent summons from the medical examiner.

"I've picked up some information . . . relating to the Arlo Nightbird murder. Strictly on the q.t. We'll need to keep mum about it till the FBI gets the official amended M.E. report."

Moon lost interest in the typewriter. Parris wouldn't look at him; that wasn't a good sign.

"Doc Simpson checked the Nightbird remains. The substitute M.E. made an error."

"I don't think I like the sound of this," Moon said.

"Mr. Nightbird didn't die of his fractured skull. His ears and balls weren't chewed off by animals."

Moon felt a coldness ripple along his spine. "You sure about this?"

"It's from the horse's mouth. Simpson is one of the best M.E.s in Colorado." Now he looked at Moon. "You haven't heard the worst part."

"Give it to me."

"Mr. Nightbird died from suffocation."

"What'd he do, swallow his tongue?"

"Not his tongue," Parris said. "Whoever cut his balls off . . ."

Moon closed his eyes. "You don't mean . . . like the V.C. did to our guys in 'Nam?"

Parris nodded. "Whoever performed the castration shoved his balls down his throat and . . . he couldn't breathe."

Moon pushed his big frame up from the chair. He stalked back and forth behind the desk. Finally, he stopped and stared blankly out the window. A lone raven sat on a cottonwood branch; the bird stared back at the Ute. "Arlo Nightbird wasn't anything to brag about," he said, "but he didn't deserve to go that way."

"Nobody does," Parris said. "How do you figure it went down?" He wondered if Moon would finally face the obvious.

"There is the explanation you suggested from the beginning. While Gorman hauls . . . his daughter to the hospital, she tells him everything. He goes back, finds Arlo half alive. Gorman remembers his threat, castrates Arlo and . . ."

"I get the picture," Parris said. "But what about the missing ears? You figure Mr. Sweetwater clipped off the ears to make it look like the bull mutilator did the job on Nightbird?"

"I wouldn't figure Gorman had that much imagination. But one thing you learn in this business," Moon said slowly, "is you don't really know people." He was staring at the blue-black raven, which had spread its left wing in the sunlight. "Not even old friends."

"So," Parris asked, "what do we do now?"

"Until there's a new M.E. report," Moon said, "we do nothing." But he would keep a close watch on Gorman Sweetwater.

It was two hours before first light. JoJo was certain that he could sense the presence of the deer. The image of fresh venison, roasting slowly over the glowing embers of his campfire, made the Ute's mouth water with anticipation. Years ago, during the last few weeks of his tour in Saudi and then southern Iraq, it was this vision that had kept him connected with home. Stalking the deer—silently, relentlessly—like the cougar. JoJo was a romantic. The slender man moved along through the darkness, inhaling the pungent fragrance of the piñon grove. He had found their droppings only last week, but by now he knew their movements by heart. Deer were much like people who got up and went to work, then came home to sleep. This group, less than a half-dozen, slept through most of the daylight hours in a tree-sheltered hollow on the top of Three Sisters Mesa. At dusk, they moved down into Snake Canyon to water at the small stream. There, they fed on the galleta grass that carpeted the low ground near the brook. Shortly before dawn, they would move up the steep trail on the side of Three Sisters Mesa, graze on the dry grasses for another hour or so, then bed down for the middle of the day. It would be easy to kill them where they slept, but one of the People would not stoop to that. Breaking hunting season laws that had been imposed on the Utes was another matter. The young man knew that the rules made sense, but he could not wait. He could almost taste the wild venison, see the yellow fat bubbling over his campfire. His hand trembled in anticipation of the small pressure on the Winchester trigger that would fulfill his fantasy.

It was at that moment that he heard the peculiar sound. It came from the Snake Canyon side of Three Sisters Mesa. JoJo was curious, but he was wary about approaching the edge of the mesa. That might frighten the deer if they were already on their way up the trail. He leaned his carbine against the crotch of a juniper and waited, trying to dismiss the odd sound from his thoughts. Presently, he heard it again. Cursing silently in his frustration that the deer might have already been frightened away from their habitual path, he crawled to the edge of an overhang. He flattened himself out on his stomach, just as he had when he watched for the Iraqi tanks on the sun-baked alkali desert. The young man peered over the edge of the cliff into the sinuous meander of Snake Canyon. Because there was no moon, he expected to see nothing at all. But there was a tiny flickering light; it must be a campfire. "Damnation," he whispered prophetically. He wriggled out of his backpack and found the binoculars. He pressed the instrument to his eyes and rotated the focus knob until he could see clearly.

"No . . . oh no," he whimpered. The young Ute, who had felt little fear when he fought the thirst-crazed Iraqis in hand-to-hand combat, was so utterly terrified that he didn't realize that he had lost control of his bladder. He had seen what no mortal was meant to see. . . . He would surely die.

20

Charlie Moon had listened to the sounds of the river for hours, but even the gentle lullaby of the Piños was not enough. The Ute could not remember when this had happened before—he could not sleep. Sunrise was still hidden behind the cloak of night when he finally gave up and rolled off the narrow bed. The tile floor was like ice under his feet. Moon pulled on his jeans and boots, then wrapped his shoulders in a tattered Truchas blanket that had belonged to his mother. He struck a kitchen match on his belt buckle and lit a kerosene lamp, adjusting the wick until the sputtering flame was barely the size of his thumbnail. Moon touched the remains of the same match to a splinter of dry pine in the iron fireplace at the center of the room. Almost immediately, flames licked at the split logs. Soon, the roar of the fire was punctuated by pistol-shot snaps as glowing embers popped onto the rough brick hearth. He sat on a straight-backed wooden chair and warmed his hands as he surveyed the room that was to have been the center of his home. And of his world. With her.

He had built this circular adobe structure on a knoll inside a hairpin bend of the river. The Piños provided natural evaporative cooling that was welcome on bright summer days, but at night the unheated house was like the bottom of a well. The stone chimney above the fireplace penetrated the conical roof at the exact center; massive redwood logs radiated out from this exit like spokes in a gigantic wagon wheel. A string of red chilies hung from this log, a small basket of onions from that, the kerosene lamp from another. He had planned to install a propane furnace and build two more rooms. A square kitchen on the north side, a circular bedroom on the south with a fine view of the rapids in the elbow of the river. There would be electricity and, when she came to be with him, a telephone. These ambitious plans seemed foolish now. Even pathetic. She would never live in this house. But some part of her was here, haunting him with dreams of what could have been. He covered his eyes with his hands. "Go away, *uru-ci*," he whispered. "You're not real." Benita's sorrowful ghost departed, but reluctantly. And with a soft promise to return with the next twilight.

Charlie Moon found the blue enameled pot which held the remains of last night's coffee. He placed it on the iron grate over the fire that was already reduced to a pile of crackling embers. This was an awfully lonely way to live. Especially the nights. This night had been filled with strange pictures that troubled his mind. A buffalo that disappeared without a trace. A mutilated Hereford bull with a cracked skull. Arlo, stretched almost naked under a bush—and missing private parts that an angry rancher had threatened to remove. A lovely girl with a swollen leg . . . who was gone. Gone.

And of course, there was always Aunt Daisy. The old woman who dreamed of a dark shadow that was transmuted into some kind of nocturnal bird that mutilated animals and men. And Oswald Oakes—the eccentric old man who, in an effort to graft some organization onto the dark chaos, had given name to the nameless shadow. Cain.

There was also, Moon mused bitterly, a Ute policeman without a clue. But something was there. A subtle hint, buzzing around his mind like a tiny mosquito. He could hear its annoying whine, but the thing remained just out of reach. Somewhere, among all these things that he had seen and heard since Rolling Thunder vanished, there was a solution to this strange riddle. The answer was like a dim star that he could barely see out of the corner of his eye. When he looked directly at it, the star was not there.

He looked through the window at the glowing promise of morning in the eastern sky.

Scott Parris removed five .38 cartridges from the cylinder of his snubnosed Smith & Wesson and dropped them into his pocket. He carefully twisted the helical wire brush through the barrel, then wiped the blued surface with an oily rag. He was interrupted by Nancy Beyal, who slammed a stack of files on the desk by his cleaning kit.

"Performance appraisals," the dispatcher said cheerfully. "Due in the tribal offices by Friday. We'll need your John Hancock on the cover memos."

He holstered the revolver and stared blankly at the stack of personnel folders on Roy Severo's desk, wishing them away. But he knew the drill. If he was late, the tribal council, not to mention the bean-counters over at Indian Affairs, would be very unhappy. He scanned a few personnel folders: Roy Severo had already made detailed notes on the performance of each member of his staff. It was primarily a matter of translating the information onto the proper forms. Parris remembered his fantasies about retiring from the Chicago force to a slower, simpler life in Colorado. Endless paperwork had not been part of the vision. And this type of work was hardly what he had in mind when he accepted this temporary position with the Southern Utes. He searched through the stack of folders until he found Charlie Moon's personnel records. Nothing special here. Moon had been on the force for sixteen years, had a good record, received annual raises that regularly fell a bit under the rate of inflation. Time off to join his Army Reserve unit and do eight months during the Gulf War. It was the same story you'd find in any police station across the country. The enforcers of the law becoming steadily poorer while the purveyors of mind-rotting drugs generated huge accounts in Bahamian banking establishments. Parris thumbed through the folder until he found Moon's employment application. The paper was yellowed and cracked around the edges. Five years at Fort Lewis College. But wait. Under the blank for Aliases and Other Names Used, someone had penciled in a few letters. A Ute word? Maybe two Ute words. He felt eyes on the back of his neck and glanced over his shoulder. Nancy Beyal had returned. "Can I help with anything?"

"Yeah. Any notion what this is?" He pointed at the penciled phrase.

She frowned at the entry. "Must be Charlie's Indian name. I'm surprised it's in his file. Mostly, Indian names are kind of private."

"You know what it means?"

"Hmmm. *Ka-Nawaa-vi.* My Ute is a little rusty, but I think it means something like 'Leaves No Tracks.' "

Parris smiled. The thought of the oversized Ute walking without making tracks was comic. "Leaves No Food," he said, "would be more appropriate."

Charlie Moon and Scott Parris arrived at Angel's Diner to discover Homer Tonompicket sitting in a corner booth, issuing a fishing license to a tourist. The pale, sunburned man's mouth hung open; his shifting eyes revealed his anxiety. "Whaddaya mean, *mink* trout?"

Homer repeated his instructions with the patience of his calling. "You can take rainbows and native browns," the game warden said evenly, "also cutthroat and greenback cutthroat, brook and brook stickleback. Creel limit and size is right here on these papers. No limit on catfish or carp or suckers. But," he assumed a frown that rolled up thick wrinkles above his brows, "no mink trout. There's a big fine if you take one." Homer was unaware that Moon stood behind him. "But I guess it's not likely *you'd* hook one. They're kinda rare." The game warden turned his attention to his breakfast and pointedly ignored the greenhorn.

The fisherman hesitated, then nibbled at the bait. "Rare, are they?"

"Mink trout," Homer said matter-of-factly, "they been on the endangered list since nineteen and seventy-five." He poured a blue packet of sweetener into his coffee. "Local breed," he added proudly.

Moon went to the counter and told Angel what he wanted for lunch; Parris stood behind the game warden and watched Tonompicket's performance.

"Why," the fisherman asked suspiciously, "do they call 'em mink trout?"

"Fur," Tonompicket said with the mild annoyance of one who must explain the obvious to an ignoramus. "Mink trout has fur."

The tourist was wide-eyed with astonishment. "Fur? You really mean . . . like hairs?"

This guy wasn't born yesterday. Maybe day before. "Well," Tonompicket said patiently, "it's more like"—he paused and looked up at the barest hint of a future beard on the young man's chin—". . . kind of a short fuzz. Like on a peach." He shoved a forkful of scrambled eggs into his mouth. "It's what you call a 'daptation. Their coat gets heavy in winter when the streams gets iced up. Them eensy little hairs trap air bubbles; for insulation." He leaned back, triumphant in his lucid explanation of this wonderful natural phenomenon.

The tourist shook his head. "Well that's just about the damnedest thing I ever heard of."

"Last time we did a survey," Homer spread a gob of strawberry jam on his sopaipilla, "State Game Department estimated less than four hundred minks left in the Animas, no more'n a couple of dozen in the Piedra. I haven't had report of any in the Piños in a real long spell." He took a bite of toast, then turned his gaze back to the confused tourist. "Not likely you'll see hide nor hair of one. But if you do," Tonompicket shook his fork in a stern gesture, "you'd best throw it back. There's a whoppin' big fine if you keep a mink. Back in eighty-three, a federal judge up in Denver fined a preacher from Salt Lake fifteen hundred dollars, and gave him thirty-four days in jail."

The tourist, who was a notary public, had no sympathy with those who trifled with the law. "Well, it was his own fault. Any damn fool ought to be able to recognize a fish with hair on it."

"Not necessarily," Homer said in a cautionary tone. "In the summer, mink trout sheds most all of their fur. They gets their thick coat back come cold weather. Between the end of May and, say, middle of October, an inexperienced fisherman," he looked pointedly at the stranger, "can mistake a mink for a native brown. Don't matter none to the law, though. Ignorance," Homer Tonompicket said firmly as he banged his cup on the table to attract Angel's attention, "ain't no excuse."

The tourist wandered off, shaking his head. Might be better to go rent a boat down on the San Juan. The guides there would know one of those minks if a fellow hooked into it. Fishing was getting to be a damn lot of bother.

Moon leaned over the game warden's shoulder. "Good morning, Homer."

"Why hello, Charlie." He nodded amiably at Parris. "Why don't you fellows take a load off."

"Nice to see you're taking good care of our visitors," Moon said.

"Have to. Tourism is the tribe's number one industry." The tribal leaders had long since given up hope of convincing Tonompicket that baiting tourists was counterproductive and unprofessional; having fun with the greenhorns was one of the few forms of entertainment that Homer Tonompicket still enjoyed. The game warden yelled at Angel, who promptly filled his coffee cup. He stirred his fresh coffee, then looked across the table at Moon. "Almost forgot to tell you. I just locked my nephew up in your jailhouse."

Moon helped himself to a sopaipilla on Homer's plate. He opened it with a spoon handle, and squirted honey from a sticky plastic bottle into the hollow pastry. "Which nephew?" Homer had an excess supply of nephews. Angel put a plate in front of Moon.

Homer watched Moon eat the sopaipilla, and licked his lips. "JoJo."

"JoJo? What'd he do?" Moon winked at Parris. "Take a mink trout?"

"He knows better'n that," the game warden said without smiling. "I think he was poachin' for deer. Over on Three Sisters Mesa."

"You *think* he was poachin' deer?" Moon renewed his interest in a greasy forkful of *chile verde*. "You got any evidence that'll stand up before the magistrate?"

Homer had a faraway look. "Caught him runnin' down the highway last night with his carbine."

"Lucky you were there." Homer had an uncanny knack of showing up exactly where he was needed. Except when Rolling Thunder disappeared. "JoJo have a deer carcass on his person?"

"Nope. But I hauled him in anyway, put him in your clink. Thought you'd want to hear his story before we cut him loose."

Moon pushed his plate aside. "You holding out on me, Homer?"

"It'd be best," the game warden said, "if you hear what JoJo has to say for yourself."

JoJo Tonompicket was hunched forward on the cell bench, his face in his hands. He didn't respond when Moon entered the dimly lit chamber; JoJo was whispering something that the lawmen couldn't quite hear, except for a brief phrase that sounded like ". . . forgive me Father for I have sinned. . . ." Parris waited outside the cell, hoping the prisoner wouldn't notice his presence.

Moon clamped a big hand on the young man's shoulder. "What's cookin', JoJo? How come you're taking up space in my jailhouse?"

The youth took no notice of the policeman's presence.

"May have to charge you rent; this is one of my choice efficiency apartments." Moon sat down beside JoJo; the chains supporting the bench groaned. "Goes for fifteen bucks a day. Ten if you eat the food."

The young man looked up through moist, bloodshot eyes. "Dammit, Charlie, you're goin' to break this bench and then we'll both fall on our ass." JoJo suddenly remembered his situation. "But I guess it don't make no difference nohow. I'm goin' to die."

Moon nodded at this logic. "Uh-huh. When do you expect this to happen?"

"Soon. Prob'ly at midnight." Bad things always happened at midnight.

He frowned at the prisoner. "You sick?"

"My soul," the young man said with a theatrical air, "has gone to the Place of the Dead. All I am now is a body. An empty shell with no soul." JoJo hugged his knees; he rocked back and forth, groaning.

Moon spoke matter-of-factly, as if they were discussing a lost puppy. "When was the last time your soul was with you, JoJo?"

"When I was hunting deer. Up by the Three Sisters."

"The way I figure it," Moon said, "taking a deer outta season, that'll get you thirty days and, if you back-talk your uncle Homer, he takes your rifle." He paused. "It don't cost you your soul."

JoJo shuddered as he recalled the apparition. "This ain't about no damn deer."

"We'll let you walk on that charge, long as you promise not to harvest any more of the People's animals out of season. Now tell me what happened to you on the mesa last night."

JoJo rocked back and forth, moaning pitifully.

"You want some breakfast? Got some glazed doughnuts. I could get you some black coffee."

JoJo paused between moans. "Not the kind of coffee you serve in this rattrap."

Moon smiled. JoJo's soul was alive and kicking. "Tell me about last night."

"It won't help none, I'm gonna die. A man without a soul can't live."

"Well, it'll help us police do our job," Moon said. "You tell me about it, I'll make sure it don't happen to anybody else. Your brothers, they hunt up there by the Three Sisters. You wouldn't want one of your family to have the same problem, now would you?"

JoJo thought about this. "No." He rubbed his eyes with the back of a grimy hand. "I guess not."

"Then tell me. You do the right thing, I'll lay you five to one your soul will come back."

The young man breathed deeply to steady his nerves. "It was before daylight. I heard this awful screeching sound, like a wail. . . . I crawled over to the edge and looked down into Snake Canyon, and there it was, dancing around this fire, making them awful noises." JoJo shuddered.

"What was it?" Moon asked gently.

"It was all hairy, with a tail. And . . ."—he laid a finger beside each temple to illustrate his nightmare—"it had horns."

Moon suddenly felt as if his blood had turned to ice. He spoke softly. "Horns?"

"It was *Kwasigeti*," JoJo said with trembling lips, "I saw the Devil dancing." He turned to look at the policeman. "And you know what else?"

"What else, JoJo?"

"The Devil . . . he only had one eye."

"One eye?" Moon felt the hair stand up on the back of his neck. This was getting to be an interesting devil.

JoJo returned to his fetal position, hugging his knees. "One eye. And it was red. Like a big coal of fire straight from hell!"

Moon wouldn't look at Parris after he locked the cell door. "You hear that?"

"I heard. Is this kid reliable?"

"He's all right," Moon said. "Drinks a little now and then, but JoJo don't generally lie."

"Where's this Snake Canyon?"

"Just on the other side of Three Sisters Mesa from *Cañon del Espiritu*."

"Near where the bull was mutilated? And Mr. Nightbird was . . ."

"Just over the mesa."

Parris's hands felt oddly numb; he flexed his fingers to encourage circulation. "You figure this kid saw our bull mutilator?"

"Most likely." Or something.

"Well," Parris said, "five'll get you ten, he also saw the fellow who found Mr. Nightbird after Benita Sweetwater left him. And took the opportunity to clip his ears and family jewels."

The Ute's nightmare danced once more before his face. A helpless, naked figure—hanging upside down in a tree. A horned beast with blood dripping from its lips . . . slowly dismembering its human victim. Screams. He turned away and suppressed a shudder. Moon tried to smile but the effort hurt his face. "Funny thing, though . . . the kid thinks he saw the Devil."

"I don't expect," Parris said, "he saw *the* Devil. But who knows," the *matukach* policeman continued with a thoughtful expression, "maybe the kid saw one of ol' Scratch's pardners." Like Cain.

21

Parris shaded his eyes; he looked up at the steep rim of *Cañon del Espiritu* and the squat, brooding profiles of the Three Sisters on the mesa top. "It's a while before dark," he said uneasily. "Why don't we drive into Snake Canyon, wait for it . . . somebody to show up. Sure would beat climbing this mountain."

"No way to drive the Blazer into Snake Canyon," Moon said, "just a deer trail along the stream bed. Besides, whatever . . . ahhh . . . whoever JoJo saw, maybe they're holed up in the canyon. Might be watching the entrance." The Ute scanned the mesa rim. "We'll get up on top where we can see into the canyon. If we spot the hairy fellow with the horns and tail, then we move in real quiet like and . . ." His voice trailed off uncertainly, as if he wasn't sure what proper police procedure might be when an officer encountered the Dancing Devil.

Parris shrugged. "It's your territory."

Moon set the squelch control on his portable transceiver and held the instrument by the side of his head. "Base? This is mobile three. You read me base?" There was an unintelligible response, lost in a sea of crackling static. "This little radio is about as useful as a boat anchor, down here in the canyon. But it should work all right, once we get on the mesa top." The big Ute hitched up his backpack and pointed toward a narrow trail that snaked along the wall of *Cañon del Espiritu.* "We'll go up there; that's the trail JoJo used."

"It's Jake with me," Parris said. He couldn't see the trail Moon had in mind.

"Only thing," the Ute policeman said, "watch your step."

"It's steep then?"

"One little slip," Moon said softly, "and all your worries are over."

Parris grinned. This would probably be a cake walk. It was not. Halfway up, he felt a coldness creeping over his limbs as he leaned against the sandstone wall, wishing that some freakish mutation had provided his fingertips with suction cups. The crumbling trail, at some points, was barely wider than his boot. Moon, despite his great bulk, seemed at ease on the narrow path. When they finally climbed over the rim between two of the massive rock formations that were the Sisters, a cold sweat was dripping from Parris's forehead, but it was not the honest sweat of exertion. He leaned against a house-sized sandstone boulder and breathed deeply of the crisp breeze that swept over the mesa top.

Moon pressed the TRANSMIT button on his radio. "Base. This is mobile three. You read me?"

Nancy Beyal's voice crackled back over the squelch. "Loud and clear, Charlie. Where are you?"

"Sittin' in the Three Sisters' laps. I'll check in again, in"—he glanced at his wristwatch—"sometime after midnight."

"Understand."

Moon dropped the transceiver into his backpack.

Parris studied the huge trio of misshapen, wind-chiseled monoliths of sandstone. Posted on the mesa top forever . . . like eternal sentries. "How come they call them the Three Sisters? Could as well be Three Dogs. Three Frogs. Three anything."

"From what I've heard," Moon said, "back in the sixteen-hundreds, three Pueblo women, they were sisters, slipped up here to hide from the 'Paches during a raid. The 'Paches killed all the men, stole the women and children and the corn. But before they headed back south," he nodded toward the New Mexico border, "one of their young men spotted the three Pueblo women. He slipped way from the war party and climbed up here after 'em. Now being caught by a 'Pache brave, that was plenty bad news for these Pueblo sisters.

"So what happened?"

Moon leaned against a gnarled piñon and folded his arms. "The women, they prayed to Sina-wa-vi."

"To who?"

"Sina-wa-vi," Moon repeated, enunciating each syllable. "Sina-wa-vi is a major spirit; the old people thought he lived up in the sky. Anyway, these women, they asked him to spare them from the

'Pache. Sina-wa-vi, he must have heard them, at least that's what the People say."

"So the prayers were answered?"

"Bet your horse and saddle, pardner. Sina-wa-vi, he sent three big bolts of lightning outta the sky"—Moon pointed a finger toward heaven—"and turned them sisters all into stone, quick as a wink. The 'Paches, all except the young man who climbed the mesa, they all ran away, hell for leather, whoopin' and hollerin' and they never did come back. To this very day," Moon added darkly, "no 'Pache will set foot within a mile of the Three Sisters."

Parris knew he was being had, but dutifully fulfilled his role as gullible outsider. "What became of the lone Apache warrior who climbed the mesa?"

Moon's face registered surprise. "Didn't I tell you? Well, it wasn't like he didn't try to make tracks, but Sina-wa-vi, he pitched down another bolt of lightning, turned that 'Pache into stone. Not nearly so big a chunk as them three sisters, but stone just the same. You're leaning right on him," Moon added.

Parris moved away from the giant boulder. "That's some tall story. Ten to one, you made it up in the past two minutes."

"Glad you liked it, pardner." The hint of a mischievous smile that flickered over Moon's face was swallowed up by the twilight that slipped over the flat top of the mesa.

Daisy Perika lit three tiny, pink birthday candles before a plaster likeness of St. Francis; the Italian monk had a tiny bluebird perched on his wrist. She closed her eyes and clasped her hands in the Roman Catholic manner. To the shaman who communed with the *pitukupf*, there was no contradiction in this act of supplication. Even the dwarf knew the power of the Word that had become flesh; as long as the little man got his occasional offering of cigarettes and trinkets, he cared little about Daisy's spiritual activities. The dwarf could be vindictive, even dangerous, but he was no fool. The *pitukupf* knew his place.

"Oh Little Brother who loves the animals," she muttered, "ask our Lord to protect those dumb creatures out there in the storm." She opened one eye and focused on the Saint to see if he was paying attention. Satisfied, she closed her eyes again. "Protect my overgrown bone-headed nephew and his ignorant *matukach* friend from the arrow of fire that pierces the clouds . . . from the foul-smelling horned beast who dances in the night . . . and," she added with special urgency, "from the dark shadow that passes over us!"

The shaman opened one eye again; she was certain that St. Francis had smiled.

There was a stirring. In a small arroyo at the bottom of the Canyon of the Snake. Under a pile of freshly cut piñon branches. Very slight, the movement was . . . subtle enough to go unnoticed by the natural creatures who lived in this place. The presence shifted its weight with an innocuous sound, much like the creaking of an old pine bending before the wind. Then, there was an audible groan . . . an awakening of a malevolent consciousness. A consciousness of overwhelming desire. Overwhelming hunger. And thirst.

Moon crawled to the edge of a sandstone outcropping. The Ute removed his hat, pulled a pair of binoculars from his backpack, and scanned the floor of Snake Canyon. Parris appeared at his side. "Don't see anything on the bottom of the canyon, nothing on the far wall," Moon said. "The kiva ruins look pretty empty."

Parris tried to see through the shadows enveloping the canyon floor. "Looks awfully still."

"Can't see much of the wall on this side," Moon said. "Somebody could be holed up in one of the caves the old people made."

"What do you think?"

"I think," the Ute said, "we wait." He winked at Parris. "From what I hear, these hairy horned devils with tails . . . they only dance late at night." Moon scooted away from the edge of the precipice. He fumbled in his backpack until he found two ham sandwiches. He pitched one to his pardner.

"I guess it's going to be a long night," Parris said as he tried unsuccessfully to see the expression on Moon's face. His hand kept moving toward the comfort of the .38 Smith & Wesson revolver strapped under his armpit. He hoped the Ute didn't notice.

"Yeah," Moon said. He was watching heavy clouds draped over the San Juans. A gray anvil writhed and hung its beak over Three Sisters Mesa. "I sure hope it don't rain."

Immediately after Moon uttered these words, Parris felt the hair on his head tingle, as if it were standing on end. Evidence of high electric fields between the cloud and the mesa top? He dismissed it as a case of the jitters. Then, there was a booming explosion. A skinny finger of lightning materialized between the cloud-anvil and the sandstone Apache warrior, chipping a watermelon-sized chunk of sandstone off the formation. The concussion was like a charge of dynamite; Parris found himself on the ground, his face pressed into a pungent carpet of fresh piñon needles. He got to his knees and tried to speak, but his lungs were gasping for breath.

Moon, who had been blown onto his back, looked toward the anvil and grunted. "Looks like Sina-wa-vi ain't done with that no-account 'Pache yet." He coughed and rubbed the back of his neck. "I expect we ought to get off this mesa top."

Parris pushed his trembling hands into his coat pockets. "Works for me."

"There's an old cave just over the edge of the cliff on the Snake Canyon side."

Parris was on his feet, dusting himself off. The pungent scent of ozone permeated the atmosphere. . . . A promise of more lightning strikes? "What're we waiting for?" Better to face the Dancing Devil than to be skewered by a bolt hurled by Sina-wa-vi!

As they crawled into the shallow cave, a light shower was splattering the dust outside the shelter with heavy drops. The "cave" was man-made, the back room of a pueblo cliff dwelling that had long since tumbled into Snake Canyon. The room was beehive-shaped, the domed ceiling not quite high enough to allow Moon to stand upright. Their boots made deep tracks in the dust of ages. The Ute lit a match and cupped it with his hand to hide the flickering light from anyone on the canyon floor. The walls had once been plastered with clay, but this was now cracked and falling off in sheets. Figures of strange animals had been scratched into the black soot that coated the plaster. There were crude representations of four-legged and odd two-legged creatures that might have been birds. One of the two-legged creatures appeared to have be malformed; the hunchbacked creature was playing a flute.

Moon dropped his pack and sat with his back against the wall of the small cavern. He pulled his hat brim over his eyes.

Parris sat down by the small entrance and peered through the mist into the sinuous form of Snake Canyon. "Maybe this devil only comes out once a month. On a full moon."

"The moon," the Ute said, "wasn't full when JoJo saw whatever he saw."

"If he's here already, maybe he saw us come over the cliff to this hole in the wall."

"Might as well relax," Moon said. Why was it so hard for Whites to accept silence? They had to fill it with words.

Parris blinked at the three kivas; the larger one had been restored and was less than a hundred yards from their shelter in the canyon wall. "I think this is a snipe hunt," He turned his head to see how Moon would react to this challenge. His friend was breathing slowly, very evenly. The Ute was asleep. Parris yawned and leaned against the sooty plaster. He listened to the sounds of Snake Canyon. Crickets conducting a great synchronous chorus. An owl hooted. A coyote cried mournfully for something that was far away. The wind made soothing whispers through the tall ponderosa that dotted the canyon floor. Cottonwood leaves rattled like chattering teeth. The canyon sung a haunting, rhythmic song of life . . . and death. Parris shuddered. It would be a long time before morning.

A saw-whet owl perched motionless on a snag in the lifeless top of a lightning-scarred Douglas fir. This feathered descendent of the dinosaurs absorbed the scene reproduced on its high-resolution retinas, waiting for a movement that would be translated into its perception of "mouse" or "lizard." There was a slight rippling movement inside the circle of stones where the small bird often snatched tasty treats of blood-warm pocket gopher or, after the rainy season, squirming tiger salamander . . . but this was odd. The owl swiveled its head a half-turn around, and back again, and blinked quizzically; it had never seen such a peculiar sight!

Scott Parris, his back arched uncomfortably against the sandstone entrance to the Pueblo back-room, was lost in a dream. He was walking with his wife, along Jackson Park Beach. Helen was on his left arm, the great glacier-scraped lake on his right, the harsh wind blowing the pungent scent of Lake Michigan across the park into Chicago's bleak streets. Helen was wearing a fluffy white dress that whipped in the gusts like crepe paper. Helen? But Helen was dead! His wife had died in Canada almost three years ago. He turned to look at her face. She was pouting, disappointed that he had remembered her departure. Now, the spell was broken, the magic dissipated. She dropped her hand from his arm and turned . . . the white dress vanished into the great forest. He followed, attempting to shout her name. No sound came from his mouth. He found himself inside this thicket of great elms and maple, standing in the edge of a small, circular clearing where the grass was freshly mowed. A small, twisted tree was rooted in the bull's-eye of the lawn. As he watched, a misty darkness drifted over the clearing. Now an undulating shadow moved in the shelter of the tree. There was the unmistakable flapping of great wings as a huge, dark bird erupted from the branches. The creature's wings became rigid; the bird soared upward, then fell directly toward him. He saw curved, yellow talons, and the talons were dripping with a scarlet liquid. He could smell the blood!

Parris awakened with a convulsive shudder. It was a long moment before he realized where he was—before he convinced himself that this was not a continuation of his nightmare. But something was different. He could hear himself breathe, even feel his heart thumping under his ribs. But he could hear nothing else. Nothing! The canyon was totally silent. Not a cricket chirped; owl and coyote were dumb as the Three Sisters of stone. Even the wind had fallen silent. Silver moonlight flooded into the gaping mouth of the archaic dwelling on the canyon wall. He could see every stone and twig on the dusty floor. The hands on his wristwatch revealed that he had slept into the small hours of morning. Impossible! But there was the moon, an apricot crescent suspended high over the opposite mesa.

He turned to see if Charlie Moon still slept, but the Ute was not there. "How did you get out without stepping on me," he muttered. In the stark moonlight illumination of the cave floor, he could see Charlie Moon's footprints. But only the footprints where Moon had entered. . . . There were no footprints leaving the dusty room.

22

Scott Parris tried to ward off the growing sense of unreality; he rubbed his eyes and strained to clear his mind of the fuzz of sleep. Was Moon now stalking the mutilator?

At the foot of the talus slope, a lone oak stood still as a tombstone even as its shadow waltzed in the moonlight. In this place, a man could easily believe that the sensible laws of nature had been supplanted by foul sorceries older than the earth itself. The deep silence was pregnant with an awful tension, as if every creature in Snake Canyon was waiting expectantly . . . for some unimaginable event. But there were dozens of reasons why the crickets would become silent. Several explanations of why the coyote and owl would slip away . . . and it was not uncommon for the wind to fall still. "No," Parris whispered aloud, "got to get my brain working."

The lawman stepped outside the small cavern and attempted to rub the stiffness from his back. He scanned the moonlit canyon floor. There . . . not far away. Something moved; he was certain. Near the large, central kiva. So. Moon was having a look at the canyon floor on his own. Maybe the Ute thought it best to leave the *matukach* policeman slumbering in the cave. Keep the city boy out of harm's way. No way was Moon going to taunt him for hiding in the cave while the Ute searched alone for the mutilator of bulls and men! He carefully made his way down the talus slope toward the ruined kiva, the crunching sound of every footstep seemed to violate the austere stillness of the canyon.

Parris had no idea that this was the beginning of an adventure that would become legendary among the Utes. A wild tale to be told, embellished, and retold by old men long after sundown as they puffed on their pipes.

Daisy Perika sat bolt upright in her small bed. The aged bowlegged man, his head and shoulders outlined by a bright light that did not hurt her eyes, was sitting on the small cedar chest not five feet away. As always, he was the soul of patience.

When she tried to speak, she barely found the breath. It must be a dream. "Nahum! Nahum Yaciiti! Is it you?"

He nodded and smiled. Everybody asked the same question.

"Are you dead?"

He looked thoughtfully at his hands, flexing his thin fingers. "Don't seem to be."

Daisy crossed herself. "When the big wind came, Armilda Esquibel, she said you were killed. Said you were carried away. By *angels*," she added doubtfully.

The old shepherd did not reply.

She pulled the old quilt around her shoulders. "Why are you here?"

"To talk."

"Talk . . . ?"

"About Charlie Moon. And his *matukach* friend."

The shaman was not surprised; Nahum had always known what was on her mind. "I'm worried about those two, out there in Snake Canyon. Between the both of them, they ain't got a teaspoon full of common sense. I've got this bad feeling they'll get in a shoot-out with . . ."

"The one they search for," the old man said firmly, "has no fear of bullets."

"Then," Daisy insisted, her fingers gripping the cotton quilt, "you've got to do something." Somehow, this old man always knew exactly what needed to be done. And did it. The old shepherd's eyes were filled with a strange melancholy that she had not seen before.

"Tonight in *Cañon del Serpiente* . . . one will bleed, another shall weep." He bowed his head. "Blood," Nahum sighed, "will be salted with tears."

Now Parris could see nothing that moved and he began to have doubts. Had the earlier sighting been a mistake? Or had Moon dropped into the kiva? There was absolutely no sound, not a breath of air whispered in the Canyon of the Snake.

He did not see the presence behind him, nor did he hear it. He *felt* it. Scott Parris was suddenly overwhelmed with the dread of a small boy who imagines a monster lurking under his bed, and wants to hide under the covers. But he was not a small boy. And there was nothing to cover himself with. As he turned, the policeman slipped the Smith & Wesson revolver from the holster under his left arm.

At first, he saw only a vague darkness. As he examined it, his mind searched the apparition and gave it shape. Broad shoulders. Hairy. Enormous head. The head had horns. And a single red ember that glowed brightly, then dimmed. A cyclops. Parris felt his breath coming in short gasps; the revolver was ice in his hand. "What is it," he muttered, "what in Hell . . ."

Something like arms . . . or wings, spread outward from the shadowy form. It was an almost graceful gesture . . . an invitation.

The policeman took a step backward, aiming the revolver at the center of the shadowy form. "It's not real," he whispered. But this was wishful thinking.

The shadow's arm-wings were lifted higher; the amorphous form now had the appearance of a great bird of prey. The creature was waving something . . . a great scepter?

It did not occur to the policeman to give a warning. Such formality has no place when you met the Devil. He pulled the trigger. The hammer fell on an empty cylinder. He remembered cleaning the gun; the bullets were still in his pocket! The shadow grew to blot out the night sky as it moved toward him. Silently, almost unconsciously, he prayed. *God protect me from the nameless terror. . . .*

Parris heard a familiar voice behind him. "What's cookin', pardner?"

23

Parris glanced over his shoulder at Charlie Moon. "Look out, Charlie, I've got it cornered!"

Moon's fingers found the bone grips of his .357 Magnum. "Got what cornered?"

Parris motioned with his empty revolver. "There." But it was gone. Now the crickets chirped. Somewhere on a perch in the canyon wall, an owl hooted.

Reluctantly, Parris holstered the .38. "You didn't see him? Big bastard, shoulders out to here." He held his arms wide, like a lying fisherman. "Seven, maybe eight feet tall. And," Parris's voice dropped almost to a whisper, ". . . horns. One big red eye." He began to tremble; he hoped Charlie Moon wouldn't notice.

The Ute policeman cocked his head quizzically. "Horns? One eye?" Moon's features were concealed by shadow.

Parris suspected that Charlie was smiling.

The Ute was not smiling.

"Horns," Parris said stubbornly. "And one red eye."

Moon's silence was response enough for his partner.

"Horns," Parris repeated. "The Tonompicket kid must have seen the same thing. No wonder he thought he'd seen the Devil dancing."

"Well," Moon said, "seems like the awful sight made you pucker your rectum a little bit too."

Parris grinned. "Lucky thing it did, or I'd be needing some clean underwear."

"Sit tight, pardner." Moon turned away. "I'll have a look around."

"Wait a minute—" But his friend had vanished, enveloped by the shadows. Parris cursed silently at the stubborn Ute. And at his own wobbly legs. He blinked at the Three Sisters to get his bearings. The restored kiva was only yards to his right; that was a good place to start looking. Caring nothing now about stealth, Parris stomped through the sage toward the edge of the ruined structure, tripping over a small boulder, brushing aside a juniper branch. There it was. He blinked into the depths of the circular structure. Nothing there. At least nothing that a man could see. But there was a sound. Behind him. A slow, rhythmic sound. Sounds of feet that danced. He reached for his revolver, then remembered the empty chambers. He pushed his hand into his pocket, frantically searching for the five thirty-eight cartridges among the tangle of coins and keys. His fingers had located two hollow-points when the figure appeared, barely two paces away. It didn't look nearly so large this time. There was no red eye. This was a man with matted, unkempt hair decorated with a pair of feathers tucked under a headband. But only a man. Something he could deal with. Parris leveled the empty .38 at the figure. "Don't you move a whisker!"

"I am . . . come to dance," the man muttered as he raised his left leg, balancing himself on the ball of his foot. He began, very deliberately, to execute a simple running-in-place step. His grunting chant sounded vaguely like something Parris had heard at a Ute Buffalo Dance.

He was about to call for Moon when the dancing man reeled drunkenly. He stumbled into Parris, instinctively grabbing the policeman's wrist for support. As the .38 went flying from his grasp, Parris attempted a hammer lock. The dancing man struggled and broke free. Parris threw his weight onto the smaller man; they tumbled over a clump of bitterbrush. He landed squarely on top of the wriggling figure, whose head made a popping sound as it landed on a flat stone. The man's body went limp, as if a circuit in his brain had been interrupted. Parris put a finger under the man's jaw; there was a strong pulse.

When Moon appeared, Parris was standing triumphantly over his quarry. "Got the sneaky bastard this time."

"You must've hit him pretty hard," Moon said. "Is he alive?"

"He's alive. And he hit his head on a rock."

The Ute switched a penlight beam onto the unconscious man's face, a pale mask with three red chevrons painted on each cheek. Moon squatted; he touched a white feather. "Looks like he plucked a chicken's wing," he said with a wide grin. "I guess these hen feathers looked like horns."

Parris bristled. "Look, Charlie, nobody likes a smart-ass. . . ."

"Hey, pardner, if you're scared of chicken feathers, it's okay by me. Maybe," he said with exaggerated gentleness, "when your momma was carryin' you, she got spooked by a rooster." Moon leaned close to examine the man's face. "You know who this is?"

Parris leaned over to look. "That poet who sells insurance? Sure . . . the hustler who conned me into that sucker memory bet."

"Right on both counts," Moon said. "Herb Ecker." He lifted the unconscious man's eyelid. "Pupils size of dimes. Kid's high on something." He directed the penlight beam onto a leather pouch strapped to Ecker's belt loop, then pulled a razor-sharp Buck knife from a beaded leather sheath. "Suppose he intended to use this blade on you?"

"Didn't notice he had a knife," Parris muttered. This had not been a textbook example of recommended police procedure. Parris got to his feet. "So. Looks like this kid's our ball-cutter. Maybe the blade's got Nightbird's blood on it."

The Ute turned to grin at Scott Parris. "Looks like you handled him pretty well in the second round. Of course, you got about thirty pounds and a foot reach on this kid."

"I didn't hit him," Parris said with a rueful grin, "but I must admit he looked a helluva lot bigger . . . when he showed up the first time."

"Well," Moon said soothingly, "guess I'd be scared too if I met up with someone decked out in war paint and chicken feathers." He paused thoughtfully. "If it was in the dark. And if I was a white man." He cleared his throat. "From the big city."

Parris was about to reply when he heard a low moan. Ecker was on one knee, then crawling on all fours toward the edge of the kiva. Before the lawmen could react, he disappeared over the edge into the near-darkness below.

Parris sprinted forward. "I'll handle this. He's my prisoner."

"Go to it," Moon said, "but take it easy this time, don't hit him so hard. You can't use that story about him falling on a rock more'n once."

Parris slipped over the edge of the kiva. Ecker, still on all fours, scurried sideways across the subterranean floor in crablike fashion, then turned to face his pursuers. Moon, standing above them at ground level, directed the flashlight into Ecker's face. The young man had a wild, terrified look in his eyes. He also had a snub-nose revolver in his hand. Ecker pointed the pistol toward Moon's flashlight.

"Now, Herbie," Moon said calmly, "it's me. Charlie. Put the gun down." Moon slowly withdrew his own revolver from its rawhide holster.

"No problem," Parris said, "I can handle this . . ."

Ecker, hearing the voice, turned the .38 toward Parris.

The Ute raised his heavy revolver and aimed it toward the crouching man. "Drop it—right now!"

Ecker muttered incoherently; Moon saw the muscles in Ecker's arm grow taut as his finger squeezed the trigger. Parris screamed at Moon: "No, don't shoot . . . it's not—" There was a booming report from Moon's revolver. Ecker's body slammed against the crumbling kiva wall. ". . . it's not . . . loaded," Parris whispered.

They kneeled over the pale body, now painted with streams of warm blood that appeared jet black in the harsh, silver moonlight. "Damn," Moon said, "where'd he get the gun!" The Ute was trembling.

"It's mine," Parris admitted.

"He was gonna *shoot* you," Moon said in a stunned whisper, as if the very idea of anyone shooting his pardner was unthinkable.

"I know," Parris said. He put his hand on Moon's shoulder. "Thanks, Charlie."

The Ute policeman shook his head mournfully. He looked at Parris with moist eyes. "I never shot anyone while I've worn this badge."

"You had no choice," Parris said. "You saved my hide, pardner." It was an absolutely necessary lie.

Moon stood up and swallowed hard several times before he could speak. "I'll climb back to the mesa top and radio for some help."

"Sure," Parris said blankly, "I'll stay with him." Now he knew the soul loss JoJo Tonompicket had felt. Hollow inside. His spirit was gone.

A heavy cloud slipped over the canyon, but it did not block the pale amber light of the moon that now hovered low in the west. A new storm was rumbling over the San Juans. Moon turned away. "At least, it's all over now." The Ute's words were punctuated with a flash of lightning, then a sharp crack of thunder that echoed off the sandstone cliffs. He disappeared over the kiva wall and was swallowed up by the night.

Parris knew better. It was never over.

Herb Ecker rolled his eyes and coughed. A foam of blood erupted in pulsating gushes from the chest wound where a splintered rib protruded from his flesh. The young man's eyes had lost their glaze. Ecker, now perfectly lucid, whispered. Parris leaned over to listen. "What is it, kid?"

"I am . . . dying."

"I know." Parris pressed his handkerchief against Ecker's chest in a futile attempt to staunch the flow of blood. The warm liquid had a sickening, sweet aroma; the policeman fought an urge to vomit.

Ecker grimaced with pain. He cried out sharply: "I came to dance . . ." He sucked in a lungful of air that immediately bubbled out his chest wound. ". . . to dance with"—Ecker gasped for air—". . . a shadow . . . dance . . . and then there came a shadow, swift and sullen, dark and drear—"

Parris tried to speak. There were no words.

The pitiful youth grasped at the policeman's sleeve, his eyes full of terror. "I am going away to . . . I do not know . . . Oh God . . . do not forget me." Ecker's jaw dropped as a final breath rattled in his punctured lung. His face was a cold mask, his eyes like stones.

Scott Parris wanted, above all else, to flee from this awful place. To hide. And forget. But there was one last task that must be done. The lawman worked the empty revolver free from Herb Ecker's death grasp. He filled the chambers with cartridges from his pocket. As he returned the weapon to Ecker's cold hand, the policeman shivered. But not from the frigid rain that had begun to fall in great sheets. He stared helplessly at the lifeless face. The death of this foolish young man was his responsibility. No. Worse than that. His *fault*. The lawman, on his knees, wept. His tears dropped onto Ecker's chest, mixing with the poet's blood.

The horned figure stood on a sandstone ledge jutting out from Paiute Mesa, across *Cañon del Serpiente* from the squat, brooding forms of the Three Sisters. Filled with a consuming hate, the hairy form shook a heavy staff at the dark heavens and mouthed obscene curses that were immediately covered by the cleansing rumble of thunder. For this small Man of the Book, the horned one had made his own plans for a painful death . . . and ritual mutilation. And, he licked his lips, delectable cannibalism. Now this precious celebration, this sacred ode to the Dark Angel, was an opportunity forever lost. The large

Man of the Crescent Moon was to have been next. But he would have to wait . . . for a time. With renewed hatred, the strange figure glared downward into the canyon at the tiny figure of Scott Parris. The policeman was foolishly guarding the pale corpse of the poet as if it had some worth. The Kneeling Man lived.

But that could be remedied.

24

FBI FIELD OFFICE, DURANGO

James Hoover searched the glum faces of the lawmen and wondered, What's wrong with this picture? These bumblers get lucky . . . they nail the mutilator. Should be ecstatic. Bragging about their success. Rubbing my nose in it. But they act like their favorite hound dog just croaked. These sneaky bastards are hiding something! But what?

He cleared his throat and tapped the glass top of his desk with the blade of Ecker's Buck knife. Forensics hadn't found any blood on the blade. So Ecker's a neat freak. He cleaned the blade. He coughed lightly to get their attention. "You want to know what I think?"

No response.

"My money says Ecker was responsible for Sweetwater's mutilated bull. And," Hoover added firmly, "for the murder and mutilation of Mr. Arlo Nightbird."

Scott Parris allowed himself a bitter smile.

"Ecker," Hoover continued, "was obviously Mr. JoJo Tonom-picket's dancing demon." He turned toward the Ute. "We've examined the little bag of junk you found on the kid's belt."

Moon spoke softly, as if to himself. "Must have been Ecker's notion of a medicine bag."

Hoover emptied the contents of the leather bag onto his desk. A small ceramic pipe with a sooty bowl. Dried plant leaves wrapped in tissue paper. A half dozen pink quartzite pebbles, a piece of charcoal. He used the blade of the hunting knife to sort the parts. "Pipe bowl had traces of crack. And there were these . . . dried weeds. Snake-weed. Golden banner. Both poisonous. I expect he was smoking this stuff along with the cocaine."

"He was pretty high on something when we found him," Parris said.

"Our psychological wizards," Hoover continued, "analyzed his journal. They diagnose Ecker as a multiple personality. By day, he's a mild-mannered peddler of insurance, scribbler of verse, student of anthropology. After the sun goes down, he expresses his dark side. Occult activities. Strange visions. Weird dances. When the feeling moves him, Ecker carries out a peculiar mission: kill and mutilate the odd animal. This experience whets his appetite for a victim higher on the food chain. Finally, he has his opportunity when Mrs. Nightbird phones and tells him that her husband is late getting home. Ecker knows that his boss is on a visit to see Mrs. Perika. He heads for the canyon, catches Nightbird with his pants down. Does the same number on his boss as he did on the bull. Except," Hoover added with a leer, "for adding a slight variation on the theme." Hoover now knew about the testicles that Dr. Simpson had found in Arlo Nightbird's throat. So did every living soul in Ignacio.

"It's a neat theory," Parris said. "But there's no hard evidence to tie this Belgian kid to the mutilation of the Hereford bull, much less to the murder of Arlo Nightbird."

"I wish," Hoover said acidly, "we'd found Mr. Nightbird's ears in Ecker's medicine bag, but things usually don't work out that neatly in the real world of criminal investigation." The special agent spoke slowly, deliberately, as if he was dealing with a slow-witted child. "We've got a kid who howls at the moon, smokes any weed he can get his hands on, wears war paint and feathers, and dances in the woods at midnight. He carries a sharp knife. When he's high, he isn't afraid of anything. Killing and mutilating a bull or," he paused, "cutting up a human being . . . that gives him big medicine." Hoover carefully replaced the items into Ecker's leather bag. "What happened is Tom and Huckleberry got lucky and stumbled over the killer. So," there was menace in his voice, "don't you guys fight me on this."

Charlie Moon was silent, but there was a hint of amusement in his eyes.

Parris understood. If Ecker was guilty of Arlo's mutilation-murder, Gorman Sweetwater was no longer a suspect. Ecker was past caring and Moon didn't want Hoover harassing Gorman. And that was that.

"Off the record," Hoover said to Moon, "I'm glad you blew him away. Saves the government a lot of time and expense." He was pleased to see the Ute's face turn to stone. "Of course it wouldn't have been necessary to shoot the suspect," Hoover said with a pretense of regret, "if Ecker hadn't managed to relieve your sidekick of his revolver. . . ."

Scott Parris opened his mouth, thought better of it, then clamped his jaw shut.

Hoover's jaw ached intermittently. Especially during the small hours when his world was eternally black and empty. And without the comfort of sleep. Scott Parris's heavy fist had left a hairline crack in the bone just below his wisdom tooth. And a deep scar in his psyche. "My written report will reflect the fact," Hoover savored the words, "that Mr. Parris was unable to exercise physical control over the suspect." He stared coldly at his victim. "It takes a young, vigorous man to perform the physical aspects of a lawman's duties." The thorn had been expertly inserted; now it needed a twist. "Maybe you're losing your edge." Then a moment to fester. "But wait—" He slapped a palm on his forehead. "I missed the obvious explanation. You didn't catch Ecker with his arms all tangled up in his coat. Sure. That's it." A sharp pain pulsated in Hoover's jaw. "You didn't have a chance to throw a sucker punch."

"Well . . . maybe you're pretty close to the truth"—Parris's thoughtful frown furrowed his brow—"guess I have kind of lost my edge." He clasped his hands and studied the worn wool carpet with an embarrassed expression. "But I figure it's because I'm out of practice. It's hard to stay frosty when all you deal with is kids and punks." He glanced up at Hoover. And barely smiled. "Problem is . . . I haven't had to fight a real man in more'n a year."

They were halfway to Ignacio when Parris muttered, more to himself than to his friend, "One thing I can't figure."

"Just one thing, pardner?" Moon turned the windshield wipers on.

"I can understand Ecker playing Indian. Chicken feathers in his hair, painting his face, smoking weed in the little pipe. But why'd he want to, want to . . . to castrate the bull. And Mr. Nightbird?"

"Who knows?" Moon shook his head in wonder. White people did some of the *damnedest* things. But he wasn't thinking about Herb Ecker. Someone else was out there. Someone with blood on his hands.

Parris rubbed moisture off the dusty glass with his coat sleeve; he looked through the mists. The crimson sun was settling comfortably onto the downy pillow of cumulus that drifted over Cortez like a great feather. This glowing picture, framed in the window of the Blazer, would vanish in a minute. Now, it was warm . . . soothing. But the autumn snows would not be long in coming. Then, the shrill winds and stinging sleet of December. Deep in the very marrow of his bones, he knew it would be a long, cold winter.

Nancy Beyal's voice crackled over static on the police radio. "Base to car three-thirty-nine. Charlie?"

Moon keyed the mike and held it by his cheek. "What's cookin', Nancy?"

"Had a call from Emily Nightbird. She's at the veterinary hospital; wants Chief Parris to stop by and see her."

Moon braked to a stop in the gravel driveway that led to the rear entrance of Schaid's Veterinary Clinic. He shut off the ignition and glanced at Parris. "I expect she's heard the rumors about Ecker. Wants to know if he killed her husband."

"Yeah," Parris said. "I expect that's it." He wondered why Nightbird's widow had asked for the out-of-town cop. Probably because he was, if only temporarily, the chief of police. The poor feared authority, but the rich and powerful preferred to deal with someone at the top.

Moon studied his friend's face carefully. "I'll go on to the station then. Call in when you're finished; we'll send someone to pick you up."

Parris got out; he paused before he closed the door. "Sure you don't want to come in?"

"Nope," the Ute said. "I've got some calls to make."

The lobby was empty, except for a tiny silver-haired woman with an orange toy poodle curled up in her lap. Emily sat behind her desk, pecking at an IBM computer keyboard; a new name plate on the desk said MS. SOMBRA. With the memory of a husband like Arlo, it was not surprising that the widow now preferred her maiden name.

Parris removed his hat. "I heard you were back at work."

"I've no time for mourning," Emily said. "We're very busy. Dr. Schaid has been advertising a half-price spay-neuter clinic. We're swamped with customers." Emily stored her file, then smiled sweetly. "But how nice of you to drop by so soon!"

This little woman was uncommonly pretty. So delicate. Parris tried to respond, but stumbled over his words. "We . . . Ch—Charlie and me," he began, "we . . . ahhh . . . got a call that you wanted to see me . . . uh . . . somebody from the station."

Emily switched her computer off and got up, pushing a stray wisp of hair over her ear. "I'm so proud of both of you!" She waited with raised eyebrows, but Parris only stared dumbly. "Well, then," she prompted, "don't keep me in suspense."

"You've heard about Herb Ecker . . . ?"

"It's all over Ignacio," she said. "Everybody's saying . . . Herb . . ." her voice grew faint, then died.

He looked at his hands. They were chapped from the dry winds and his nails needed clipping; he felt like a small boy reporting to his teacher. "FBI figures it was Ecker who was responsible for your husband's . . ." But how could you say it?

Sensing his embarrassment, Emily spoke up quickly. "Herb . . . it's really so astonishing." She furrowed her pretty eyebrows in concentration. "You never really know people at all, do you?" She moved close, put her hand on his arm. "I'll want to hear about it, but not right now." The woman with the toy poodle increased the volume control on her hearing aid. She wasn't missing a syllable. "But not here," Emily added.

He understood. Or thought he did. "It'll keep till you're ready."

Emily caressed his forearm. "Drop by my house tonight. About dinner time."

"I had a late lunch," he said, "don't think I could hold much dinner."

"What I had in mind," she whispered in his ear, "was *dessert*."

"You want some coffee pardner?" Moon's casual tone seemed oddly contrived.

Parris exhaled as if he had been holding his breath for an hour. "If it's strong."

"Melts the spoon."

"Sounds like just the ticket."

Moon found a dingy mug. "You tell Emily about Herb Ecker? How he must have cut up her husband and stuffed his—"

"I lack your extraordinary gift for graphic expression, but I think she got the idea."

"Arlo," Moon said as he studied the faraway look on Parris's face, "hasn't been away from her bed all that long, but talk is that Emily's comb is already turning red."

Parris looked up. "Comb?"

"Old barnyard observation," the Ute said. "When a hen is ready for a rooster, her comb turns red."

"Barnyard," Parris sighed, "I should have guessed."

"You want to go get some supper? Angel's got a taco special tonight."

"No," Parris said with a great counterfeit yawn. "Been a long day. Guess I'll turn in early tonight." But perhaps, just perhaps . . . not before dessert.

"Early to bed," Moon said, "good idea for a fellow your age." The Ute looked sideways at the clock on the wall. The telephone rang. Without waiting for Nancy Beyal to perform her duty, Moon yanked the receiver to his ear. "Tribal police." He paused and grinned. "Sure he is, and he'll be tickled pink." He winked at Parris. "It's for you."

He pressed the receiver to his ear. "Parris here."

"Scotty?"

It was *her*. "Anne? Is it really you?" He spilled the coffee on his trousers and didn't notice. "Where are you? About to leave for the airport? You'll be in Denver in . . . no, don't rent a car, I'll be there at . . ."—he glanced at his watch—"about ten-thirty. No. Make that ten."

After listening to her quick good-bye, he dropped the receiver into its cradle and grinned at Moon. "Anne's flying in. All the way from Washington. . . . I can't believe it!"

Moon grinned back. "Imagine that!"

"I'm driving up to Denver. To meet her. You know," he added hesitantly, "Chief Severo's due back in a few days. Maybe you could stand in as acting chief until then."

"I'll see it's taken care of, pardner." Sally Rainwater would make a fine chief of police, acting or otherwise.

Parris shook Moon's big hand. "Thanks."

"You'd better get moving then." Moon assumed a concerned expression. "You want me to give Emily a call, tell her you won't show up?"

Parris was puzzled. "Emily?"

"Emily Nightbird, your late date. You remember; the poor widder woman who has the red comb for you?"

Parris blushed. "How did you know . . . I mean about our . . . my appointment with Em— Mrs. Nightbird?"

Moon winked. "Heard it through the talking drums, pardner." The woman with the orange poodle had called Nancy Beyal.

Nancy left her station at the radio console after Parris was out of sight; she touched Moon's elbow. "Scott'll be pretty upset if he finds out you called Miss Foster, telling her to come home because he missed her so much he was starting to act crazy." Nancy actually thought it was a terribly romantic thing to do.

"He's my pardner," Moon said. "It's hard for him, Anne being so far away." Moon had some idea of how hard it really was.

"Or," Nancy whispered as she ran her fingertips along his sleeve, "maybe you want Scott out of the way because you're interested in Emily Nightbird for yourself." Emily was a pretty woman. Very pretty. And rich. Nancy pressed her sharp fingernails through his shirt sleeve, but Moon didn't notice. He was remembering. He was a child, back at the camp meeting with his parents. They had sat on hay bales under the junipers to listen to the words of the Navajo elder. This old evangelist who followed the Jesus Way had thundered the Good News to the forlorn little band of people whose ancestors had lost their land to the swarms of European invaders. It had seemed so foreign to him then, but now the words his mother sang rippled over the silence of the years. Charlie Moon could smell the pungent tang of the juniper, taste the alkali dust. The small child could see the Navajo evangelist raising his arms in adoration of the Source of all that was holy. He remembered every detail. His father's tears. His mother's sweet voice, so small, yet rising above the others as she sang.

". . . filled with His goodness . . . lost in His love . . ."

His eyes tried to see through the curtain of darkness. Far, impossibly far away. Toward a place filled with goodness. Scented with the fragrance of wild spring flowers, filled with the song of the Spirit. Where the Good Shepherd wiped every tear from the eyes of those who loved him. Where Benita Sweetwater lived.

Lost in His love.

25

Scott Parris was at the gate when the lumbering jet rolled to a stop. Anne was among the first to exit the plane, but they were still locked in an embrace after the other passengers had disappeared. If it was possible, she was even more wonderful than he had remembered. Scarlet hair still fell over her shoulders in great waves, her eyes were still great pools of blue fire. And she still carried the faint scent of honeysuckle.

From the moment he pulled the Volvo out of the short-term parking lot, Anne talked nonstop about her hot stories on the firing of the president's press secretary, the deepening rift between Russia and the Ukraine, the latest gossip on the vice president's feud with NASA. They were an hour south of Denver when she finally ran out of steam. "Sorry, Scotty. I've hardly let you say a word. What have you been up to in Ignacio while I've been away?" Charlie Moon's urgent call had been suggestive, even mysterious. But the Ute had really told her nothing except that Scott needed her.

For the second time in twenty-four hours, he blushed. Fortunately, it was too dark for her to see this guilty reaction. "We've had a really strange case. A mutilated bull, then a murdered man who was mutilated exactly like the bull. On top of that, a couple of college kids are dead, a Ute girl and a Belgian exchange student. And the old Ute woman, Daisy Perika, is dreaming her dreams. You remember Daisy."

"How could I forget her? But a murder! Have you caught the killer?"

She noticed that he hesitated. Just a little. "The FBI thinks the Belgian kid, stoned on drugs, killed the bull and the Ute guy."

She snuggled close. "I want to hear the whole story. Every awful, gory detail."

He recounted Daisy Perika's strange vision of shadows, an owl that killed men, Benita Sweetwater's deathbed confession, the wild encounter with Herb Ecker. He didn't mention the fact that Ecker had died because he had threatened Charlie Moon's friend with an *empty* revolver. That particular secret, he would take to the grave.

Anne listened silently. When he was finished, she frowned. "So this Herb Ecker killed the bull, then murdered this awful Nightbird person?"

"Looks that way."

She sensed a certain reservation in his tone. He was not certain.

Parris watched the endless trail of headlights heading north on Interstate 25. "You know," he said, "with you here, everything is just perfect. Nothing could happen that would ruin this night."

The jazz on the FM radio was interrupted by a perky female voice. "This is Nightbeat, the pulse of metropolitan Denver. Our guest tonight is FBI special agent James E. Hoover. No relation to the famous J. E. Hoover." She laughed automatically, as if it were in the script.

Parris turned the volume up.

". . . I understand the FBI has solved the mutilation-murder case on the Southern Ute Reservation with the identification of a Belgian student as the criminal. You must be very gratified. . . ."

Hoover's tone was flavored with a smooth, almost folksy humility. "Well, you must understand that I didn't do it all by myself. In addition to the Bureau's excellent forensics laboratory, I had the entire staff of the Southern Ute Police under my direction. Without their tireless footwork, my development of the evidence leading to Herb Ecker might have taken much longer."

Scott Parris felt a sense of unreality, disconnection. This wasn't happening.

The female voice continued: "What evidence links this suspect to the mutilations?"

Hoover's voice barely betrayed his uncertainty. "The suspect precisely fits our profile of the murderer-mutilator. He had motive and means and opportunity."

"I understand that Mr. Ecker was killed before he could be interrogated about the mutilations. . . ."

"Yes," Hoover said sorrowfully. "The officers responsible for that action were not operating under my direct supervision when the shooting occurred. There will be a thorough investigation of Mr. Ecker's death, but the Bureau has no solid evidence . . . uh . . . at this time . . . that Mr. Ecker's civil rights were violated by the two policemen responsible for his death."

Parris gripped the steering wheel with white knuckles. "That sanctimonious little son-of-a-bitch!"

The interviewer continued. "I understand that you are somewhat of an authority on Ute culture." Hoover had told her as much in the pre-interview conference.

"Well," Hoover said modestly, "I'm still learning, but I do pride myself on understanding the psyche of the Utes. They're really a great bunch of folks. With a little assistance from the Bureau, the Southern Ute Police have real potential of becoming a first-rate law enforcement operation."

"Would you like to tell us who, among the Ute policemen, helped you the most in solving this case?"

"Well . . . I'd really like to name some names for your audience, but you know how it is, if you forget even one person you're in big trouble." Hoover chuckled amiably. "I'd just like to congratulate the entire staff on the Southern Ute police force for their excellent support of this important FBI case."

When the interview was completed, the station cut to a commercial spot hyping a deodorant soap. Anne shook her head in wonder. "He practically accused you and Charlie Moon of misconduct. That is simply astonishing."

"Not when you get to know him," Parris said bitterly. "It's vintage Hoover." He wondered why Sam Parker didn't sack this idiot. Did Hoover have some political juice?

Anne was using the mirror on the sun visor as she touched up her lipstick. "Tell me, once more, word for word, what Daisy Perika said about the owl dipping its talons in blood."

"I can't remember it that precisely," Parris said wearily. "There was this shadow that turned into an owl. It killed a Ute. That'd be Arlo Nightbird. Then it became a shadow again."

"An owl. Shadows. Symbols," Anne whispered. "Her visions are in symbols. But remind me; what did that poor boy say just before he died?"

"Said he'd come to dance. Then, he said something about a

shadow coming. Swift and sudden. Dark and dreary. Stuff like that."

"Robert Service poetry," she said sadly, " 'March of the Dead.' Not particularly cheerful." Anne leaned over and kissed him on the neck.

He swerved onto the shoulder, then back onto the pavement.

"You can do that again."

She did.

Daisy trudged along the deer path. When she got to the barbed wire fence that kept Gorman's Herefords in Spirit Canyon, she moved to the canyon wall and squeezed past the last cedar post. As she climbed the slight grade into *Cañon del Espiritu*, the old woman stopped several times to lean on her oak staff and catch her breath. With every year, the walk seemed longer, the path steeper. Before a long time would pass, her breath would be gone forever and she would walk through *Na-gun-tu-wip*, where the spirits of the wandering dead dwell. As she passed through, wolves would howl and threaten her with bared teeth; serpents would hiss at her bare feet—but if she could maintain her courage she would pass over that great chasm to that land of everlasting light where she would put on a new, strong body. A body that would never grow old.

But that would come later, at the appointed time. Now, she was old and her back ached. Daisy consoled herself with the comforting knowledge that the path back to her trailer home would be downhill.

As she approached the abandoned badger-hole that was the entry into the home of the *pitukupf*, she paused and carefully dropped an offering of corn pollen onto the sandy canyon floor. The figure she drew with the pollen was a circle within a circle: the sun encircling the moon. This done, she approached the hole cautiously and squatted, hugging her staff with one arm. How long had he lived here? A thousand years? A thousand centuries? The shaman removed a brown paper parcel from her apron pocket and unwrapped it as she gave thanks to the One Spirit who guarded all creation. Daisy placed two new packages of Flying Dutchman pipe tobacco on the sand beside the badger hole. It was the *pitukupf*'s favorite brand, much to be preferred over *kinnikinnik*, the wild tobacco that grew in the canyon. She spread a yellow paper napkin beside the tobacco and placed a shiny pocket knife with red and green plastic handles on the center of the napkin. The pocket knife was inexpensive, but the dwarf had no concept of money. And he would appreciate the bright colors. It would never have occurred to the shaman to doubt that soon after she left, the little creature would retrieve the tobacco and the pocket knife.

When her task was completed, Daisy used her heavy oak staff to push herself erect. Before beginning the long walk home, she turned to look at the nearly vertical cliff wall adorned with ancient petroglyphs. Daisy's eyes, as always when she stopped at this sacred place, scanned the figures scratched into the sandstone canvas. She frowned and squinted to focus her eyes. . . . Something was wrong. There was a figure on the wall she had never seen before. It was very faint, perhaps the evening sun was just right to cast shadows in the shallow lines scratched into the stone. Or was it something new? She moved closer, looking up at the etching of a figure. A figure with hundreds of tiny rays covering its surface . . . a hairy creature. A creature with a tail. A creature with horns!

She crossed herself, and hurried away.

26

Daisy Perika walked stiffly down the road to her mailbox, thankful for the cool breeze from the northwest. It had been an unusually mild autumn, but soon the first frost would kill the pesky deerflies that bit her ankles. Then the heavy blanket of snow would drape its soft shawl around the Three Sisters who kept their faithful watch over *Cañon del Espiritu*. The old woman opened the dented steel box and removed a thick stack of mail. That very strange man from the old Carson show still wanted to give her millions of dollars. There was an official looking envelope from the alcoholic's shelter in Denver, a plea for another donation from the Jesuit Father in New York. She sighed. You sent these people a few dollars and they never let you rest!

The tribal newspaper was welcome mail. She unfolded the *Southern Ute Drum* and read the front page as she slowly made her way up the lane toward her trailer home. A powwow at Shiprock. A cut-rate spay-neuter clinic at Dr. Schaid's animal hospital. The Navajos were promoting another boycott against the business community in Farmington. She turned the page. A fishing contest at Capote Lake. The Nightbird Insurance Agency would be reopened under Emily Nightbird's maiden name. When she turned the page again, she saw the story. The Economic Development Board intended to pursue Arlo Nightbird's quest to turn *Cañon del Espiritu* into a "Spent Nuclear Fuel Holding Facility." Ahhh . . . the *pitukupf* would not be pleased with this plan to dump garbage in the place where he lived!

The shaman tarried in the foot path, flipping the pages of the newspaper slowly, absorbing these fascinating bits of information, correlating them, searching for connections. There was something here, but she could not quite see it. Almost unconsciously, she whispered: "maybe the *pitukupf* will show me."

The tired old woman was climbing the front porch with the warm sun on her back when she noticed her shadow on the aluminum wall of her trailer.

Her short, thick shadow began to grow. It became tall, the shoulders broad.

The mail slipped from Daisy's hand; she gripped her skirts with cold, bloodless fingers.

The shadow raised its arms. The arms became great wings, with feathers that fluttered as if troubled by a wind.

The shaman stood frozen, unable even to cry out. Trembling, she watched the shadow wings spread as if for flight; they began to move in a slow rhythmic motion. Would they carry her away?

She closed her eyes. "Dear Jesus," she whispered, "you can make it go away." When she opened her eyes, her ordinary shadow was on the aluminum wall—the shadow arms were at her side where they belonged. Immediately, the shaman understood the meaning of her vision. She knew who had killed Arlo Nightbird.

That night, Daisy tossed uneasily in her bed staring alternately at the ceiling, then through the small window into the frigid darkness. What to do? Perhaps this dark knowledge was best kept secret. Or forgotten altogether.

27

She shivered. Cold as frog spit, that's what it was. The top of Chimney Rock was just now catching a faint glow of light from the east. Daisy trudged unsteadily along, eager to feel the warm light from the sun that would soon rise above the blue profile of Eight Mile Mesa. The paved road was a dark ribbon at her left hand, the waters of the Piedra rushed by at her right. She would occasionally pause to lean on her oak staff and wait until her breathing slowed. Ignacio was miles away and there was no traffic on the road at this early hour.

Her troubled thoughts were on her vision of the dark shadow that became an owl. And the owl was transformed back into a misty shadow. Sometimes what you saw in a vision wasn't the real thing, but just a hint of what the actual thing was. It had been that way in the ancient days, when Joseph had explained the meaning of the old Pharaoh's troublesome dreams. Fat cattle meant good crops—thin ones meant famine. Shadows and owls and other symbols were like arrows that pointed toward the truth.

There was still no explanation for the mutilation of Gorman's bull, or of the strange disappearance of Rolling Thunder, but the shaman had worked out a part of the puzzle. There was no doubt about who had killed Arlo Nightbird. But Arlo was dead. *Cañon del Espiritu* still lived. And the canyon was the only home the dwarf had ever known. Or, she supposed, the only home he could ever know. Like Daisy, the *pitukupf* was too old and set in his ways to move. Aside from the dwarf, there were the peaceful old spirits that inhabited the ancient canyon. How could they rest if the *matukach* buried these dangerous things under the floor of their home? The old woman had awakened before daylight with an overpowering sense that she must take personal action.

As she leaned on her staff and considered all of these things, the river began to speak to the shaman. The Piedra, which normally whispered in that secret language of all rivers, now muttered words that she could understand. *Bloody bloody bloody . . . trouble trouble trouble*, the waters said. She began to walk. As her halting steps brought her near a small rapids, the voices were much louder: *BLOODY TROUBLE . . . BLOODY TROUBLE . . . BLOODY TROUBLE*. The shaman paused; she frowned at the rolling surface of the river, which briefly assumed a crimson cast in the first direct rays of morning sunlight. These urgent words and scarlet colors from the waters were warnings; as clear as the painted signs along the highway.

With an arm that trembled, the old woman raised her walking staff toward the mountains. "It's me, God," she whispered hoarsely. "I am very old now. My legs hurt when I walk and my ankles swell up. My hands . . . they shake like the leaves on the aspen." She held one hand out so that God might see this slight palsy. "I'm all worn out . . . can't take another step. It's up to you to do something." She sat down by the roadside. To wait.

After a time, the urgent voices of the river quieted to a whisper, then fell completely silent. The surface of the Piedra was like a pond. The shaman sensed, rather than heard, a gentle voice speak to her. This message was also clear. Because of her stubbornness, Daisy would be permitted to go to Ignacio, to witness what would happen there. To learn the folly of it. Above all, she was not to do battle with the tribal council to save her home at the mouth of *Cañon del Espiritu*.

Another home was already being prepared for her.

In most of his dealings, Albert Gibbons was a man with a whimsical, even gay disposition. But when he traveled, the Reverend Gibbons was a most cautious man. He made meticulous plans and he stuck to them. Albert was, so he believed, on his way to Colorado Springs to deliver a learned paper that would electrify the annual convention of Wisdom Literature Theologians. In fact, he was rolling down Route 151 toward Arboles and the northern finger of Navajo Lake. His right brain rehearsed his erudite speech on subtle parallels between sections of Ecclesiasticus and the *Sama-Veda*, while his left brain raised questions that were of some practical importance:

Can this narrow little road possibly be the highway that will take us through Alamosa and thence to Walsenburg and Interstate 25? And should the sun not rise before us? Wake up, Albert!

He shifted his gaze between a crumpled map and the highway and his sleepy wife. "Can't figure how we got off on this little back road," he muttered. It was partly Pamela's fault. She should have been paying attention. He glanced at the sun rising on his left. "We must be heading south."

"I gotta go pee-pee," little Billy bawled from the backseat.

"Albert," his wife said, "look at the old woman sitting by the road." She tugged at his sleeve, causing the station wagon to swerve slightly. "I think she's an Indian. She looks so . . . so forlorn."

Albert corrected his steering. "We'll stop and see if she needs some help."

"Neato," Billy squawked, "I ain't seen no real Indians yet." The child's stubby vocal chords vibrated with that nerve-jarring quality of broken fingernails scraping over a chalky blackboard.

Albert braked the big automobile to a crawl.

Pamela pushed a button to lower the window. "Dearie," she called out, "over here. You need a ride?"

"It's about time you got here," Daisy said gruffly as she pushed herself erect with the wooden staff. "Open the door for me, I got the arthritis in my hands."

"I'm Albert," the driver said, cheerfully resigned to his fate. "This is Pamela. That's our son Billy in the backseat."

"I'm tired," the old woman said. "My feet and knees hurt." She noticed his clerical collar. "You a priest?"

"That I am," Albert replied. But he did not wish to be mistaken for a priest with pastoral duties. This woman was very old and feeble. And there was a hint of guilt in her expression. Neither last rites nor confessions were his cup of tea. "I teach at a small seminary in Arizona." Five years and still no tenure.

The old woman leaned on her staff and squinted suspiciously at this *matukach* and at the woman seated next to him. "We have us a priest over in Ignacio . . . but that Pope over in Rome won't let him have a wife." Daisy turned her glare upon the homely child in the rear seat, who had his nose pressed hard against the glass. He resembled a little pig with freckles; Daisy shuddered inwardly.

=227=

Pamela turned to open the rear door for the old woman. "It's all right, dear. We're Lutherans."

Daisy got in beside Billy, who scooted away quickly. "Well—I need a ride." She could not afford to be choosy, but this development was a great puzzle to the shaman. The country between Durango and Pagosa had enough good Catholics to fill a dozen churches and here was God, sending her a Protestant. Maybe it was The Great Mysterious One's notion of a little joke. Well, that could be a good sign. Someday soon, she would have a lot of explaining to do and it would help if God had a sense of humor.

"We're on our way to Colorado Springs," Pamela shouted over her shoulder. She always spoke loudly to the elderly, as if the entire lot had defective hearing.

"God," Daisy said, "wants you to take me to Ignacio. I got important business there."

Albert found Ignacio on his road map. He finally understood where he was, and sighed. The Forty-Fifth Annual Convention of Wisdom Literature Theologians would have to wait. God's will be done.

Little Billy eyed the wrinkled woman with frank suspicion. "You a real Indian?"

She glared at him. "Sure as Columbus was a foreigner."

"I don't think you're a sure-enough Indian," the boy squawked.

"Now, son," Albert cautioned, "remember your manners." The boy had little to remember.

"Sure-enough Indians live in Calcutta," the shaman said. Daisy leaned over, her face close to the boy's. "Besides, how would you know a real Indian if you saw one?"

Billy paused to consider this, then smirked at the supposed impostor. "Real Indians can make fire"—he rubbed his grubby little palms together to demonstrate—"by rubbing two sticks together." He grinned, exhibiting a set of red gums from which sprouted about nine teeth. "Till they get red hot!"

Daisy tilted her head and winked. "Watch this." She closed her eyes and raised her hands, fingertips touching as if in prayer. "O ghosts of my ancestors," the shaman moaned, now raising her arms in a theatric gesture, "put the spirit of fire in the hand of your daughter!" She cracked one eye to watch the child, who waited with no little apprehension.

"I don't see no fire," he said sullenly. As he spoke, a thin blue flame leaped up from the shaman's index finger. Billy was startled. Billy peed in his pants.

Albert braked the station wagon and glanced over his shoulder at the old woman. "This close enough to your destination? We don't mind taking you. . . ."

Daisy unbuckled the seat belt. "No. This'll do fine."

"Good-bye, dearie," Pamela said as she waved at Daisy's back. "Albert," she whispered, "how do you suppose she did that fire thing with her hands?"

He made an illegal U-turn. "Some kind of Native American magic, I suppose." The priest, who had watched the episode in his rearview mirror, smiled with satisfaction at the secret he shared with the hitchhiker. He had seen the old woman palm the plastic cigarette lighter.

Charlie Moon arrived barely two minutes before the fire engine; both were too late to make any difference in the outcome. The Economic Development Building was wrapped in flames. The scorching heat kept the curious onlookers well away. Moon was interviewing potential witnesses when he noticed a familiar face under a maple tree. He turned his task over to Sally Rainwater and made his way through a throng of onlookers to the solitary figure. Moon pushed his hat brim back a notch. "What brings you here, Aunt Daisy?" What, indeed.

The old woman looked up and blinked innocently. "Had to come to town. Things to do."

Moon had no doubt that his aunt had seen the *Drum* article. Daisy would have read about the Economic Development Board's decision to revive the late Arlo Nightbird's plans to convert *Cañon del Espiritu* into a nuclear waste repository. Arlo's extensive files had been stored in the EDB building. Now, the valuable papers were ashes. Without the stacks of documents, the plans for the canyon were as good as dead. The policeman wanted to ask the question; the nephew didn't want to hear the answer.

The old woman watched the flames. She looked guilty. Extremely guilty. Moon turned to see the remains of the building collapse. "Good thing it happened so early in the day; nobody was inside." He cocked his head and stared down at his aunt. "Don't suppose," he said casually, "you have any secrets you want to share with your favorite nephew?"

"You want to learn yourself some secrets," she said with a poker face, "maybe you should go over to *Cañon del Espiritu* and have a long talk with the *pitukupf*."

"Maybe I'll drop by later and have a chat with the dwarf," Moon replied. "But in the meantime, I need to figure out how this fire got started. Anything you want to tell me?"

"Was on my way to the grocery store," she said. The shaman had learned this trick from the politicians she watched on television. Someone asked them an unwelcome question, they answered a *different* question with the intention of sowing confusion. It was a very clever ruse and it usually worked.

Moon's brow furrowed. "The grocery store's way over on Goddard Avenue. Isn't this stop a bit out of your way?"

And sometimes it didn't work. "Meat," she said darkly, "need to pick up some . . . fresh meat." Daisy had no intention of stopping at the grocery.

Moon grinned down at his aunt. "Don't suppose you brought any matches with you?"

Daisy closed her fingers over the plastic cigarette lighter in her pocket. "I read in the *Drum* that there's going to be a fishing contest at Capote Lake." Any mention of fishing always distracted her nephew.

"Uh-huh," Moon said absently. "Maybe I'll go wet a hook."

The fire chief waddled up in his oversized rubber boots. Abe Workman pushed his helmet back and wiped sooty sweat from his forehead. He nodded politely at Daisy Perika, then turned to the Ute policeman. "I got something for you, Charlie. Federal Express lady stopped next door to make a delivery. Navajo woman, her name's Martha George. Said she saw something . . . ahhh . . . somebody near the building right before she smelled the smoke."

Moon looked for the familiar van and didn't see it. "Where is she?"

"Already took off. Had some deliveries to make in Bayfield."

Moon knew about this Martha George. The Navajo woman was rumored to be some kind of clairvoyant. Her father was a traditional Navajo healer . . . performed the Blessing Way. The policeman found his notebook. "She give you a description?"

"Not much. Except . . . she says the suspect was . . . uh . . . not more'n two feet tall." Workman blushed under Moon's stare. "Must have been somebody's kid, Charlie. Playin' with matches, maybe."

"Yeah. A kid." The policeman put his notebook in his shirt pocket.

Daisy's face was impassive. Reflections of the flames danced in her dark eyes.

28

His face, she thought, had a hollow look. Almost haunted.

Anne Foster frowned at the dark patches under his eyes. "You look absolutely exhausted." She caressed his hand. "You simply must take a few days off. Get away from the pressures at work."

"I'm fine." Scott Parris forced a smile, and it hurt his face. "All I need is a few hours of good sleep." Sleep without dreams.

But first there was work to do.

And promises to keep.

She knew that he was driving himself much too hard. Anne would have been astonished to know how he was spending every spare moment. But she would never know. No one would.

Not unless the dead knew.

The coyote paused to sniff tentatively, interrupting a determined search for the scent of the cottontail. The hungry canine turned, orienting her sensitive ears toward the source of the barely audible sounds. *Scuff-scuff*, the sounds said. They would pause, then start again. *Scuff-scuff*. The clever animal, long acquainted with the threat of the two-legged creatures and their dogs, sensed that something far more sinister approached along the floor of the canyon. The coyote moved into a patch of dead chamisa and waited with apprehension as the source of the scuffing sounds approached. The animal tilted her head in puzzlement at first sight of the *thing*—this unnatural apparition that moved in undulating motion like a shadowy wave over the moonlit sand of the canyon floor. At first, the shape of the intruder was indistinct, an amorphous patch of dark fog floating over the ground. Then, as if it could change its shape at will, the presence seemed to take on substance. The thing paused, raised itself to a standing position . . . like a great bear. But it was not a bear. . . . This creature had broad shoulders, no neck, and a peculiar, flattened head. The head had horns. And a single red eye. Now it would glow brightly, like an ember in a fire. Then it would dim, as if the creature had blinked. The coyote could not deal with abstract concepts, like Good and Evil. But there were primitive instincts deep within her breast that drummed an urgent warning: Be still, be still!

29

He had blood on his hands.

For the tenth time in an hour, he washed carefully, using a miniature brush to scrub his knuckles and cuticles. He examined his fingers
carefully in the dim light—his hands appeared to be clean but he was
certain that traces of blood remained. Patiently, he lathered his
hands again with the yellow disinfectant soap and scrubbed with the
brush until it seemed that the skin itself might slough off into the
basin. He rinsed under the faucet, then dried his hands gently on a
soft cotton towel.

As he locked the front door behind him, his thoughts were occupied with a bit of food and early to bed. But first, a walk. A long,
quiet walk along the bank of the river. Contemplating his lonely
evening, he didn't notice the small figure waiting in the quivering
shadow of the willow.

"Hey," she said.

He paused in mid-stride, then leaned forward slightly to get a better look. "Yes?"

Daisy's back was to the street lamp, her face masked in shadow.
"Need to talk."

He didn't like the sound of this, but he managed a casual tone.
"Want to come inside?"

Daisy considered the dark windows. Like little square eyes in the
flat face of the structure. The door was an open mouth. "No," she
snapped.

"Well, then," he said, "what'll we talk about?"

The shaman realized that she had not prepared herself for this
encounter. How could she say it? "It's about what you've been

doing. . . ." She paused, drawing a deep breath, ". . . to those ani-mals."

He felt a warning premonition chill his blood. He tilted his head and blinked at this unwelcome visitor. "What . . . exactly," he asked, "do you want?"

She told him.

30

BURNT CREEK RANCH, POWDERHORN, COLORADO

The ranch foreman did not have cattle on his mind as he steered the battered Jeep pickup between ruts in the gravel road. Toby Aucliffe wasn't even thinking of rain or, more to the point, the lack of rain—the western rancher's eternal preoccupation. Toby, with a stub of a cigar clamped between his nicotine-stained teeth, had a woman on his mind. A particular woman who had skin as pink as a fresh slice of ham, a woman with a voice that was slow and sweet, like thick maple syrup dripping off a stack of hot buttermilk pancakes. Roy enjoyed his food almost as much as his women, and tended to compare and intermingle these two categories of pleasure in an almost seamless fashion. He let up on the accelerator and eased the little truck around a hairpin curve that hugged a deep arroyo.

He smelled the carcass before he saw it.

Toby slammed the pickup door, threw the unlighted cigar onto the gravel road and ground it savagely under his boot heel. Damn cows. Almost as bad as horses. Turn your back, and, just to spite you, they'd fall over deader'n a stone. In his view, the animals got sick or died just to annoy him, to ruin his plans for a Saturday night in town. He hesitated, then stomped across the dry meadow toward the still form in a patch of sage. From the road it looked like a boulder, but the cowman knew every boulder on his turf. This was a purebred Hereford, one of more than six hundred head on the Burnt Creek ranch. As he approached the carcass, he realized that this was a big animal. This was one of the bulls. Toby cursed silently. Purebred Hereford bulls cost serious money. The consortium of Dallas chiropractors who owned the ranch would demand a full report on this one. "A written report, listing all the pertinent details," he muttered aloud, imitating the whining tone of their bespectacled accountant. The barely literate cowman hated accountants almost as much as he hated beeves that croaked for no good reason. Toby cursed again, this time his fury directed toward the rich chiropractors who played at ranching.

When he was within a few feet of the remains, Toby Aucliffe stopped suddenly, bouncing back like a drunk who had stumbled into a glass door. "Oh no. . . ." He turned away in horror, closing his eyes to blot out the picture of the mutilation. Then, the hard case vomited up his breakfast.

The package arrived at the Granite Creek Police Department by United Parcel Service. Scott Parris read Nancy Beyal's return address; he cut the heavy tape with his pocket knife and unwrapped the brown paper. Inside, he found the paperback romance that the dispatcher had been reading on the day he arrived at the Southern Ute Police Station.

Parris smiled at the teasing note taped to the lurid cover of the Mexican romance novel.

> Dear Scott P.:
>
> Thought you might enjoy this on some lonely night when Anne is traveling.
>
> Luv. Nancy B.

His smile vanished as he saw the cover of the paperback. The policeman put his hand into his coat pocket. It was still there. A crumpled copy of the liturgy that veterinarian Harry Schaid had passed out to the mourners at Benita Sweetwater's funeral. He searched the wrinkled surface until he found the words:

> *Yea, though I walk through the valley of the shadow of death. . . .*
> *De esta suerte, aunge caminase yo por medio de la sombra de la muerte. . . .*

Of course.

Emily brushed aside a moist wisp of hair and looked up from the deep furrow where she was planting the Parrot tulip bulbs under precisely eight inches of lightly fertilized soil. Fidel Sombra slammed the truck door and sat down on the edge of the front porch. He removed his new straw hat and scratched at his grizzled head. "Hello, dotter."

Emily wiped the rich soil from her delicate hands. "Good morning, Daddy." She wrinkled her pretty nose and smiled. The old man hadn't bathed in a week; he smelled like his pigs. "I've got some coffee on. Shall I bring you a cup?" Better that he didn't come inside, stink up the house.

"Nope. I've already drunk so much coffee today, it'd squirt out my ears." He had killed a six pack of Mexican beer. The old man removed a sheath knife from his belt and used the curved tip of the gleaming blade to scrape the dirt from under his horny fingernails. "Besides, your coffee ain't worth a sh— I mean, it's altogether too weak for me."

She watched her father and frowned thoughtfully. Instinctively, Emily sensed that something was wrong. Something. But what?

Charlie Moon sat across the booth, having lost interest in a piece of Angel's pecan pie. "I can't make an arrest with nothing to go on but your notion about Aunt Daisy's . . . uh . . . vision. It's not evidence."

"But it does fit," Parris said stubbornly.

"I expect," Moon admitted cautiously, "it could have happened that way."

Parris wondered whether the old woman had actually witnessed the mutilation of Arlo Nightbird from her perch on the side of Three Sisters Mesa. Perhaps she rejected the horrible scene from her conscious mind. Then, maybe she slept . . . and dreamed the vision. A collection of graphic symbols representing the victim and the mutilator. "So what do we do?"

The Ute's face was impassive. "Hoover," he said slowly, "believes Herb Ecker killed and mutilated Gorman's bull. And likewise for Arlo Nightbird. He's closed the case." Moon pushed the pie away; he dipped a spoon into his cup of lukewarm coffee. He stirred. "But maybe I should stir the pot . . . see what floats to the top."

CAÑON DEL SERPIENTE

Once again, the long finger dipped blood from the ancient depression in the boulder. The finger drew. Now there was a new representation of a human being on the sandstone. This new stick-man kneeled above the earlier figure of the Man of the Book. The scarlet fingertip made many small spots between the figures; they were tears. Kneeling Man wept tears of blood onto Dead Poet.

Soon, they would be together.

"I don't see why this couldn't of waited till tomorrow." The old farmer's back ached and he had an overwhelming desire for a drink. A strong drink. Fidel Sombra rubbed a dirty sleeve across his mouth. "A bunch of my pigs got loose last night, and I been chasing the greasy little bastards all over La Plata County, from here to hell and back. I'm awfully tired." He waited in vain for the least bit of sympathy.

Emily had her little hand out, palm up. She spat the words at him. "That knife you were using for your manicure the other day; I was certain I had seen it before. Last night, I remembered. That was Arlo's knife. Give it to me. Now!" His daughter had that stubborn look that he remembered from her mother's face. It would be pointless to lie. Fidel sullenly removed the sheath knife from his belt and offered it to his daughter.

"I had assumed that animals chewed Arlo's ears off," Emily said. "But you had his knife. You must have . . . removed his . . ." Her words were interrupted by a shudder. "What did you do with . . ."

"No need to worry about it." He winked. "Fed 'em to the hogs."

She closed her eyes and shook her head in disbelief. Now her voice was soft, as if she was attempting to communicate with a moron. "Daddy . . . tell me what you did with Arlo's turquoise ear stud."

Fidel stiffened his back. That had been his favorite keepsake from the memorable trip to Spirit Canyon. "Don't have it no more."

Emily stamped her tiny foot. "Don't lie to me, Daddy. I'm not leaving this house until you give me the ear stud!" She was clenching the hunting knife in a tight little white-knuckled fist.

Emily was her mother's daughter, and Fidel was certain that she could tell when he was lying. "Honest, dotter. I don't have it no more."

"How," she said evenly, "could you *not* have it?"

Fidel was trembling; he couldn't take his eyes off the knife. "I . . . well . . . I kind of lost it."

Emily realized that he was terrified. She dropped the knife into her purse. "That's absurd, Daddy. How could you lose it?"

The old farmer explained precisely why he no longer had the turquoise ear stud in his possession. At first, the remembrance of his drunken prank made him smile. Then, he interrupted his narrative with snickers. Finally, it was too much to bear. Fidel Sombra cackled and wheezed until his ribs ached.

33

Charlie Moon wondered—had he been foolish to take up police work? There wasn't much money in it, and he had nothing better to do than answer another urgent call from Louise Marie LaForte. It was like he was her personal policeman. The old woman was a bit pecu-liar on her best days, and on her worst days she saw things. Louise Marie saw haunts. She saw the *loup-garou*. Louise Marie had probably had a taste of her homemade wine. Moon smiled—maybe she had tasted a quart. He turned the Blazer into her gravel driveway and, from long habit, glanced at the dilapidated house next door. A shade was quickly pulled in the upstairs window, blocking the flickering light from a kerosene lamp. So, the writer-taxidermist-lunatic was, despite repeated warnings, still spying on his neighbor. Taxi was get-ting to be a nuisance. The old woman was waiting on her porch swing. Moths danced a frenzied jitterbug in the dim yellow light fil-tering through a closed window shade; a small crockery pitcher was on a tray by her knee.

Moon tipped his hat. "What's cookin', Louise?"

She pointed to an extra cup by the pitcher. "Would you like some tea?"

"Never touch the stuff. What's the problem this time?"

Louise Marie drained the last swallow of "tea" from her cup, then hiccuped daintily. "This time it's bad," she said with an air of deli-cious mystery, "*very* bad."

"What's bad?"

She waved her little hand in a dramatic arc toward the heavens. "I have seen the northern lights dance over the earth, flapping her long skirts of blue fire." There was a long, thoughtful pause before she continued. Louise Marie had a sense for dramatic timing. "I have seen the *loup-garou* many times. *Oui*, I once even saw the great water monster with the long neck swimming in Missisquoi Bay in Lake Champlain, but," she murmured as she solemnly crossed herself, "I am a good Catholic so I never believed in reincarnation." Some things, of course, happened whether you believed in them or not.

Moon sat down beside her in the porch swing. The chain creaked ominously under the strain of his weight. "You mean like when dead folks come back as somebody else?" There was a vague memory he couldn't quite connect with. A memory of a dream.

"*Oui*," she said darkly, "or if they were very naughty, they may come back as some*thing* else."

He squinted at the thin sliver of moon rising over the Piños. "Well, don't know as I ever thought much about it." He put his arm on the swing behind the old woman and patted her on the shoulder. "Is that why you called me out in the middle of the night, to talk about reincarnation?"

"He's back," she whispered. There was a sweet fragrance of raspberry wine on her breath.

"The *loup-garou*? I figured he was gone for good."

"Worse than *loup-garou*." Louise Marie shuddered. "Arlo Nightbird is back."

Moon stopped swinging and the old woman almost pitched forward onto the porch floor. "What'd you say?"

"Arlo," she said as she regained her composure, "he's come back. I heard this funny noise, just a little while ago." Louise Marie paused to pour scarlet liquor from the pitcher into the cup; she had a sip to steady her nerves. "Went out to check with my flashlight. Saw him in my garden. Then I called the police."

"You know," Moon said sternly, "you don't live in Southern Ute jurisdiction and you're not a Ute. You're not even any kind of Indian. You should have called the Ignacio police."

"The Town Police always say 'Call Charlie Moon,'" she said pitifully. "You're the only policeman who will come out to help a poor old lady." Louise Marie scooted closer to the big man.

The Ute policeman tilted his head back. He watched the countless stars. He could almost feel the whirling power of the galactic arms, flinging the earth through deep space. "What was Arlo up to in your garden?"

"He was rooting around, probably for some old potatoes. Or maybe grubs."

"Grubs?" Moon grunted. "Can't imagine Arlo having a taste for grubs."

"*Oui*. But he does now," she said patiently. "He came back as a swine, you see."

Moon smiled at the Big Dipper. "Well, I can understand how a person might have a hard time telling the difference between Arlo and a pig."

Her shoulders stiffened. "This is not to be taken lightly, Charles Moon. That pig was definitely Arlo Nightbird, come back to torment me."

Reason, the Ute decided, was his only weapon in dealing with the old woman's fantasies. "But why would Arlo visit *you*, Louise Marie?"

She shrugged, as if it was a great mystery. But Louise Marie had no doubt that the visitation was Arlo's revenge. She had, after all, called him a swine!

Moon turned his head to look down at the sharp little eyes peering up through a mound of wrinkled flesh. "What makes you so sure this particular porker was Arlo Nightbird?"

"Well," she said with firm assurance, "it couldn't have been nobody else."

"And why not?"

"That pig was wearing Arlo's big turquoise stud," she touched her left ear lobe, "Right here."

Charlie Moon trudged around the farmhouse, slogging through the mud that would turn into a hard plaster on his new boots. He paused, shaded his eyes from the sun, and shouted toward the barn. "Fidel . . . you out here?"

The old farmer appeared in the barn door. He removed his tattered Farmall hat, pushed a swatch of matted gray hair off his forehead, but didn't speak. Moon took long steps across the barnyard, hoping this would minimize the accumulation of mud on his boots. It didn't.

"How you doing, Fidel?" The policeman sat down on a moldy bale of hay and attempted to clean his boots with a handful of straw.

"Lots of chores to do," the old man answered sharply. "What brings you out to my place?"

"Heard some of your pigs got loose."

Fidel Sombra's hands tightened into fists. "You come here to talk about pigs?"

Moon didn't look up from his boot cleaning. "Wanted to talk about Arlo's murder."

The old man felt his heart racing. "You're . . . you're outta your juris— whadayacallit."

"Guess you're right." Moon wiped his boot heel on the hay bale. "But this isn't official. Kind of a personal visit."

The farmer turned up a burner on his Coleman stove until the black liquid in the blue enameled pot bubbled. "Why d'you care about that little horse's-ass. . . ."

"It's kind of a puzzle," Moon said, "can't get it off my mind."

"You wonderin' why that foreign feller killed Arlo?" Fidel poured coffee into a filthy ceramic cup. "Why, that crazy drugged-up kid didn't need no reason."

"Ecker didn't kill Arlo." Moon continued to clean his boots. "We both know what happened, don't we, old man?"

The farmer sat down on a three legged milking stool. He glared at the Ute policeman. "You know so damn much, you tell me—then we'll both be smarter."

"I've been checking the telephone records. You called your daughter on the same evening Arlo went into *Cañon del Espiritu* with . . ."—Moon choked on Benita's name and started again—". . . with Gorman's daughter."

Fidel dropped his gaze to the ground. "Don't mean nothin'. I call my dotter almost every night."

"Emily told you Arlo was late for their anniversary dinner date. Then," Moon continued, "the record shows you called the Nightbird Insurance Agency. Talked for about four minutes."

"I can call anybody I damn well please. . . ."

"You bullied Herb Ecker into telling you that Arlo had gone up to the canyon to see my Aunt Daisy." It was a reasonable speculation. "So you knew where Arlo was and . . ."

The old man bristled. "You got no business here. This ain't no part of the reservation." Fidel regained some of his composure. "Besides, all you got is a pocketful of guesses."

Moon smiled; he got up and hitched his thumbs behind his gun belt. "What if I told you we'd picked up one of your runaway pigs?" He saw a sudden fear flicker in Fidel's eyes. "And what if I told you it was a real stylish porker—wearing Arlo's turquoise ear stud?" The

Ute hadn't seen a sign of the pig with the jeweled ear, but Fidel wouldn't know that. Not unless Fidel had recovered the pig himself.

The old farmer deliberately poured his coffee onto the straw; he stared at the spilled liquid as it gradually disappeared into the soft earth. "I was drunk as a skunk when I prettied that pig up," he whispered, "but it seemed like the right thing to do at the time." The old man wiped his eyes with a grimy sleeve. "What're you gonna do?"

"Can't leave this thing like it is," Moon said. "I'll have to tell Emily what I know."

Fidel turned his coffee cup thoughtfully in his dirty hands, studying the ceramic object as if he had never really seen it before. "I'd as soon you'd leave my dotter outta this."

Moon closed his eyes and tried to remember Benita's face. Every day, the picture faded in his mind. But one thing didn't fade away—Arlo was responsible for Benita Sweetwater's death. But Arlo had been murdered too, and payment must be made for that death. "I've been thinking about that a lot," he said. "I'll have to do what's right." He watched Fidel's face. "You understand."

"Sure," the farmer said. "I know." Everybody in Ignacio knew that you could count on Charlie Moon to do the right thing. Fidel cursed, then stomped the coffee cup into a thousand fragments under his heel.

The pretty clerk in the Durango flower shop beamed up at the tall, somewhat awkward figure, who shifted his weight from one foot to another and back again. "And what sort of message should I put on the card?"

"Well . . ." he hesitated, "just say it's from Charlie." It was the right thing to do.

The sales clerk scribbled on the card. "Very well, sir. That's one dozen long-stemmed roses." The Chicano girl beamed at the big Ute and wished she had a man like this to send her roses. "She's a very lucky lady."

"Yeah," Moon said. "I guess she is at that." Very lucky indeed.

This girl's big brown eyes were almost as pretty as Benita's eyes, but her lips were not as full. And her voice wasn't sweet music . . . but that, he reminded himself, was finished business. An opportunity forever lost.

She saw the shadow pass over his face, and turned to answer the telephone. He idly watched the figures on her portable television set.

oon took a deep breath. Now or never. "Because he . . . uh . . . you a disease?" He hadn't intended to make it sound like a ques-

nily's mouth dropped open. "How . . . how could you know about ?"

Cecelia Chavez visited you that same night Arlo was late." True gh. The public health nurse had admitted to the visit, but noth-nore. Now for the big guess. If he was wrong, Emily would realize little he really knew and the game would be over. "She came to you that the blood you donated didn't pass the test." He watched ace. Emily's pupils dilated ever so slightly. Time to play the hand "I've had a talk with Doc Anderson." Moon's expression was ident, as if he knew everything. Emily's personal physician had refused to discuss his visit to the Nightbird residence, had even atened to destroy Emily's medical files at the least hint of a court r. The doctor was hiding something, but what? There was a long ce. Moon wondered if he'd gone too far. Too fast.

nally she spoke, barely above a whisper. "So you know." She ed at a rose, rubbed her finger across the delicate petals. "HIV-ive. AIDS. That's what Cecelia said the test on my blood indi-d." Emily found a lace handkerchief in her purse. "I was awake all t. First, I cried." She trembled at the memory. "I was afraid to By first light, I was furious. I called my father, told him every-g. When we found Arlo, he had a lump on his head but he wasn't l. He opened his eyes." She squeezed the handkerchief into a tiny "The filthy little bastard grinned at me! I must have went erk. It was like I was outside my body . . . floating up above . . . hing someone else. Arlo's knife was on the ground beside him. I it to . . ." She couldn't go on.

So you castrated him," Unconsciously, Moon pulled his knees ther.

ne patted the handkerchief on her eyes, but there were no tears. as the surest way to make sure he wouldn't infect someone else." he logic, he realized, was unassailable. "But . . . you shoved his down his throat." The policeman tried, without success, to swal-

He started screaming. I had to make him stop." Emily's voice ed off. "You have to believe me, Charlie. Angry as I was, I ldn't have done anything like that . . . if I'd been in my right l."

It was the final scene of a hilarious James Herriot tale from the York-shire Dales. Siegfried was, as usual, furious with his younger brother. Tristan had terrified the neighborhood by donning a cloak and appearing nightly at a ruined monastery as the tortured "ghost" of an unhappy monk. A brawny constable, who did not believe in such nonsense, had almost run him to ground. The scene was abruptly replaced with an advertisement for "veterinary-approved" animal foods. "Your puppy will love Peter's Perky Puppy-Chow," the announcer insisted. The counterfeit veterinarian in the white smock droned on, listing the benefits of "enhanced vitamin and mineral content." This commercial was followed by others. Ford pickup trucks with a factory rebate. Salsa, a grizzled cowboy guaranteed, that wasn't made in New York City. An astonishingly beautiful woman leaned on a stuffed leopard, extolling the virtues of a new perfume from Italy. "My Confession," she whispered huskily, "is subtle, barely touching his consciousness." Then, a seductive smile as she unfas-tened the top button of her silk blouse.

The clerk hung up the telephone and turned to flash a smile at the policeman who was frowning at the television set. "Now," she said, "will this be cash or credit card?"

Moon didn't hear her. The revelation had been like a sudden illu-mination of a dark landscape that was already there. A strike of sum-mer lightning at midnight. The Ute policeman already knew who killed Arlo Nightbird. Now he thought he knew how Gorman's Hereford bull had met its death. But he didn't have a shred of evi-dence.

34

Charlie Moon looked up from his desk. Emily Sombra-Nightbird had appeared without a sound. It was not an unexpected visit.

"Hello, Charlie."

He got up and nodded toward an uncomfortable wooden chair. "Have a seat."

"I stopped by to thank you. For the lovely roses." She had the bouquet in her hands, a question in her eyes. Why the sudden attention from this big, taciturn Ute?

Moon tried to appear relaxed, but his heart was kicking against his ribs. "Hoped you'd like 'em."

Emily moved close to him; he enjoyed the wonderful fragrance in her hair. "I can't remember the last time anyone sent me flowers."

Moon nodded dumbly. Emily would be shocked if she knew why he sent the roses. Benita Sweetwater owed her a debt; the roses were a token of that debt.

She touched his sleeve. "You know, I've always had a soft spot for . . . strong, decisive men."

Moon swallowed hard. "We need to talk."

"I hope it's not about Arlo's death." Her eyes went flat. "I'd like to put that far behind me." As East is from West.

The Ute studied Emily's face, especially her eyes. "Been doing some checking." He tried to sound casual, but his pulse throbbed under his shirt collar. "On that evening Arlo was late for your anniversary date, phone company records show your daddy called you, then called the insurance agency."

Emily raised her immaculate eyebrows. Her face said So?

"Herb Ecker must have told him where to find your husband. It

looks like Fidel went to the canyon, found Arlo h[...] knows Fidel hated Arlo. And," Moon added, "[...] nasty temper."

"My father didn't . . . wouldn't . . ." She hesita[...] a tight red line across her face.

"I've been out to Fidel's farm. We had a long ta[...] wears a turquoise ear stud."

Emily's face seemed to be frozen; her normally [...] vacant.

"You'll want to hire your daddy a lawyer." Moo[...] sink in. "A real good lawyer." He waited.

"My father," she said finally, "did not kill my h[...]

"I understand you want to protect your daddy[...] hand to indicate a stapled sheaf of papers on his [...] dence against him is pretty solid." The papers wer[...] line receipts.

Her gaze followed the impressive document as [...] desk drawer. And turned a key in the lock. "I [...] alibi."

"Sure." Moon did his best to sound skeptical. "[...] somewhere else, I'll listen." This was it. Either [...] wouldn't. "But I doubt it'll help Fidel."

"How do I know you won't use something I say [...] problem for me?"

"Whatever you say is off the record." He saw th[...] eyes. "You have my word."

Emily put her face in her hands and sighed. You [...] lie Moon. That was one of the few constants in Ign[...] did tell my father that Arlo had gone to visit your [...] went to look for him early the next morning. [...] stalled on the gravel road. Daisy wasn't at home, so [...] up into the canyon." She closed her eyes. "We fo[...] scrub oak . . . almost naked . . . head bleeding . . ."

Moon's tone was sympathetic. "I imagine you go[...]

She glared back at the policeman. "Of course I w[...] in shock."

"And angry?"

Emily squeezed a rose stem, pressing a tiny thor[...] "Angry? Why would I be angry?" She sucked the d[...] her finger.

So. She was already considering an insanity plea. Wouldn't need it. She had his word that this conversation was off the record. But that promise was academic. He hadn't read Emily her rights, so the confession wasn't admissible in any case. And no Colorado jury would convict her. Not after her husband had infected her with a deadly disease, then attempted to rape Benita Sweetwater. Moon's hands were cold; he flexed his fingers to encourage the blood to circulate. "Then," he said softly, "you . . . uh . . . cut off his ears so it'd look like whoever mutilated Gorman's bull also butchered your husband?" A pretty calculated plan for a woman who was out of her mind.

She winced at the word 'butchered.' Emily passed a delicate hand over her eyes, as if to erase the ghastly picture from her memory. "Having some kind of plan was the farthest thing from my mind. I simply dropped the knife and walked back to Daddy's truck. I don't remember much after that."

"Then it was Fidel that . . ."

She sighed. "Daddy took Arlo's knife. And . . . I didn't find out until later . . . he also . . . removed Arlo's ears." Her eyes were now blank, like a large pair of black buttons sewn on a doll's face. "You already know what he did with Arlo's turquoise ear stud." At the edge of hysteria, she began to giggle.

Moon leaned over to put his hand on her shoulder. When she became quiet, he spoke. "Emily, you can't just kill your husband because he's . . ."

Her delicate little face was a picture of genuine puzzlement. "Why?"

He tried to think of a reason that would sound credible to this fascinating half-Apache woman. He couldn't. "It's against the law," he said lamely.

Emily Sombra was quiet for a long time before she looked up at the Ute's face. "Charlie, I solemnly promise *never* to do anything like that again." She waited. "You do believe me?"

"Sure I do." Anyway, no more than a fifty-fifty chance. If a future husband trifled with her, murder would be much easier the second time. But Moon didn't want to arrest this woman. There were, after all, good reasons to leave her be. First, Arlo pretty much deserved what he got. Well, almost. Second, Emily was half Indian, even if that half was 'Pache. But something nagged at his conscience: James Hoover had pointed out that the wife was the killer (in sixty percent of the cases?) where the murdered husband was unfaithful. Moon told himself that the distasteful prospect of proving Hoover right had nothing to do with his decision to forget about Arlo's murder. But there it was.

She inhaled the sweet fragrance of the roses. "You tricked me with that story about my father." There was no hint of accusation, only curiosity. "You knew I did it. But how?"

He couldn't tell her that it had begun when Scott Parris had received Nancy Beyal's paperback romance. *Village of Shadows. Aldea del Sombras*. Parris had a hunch that Daisy's vision of the shadow was related to Emily's father's name. *Sombra*. Shadow. But his *matukach* friend, who wanted to pin the murder on Fidel Sombra, had not understood the full meaning of Daisy's vision. There was, after all, the owl with blood on its talons. But Parris probably didn't know that Emily had taken up her maiden name after Arlo's death. Somehow, Aunt Daisy had gone to that dark place and seen it all: Shadow that was transformed into Owl and dipped its talons in the warm blood of the *Nuu-ci*. And then became Shadow again. The Sombra woman had married Arlo and become a Nightbird. Then, she had dipped her hands in the blood of the People. She was now, once again, a Sombra. A Shadow. He wondered whether his aunt had made the connection between her strange vision and Emily Sombra-Nightbird-Sombra.

"It wasn't really my fault," she whispered almost to herself, "it was all a silly mistake."

Moon raised an eyebrow. "Mistake?"

"Certainly. I called Dr. Anderson, reported what the public health nurse had told me about my blood donation. He came over, just before you and Scott . . . Mr. Parris arrived, and took another blood sample."

So that, Moon realized, had been what Scott Parris had seen when he thought Emily was getting an injection. "You said he'd given you a shot, to calm your nerves."

"Well," she said flatly, "I was nervous when you arrived early and saw the doctor in my home. I lied."

Nervous—that was almost funny. The woman had nerves of steel. Cold, hardened steel. Moon noticed the roses in her hand; they were wilting.

"Anyway," she added quickly, "the second test, performed at a laboratory in Kansas City, showed no evidence of the AIDS virus. Just to be sure, Dr. Anderson drew blood for another test, sent it to

Atlanta, to the Centers for Disease Control. That one was negative too." She raised her eyebrows hopefully, like a small child explaining a report card to a parent. "So, I have a clean bill of health. The government scientists in Atlanta said the first test result was a 'statistical fluctuation.' A silly mistake. Arlo didn't give me a disease after all. I feel so *silly*." She paused and wiped at her eyes. Still no tears. "I hope you'll keep all this to yourself, Charlie. I'd be eternally grateful."

"What you've told me is between us. I don't plan to take any official action. Not unless some new evidence on Arlo's death turns up." Fat chance. Of course there was always the missing pig with the bejeweled ear. . . .

"Oh no," she said with a wave of her tiny hand, "I didn't mean about how Arlo died. I know you won't mention what I told you about his death." She had his word. "What I meant is, I wouldn't want anyone to know that I ever tested positive for the AIDS virus! You know how tongues will wag."

The Ute shook his head in amazement. Emily was half 'Pache, on the female side of her family. The 'Pache women had their own special rules to live by. For giving birth and for burying. For cooking and bathing. And for dealing with faithless husbands. "You," he said, "are some kind of woman." He meant every word.

"Well, thank you, Charlie. But I do sense that you are . . . disappointed in me."

"Well, I don't exactly buy that story about why you shoved his—"

"Well, Charles, that's because you're a man and you don't realize how a woman reacts under such terrible stress. I was very, very upset with Arlo," she said sternly. "It isn't fair for you to judge me so harshly." She stuffed the handkerchief into her purse and snapped it shut. "You really don't understand how awful it was for me. You had to be there."

Moon's back stiffened as if he had taken a stiff jolt of electricity. "What?"

"I was just saying that . . ." Her voice trailed off as she puzzled over the peculiar expression on his face. Such a strange, fascinating man.

The policeman stared at the woman without really seeing her. That was it. It was like she said. You had to be there!

She pouted prettily. "Will you remain cross with me forever?"

Moon barely heard her. Now he knew for certain who had killed and mutilated Big Ouray. But there was not enough evidence for an arrest. And that killer of animals might turn out to be very dangerous. Even more dangerous than this fascinating woman.

"Charlie Moon!" She stamped her delicate little foot. "You are not listening to a word I'm saying." She moved close to him, so that her skirt brushed against his knee. "You know . . . it's awfully lonely in that big house after the sun goes down." She touched his sleeve, then smiled shyly. "Why don't you drop in this evening . . . around dinner time."

Moon had no appetite. "Thanks. I don't feel much like having dinner."

"I was thinking about something," she said, "more along the lines of . . . *dessert*."

Nancy Beyal pushed a flashing button on her telephone console. "Southern Ute Police." The dispatcher listened to the excited caller, who demanded to speak to "Charles" Moon. "No, Mr. Oakes. Charlie's on vacation." She scribbled a few words on her yellow pad as she listened to his questions. "For a week. Maybe two." Nancy nodded as if the caller could see her. "Charlie said he was going to borrow a dog, maybe go hunting." She listened again, with characteristic patience. Oakes was excited, claimed he was "on to something." "Okay. I'll write it down. Maybe he'll call in for his messages." She paused to hear another urgent question. "No, Scott Parris isn't here anymore . . . but I can give you his Granite Creek number." This seemed to satisfy the agitated man.

Scott Parris used his pocket knife to cut the masking tape on the parcel from Charlie Moon. It felt like a book. He unwrapped the heavy brown paper. It was a photocopy of Herb Ecker's journal. A note from Moon was attached:

GREETINGS TO MY FRIEND

KNEW YOU WOULD WANT TO SEE THIS.

—Charlie

Parris leafed through the stapled pages. The entries were in a meticulous hand that was easy to read. There were bits of verse, lines about the inevitability of death and decay. It ranged from the dreary to the bizarre. Except when Ecker penned romantic lines about a young woman. Benita. Embarrassed at this violation of the dead man's privacy, he skipped over these sentimental sections quickly. There were detailed accounts of the young man's expenses. Rent. Groceries. A new battery for his motorcycle, an assortment of books. And notes. Pages of notes. Some of the entries bordered on the mystic.

> Interesting event approx. 12 km S.E. of Dulce. Apache's quarter horse killed and mutilated. Tongue, tail, genitals removed. But this is not the work of the Horned Beast.

There was an entry on the day after the Sweetwater bull's death had been reported to the Nightbird Insurance Agency.

> Benita's father reports Big Ouray dead. Dr. Schaid says mutilation is work of coyotes. The veterinarian conceals the truth. H. B. strikes again! Benita, sweet princess, stopped to talk with me.

A few days later, Ecker had written:

> Of all the inhabitants of Ignacio, only I understand the mystery of the Horned Beast! Perfect Knowledge is Perfect Power!

Parris flipped through the pages, past more strange verse, more listings of grocery bills and rent paid. Ecker's hand had been slightly shaky when he recorded the fact of Arlo Nightbird's death.

> Mr. Nightbird is dead. It was to be expected.
> He had offended the Gods!

Then, there was the final entry:

> JoJo Tonompicket arrested for poaching—says he saw 'Dancing Devil' in Snake Canyon. Police believe this man is crazy. No! J.J. has seen the Horned Beast. Tonight I use the vision-medicine. I will dance the old dance, sing the old song. I will see into the dark corners.

What did this all mean? Were the FBI shrinks right? Had Ecker's brain expressed two personalities, the poet by day, the Horned Beast by night? Or . . . was something else out there? It was a particularly unpleasant thought. Ecker had certainly not killed Arlo Nightbird. But Ecker had gone to Snake Canyon to dance. Was he a solitary dancer, or did he intend to dance with . . . with what? And he was dead. Dead because he went to dance. No. Tell the truth! Dead because a careless policeman had lost an unloaded gun in a scuffle. Because Charlie Moon, that gentle man, had his limits. Moon would kill to protect his friend.

The telephone jangled. The policeman pressed the receiver to his ear. "Parris here," he barked.

"This is Oswald Oakes." The voice quavered with ill-concealed excitement. "I called the Southern Ute Police; Miss Beyal told me you had returned to Granite Creek. She gave me your home telephone number."

It took Parris a long moment to connect the name with a person. This was the guy Moon called "Oz." The eccentric antiquarian. The gambler with the Indian artifact collection and the computer files on animal mutilations. "I'll remember to thank Nancy for that," he muttered. "What's on your mind?"

"There has been another bull mutilation. On a ranch in Gunnison County, just south of Powderhorn. Precisely the same as the Sweetwater animal. Ears and testicles were removed."

Parris felt a sick sensation grip the pit of his abdomen. He silently cursed his decision to accept the stint with the Ute police.

Oswald nervously drummed his fingers on the marble top of an antique table as he waited for a reply. "There are some very intriguing aspects to this particular mutilation; I was certain you would want to . . . to see for yourself. You could meet me at the kill site." He waited. Did this dull policeman have not the least interest in identifying the mutilator? "I will be leaving within the hour."

Parris hesitated. "I don't know . . . it's only a couple of hours before sundown and—"

"Suit yourself," Oswald interrupted crisply, "but this mutilation could be a breakthrough. There is unusual evidence that may lead to the identity of the mutilator."

"Well . . . I'd like to see what you've found. But it's a long way from my jurisdiction and I'm pretty busy these days." Promises to keep. "Doesn't Charlie Moon want to have a look?"

"The redoubtable Sergeant Moon is not at his post. Your aboriginal colleague has left on vacation." Oakes's tone betrayed his annoyance.

"Okay," Parris sighed. "Tell me where to meet you."

It was back.

Louise Marie LaForte stood among a forlorn patch of frostbitten tomato plants; her tiny hands trembled. She closed one eye and squinted down the long, rusty barrel of the antique revolver. Her wrists ached. She would decide to fire, then the weight of the pistol would inexorably lower the barrel and spoil her aim. The small woman strained to raise the sight well above her target, then waited for gravity to do its work. When she pulled the trigger, the booming report was so loud and the recoil so unexpected that she shrieked and dropped the weapon. The pig also squealed; it took a few halting steps, then crumpled to the ground in her vegetable garden. She leaned forward, her hands braced on arthritic knees. Yes, this was the very same swine that she had reported to Charlie Moon. The turquoise stud glistened in the pig's ear. Her chin trembled as she glared at the swine. "Damn you, Arlo Nightbird."

Louise Marie straightened her back with a grunt, and scratched at her wrinkled neck. *Oui*, it was a difficult problem, this. A good citizen should report such a matter to the police. Then, they could take the pig's carcass and dispose of it properly. Dismember it. Burn it! But what if they merely buried the creature. . . . Arlo's evil spirit might slip away from the swine's body. . . . He might come back to haunt her again . . . in another, even more dreadful form? Her lurid imagination was well equipped to give dramatic dimension to her fears. Louise Marie pictured a long striped snake, big around as a lard bucket. The serpent would crawl under her house at night . . . slither through a hole in her bedroom floor. Slip under the covers while she slept . . . and then? Never! Louise Marie realized the need to act decisively and destroy the pig's corpse so that not a trace remained. There was a particularly tempting solution. And the turquoise ear stud would make a delightful addition to her box of pretties.

"But, no, I must not," she whispered with an entirely satisfying rush of self-pity, "even though I'm a poor old woman, with nothing but a little pension to live on." The vision of fresh strips of bacon, tender slices of rose-colored ham—she could taste the crimson grease

. . . pork chops slow-broiled in the oven. It made her little mouth water. But it was almost like—she hesitated to admit it to herself— cannibalism! Her conscience argued against this solution.

Hunger won the argument.

35

Oswald Oakes felt an almost dizzy sense of exhilaration as the convertible hummed along the narrow blacktop highway, over the gentle slopes, the speedometer needle jittering around the seventy-mile-per-hour mark. He flicked a spent butt out the window and lit a fresh cigar. He leaned into a curve around a low ridge; the Miata's radials gripped tenaciously at the blacktop, as if the rubber treads were magnetized to the road. He felt wonderful . . . but there was something else. Something that tickled at the base of his brain, the animal part that knows without knowing how it knows. He glanced at the rearview mirror, but there was no one in sight. He tried to shake off the absurd notion that he was being followed. Hunted like an animal. There was nothing, no one, back there. Oakes realized that the suggestion had been implanted in his mind by the recurrent dream. The nightmare where he was being followed across the rolling Colorado plateau. Pursued by someone who would kill him after the sun slipped behind the jagged granite mountains. The gambler reminded himself that he was a rational man; he attempted to dismiss the fear from his mind.

But it followed closely, on the road behind him.

Scott Parris lifted his boot off the accelerator pedal, allowing the Volvo to slow to a crawl as he approached the gravel road that turned east off Route 149. He checked the rough sketch he had made from Oswald's instructions and tried to make sense of the hasty scrawls. It was possible that the old eccentric's directions had been confused. Oswald, unless he had already arrived, would be heading almost due north on 149 from Slumgullion Pass, but Parris was heading south, out of Gunnison. The policeman took the turn onto the sinuous trail that followed the crumbling bank of a dry arroyo.

He glanced to his right. There was a low ridge that was a good match for Oswald's description, a hogback of fractured basalt supporting a sparse population of juniper and piñon. When he was, according to his odometer, one and three-tenths miles off the main highway, the policeman saw the weather-worn wooden sign nailed to a ponderosa:

BURNT CREEK RANCH—PUREBRED HEREFORDS

The mutilated bull, according to Oswald's directions, should be within a hundred yards of this spot. But where was Oswald? Then he saw a flash of blue; it was a small convertible, parked off the road behind a clump of scrub oak.

The Miata door was open, as if the driver had left in a hurry. But there was no sign of Oswald. Parris smiled as he imagined the old man's urgent desire to visit the carcass of a mutilated bull. It took all kinds. The policeman was in no hurry to get acquainted with a half ton of rotting beef. But it was a pleasure to stretch his stiff legs. The air was both sharp and sweet; the only sounds were a light breeze playing with the sage and a melodious bird song he didn't recognize. The late afternoon sun, about to sink behind a heavy cloud bank on the western horizon, was pleasantly warm on his face. He watched the silver gleam of a southbound jet gliding along at thirty thousand feet, painting a wavy discontinuous ribbon of contrail across the face of the intermittent winds. He leaned on the Miata; the hood was warm under his palm. The key was still in the ignition switch. Strange. Door open, a key chain dangling from the ignition, and no sign of Oswald. The fellow had clearly been in a big hurry to leave his little automobile.

Then, unbidden and unwelcome, the darkness came to call. The Dread blew its cold breath on his neck . . . touched his groin with an icy finger. The lone bird interrupted its sweet song and flew away in a frantic flurry of thumping wings. Parris removed his revolver from the shoulder holster. He checked the cylinder to satisfy himself that his .38 Smith & Wesson was fully loaded, then jammed it back under his left armpit. The first thing to do, he reasoned, was to find Oswald.

He had no idea what the second thing to do might be.

He left the Miata and headed off at a right angle to the gravel road. There might be some sort of trail, maybe a heel print in the sand. But now the sun was touching the dark cloud to cast a premature gray shadow over the high country. He buttoned his leather jacket against the gathering chill, grateful for the wool lining. The expensive garment was a birthday gift from Anne. He wondered where Anne was at this very moment. He hoped she was warm. And safe.

The almost barren landscape was punctuated with gnarled piñon, fragrant juniper, clusters of yucca spears, and massive black basalt boulders. A muddy stream ran through a shallow valley to the west. The policeman made a turn to the north, paralleling the road. He was groping his way through the shadow cast by a large basalt outcropping when he nearly stumbled onto the rotting carcass of the Hereford. Parris instinctively backed away, shielding his face from the stench that had not been noticeable a few yards away. The stark profile of the animal, legs jutting out like huge toothpicks stuck in a gargantuan plum, was unreal. An amateurish stage set. The policeman silently cursed himself for agreeing to this hurried meeting with Oswald. What did he care about some perverted fiend who took pleasure in the killing and mutilation of cattle? Thousands of cattle were slaughtered every day to sate the nation's appetite for hamburgers. Besides, the animal mutilations had nothing to do with Arlo Nightbird's murder. He paused to lean, almost sitting, against the east side of the stone outcropping. The basalt monolith's shadow was moving eastward as the cloud-filtered sunlight dropped under the western horizon. Funny, he mused as he examined the shadow stretched out in front of him, there's a tree on top of the boulder. But how could a tree grow out of a rock? At that moment, a shaft of sunlight beamed thorough a small tear in the cloud, casting a crisp shadow of the boulder. And of the Thing that stood on the boulder behind the policeman. It was not a tree. Tall. Broad shoulders. No visible legs. One arm holding something upward, as if in a salute. And the head of the beast was the terrifying visage that haunted his dreams. The enormous head, like an oversized Wagnerian Viking, had horns.

Barely able to breathe, he slowly unzipped his jacket, then moved his fingertips toward the short grip of the .38. Inches away. Miles away. After an eternity, he felt the checkered grip under his fingers. Then, the sky fell.

When a mere wisp of his consciousness returned, Scott Parris was immersed in an impossible dream. His universe was upside down. The night sky had fallen far below his feet, the earth was suspended barely above his head. His hands were tied securely behind his back; he tried to speak but his mouth was filled with a coarse mixture of sand and pebbles. A frigid wind troubled the piñon branches; he shivered convulsively. It was at this moment that Scott Parris realized that he was entirely naked.

A shadowy form moved forth from the gloom; the beast was also inverted. The shaggy creature had waited patiently for his victim to become fully aware of the fate that awaited him. The hairy phantom moved closer, wagging its great head, the short curved horns glistening wickedly in the moonlight. The single red eye winked twice, then disappeared. Parris felt something grasp his hair; the beast held a long obsidian blade before his eyes, allowing him ample time to see and understand. The blade disappeared from his view; the policeman felt its serrated edge move under his right earlobe. *No,* he thought as he closed his eyelids and clenched his teeth into the dirt that filled his mouth. No. This is not real. In a moment, I will wake up. And thank God that this was only a terrible nightmare.

The obsidian blade began to saw back and forth under his ear. Slowly. Deliberately. The beast would not hurry this experience.

This was no dream. He had but one overwhelming desire, and it was not for an end to the pain. Above all else, he strained for the ability to fight back. But it was not to be. He tried to cry out, but that was also impossible. Blood flowed in a scarlet stream from his partially severed ear, soaking his hair, dripping in heavy plops onto the ground under the piñon.

This excited the beast, who touched a fingertip to the blood, then to hungry lips, then sawed again. More vigorously now.

Parris had no doubt of his immediate future. After his right ear was severed, then the left would be sawed off. He knew only too well which portions of his body would be removed after that. Parris strained against the bonds that held his wrists. There was a sickening pop as he dislocated his right shoulder. *Merciful God,* he prayed in a silent scream, *help me.*

The beast paused sawing and licked the blood directly from the fresh wound.

Parris's mind began to slip away from this horror. He was no longer aware of the star-studded sky under his feet, nor could he see the featureless earth above his head; this was replaced by a rolling swell of iridescent blue waves breaking on a beach of black volcanic sand. Then, a turquoise sky over snow-blanketed peaks. Now he was in another place, standing on the banks of a wide river. The waters rolled over ebony boulders; the waters sang to him. Of peace and joy. His ears were filled with a cacophony of old, sweet sounds . . . and a great light. It was all there for him, across the river. Somewhere on the far bank, a small child laughed . . . there was the unmistakable sound of a waterfall . . . and then, a woman's voice. A voice that he did not recognize, singing clearly over an infinite void, calling to him: . . . *echoes of mercy . . . whispers of love . . .*

He stood upright now, unbound. Alone on the mossy bank of this great, rolling river. Filled with longing to cross to the distant bank. Memories of the past world were fading.

Now there was a small light on the other side. The light grew larger, more luminous. More inviting. Come to Me.

Yes. I will! He stepped toward the water.

At this moment Scott Parris heard the harsh, unmistakable sound of a carbine being cocked. And the sound of another voice, this one familiar. It was loud, but it came from an impossibly distant place— a place in that other world that held dark terrors.

The Ute was, once again, imprisoned in his nightmare. "Get away from him." I know who you are. I don't want to do this. Not again.

The dark form swung its massive shoulders to glower at Makes No Tracks. The apparition wagged its shaggy head in fury and spat blood toward the Ute. Moon watched the form raise its arms to exhibit a heavy club in one hand, a glistening blade in the other. But the blade was not blue fire as it had been in his nightmare. And the only barrier between the Ute and the Beast was a deep dread. Of death. And killing.

The Beast poised, as if to attack.

The Ute stood his ground. "It's finished," he said softly.

The Beast knew this was true. It was finished. The adventure was almost over. But for who?

Moon motioned with the barrel of the carbine. "Move away."

There was the briefest of hesitations before the shaggy figure plunged the obsidian blade toward the throat of the man who hung from the piñon branch. As the blade moved, Moon pulled the trigger. The beast did not flinch, nor did it cry out. The Ute cocked the carbine and fired again. And again.

Parris was flat on his back, looking up at the dark outline of the big Ute policeman. He rolled over and pushed himself up on one elbow. He coughed, spat sand and pebbles from his mouth, gagging in the process. He was bleeding and terribly weak; his hands were like ice and he couldn't yet feel his feet. But life was never so sweet as at this moment. Even now, he could hear the distant sound of the woman's song. Perhaps, his mind argued, it is only the wind in the piñons. "No," he muttered aloud, "it's not the wind."

The Ute was on one knee beside him. "What'd you say?"

"It's . . . it's not the wind."

Moon nodded. "No. I guess it's not." Delirium was not surprising, considering what the man had been through. "I sure do appreciate you holding the prisoner in custody till I got here pardner, but you just about lost an ear." It was hardly necessary to mention what other parts his friend had almost lost. The Ute pressed a handkerchief firmly against Parris's head. "Hold that snug. You've bled some."

Parris became aware of a dark form half covered by a large animal skin. "What . . . who is it?" Cain, of course.

Moon would not look toward the corpse or speak the name of the dead man. "He's there. Head, horns, tail, and all." Wrapped in a buffalo hide. Rolling Thunder's hide.

Moon switched on his flashlight; he illuminated the corpse. The face had a well-trimmed mustache. It was Oswald Oakes. His entire body was painted black, except for yellow circles around his eyes. Around the man's neck was a rawhide thong decorated with tooth of elk, shell of periwinkle, quill of porcupine. And there were trophies on the necklace—the shriveled ears of deer and elk and horses and bulls. Here was JoJo's Dancing Devil and Louise Marie's *loupgarou* and . . . and the beast he had seen in *Cañon del Serpiente*. The beast that Herb Ecker had come to dance with.

"He lured me out here," Parris spat dirty saliva, "to see a dead bull."

"I know," Moon said. "Been watching him for a week or so."

Parris heard himself answer; he felt oddly detached from his voice. "What kept you?"

"Busted a fan belt out on the main road. Had to walk in." Moon held a small object close to his friend's face. "He always had one of these things stuck in his mouth."

Parris blinked and sniffed. It was the stub of a cigar; the smoking tip was a dull red ember. So this was the beast's single red "eye," that blinked in synchrony with his breathing. "How did you figure out it was . . . ?" Parris left the question hanging in the night air.

"Hunch." Moon pitched a rumpled pile of clothes at Parris's feet. Later, when the time was right, he would tell his friend that he'd had his inspiration in the flower shop. From a television perfume commercial. My Confession. That was when he remembered Oswald's sarcastic suggestion that he pray for a confession. "My Confession," the lovely woman on the television screen had whispered, "is subtle, barely touching his consciousness." And that, of course, was exactly how the confession had been offered. Subtle. Barely touching the Ute policeman's consciousness.

Oswald's "confession" played and replayed in his memory, much like the lines of an old song that would not go away: ". . . surely the mutilator will confess his crimes to you . . . you were quite right to come to me . . . I can describe precisely how the bull was mutilated." The old man had described the mutilator as if he knew the criminal intimately. But the Ute policeman had dismissed these statements as the foolish ramblings of an overzealous eccentric—a self-deluded old man who believed he could understand the mind of a madman he had never met.

And what had Oswald said when they were barely inside his door? Something about wanting to try a new contest. "One that challenges the intellect."

The compulsive gambler's final hint now surfaced from the Ute's memory; it whispered in the frigid breeze that shook the little trees: "It is only a game, don't you see?" A sudden gust whipped at a juniper and the writhing branches repeated the whisper. . . . *Only a game . . . don't you see . . . don't you see . . . don't you see?*

But Moon hadn't seen. This confident player had purposely shown his hand to his opponents. And, Moon realized bitterly, he hadn't bothered to look at Oswald's cards. Oswald had even presented the lawmen with the weapon he had used to kill Big Ouray. The old man had taken pains to guide them away from false assumptions about the physical strength required to crush the bull's skull, insisting that a twelve-year-old could swing the club with sufficient force to do the job. It was only a matter of accuracy, and that required nerve. Oswald was not short on that commodity.

Rolling Thunder had probably been killed in the same manner, to provide Oswald with the skin to wear on his midnight prowls. Moon leaned over to pick up the Mayan club with the smoky yellow quartz head. Oswald had gone straight to the book with the figure of a bovine skull, recited the thickness of the bone, pointed out the precise location where a fatal blow must fall. He must have enjoyed that mocking game; demonstrating to the slow-witted lawmen exactly how he had bludgeoned the animals. Knowing they wouldn't understand the significance of his testimony. Certain that he would eventually win the game. And he had come close. Too close.

But it was Emily Nightbird who had unwittingly unlocked the vital knowledge buried deep in the Ute's subconscious. It was what she had said to justify the brutal castration and suffocation of her husband. "You had to be there." Almost as she spoke the words, Moon had remembered the conversation in Oswald's parlor with crystal clarity. The old man had made the teasing remark: ". . . this mutilator certainly was not the *pitukupf*. Or one of those old Anasazi spirits defending his resting place."

Oswald, that tireless collector of such arcane facts, would know that the *pitukupf* reportedly lived in *Cañon del Espiritu*. And the Canyon of the Spirits was also where the local Anasazi had left their impressive petroglyphs on the flat sandstone walls. But how did Oswald know that the Hereford bull had been killed in *Cañon del Espiritu*? He had only been told that the bull was killed in a canyon. There were hundreds of canyons on the reservation, dozens with enough water and grass to support livestock. But Oswald had known precisely where Big Ouray was slain because he had wielded the club that cracked the skull. It was like Emily had said. He had to be there.

Parris shivered as he buttoned his shirt, but not from the cold. "I still can't imagine this old guy taking on a full-grown bull . . . armed with nothing but a stone club."

"He was," Moon said, "one of a kind." One hoped it was so.

There was a long silence before Parris spoke. "But why?"

Moon helped his friend to his feet. "For Oz, it was a game." That was all. Life, the gambler had often asserted, was a game. Oswald had sweetened the pot on this ultimate contest. And lost.

Parris nodded toward the painted body. "He's dead?"

The Ute nodded. Between the Moon of New Grass and the Moon

of Dead Leaves Falling, he had killed two men. It was time to think about another line of work.

Parris thought he saw a leg twitch. "You sure he's dead?" In the horror movies, this would be the time when the body of the beast would be reanimated.

"I'm sure." The Ute, who remembered his bitter frustration when Benita died . . . and Arlo Nightbird was beyond his reach, was certain that his friend wanted Oswald to live. So he could get his hands around a throat that still pulsated with life.

But Moon was mistaken. Hatred, while the vision lived, was not possible. Faint whispers of the sweet song lingered in Parris's senses like the remnant of a delicate fragrance. Music infinitely pure, more lovely than could be imagined. He closed his eyes and thought he saw a faint afterglow of that bright light across the singing river.

But he wondered. What did the spirit of Oswald Oakes hear, what awful visions did he see? And what dark mansion had been prepared in *his* father's house . . . across that other river?

Scott Parris bowed his head and closed his eyes. And prayed. For lost souls.

36

Daisy Perika held the *Southern Ute Drum* under the sunlight that streamed through her kitchen window, illuminating a trillion tiny particles of floating dust. She read the story on the front page carefully, forming each word with her lips. Oswald Oakes had killed the tribe's buffalo for its skin—then he had killed and mutilated Gorman's prize Hereford bull! But she remembered something about Oakes—this was the man that Charlie Moon played poker with. Oakes was a compulsive gambler. She thought about this and smiled. Of course. And the buffalo spirit had pointed her toward this man! The shaman closed her eyes and remembered. She could see the deep forest . . . and the chalklike skeleton that dropped the rectangles of pottery on the moss, then gazed anxiously at them to see the result. The skeleton was playing some form of ghostly solitaire, like an old warrior playing *wisa-nipi* with his painted wooden disks. The skeleton was a gambler.

Daisy sighed. It was a dark world, where a man would play such dark games as Oswald Oakes had lost himself in. Enough to make you want to cry. But there had been enough tears. What an old woman needed, from time to time, was a good laugh.

Special Agent James E. Hoover, accompanied by Sam Parker, was ushered to his customary table by the window. The owner, who was also the cook and waiter and janitor in the ten-table hole in the wall, rubbed his hairy hands on a filthy apron and grinned crookedly at this regular customer. "Good ta see ya, Mr. Hoover." He glanced at Parker. "What'll ya have, gents?"

"Something wholesome, Percy," Hoover said. "Brought my boss along, so help me make a good impression."

Percy faked a chuckle.

Parker tilted his head to read the handwritten menu through the bottom of his bifocals.

Hoover unfolded a napkin. "So what's good tonight?"

"Well, for eight-fifty, I could broil you a steak with baked spud and sour cream. And the barbecue is six ninety-five with wedge fries. Or," Percy added seductively, "you could try the special."

Hoover's eyebrows peaked. "Special?"

Percy twisted his face into an evil grin. Hoover was a cheap bastard who left lousy tips. And always ordered the special because it was a bargain. "It's our S-Q special. Fresh sausages, mashed spuds with cream gravy, and two veggies," the manager said, "for three-twenty-five."

Hoover hesitated.

Percy leaned forward. "And dessert is free with the special! Cherry cobbler. With vanilla ice cream."

The special agent considered the value and was hooked. "Bring on the special." He looked across the red-checkered oil cloth at his boss. "What'll you have, Sam?"

Sam Parker studied the menu. "Maybe I'll have the special. And decaf coffee."

Percy nodded. "Sorry, bud. Only one order of the special left. Try the barbecue. Or I got ham steak with brown sugar and pineapple slices."

Except for occasional bits of small talk, they ate their meals in silence.

Hoover's hands shook slightly; a muscle in his jaw twitched with an unseemly rhythm. It was apparent that the other customers paid the employees of the Federal Bureau of Investigation not the least attention, but he could not shake the unsettling sensation that unseen eyes watched his every move. He repeatedly glanced over his shoulder toward the dirty plate glass window, but it was impossible to see what might be lurking in the darkness outside. Only the occasional flash of headlights was visible.

Sam Parker was making mental notes about this troublesome employee. The bloodshot eyes. The nervous pattern in Hoover's speech. The tic in his jaw. There had been other subtle indications that the man was . . . emotionally unstable. Hoover was short-tempered. And nervous. And mildly paranoid. But worst of all, Hoover had been seeking attention from the press. The greenest rookie knew that publicity was the exclusive domain of the public relations officer. Not only had Hoover made unauthorized public announcements to the effect that Herb Ecker was guilty of the Nightbird murder, but it appeared that he had been wrong. Charlie Moon had made a solid case against the late Oswald Oakes for the mutilation of the Hereford bull and the killing of a tribal buffalo. And Oakes had viciously assaulted Scott Parris. It seemed a reasonable extrapolation that Oswald had also killed and mutilated Arlo Nightbird. But Charlie Moon had made no move to charge Arlo's death against Oswald Oakes's bill. Parker suspected that Moon, as usual, knew a great deal more than he cared to reveal. Maybe another tribal member had mutilated and murdered Nightbird. But that might as well remain Ute business. Parker had a rare gift; he knew when to keep his nose out of tribal affairs.

James E. Hoover was Sam Parker's immediate concern. A single misfit could tarnish the image of thousands of dedicated, capable investigators who routinely risked their lives to protect the citizens of this great republic. Patience, that was the thing. Sooner or later, there would be an excuse to write up a personnel action on this nasty little bastard. Hoover had skirted the edge of unacceptable behavior; something more concrete was needed to put this guy away. Parker excused himself and visited the grimy rest room to empty his bladder.

For the tenth time in as many minutes, Hoover glanced over his shoulder and squinted suspiciously toward the plate glass window. Aside from a few headlights, nothing moved on the street. But the skin on the back of his neck was tingling. Worse still, his hands were shaking uncontrollably. He removed the small bottle from his coat pocket and washed two of the bitter yellow pills down with a swallow of tepid coffee.

Percy returned with a coffee pot. "See you've cleaned your plates. Ready for dessert?"

Hoover patted his belt buckle. "Bring on the pie, Percy. That was a passable dinner." The special agent burped.

The cook grinned. Like a possum, Hoover thought. "Glad you 'preciated it."

"Tasty sausages," Hoover said. "I'd like to try it again sometime, but I didn't see the S-Q special on the menu." He frowned. "I guess the 'S' is for sausage. What's the 'Q' stand for, 'queasy'?"

Percy smiled broadly, displaying a mouthful of nicotine-stained teeth. "*Sarichi Cuquavi* ain't gonna be on the menu. That," Percy said sarcastically, "is why I call it 'special.'"

Hoover removed the paper napkin from his shirt and wiped at his chin. "My French is kind of rusty. What's it mean?"

"Well," Percy frowned thoughtfully, "*Sarichi Cuquavi* is . . . them is Ute words."

Hoover paled. "Did you say *Ute?*"

"Don't ask me for more'n that." Percy held his palms up in a defensive gesture. "I understand it don't translate too good into American."

A burly Ute rancher at the next table looked up from his barbecued chicken and laughed. "That's easy to translate. You want to know what it means?"

Hoover buried his face in his hands and groaned. "No. Please don't tell me."

The Ute, not to be denied the opportunity to display his bilingual abilities, told him.

A wave of nausea rippled through Hoover's groin; he fought back a gag.

Percy's eyes widened. This was news to him, but it served the cheap bastard right. Anyway, he had a twenty dollar bribe in his pocket and it was no crime to serve Native American dishes in his restaurant.

As Percy hurried back to his grimy kitchen, Sam Parker returned from the rest room. He was alarmed to see James E. Hoover's face; it was the color of dirty cotton. And his hands shook.

Hoover's body rippled with a great shudder. "Those damn Utes," he said between sobs, "you know what they did to me?" He ducked his head and made a low groaning sound. He wanted to vomit, but could not.

Now, Parker noticed with an odd mixture of embarrassment and satisfaction, several customers were showing considerable interest in Hoover's behavior. Customers that could, if necessary, be called as witnesses in a departmental fitness hearing.

Sam Parker put a hand on Hoover's trembling shoulder. "Sure, James. I know it's been tough." Parker nodded apologetically to the

=271=

Ute family at the next table and whispered. "He's not well." The man grunted and returned his attention to a slab of greasy chicken, but his plump wife had lost all interest in her plate of Polish sausage and sauerkraut.

Hoover was wiping at his eyes. "If I told you, you wouldn't believe . . ."

Parker's problem was solved. "Don't worry James. The Bureau takes care of its own."

Daisy Perika, who had watched Hoover savor every morsel, shuffled slowly down the Durango street to the spot where her niece had parked her aquamarine Saturn. She was twenty dollars poorer, but it had been a good investment. The shaman's face ached from the strain, but she couldn't stop smiling.

The solicitous niece helped the old woman into the sedan and drove away.

Daisy was a good Catholic. She knew that revenge was wrong, but she rationalized that this was a special case. This FBI man had accused her of serving dog meat to a guest, and in doing so he had insulted the People. That could not go unanswered. Justice must be served. Sometimes, of course, justice could be served on a platter. With mashed potatoes and gravy. Now the shaman laughed. She laughed until streams of tears blinded her.

Daisy's niece glanced at the elderly woman, but she dared not ask any questions. When this old woman had been up to something, it was best to remain ignorant.

Daisy recalled Hoover's rapt expression as the special agent gobbled up the delectable sausages. She also remembered Dr. Schaid's alarmed expression when he heard her bizarre request. The animal doctor was worried about getting into trouble with the authorities. He had hesitated until she assumed her most solemn expression and insisted that the tissue specimens were needed for a secret Ute sacrificial rite. The *matukach,* who entertained absurd notions about mysterious Native American ceremonies, were so gullible.

And, in a way, she had not lied. It had been a sacrifice. The neighborhood *sarichi* might be howling high notes at the moon tonight, but they sure wouldn't be chasing bitches in heat. Not after sacrificing their *cuquavi!*

The shaman's laughter shook her small frame, leaving her weak and drained.

37

Scott Parris pulled the stiff collar of the leather jacket over his throat; he squinted against the wind-driven sleet that stung his eyes. He pushed his battered felt hat down until a stabbing pain from the fifteen stitches at the base of his right ear took his breath away.

The rocky, treeless hillside was disfigured with intermittent clumps of dead sage and chamisa. The markers were starkly simple. This lonely place was not a cemetery. This was a graveyard. Forlorn acres where the bodies of the poor were interred in sixty-dollar plastic caskets paid for by the good citizens of La Plata County. It was a resting place for the unknown. The forgotten. The policeman had promised himself—he would never forget! Every year on this day, God willing, he would be here.

This grave, like most of the others, had no tombstone. Just an aluminum tube supporting a plastic holder. He pulled a tumbleweed off the marker. The paper card behind the cracked cellophane window had a typed entry:

HERBERT ECKER

The anonymous typist had not bothered to enter the date of birth. Or of death. Parris looked over his shoulder, making sure he was alone. But there was no need for concern about privacy; hardly anyone visited this place. Especially on this day. He focused on the card in the plastic holder and held onto his hat brim as a gust of wind snatched at the dead weeds on the grave mound. The shrill voice of the wind promised a blizzard before the year was new.

"Well, kid," he said hoarsely, "time rolls on down the road, and I guess we're along for the ride." The policeman felt enormously self-conscious, speaking over a grave . . . as if the dry bones could hear his voice. He removed his hat, braving the stinging crystals of ice.

"It's already Christmas Eve. You can see I made it with a day to spare." His throat was tight; he wiped at his eyes with his sleeve. He paused for a few seconds, taking deep breaths of the frigid air. A promise made. A debt unpaid. The little book was in his coat pocket, but he was determined not to use it. After endless hours of rehearsal, he would get it right. Word for word, from beginning to end. Scott Parris cleared his throat. And began . . .

"*A bunch of the boys were whooping it up, in the Malamute Saloon;*
The kid that handles the music box was hitting a jag-time tune. . . ."